"I'LL START BY TAKING YOUR GUNS."

"Ma'am," Dusty said, "would you mind waiting outside? If Columbo tries to t⬛⬛⬛⬛⬛⬛⬛⬛⬛⬛⬛⬛⬛⬛s blood before a beautiful a⬛⬛⬛⬛

"You just got you⬛⬛⬛⬛⬛⬛⬛⬛⬛⬛⬛⬛⬛⬛⬛at out. Already as tense a⬛⬛⬛⬛⬛⬛⬛⬛⬛⬛⬛olumbo needed little stimul⬛⬛⬛⬛⬛⬛⬛⬛⬛nd his right hand started t⬛⬛⬛⬛⬛

Crossing so fast th⬛⬛⬛⬛⬛⬛⬛ould barely follow their movements, Dusty's hands closed on the bone handles of his Colts. Half a second later, the guns had left their holsters, been cocked, turned outward, had the triggers depressed and roared so close together that the two detonations could not be detected as separate sounds. At almost the same instant, a .45 of an inch hole opened in the center of Pinter's forehead and a second bullet caught Columbo in the center of the chest. . . .

Also by J. T. Edson

THE NIGHT HAWK
NO FINGER ON THE TRIGGER
THE BAD BUNCH
SLIP GUN
TROUBLED RANGE
THE FASTEST GUN IN TEXAS
THE HIDE AND TALLOW MEN
THE JUSTICE OF COMPANY Z
McGRAW'S INHERITANCE
RAPIDO CLINT
COMANCHE
A MATTER OF HONOR
RENEGADE
WACO RIDES IN
THE BLOODY BORDER
ALVIN FOG, TEXAS RANGER

Hell in the Palo Duro

J. T. EDSON

A DELL BOOK

Published by
Dell Publishing
a division of
Bantam Doubleday Dell Publishing Group, Inc.
666 Fifth Avenue
New York, New York 10103

ISBN: 0-440-21037-2

Printed in the United States of America

Published simultaneously in Canada

December 1991

10 9 8 7 6 5 4 3 2 1

OPM

1
DON'T COME AFTER ME

The Ysabel Kid, Waco and Sheriff Ian Laurie agreed that there were several puzzling aspects about the way in which the Glover gang had been acting since robbing the bank in Wichita Falls.

It was not so much the fact that Andy Glover had quit his normal hunting grounds in Eastern Texas. Having received orders from Governor Stanton Howard, the Texas Rangers had launched a vigorous campaign to stamp out the lawlessness that was flourishing in the Lone Star State. Naturally the owlhoots in the more civilized eastern counties were the first to feel the pressure.

Nor was there too much of a surprise in discovering that, having brought off a successful robbery, except for the loss of one man, the gang did not cover the twenty or so miles to the Red River to cross into the Indian Nations. Working in conjunction with the Texas Rangers, the Army and U.S. marshals

planned to run out the outlaws who had settled in that territory.

Having learned of that policy, which had not been kept a
secret, Andy Glover might have decided that Indian Nations
no longer afforded a safe refuge. Yet, on the face of it, neither
did the route he and his men had been following for the past
three days.

During the gang's flight from Wichita Falls, the Kid had
shot and wounded one of them. Questioned about his companions' destination, the dying outlaw had replied to the effect that
they were going to hell in the Palo Duro. He had died before he
could clarify the statement. At first, the sheriff of Wichita
County had regarded the words as a lie designed to send his
posse off in the wrong direction, or the deranged utterings of a
man in mortal pain. All the evidence now pointed to Billy
Robinson having told the truth.

There had been some debate on the first afternoon of the
hunt about whether the posse should make camp on the gang's
trail at sundown, or head for the Red River and search out
Glover's crossing point in the morning. Accepting the Ysabel
Kid's suggestion, Laurie had decided to make camp. It had
proved to be the correct decision.

Soon after moving off the next morning, the posse had found
that the gang's tracks veered sharply to the west. Using the old
cavalry technique of riding for an hour at a fast trot, then
halting, removing the saddles and allowing the horses to roll,
graze and relax for fifteen minutes, they were able to make
better time than the outlaws. Slowly but surely, they were closing the distance between them and the Glover gang.

Continuing the process of riding and halting until some of
the horses were too tired to roll, the posse had reached the
Pease River about twenty miles above its junction with the Red
by nightfall. They had been in the vicinity of the Box V ranch
house and Laurie had sent men in search of information and
fresh horses to keep up their rapid pace.

The gang had swung well clear of the ranch, but returned to
the river and kept going upstream. On reaching the point where

the North Pease—as it had become—swung sharply to the southwest, the gang had gone north.

Making good time, the posse had tracked their quarry across what would one day become Hall and Briscoe counties to the Red River's Prairie Dog Town Fork. On crossing over, they had discovered that the gang had once more headed west. That appeared to rule out the possibility of Glover returning to the Indian Nations after having laid a long, false trail. It could also mean that he had selected his route in the hope of bluffing the posse into turning back.

On coming to the junction of the Swisher Creek and the Prairie Dog Town Fork, Laurie had once more sought information and fresh mounts. Each had been found at Dan Torrant's Lazy T ranch. According to Torrant, there had been no sign of the outlaws near his house. However, one of his men had claimed to have seen signal smoke to the west. Torrant was of the opinion that the gang would turn back once they had become aware of it.

Sheriff Laurie had faced a difficult decision. Although he wanted to take back the gang and its loot, he felt himself responsible for the lives of his posse. In addition to the Ysabel Kid and Waco, he had along his brash, hotheaded young deputy, Eric Narrow, and four citizens. Skilled fighting men, the latter quartet each had a family in Wichita Falls. So Laurie had wondered if he was justified in taking them into the Palo Duro country.

While the other Comanche bands had made peace a few years earlier, due in some part to the Ysabel Kid's efforts,[1] the *Kweharehnuh* (Antelope) band had refused to do so. Returning to the wild, virtually unexplored canyons, draws and hillocks of the Tule and Palo Duro country, they had continued to live in the traditional *Nemenuh*[2] manner and were known strenuously to resent trespass on their domain.

After long, deep thought, Laurie had concluded that Glover

1. Told in *Sidewinder*.
2. *Nemenuh* (The People): the Comanches' name for their nation.

knew he was being hunted and intended to bluff them into quitting. Believing that the gang would turn away before reaching the area from which the signal smoke had been seen, he had told the Kid to keep following their tracks.

Now the sheriff wondered if he had guessed wrongly.

Instead of turning away, the gang's trail had led the posse straight toward the location of the smoke. Then the Kid had made an interesting—and puzzling—discovery. A man had met Glover's party. Telling the sheriff to let the horses rest, the Kid had backtracked the newcomer. Returning thirty minutes later, the Kid had said the man had sent up the smoke signal from the top of a hill that offered an excellent view of the surrounding terrain. He had also claimed that the man walked like an Indian, but rode a shod horse, hinting at mixed blood. Whoever he might be, he had accompanied the gang westward after the meeting.

Much to Deputy Narrow's undisguised annoyance, Laurie had consulted the Kid on what the posse ought to do next. They had closed the distance separating them from the gang to slightly over a mile. Given reasonable luck, they would catch up and capture the outlaws during the night. Against that was the danger of coming across a *Kweharehnuh* hunting party. If it should happen, the Kid believed that he could avert trouble and might even be granted permission to keep going after the gang.

On Laurie putting the situation to the posse, they had agreed to stay with him. Apart from Narrow, they had faith in the judgment of the Ysabel Kid. Possibly the deputy shared it, but he had no intention of letting it be known. To someone who did not know the facts, that faith might have seemed strange, or even misplaced.

Around six foot in height, the Kid had a wiry frame suggestive of untiring and whipcord-tough strength. Every item of his clothing, from the low-crowned, wide-brimmed J. B. Stetson hat, through bandana, vest, shirt, Levi's pants to the flat-heeled boots, was black in color. On a gunbelt of the same sober hue he carried a walnut-handled Dragoon Colt butt forward in a low cavalry-twist holster at the right and an ivory-hilted James Black bowie knife sheathed at the left. Across the crook of his left arm, encased in a fringed buckskin pouch of Indian manufacture, rested a Winchester Model '66 rifle.

The armament appeared out of keeping, taken with the handsome, almost babyishly innocent aspect of his Indian-dark face. Or might if one discounted his red-hazel eyes. They implied that a savage, untrammeled wildness lay behind the black-haired Texan's youthful exterior.

Slouching apparently at ease on a horse borrowed from the Lazy T, with his magnificent white stallion—which looked as untamed as its master—loping barebacked at his side, he exuded a sense of being more Indian than white. People who knew him were aware of how close that came to being true.

Although his mother had died giving birth to him, Loncey Dalton Ysabel had survived to be raised as a member of the *Pehnane* (Wasp, Quick-Stinger, Raider) Comanches. His maternal grandfather, Long Walker, was war chief of the Dog Soldier lodge. From that source, his father—an Irish Kentuckian called Sam Ysabel—being away much of the time on the family's business of smuggling, the child had learned all the subjects a brave-heart warrior was expected to know.[3]

By his fourteenth year, when he had ridden off on his first war trail, the boy had already gained the man-name *Cuchilo* by virtue of his skill in using a bowie knife. To the Mexicans along the Rio Grande, where he had helped his father on contraband-running expeditions, he became known as *Cabrito* (the Kid). The Texans with whom he had come into contact called him first Sam Ysabel's Kid, then changed it to the Ysabel Kid. Members of all three races were unanimous in their opinion that he would become a fighting man second to none, and he had fulfilled the predictions. Maybe he was not *real* fast with his old Dragoon, but he could claim few peers when it came to accuracy in using a rifle.

At the outbreak of the War Between the States, the Kid and

3. Told in *Comanche.*

his father had joined Mosby's Raiders. The Confederate States' government had soon found an even more useful purpose in which their specialized talents could serve the South. So they had spent the remainder of the hostilities collecting shipments of essential materials from Matamoros and delivering the goods across the Rio Grande to the authorities in Texas. While doing so, the Kid had increased his reputation of being a bad man to cross.

Bushwhack lead had cut down Sam Ysabel soon after the war had ended. While searching for his father's killers, the Kid had met a man who changed the whole course of his life. The Rio Hondo gun wizard, Dusty Fog, had been conducting a mission on which the peace between the United States and Mexico hung balanced, and the Kid had helped him bring it to a successful conclusion.[4] At the same time, the Kid had also avenged his father's murder. That had left him with the problem of what to do next. Smuggling was unprofitable in the war-impoverished Lone Star State, and without his father along, it had no longer appealed to him. So he had accepted Dusty Fog's offer and joined the OD Connected ranch's floating outfit.

In that way, a potentially dangerous young man had been transformed into a useful member of the community. The people of Texas could be grateful that he had. His Comanche-trained skills—silent movement, locating hidden enemies and remaining concealed from keen-eyed searchers, how to follow a track or hide his own trail, exceptional ability with a variety of weapons and at horse-handling—would have made him a formidable outlaw with no exaggerated notions about the sanctity of human life. However, since joining the elite of General Ole Devil Hardin's ranch crew, he had used his talents solely for the cause of law and order.

On resuming the hunt, the Kid had told Waco to handle the tracking. Instead of studying the marks on the ground, the Kid concentrated his efforts on scouring the terrain ahead. Having seen the youngster, whose only name was Waco, read sign dur-

4. Told in *The Ysabel Kid.*

ing the hunt, Laurie raised no objections. The sheriff knew that the Kid was acting in a correct manner and was better occupied in locating an ambush should one be attempted.

Maybe two inches taller than the Kid, Waco had a spread to his shoulders that hinted at a powerful frame fast developing to full manhood. In dress and appearance he was a typical Texas cowhand. Blond, blue-eyed and handsome, he wore two staghorn-butted 1860 Army Colts in the carefully designed holsters of a well-made gunbelt. He too sat a borrowed horse and led his big, powerful paint stallion. A Winchester Model of 1873 rifle dangled from his right hand.

Like the Kid, Waco had once teetered on the verge of the owlhoot trail. Where smuggling might have brought the Indian-dark young man into conflict with the law, Waco could easily have turned into a wanted, desperate killer.

Left an orphan almost from birth by a Waco Indian raid, the blond youngster had been raised as part of a North Texas rancher's sizable family. Guns had always been a part of his life, and his sixteenth birthday had seen him employed by Clay Allison. In that tough wild-onion crew, noted for their boisterous ways and generally dangerous behavior, Waco had perfected his ability to draw fast and shoot accurately. Living constantly in the company of older men, he had grown sullen, quick to temper and ever ready to take offense. It had seemed only a matter of time before he would become involved in that one shootout too many which would have seen him branded as a killer, with a price on his head.

Fortunately for Waco, that day did not come. From the moment that Dusty Fog had saved his life—at considerable risk to his own—the youngster had started to change for the better.[5] Leaving Allison, with the Washita curly-wolf's blessing, he had found himself accepted as a member of the floating outfit. From the other members, who treated him like a favorite younger brother, he had learned many useful lessons. His skill in han-

5. Told in *Trigger Fast*.

dling revolvers had not diminished, but he now knew *when* as well as *how* to shoot.

Six miles had fallen behind the posse since the Kid had relinquished his post as tracker. Suddenly he brought his horses to a halt.

"Stay put, boy!" he ordered as Waco's head swung in his direction.

"Yo!" the youngster answered.

"Hold it back there, sheriff," the Kid went on, looking over his shoulder. "I'm going to make some talk to them *Kweharehnuh* bucks up ahead."

"*Kweh*—!" Laurie began, motioning to Narrow and the townsmen to stop and advancing to join the cowhands. "I don't see 'em!"

"They're there," the Kid assured him. "So stay put. No matter what happens, don't start shooting and don't come after me."

"We won't," promised Laurie.

"That goes for you more than any of them, boy," the Kid said, eyeing his companion coldly.

"I hear you," Waco drawled.

"Mind you do it then!" growled the Kid.

"You'd reckon he didn't trust me to do it," Waco commented to the tall wiry peace officer, as the Kid transferred to the white stallion's bare back without setting foot on the ground.

"Maybe he knows you," Laurie replied.

"I'll fix his wagon," threatened the young blond, without denying the allegation. "When we get down to home, I'll lay all the blame on him for us being late back."

On their way home after a successful and profitable trail drive to Mulrooney, Kansas, the floating outfit had called at Bent's Ford in the Indian Nations. Dusty had found a telegraph message from Ole Devil awaiting his arrival, telling him to call and see the governor of Texas at Austin. Doing so had created something of a problem. Part of the trail herd had belonged to a friend who ranched near Throckmorton and had been unable to make the drive. After some discussion, it had been decided that the Kid should deliver the friend's share of the money brought in by the cattle.

Sharing the Indian-dark cowhand's aversion to wearing formal clothes and a necktie—which would most likely be expected of him when visiting the governor—Waco had volunteered to accompany the Kid. They had been in Wichita Falls during the bank robbery and offered their services to the sheriff. Before setting out with the posse, the Kid had notified Dusty of their actions by telegraph. Neither of them felt any qualms at turning aside from their duty, knowing that Dusty and Ole Devil would approve of them doing so under the circumstances.

"What's up, Ian?" Narrow demanded as he and the four townsmen gathered around the sheriff.

"The Kid's seen some *Kweharehnuh* and's going to talk to them," Laurie replied. "Keep your rifles on your saddles and don't nobody shoot unless I give you the word."

A low rumbled mutter of surprise rose from the men. They all tried, without success, to locate the Indians that the Kid had claimed he was going to interview. Ahead, the range was little different from the kind of terrain through which they had traveled all day. Rolling, broken by folds, mounds and draws, it hardly seemed capable of offering hiding places for a large body of men. Apart from the solitary, black-clad figure on the huge white stallion, there was no sign of human life in front of them. As usual, Narrow was inclined to scoff.

"They must be a hell of a long ways off," the deputy declared. "I can't see hide nor hair of them."

"Which's likely why the sheriff had Lon and not you riding the point," drawled Waco.

Although Narrow let out a hiss of annoyance, he made no reply. Early in the hunt, he had found out that his assumption of tough superiority did not impress Waco. So he sat back in his saddle and watched the Kid with an air of disbelief. At the moment, Narrow found himself torn between two desires. While he looked forward to a fight with the Indians, he also hoped the Kid would prove to be wrong. Then the sheriff would stop listening to the cowhand and pay more attention to his deputy's opinions.

"Reckon he's joshing us about them *Kweharehnuh,* Waco?" asked a posseman called Bretton.

"He wouldn't know how at a time like this," the young blond replied.

With each sequence of hoofbeats in the stallion's walking gait carrying him deeper into danger, the Kid maintained his ceaseless vigilance. Detecting the whole of the Antelope party might spell the difference between life and death. So, although he slouched casually as if a part of the horse, he had never been more alert.

Give them their full due, the *Kweharehnuh* braves sure knew how to keep out of a man's sight. Like the Kid, they must have taken seriously their childhood games of *nanip'ka* (guess over the hill), in which the players had to hide so that the one who was "it" could not locate them. It offered mighty good training in concealment as well as for the discovery of hidden men.

That is, all but one of them remembered the lessons of *nanip'ka.*

Flattened on a slope behind a fair-sized rock, the solitary transgressor had allowed the single eagle's feather of his head-dress to rise into view. He must be a *tuivitsi*[6] fresh from horse-herding and on his first man's chore. Happen he did not improve his technique, he would never make a *tehnap,*[7] much less reach the honored state of *tsukup.*[8] The feather's movement in the breeze had been sufficient to attract the Kid's attention and so spoiled what would have been an effective ambush.

The nearer the Kid rode, the more uneasy he became. So far, he had picked out twenty braves and feared that there might be others still hidden from him. A gentle touch on the reins of the stallion's hackmore ended its forward motion about sixty yards from the nearest located Indian. That ought to leave him suffi-

6. *Tuivitsi:* an adolescent.
7. *Tehnap:* an experienced warrior.
8. *Tsukup:* old man.

cient distance to turn and get the hell back to the posse happen things should go wrong.

Gripping the rifle at the wrist of the butt and end of the barrel, he elevated it above his head. That allowed the *Kweharehnuh* to see the red, white and blue patterns on the buckskin container. With such a well-planned ambush, there must be a *tehnap* present who would be able to identify the medicine symbols. If so, they would know the container to be a Dog Soldier's medicine boot, given to each member of that hardy, savage lodge on his initiation.

Three times the Kid raised and lowered the rifle. Then, taking his right hand from the butt, he turned the rifle so it pointed forward with the barrel still in his left fist. After that, it was just a matter of waiting. He had let them see the medicine boot and made a sign identifying himself as a Dog Soldier who asked to make talk. That put the play into the *Kweharehnuh*'s hands. The next move must come from them.

It came!

Rearing to kneel on the rock, the *tuivitsi* who had betrayed the ambush flipped the butt of his rifle to his shoulder and pressed its trigger.

2

YOU'RE NOT ABOUT TO
BE COMING BACK

"They're attacking him!" screeched Bretton as the young *Kweharehnuh* brave appeared and fired in the Kid's direction.

"Come on!" Narrow shouted, starting his horse moving. "Let's go!"

Remembering the Kid's orders and seeing that his *amigo* had not been hit, Waco jumped his horses to swing into the other men's path.

"Stay put!" the youngster snapped, and the foregrip of his Winchester slapped into his left palm as he prepared to enforce the demand should it become necessary. "Lon's all right and he's not hightailing it back here."

"Do like Waco says!" the sheriff commanded. "Form a line, just in case, but hold your fire unless I tell you different."

When the bullet flung up dirt less than a yard in front of his horse, the Kid uttered a silent prayer that the posse would not attempt to intervene. He stiffened just a trifle, alert to pivot the stallion around and go like a bat out of hell should the need become apparent. So far, only the *tuivitsi* had thrown lead. Other *Kweharehnuh* came popping out of their hiding places, many of which hardly appeared to offer enough cover to conceal a jackrabbit. However, they made no hostile gestures.

With a sensation of relief, the Kid noticed that a few obvious *tehnap* and a warbonnet chief were present. The latter barked an order for the *tuivitsi* to refrain from further shooting. That indicated a willingness to talk. On the other hand, to add to the Kid's concern, he observed that every man—even the youngest *tuivitsi*—carried a rifle.

And not just *a* rifle!

The weapons they held were all *repeaters!*

Looking closer, the Kid saw the big sidehammers and distinctive trigger guards of Spencer carbines. In addition to brass-framed Winchester Model of 1866 "yellow boys," there were a few all-steel Model '73's. What was more, from the raw *tuivitsi* to the warbonnet chief, each warrior had at least one belt with bullet-loaded loops on his person.

"Who are you, white man?" called the chief in the quick-tongued dialect of the *Kweharehnuh*. "You wear the clothes of a ride-plenty, but signal that you are a *Pehnane* Dog Soldier."

"My name is *Cuchilo,* the Knife," replied the Kid, using the slower-spoken *Pehnane* accent fluently. "My grandfather is Long Walker. I come to make peace talk with my *Kweharehnuh* brothers."

"I have heard of Long Walker, and of *Cuchilo,*" the chief admitted as the Kid rode up to him. "But it is said that you are now a white man. And all men know that Long Walker eats the beef on the reservation."

"Long Walker has made peace with the white men, as did chiefs of other bands," answered the Kid, watching the braves coming closer to hear what might be said. "Just as I now live with them. But if any man doubts that I am still one of the *Nemenuh*—"

While addressing the chief, the Kid had eased the boot from his rifle and draped it across the stallion's neck. Giving no hint of what he planned to do, he let the one-piece reins fall, swung his left leg forward and up, jumping to the ground on the horse's Indian side.[1] As he landed, he snapped the Winchester to his shoulder. Now his left hand held the foregrip, while the right inserted its forefinger into the trigger guard and curled the other three through the ring of the lever. Almost as soon as his feet touched the ground, he had the sights laid. Three times in a second and a half, blurring the lever through its reloading cycle, he sent .44-caliber bullets spinning from the muzzle.

Once again Waco displayed his quick grasp of the situation. Realizing from the Kid's apparently passive acceptance that the *tuivitsi*'s shot had been no more than a test of courage, the blond cowhand had been waiting for his *amigo*'s response. Knowing him, Waco had expected the answer to the challenge to be something sudden and dramatic.

"Keep the guns down!" Waco warned, even before the Kid's Winchester had started to crack. "He's all right."

Shock twisted at the *tuivitsi*'s face as he realized that the black-dressed ride-plenty (cowhand) was lining a rifle at him. Before he could make a move to counter the threat, bullets started slamming between his spread-apart knees and spattering his bare legs with flying chips of rock. Letting out a startled yelp, he bounded into the air. Coming down, he slipped from his perch and landed rumpfirst on the ground. Although the descent and arrival proved painful, he retained his grip on the Spencer carbine. Spitting out furious words, he tried to raise it and avenge his deflated ego.

Having expected such a reaction, the Kid was already bounding forward. Giving the *tuivitsi* no opportunity to point the Spencer his way, he lashed up with his left foot and kicked it from the other's hands. In a continuation of the attack, the Kid elevated his Winchester and propelled its metal-shod butt against the side of the brave's head. Down went the *tuivitsi*, flopping limply onto his side. Without sparing his victim as much as a glance, the Kid returned and vaulted afork the stal-

---

1. Unlike the white man, the Indian mounted and dismounted on the right side.

lion's seventeen-hand back as if it stood no higher than a newly born foal.

Hoots of laughter burst from the stocky, thick-bodied warriors in the antelope-hide clothing. Like most Indians, the Comanches had a lively sense of humor when among their own kind. They had appreciated the manner in which the Kid had handled their companion. That had been the way of a *tehnap* dealing with a *tuivitsi* who had forgotten his proper station in the band's social structure. Fast, painful and very effective.

No matter how the Kid might be dressed, the *Kweharehnuh* braves now accepted that he was a Comanche. Every action he had made since being fired at by the *tuivitsi* had been that of an experienced name-warrior.

"Well, chief," challenged the Kid. "Am I still *Nemenuh*?"

"You are still *Nemenuh, Cuchilo,*" confirmed the chief. "I am called Kills Something."

"The fame of *Pakawa* has reached my ears," the Kid said conventionally, using the other's Comanche name.

"Why do you bring white men into the land of the *Kweharehnuh, Cuchilo*?"

That had an ominous ring to it. Normally there would have been more talk: a lengthy delivery of compliments, or an exchange of tribal gossip. So the Kid felt puzzled by its omission. Something else was wrong, too. With Glover's gang so near, the warriors must have seen them. Yet there had not been time for the *Kweharehnuh* to have killed the five men silently and then taken up their ambush positions. It seemed unlikely that *Pakawa* would permit the smaller party to pass and go for the larger.

"We are hunting for thieves," the Kid answered frankly, knowing that stealing from one's own people rated as a serious crime among the Comanches. "The men who went by here not long ago."

"What is it you want from us?" Kills Something inquired, but his voice held no hint of making an amiable request for information.

"To go after them and take them back to their people."

"No!"

"They are like mad wolves, *Pakawa*," the Kid pointed out. "As long as such live, nobody, red or white, is safe from them."

"I must still say no," the chief stated.

"Can I ask why?"

"It is the order of *Paruwa Semehno* and the medicine woman *Pohawe*. They say that no white men, except the chosen, may enter our land."

"And the four white men and the half-breed are the chosen?"

"Yes. The man of no people has the medicine, so we let them pass. Tell the men with you to turn back, *Cuchilo*."

"What if they won't do it?"

"You are a *tehnap, Cuchilo*," Kills Something replied. "So you will know when it is time to fight and when to ride away. There are three of us, each with a repeating rifle, for every one of you. If you come, there will be dead men in the Land of Good Hunting. I do not think they will be *Nemenuh*. And tell the one with the star to think well on what he orders. There are young braves with me who want to count coups. Let them taste blood, and they will go looking for more. If they do, many will die."

"All this I will remember, *Pakawa*," promised the Kid. "May your squaws give you many children."

With that, the Kid turned his stallion and rode toward his companions. He did not look back. To do so would be discourteous in that it would imply a lack of trust in the warriors he was leaving.

"When do we take out after 'em, Kid?" demanded Narrow, before any of the others could speak.

"I don't reckon we can," the Kid replied flatly.

"But we're not more'n a mile behind 'em," the deputy protested.

"And there's twenty or more *Kweharehnuh* brave-hearts less'n half a mile ahead of us," warned the Kid.

"So?" grunted Narrow. "They was talking peaceable enough to you."

"Why, sure," the Kid agreed. "Only they'll stop acting peaceable happen we try to go by 'em."

"I'll be damned if I've rid' this far to be turned back by a handful of tail-dragging Injuns!" Narrow bellowed, still refusing to let the others get a word in. "I say we go on and the hell with what they figure to do about it."

"You try it, deputy," drawled the Kid, "and you're not about to be coming back."

"It's as bad as that, huh, Kid?" the sheriff put in, silencing his deputy with a scowl.

"It's that bad," the Kid confirmed. "Every one of them, down to the youngest *tuivitsi*'s toting a repeater and enough bullets to start *two* wars. And they've been told by old Chief Ten Bears 'n' their medicine woman to keep white folk out of the Palo Duro. Unless that 'breed who met Glover's with 'em."

"We could go 'round 'em—" Narrow began.

"There's not even part of a hope of doing it," the Kid declared. "They'll have a couple of scouts trail us, and happen we're *loco* enough to try, the rest'll be on hand so fast you'll think the hawgs've jumped us."

"Damn it all, Kid!" growled the sheriff. "Why should they let owlhoots go through and stop us?"

"I don't know, sheriff. It's medicine business, and rightly, they don't talk about *that* even to a feller from another *Nemenuh* band."

"So you're saying we should go back, Kid?" asked posseman Hobart.

"That's what I'd say, was I trail-bossing this posse," the Kid answered. "If we push on and get wiped out, those young bucks'll think they've got real strong war medicine and set off to try it out. Folks'll die then. But I'll go along with whatever the sheriff says we do."

"Couldn't we set up camp here and wait 'em out?" asked Bretton.

"Happen they got short on patience, they're more likely to jump us than head for home," the Kid replied. "I could maybe get through alone and talk to old *Paruwa Semehno*. Only, way

Paruwa spoke, I reckon I'd be wasting my time. For some reason, he's shielding them owlhoots and a whole lot farther east than I'd've figured on. Fact being, I was counting on taking Glover tonight and well clear of the *Kweharehnuh*'s range. Those bucks won't let it happen."

"So was I," Laurie admitted.

By bringing only a small, handpicked posse, the sheriff had hoped to catch up with the gang before they penetrated too deeply into the Palo Duro country. Faced with the present situation, he could see only one answer. To go on meant fighting, probably getting killed. Given a victory to whet their appetite, the young bucks would sweep off on a rampage of looting and slaughter.

"What'll we do, Ian?" Bretton wanted to know.

"We go back," the sheriff replied quietly and bitterly.

Although the townsmen, the Kid and Waco nodded their agreement, Narrow registered his disapproval.

"So we're going back with our tails dragging 'tween our legs?" the deputy snarled. "That'll look good comes next election."

"So'd going on and stirring up an Injun war, *hombre*," drawled Waco.

"It's easy enough for you to talk about pulling out," Narrow answered. "You didn't have money in our bank."

"I did!" Poplar, the third member of the posse, injected coldly. "Likely more than you did, Eric. But I'm still ready to go along with whatever Ian says we should do."

"There's no way out, Kid?" Laurie asked.

"It's turn back, or go all the way and likely stay permanent. You want me to, I can maybe sneak by the *Kweharehnuh* in the dark and go after Glover. Only there'll be none of them coming back with me, and way I'll have to travel after it's done, I'll not be able to fetch back your money."

"I want justice, not that kind of revenge," Laurie answered. "No. We'll all go back."

Guiding their horses around, the dejected posse began to ride in the direction from which they had come. Without making it obvious, the Kid kept a watch to the rear. As he had expected, they were followed at a distance by two braves. After they had covered about three miles, the sheriff joined the Kid and Waco behind the party.

"You said *all* them bucks had repeaters, Kid?" Laurie asked.

"Every last blasted one."

"That's not usual, is it?"

"It's damned *unusual,* sheriff. You'll mostly find a few repeaters in each village. But it's near on always the chiefs and name-warriors who own 'em. And bullets're mostly in short supply."

"Then somebody must've been selling them to the *Kweharehnuh,*" Laurie said.

"What'd the *tuivitsi* have to buy them with?" countered the Kid. "It'd take a whole heap of trade goods to buy a repeater. More than a *tuivitsi*'d be likely to own."

"Couldn't the *tuivitsi*'ve had the rifles give' 'em?" Waco inquired. "You told me a warrior often gives his loot away."

"Not a repeater, especially if there's so much ammunition around for it," corrected the Kid. "And, happen a war party'd pulled a raid that brought in so many rifles, we'd've heard about it."

"It could've happened a fair time back," the sheriff pointed out.

"Not all that long," objected the Kid. "Some of them were toting Model '73's and they've not been around a year yet."

"What worries me as a peace officer," Laurie said soberly, "is why they let a bunch of owlhoots through."

"And me," admitted the Kid. "Comanches don't cotton to thieves."

"How about when they're wide-looping hosses?" challenged Waco.

"That's not stealing, it's raiding," the Kid explained. "And they don't do it again' another *Nemenuh.*"

"Do you think that old Ten Bears's been paid, either with money to buy them or the rifles and ammunition, to let Glover and his men through?"

"You mean that Glover'd fixed it up, through the 'breed they met, sheriff?" Waco asked. "It could be, Lon. If Glover was getting hard-pushed by the Rangers and figured the Nations to be unhealthy for white owlhoots, he might've decided to come this way."

"And sent the 'breed on ahead to dicker the way by the *Kweharehnuh* for them?" asked Laurie.

"Something like that," agreed the blond youngster.

"Would Glover've made enough money to be able to pay for that many rep—" the Kid began, then his head swiveled around and he pointed. "Hey. Look there!"

Following the direction indicated by the Kid, Waco and Laurie found that a cavalry patrol was coming toward them. Fanned out in line abreast, ten privates flanked a first lieutenant, sergeant and civilian scout. Unlike the posse, who had returned their rifles to the saddleboots, the soldiers carried their Springfield carbines in their hands.

"Halt!" yelled the officer, apparently addressing the posse, for his own men kept moving. "Halt in the name of the United States government."

"Means us, I'd say," drawled the Kid.

"Best do it," Waco commented, studying the officer's nonregulation white planter's hat, shoulder-long brown hair, the buckskin jacket over an official blue shirt and Western-style gunbelt. "He reckons he's ole Yellow Hair Custer."

Stopping their horses, Laurie's party watched the patrol advancing in what looked suspiciously like a skirmishing line. Instead of riding straight up, the lieutenant brought his men to a halt about fifty yards away. The soldiers did not boot their carbines. Rather they shifted the weapons to a position of greater readiness, which the Kid, for one, found disconcerting and annoying.

"Who are you men?" demanded the officer in a harsh, challenging tone.

"The sheriff of Wichita County and his posse," Laurie called back, moving slowly around so that his badge of office would be visible. "Don't you remember me, Sergeant Gamba?"

"It's him all right, sir," declared the stocky Italian noncom.

Not until he had received the assurance did the officer show any sign of relaxing. Ordering his men to sling their carbines, he rode forward. Asking the Kid to accompany him, Laurie went to meet the patrol.

"What brings you out this way, sheriff?" asked the officer, without the formality of an introduction.

"I was after the Glover gang," Laurie replied. "They robbed the bank at Wichita Falls."

"Did you catch them?"

"Nope. The *Kweharehnuh* turned us back."

"*Kweharehnuh*!" repeated the officer eagerly. "Did they attack you?"

"Just told us to turn back," corrected the sheriff.

"And, of course, you obeyed," the lieutenant said dryly.

"Seeing's how there was twenty or more of 'em, all toting Winchesters or Spencers," the Kid put in, "it seemed like a right smart thing to do."

"There were only twenty of them?"

"Maybe twenty-four, or -six. I didn't stop to take no careful trail count on them, mister. 'Specially when they could right soon get more to help out should they need 'em."

"Where do I find them?" the officer demanded, and a light of battle glowed in his eyes.

"Was you *loco* enough to go looking, they're maybe four, five miles back," the Kid replied. "All 'cepting two scouts who're watching us talking to you."

"I don't see any scouts," announced the lieutenant, after taking a cursory glance at the surrounding country.

"That figures," the Kid sniffed. "They're not fixing to be seen."

Although the officer—his name was Raynor—heard the words, he ignored both them and the speaker. An ardent admirer of General George Armstrong Custer and a disciple of his policy toward Indians, Raynor saw the chance of coming to the notice of his superiors. Oblivious of the fact that he commanded a mere ten men, and they barely beyond the recruit stage, he was prepared to take on whatever force the *Kweharehnuh* might have at hand. If there was honor and distinction to be gained, however, he did not intend to share it with an obscure civilian peace officer.

"Wait here for an hour, sheriff," Raynor ordered. "Then we'll accompany you after the outlaws."

"But—!" Laurie gasped, realizing what the officer meant to do.

"Handling Indians comes under the jurisdiction of the United States Army," Raynor interrupted pompously. "And this is far beyond the boundaries of Wichita County."

"You mean you're fixing to lock horns with them *Kweharehnuh,*" growled the Kid, "knowing they're all toting repeaters?"

"I shall do my duty as I see it, cowboy," Raynor replied. "If you'll wait here, sheriff, I'll send back word when it's safe for you to join me."

3

YOU'RE LETTING THEM GET KILLED

Riding westward once more at a slow walk, the posse heard the crashing of many shots from where the cavalry patrol had disappeared into a valley. It could not be said that the sound came as any great surprise to Sheriff Laurie and his companions.

Stubbornly refusing to listen to the Kid's warning, and overriding the sheriff's offers of assistance, First Lieutenant Raynor had insisted on taking his small body of men in search of the *Kweharehnuh*. Nothing anybody had said came close to persuading him that he was acting in a foolishly dangerous manner. The two scouts had either concealed themselves exceptionally well, or withdrawn at the sight of the posse meeting the patrol. So, on his own scout failing to locate them, Raynor had made it clear that he doubted if they had ever existed.

When the Kid had tried to pass his warning to Sergeant Gamba, Raynor had flown into a rage and threatened to arrest him for trying to seduce members of the United States Army from their duty. Laurie's intervention had saved the officer from paying the penalty for such incautious, ill-advised behavior. Unfortunately, the damage had been done. Filled with an overinflated sense of his own importance, Raynor had taken the Kid's words as a personal affront and refused to discuss the matter further. Repeating his order for the posse to remain at that spot until his men had cleared a way through the Indians, Raynor had set off to meet his destiny.

If it had not been for the very real danger of Raynor stirring up an Indian war, Laurie might have left the officer to his fate. As things stood, the civilians knew that they must back up the military. Allowing the patrol to cover about three quarters of a mile, the sheriff had followed with his men.

Absorbed in daydreams of the acclaim his victory over the *Kweharehnuh* would bring, Raynor had remained in ignorance of the flagrant disobedience shown by the civilians. Concentrating on the range ahead, for they had taken the Kid's warning seriously, Gamba and the scout had evidently decided that they could forget the danger of an attack from the rear. None of the other soldiers had seen sufficient service to take the precaution of maintaining an all-round watch in such a situation.

"Come up careful!" snapped the Kid, making another of his spectacular changes from the borrowed horse—remounted on his return from the interview with Kills Something—to his stallion and sending it leaping forward.

Before starting to follow the soldiers, the members of the posse had drawn their rifles. Armed and ready for battle, they set off after the Kid. Their horses might still have been walking, the way the big white—unburdened by a saddle and other equipment—drew ahead of them.

Despite the urgency of the situation, the Kid did not forget his lessons in the art of making war *Nemenuh*-fashion. He scanned the rim of the valley, searching for any scouts the *Kweharehnuh* might have placed there. Not that he really expected to find them. Acting as scouts was work for the younger braves, but not at such a moment. No properly raised *Nemenuh* warrior would be willing to take such a passive role when there was honor to be won, coups available to be counted and loot for the gathering. So the whole bunch he had met earlier would be involved in the ambush.

Given just a smidgin of good Texas luck, the posse's arrival might not be detected until it was too late for the *Kweharehnuh* to deal with them.

Approaching the rim, the Kid signaled for his horse to stop. Even before its forward momentum had ceased, he quit its back and ran on. Dropping to his stomach, he wriggled to the edge of the valley and looked over. He had expected to find the patrol in difficulties, but not in that deep.

Below the Kid, the slope descended at an easy angle and was covered with a coating of rocks and bushes. It formed one side of a narrow, winding valley through which the posse had earlier followed the Glover gang. At the time, it had struck the Kid as a good place for an ambush. Studying what lay before him, he found that his judgment had been very accurate.

Raynor sprawled motionless on his back halfway across the bottom. Close by lay his scout, his skull a hideous mess where a heavy-caliber Spencer's bullet had torn through it. One private and four dead horses completed the toll taken by the *Kweharehnuh*'s opening volley.

Hunched behind a rock at the foot of the slope, his right arm dangling limp and bloody from where a .44 Winchester ball had struck it, Sergeant Gamba held a long-barreled Peacemaker in his left hand and yelled encouragement to his remaining men. They had lost all their horses, the Kid observed, and apparently most of their ammunition. Crouching in whatever cover they could find, they still returned the hail of lead that came hurtling their way from various points on the other slope. So far, the *Kweharehnuh* remained concealed except for brief appearances to rise and throw shots at the soldiers.

Nearer rumbled the hooves of the posse's horses. The sound slammed the Kid back to reality. There was only one way in which his party could hope to save the remnants of the patrol. Done properly, it would inflict such a defeat on the *Kweharehnuh* as to chill their desire for further riding of the war trail.

Swiftly the Kid backed away from the rim and rose. Turning, he sprinted toward his companions, waving for them to halt. While uncertain of what he wanted, the sheriff was willing to back him up. Reining in his own horse, Laurie yelled for the others to stop. All but Narrow obeyed. Every bit as hotheaded and reckless as the late Lieutenant Raynor, the deputy was too excited by the prospect of a fight to take notice of what went on around him.

The Kid spat out a curse. All too well he knew the way of the Comanche braves in that kind of a fight. Only by acting as he wanted could the posse hope to be effective in their rescue bid. So he did not mean to let the deputy spoil the plan he had in mind.

Flinging himself forward, the Kid shot out his left hand to grab the reins of Narrow's horse close to the bridle's curb chain. With a jerk, he caused the animal to turn so abruptly that it nearly fell and almost unseated its rider. By dropping his rifle and clutching the horn in both hands, Narrow saved himself from being dislodged. Rage flared in his eyes as he glared down at the Kid's unsmiling, Comanche-savage face. At that moment, the Indian-dark cowhand looked anything but young and innocent.

"What the hell—?" the deputy snarled.

"Get down, *pronto!*" answered the Kid, still holding the reins. "If you don't, I'll gut this critter and you for making me do it!" Then he swung his gaze to the other men. "Get off them hosses and head for the rim. Be careful. Don't let the Injuns see you and don't start shooting until I give the word."

"Do it!" Waco advised, leaping to the ground. The fact that the Kid had said "Injuns" instead of *"Kweharehnuh"* gave the youngster some notion of how urgently and seriously he regarded the situation.

"Come on, boys!" Laurie went on, and set the townsmen an example by dismounting to dart after Waco on foot.

Leaving their horses ground-hitched by the trailing reins, the four men headed toward the rim. Retaining his grip on Narrow's reins, the Kid watched them. He nodded in satisfaction when he saw that his orders were being carried out to the letter. Then he turned his eyes to meet the deputy's.

"On your feet, or not at all, *hombre*," the Kid warned. "And make up your mind fast."

"All right," Narrow answered, and swung from his saddle.

While the deputy checked his rifle, the Kid joined their companions on the rim. Still the steady rain of bullets flew from the opposite slope, being answered by an ever-decreasing response from the soldiers. So far, fortunately, the *Kweharehnuh* did not appear to have realized that a new factor had entered the game.

"No shooting!" the Kid gritted, hearing Hobart's low-spoken exclamation of anger and seeing him lining his rifle.

"You're letting them get killed!" Narrow raged, having arrived and flattened himself alongside Waco. "And I'm damned if I'll stand by—"

"You shoot and so do I," the blond threatened, twisting to thrust the muzzle of his rifle into the deputy's side. "Lon knows what he's doing."

"Get set!" ordered the Kid, moving his rifle into position and watching the way in which the *Kweharehnuh* braves exposed themselves for longer periods when rising to shoot at the soldiers. "They'll be charging—*Now!*"

Suddenly, bringing the final word of the Kid's warning in a sharp, loud crack, stocky warriors seemed to spout from their places of concealment.

"Brave up, brothers!" roared a young *tehnap* who wore as his war medicine a headdress with a pair of pronghorn antelope horns large enough to turn a white trophy hunter wild with envy. "This is a good day to die!"

With their repeaters cracking as fast as the levers could be worked—and, in the case of the Spencers, the hammers cocked manually—the warriors hurled themselves eagerly toward the soldiers.

It was an awe-inspiring sight, made more so by the earsplitting war whoops that burst from each brave's lips as he charged. No bunch of unblooded soldiers, especially after having been so badly mauled, could be expected to remain unaf-

fected in the face of such an assault. Their heads having been
filled with old soldiers' stories of the consequences of defeat
when Indian-fighting, the remnants of the patrol showed signs
of panic. Desperately Sergeant Gamba tried to rally them.

Everything seemed to be going exactly as the *Kweharehnuh*
wanted.

All but for one small, yet very significant, detail.

In their excitement, the Antelopes had either overlooked or
discounted the posse. Even worse for them, they had forgotten
the presence of the black-dressed ride-plenty who had been ed-
ucated as a Comanche and won himself the man-name *Cuchilo*.

The Kid had known that, no matter how advantageous it
might be, the younger braves would not content themselves
with a long-distance fight against an all but beaten enemy.
Coups counted by personal contact rated too highly for that. So
he had been determined to keep his party's presence unsus-
pected until the moment when their intervention would carry
the greatest weight.

"Fire!" snapped the sheriff, at last understanding why the
Kid had insisted upon waiting.

Seven rifles crashed in a ragged volley, followed by the eighth
as Waco swung his Winchester away from Narrow. Down went
the young *tehnap,* hit by three bullets. His antelope horn medicine had proved ineffective. Death took two more of the braves
at almost the same moment. A fourth screamed and crumpled
forward as red-hot lead drilled through his thigh, and a fifth's
"yellow boy" was sent spinning from his grasp.

"Pour it into them!" Laurie roared, his sights swinging away
from the *tehnap* who had led the charge.

Even as he worked the lever of his Winchester, the Kid knew
that he had not been the only one to send a bullet into the
tehnap. Waco would have selected another warrior, knowing
how the Kid's mind worked. Probably the sheriff and that loud-
mouthed deputy had gone for the buck as the most profitable—
or in Narrow's case, the most impressive—target. Not that the
Kid devoted much attention to the matter, being more concerned with saving what was left of the patrol.

Caught in the withering blast of fire, the braves' assault wavered. Another two warriors tumbled to the ground and the rest came to an uncertain halt.

"Get at them!" bellowed the Kid, leaping to his feet.

Giving the ringing war yell of the *Pehnane,* the dark cowhand bounded down the incline with the agility of a bighorn ram in a hurry. He knew that the posse must press home its advantage and avoid permitting the braves to recover. There was no sign of Kills Something, or the three oldest *tehnaps.* That figured. Warriors of their standing had earned sufficient honors and would be more respected if they stayed in the background and increased the chances of the younger brave-hearts to count coup. Seeing the attack brought to a halt, they would either rush up to give their support, or remain concealed ready to cover the other braves' retreat. In either event, they would be a force to be reckoned with. So, as he ran and cut loose with his rifle, the Kid kept a careful watch for the quartet of experienced fighters.

Waco was the first to follow the Kid's lead, beating Laurie to it by a fraction of a second. Not that the four townsmen lagged behind. Thrusting themselves to their feet, they rushed after the sheriff and cowhands. Only Narrow remained on the rim. Already his Winchester had accounted for the buck with the pronghorn headdress and, he felt sure, cut down another *Kweharehnuh.* He wanted to increase his tally, and shooting on the run being notoriously inaccurate, he doubted if he could do it by leaving his present position.

Twisting around ready to run away, a soldier saw the approaching figures. For a moment he seemed to be on the verge of raising the revolver that dangled in his right hand. Then, recognizing that help was on hand, he turned to use the weapon against the Comanches. By his actions, he spurred his companions into continuing their resistance. They resumed their firing, adding to the *Kweharehnuhs'* confusion.

An uneasy sensation of having missed something began to eat at the Kid as he passed the soldiers. Another two strides brought him almost to the foot of the slope and produced a realization of what he had missed. While Kills Something and the older *tehnaps* would have allowed their less experienced companions to carry out the ambush, they ought to be taking a hand now things had gone wrong.

So where in hell might they be?

The outcome of the affair could easily hang upon the answer to that vitally important question.

Catching a slight hint of movement from the corner of his left eye, the Kid swung his head in that direction. What he saw handed him a shock. Instead of remaining behind the men laying the ambush, at least one of the *tehnaps* had crossed the valley. Rising from behind a large rock, the brave lined his Winchester '73 at the black-dressed cause of his companions' misfortunes. Instantly, showing the superb coordination of mind and muscles developed in his formative years, the Kid hurled himself down in a rolling dive. While his speedy response saved him from the *tehnap*'s first bullet—the wind of which stirred the back of his shirt—he felt sure the next would be better aimed. So he landed expecting to feel the flat-nosed .44.40 bullet strike his body.

As he followed the Kid, Waco saw a shape rising from among a clump of buffalo-berry bushes to his right. Behind the blond, the sheriff found a greater need to notice the warrior. Cradled at his shoulder, the brave's rifle was pointing at Laurie's chest. Like Waco, the sheriff held his Winchester so its barrel was pointing to the left. He doubted if he could turn it quickly enough to save his life. Waco's thoughts paralleled the sheriff's, but he came up with a different answer. Instead of trying to use the rifle, the blond held its foregrip in his left hand. Leaving the wrist of the butt, his right flashed to the staghorn butt of his off-side Army Colt.

To Waco's rear, Laurie watched everything. In his time as a peace officer, he had seen a number of real fast men in action. That tall, blond youngster, in his opinion, could have matched the best. All in a single, incredibly swift motion, Waco produced and fired the revolver. Its bullet took the *tehnap* in the center of the torso. The breastbone cracked, the sound mingling with his cry of pain. He staggered and disappeared as suddenly as he had come into view.

On the rim, Narrow had found the rapidly departing braves an elusive and hard-to-hit target. Six times his rifle had spoken, without the sight of an Indian falling to delight him. So he decided that he might as well join the other members of the posse. Standing up, he observed the *tehnap* rising at the Kid's left. Presented with a stationary target, Narrow hurriedly revised his plans. Taking aim as the warrior sent the shot at the Kid, Narrow fired in echo to it.

"That's another!" the deputy enthused as the *tehnap* collapsed.

Completing his roll by springing to his feet, the Kid turned to the left and wondered why he had not been shot. He saw the *tehnap* going down and commenced a silent vote of thanks to whoever had saved his life. Even as he did so, a savage war screech caused him to forget all thoughts of gratitude.

The young *tuivitsi* was not among those making good their escape. Although he had fallen, he was unharmed. Since his humiliation at the Kid's hands, he had suffered from the mockery of his companions. So he had decided to perform a deed that would retrieve his lost honor. It had been his intention to let the newcomers join the soldiers, then rise and open fire on them—without having given any thought to how he might escape after doing it.

Seeing that his humiliator led the rescuers, the *tuivitsi* had hastily revised his scheme. There would be greater honor if he killed the man who had been responsible for his shame. Looking up, he found that the *Pehnane* was facing to the left and unaware of his presence. Thrusting himself erect with a wild yell, the inexperienced *Kweharehnuh* called attention to himself.

Snapping up his rifle, Laurie took aim and fired. Four more weapons hurled lead at the *tuivitsi*. Two of the bullets missed, but any one of the others would have been fatal and he was thrown backward by their impact.

The Kid spun around. With the *tuivitsi* and the *tehnap* no longer menacing his existence, he looked for Kills Something. Although he figured that the chief would also be on his side of the valley, the Kid was just a shade too late in locating him.

Having positioned himself closer to the rim than the two *tehnaps,* Kills Something had found himself cut off from his companions. There was, however, a way in which the loss of honor could be lessened if not entirely removed. Already Old Man and two of the *tuivitsi* had gathered and driven off the soldiers' horses. So *Pakawa* would take the mounts of the *Pehnane* and the other white men.

Approaching the top of the slope, Kills Something had seen Narrow. Unfortunately for him, the deputy had not been equally observant. Standing erect and in plain sight, thinking of the story he would be able to tell to his cronies on returning to Wichita Falls, Narrow paid the price for his carelessness. Raising his rifle, the chief laid his sights and squeezed the trigger. Puncturing Narrow's left temple, the bullet shattered through the other side of his head. He died without knowing what had hit him.

While turning in search of the chief, the Kid had cradled the butt of the old "yellow boy" against his right shoulder. On detecting Kills Something, he made a rough alignment of the barrel rather than the sights and started shooting. Five times, as fast as he could operate the mechanism, lead spurted from the rifle's barrel. As he fired, the Kid moved the muzzle in a horizontal arc. Fast though he acted, he failed to prevent Narrow from being killed. An instant before the first of the Kid's bullets struck him, the chief had made wolf bait of the deputy. Three of the Kid's shots found their mark and Kills Something fell out of sight beyond the rim.

Lowering his rifle, the Kid snarled out a curse at Raynor's stupidity. Then he swung back to the bottom of the valley and his companions. They showed every sign of continuing to pursue the fleeing braves and he understood the danger of doing it. Chasing surprised, dismounted Comanches was one thing. Going after them once they had reached and boarded their war ponies was a horse of a very different color.

By the time the posse reached the top of the other slope, the braves would be in what had become a Comanche's natural state—on the back of a horse. They would then be ideally suited to escape—or to launch a counterattack. If they selected the latter course, the posse might find them a vastly different and more dangerous proposition.

"Hold it, sheriff!" the Kid yelled. "Let them go!"

Having reached much the same conclusions, Laurie needed only to hear the Kid's words to respond. Nor did any of the other members of the posse raise objections when Laurie called for them to stop.

"Looks like we can get after Glover's bunch again, Ian," Poplar suggested as the men gathered about the sheriff.

"Like hell we can," answered the Kid. "This neck of the woods'll be all aswarm with *Kweharehnuh* once word of the fight gets around. And that'll not be long. We're going to need luck to hit Torrant's afore they jump us, with all the wounded soldiers along. The sooner we get headed that way, the better our chances of doing it."

4

THERE'LL BE A PRICE
ON YOUR HEADS

"We got back to Torrant's without any more trouble from the *Kweharehnuh,* borrowed some hosses from him and got the wounded to Wichita Falls," the Ysabel Kid concluded, after describing the hunt for the Glover gang and its consequences. "Found your telegraph message waiting for us, Dusty, and come down here as fast as we could make it."

Dirty, unshaven, showing signs of having traveled hard and at speed over a long distance, the Kid and Waco sat at the dining-room table in the log cabin maintained as a base for hunting by the governor of Texas. Situated on the banks of the Colorado River, the building was sufficiently far from Austin to ensure Stanton Howard's privacy, yet close enough for him to be reached in an emergency.

Three more men shared the table. Big, handsome, impressive even in his hunting clothes, Governor Howard sat drumming his fingers on the wood. To his right, tall and slim in his undress uniform, Colonel Edge of the U.S. Army's Adjutant Gen-

eral's Department frowned at the roof. However, the Kid and
Waco gave most of their attention to the third of their audience.
He was the segundo of their ranch, a man for whom either of
them would have given his life without hesitation. His name,
Dusty Fog.

Ask almost anybody in Texas about Dusty Fog and they
would have plenty to tell. How, at seventeen, he had commanded Company C of the Texas Light Cavalry and earned a
reputation as a military raider equal to that of John Singleton
Mosby and Turner Ashby. In addition to harassing the Yankee
forces in Arkansas,[1] he had prevented a plot by Union fanatics
to start an Indian uprising that would have decimated the Lone
Star State.[2] It was whispered that he had assisted Belle Boyd,[3]
the Rebel Spy, on two successful missions.[4]

With the war over and Ole Devil Hardin crippled in a riding
accident,[5] Dusty had handled much business on his behalf. He
had become known as a cowhand of considerable ability, trail
boss equal to the best and the man who had brought law and
order to two wild, wide-open towns.[6] He was said to be the
fastest and most accurate revolver-toter in Texas. According to
all reports, he topped off his talents by being exceptionally capable at defending himself with his bare hands.

By popular conception, such a man ought to be a veritable
giant in stature and handsome to boot.

Dustine Edward Marsden Fog stood no more than five foot
six in his high-heeled, fancy-stitched boots. Small, insignificant
almost, the dusty blond Texan might appear, but he possessed a
muscular development that went beyond his inches. There was
a strength of will about his good-looking face and a glint in his
gray eyes that hinted that he was no man to trifle with. Al-

1. Told in *Kill Dusty Fog!* and *Under the Stars and Bars.*
2. Told in *The Devil Gun.*
3. Some of Belle Boyd's history is told in *The Bloody Border, Back to the
Bloody Border, The Bad Bunch* and *The Hooded Riders.*
4. Told in *The Colt and the Saber* and *The Rebel Spy.*
5. Told in the "The Paint" episode of *The Fastest Gun in Texas.*
6. Told in *Quiet Town, The Making of a Lawman, The Trouble Busters.*

though his range clothing had cost good money, he gave it an air of being somebody's castoffs.

Studying Dusty, the Kid and Waco felt puzzled. Like them, he was unshaven and untidy. Nobody expected members of a hunting party to dress as neatly as if they were going to a Sunday afternoon prayer meeting, but Dusty's appearance went beyond the usual bounds. Taken with the pair having seen their work mounts[7] in the corral, guarded by the OD Connected's wrangler, Dusty's appearance suggested that something unusual was in the air.

"Why didn't the *Kweharehnuh* come after you?" asked Colonel Edge.

"We'd dropped their warbonnet chief and spoiled their medicine," the Kid explained. "A scout trailed us to Torrant's, watched us pull out again and turned back."

"We wasn't a li'l bit sorry to see him go," Waco drawled.

"They wouldn't let you go after Glover's gang then?" Dusty asked.

"Nope," confirmed the Kid. "I'm damned if I can figure out why not. 'Less that 'breed had bought a way through for 'em by handing out repeaters."

"You say that they *all* had repeaters, Lon?" Howard inquired.

"Every last son-of-a-bitching one, Governor," replied the Kid. "And plenty of shells to use in 'em."

"Then it's true, Dusty!" Howard ejaculated.

"It's starting to look that way, sir," the small Texan agreed. "We know now what the *Kweharehnuh*'s price was for their part in it. A repeater and ammunition for every man'd go a long way to making them act friendly to the right sort of folk."

"What's it all about, Dusty?" Waco asked.

"There may be a town in the Palo Duro where men on the dodge can go and hide out safe from the law," Dusty answered.

"Hey, Lon!" Waco said. "Maybe that's what the feller you

7. A Texan used the word "mount" and not "string" for his work horses.

shot meant when he said the gang was going to hell in the Palo Duro."

"According to Jules Murat," Dusty put in, "that's the name of the town."

"What?" asked Waco.

"Hell," Dusty elaborated. "Jules says that the town's called 'Hell.' "

With his two *amigos* listening and taking in every word, Dusty went on with the explanation. Captain Jules Murat of the Texas Rangers had been trying to locate the notorious Siddons gang, without any success. Then an informer had claimed that they had gone to a town called Hell in the Palo Duro. At first Murat had been inclined to scoff at the idea. Not for long. Checking with the heads of other Ranger companies, he had learned that several badly wanted gangs had formed the habit of disappearing as if the ground had swallowed them when things grew too hot. So he had done some more investigating and believed that the town did exist.

"From what I saw of the *Kweharehnuh* at the Fort Sorrel peace meeting, I'd've said it wasn't possible," Dusty finished. "Only what you'd told us is making me change my mind."

"Jules isn't an alarmist," Howard continued soberly. "Such a place would be a blessing for outlaws. If I discarded the idea, it was only because I couldn't see how they could reach it in the heart of the Antelopes' country."

"You've given us the answer," Dusty told his friends. "According to Jules's informers, the folk who run Hell have done a deal with the *Kweharehnuh*. On top of that, they put out scouts to watch for white folks coming. Said scouts check on who they are and, if they're all right, take them past the Antelopes."

"What's your opinion, Kid?" Edge wanted to know.

"It's possible," the Kid admitted. "We saw the repeaters and shells that bunch was toting, 'n' Kills Something allowed he'd had orders from old Ten Bears to keep most white folk out."

"That 'breed was a scout for the town," Waco declared. "He saw Glover's bunch coming and sent up the smoke. Anybody's didn't know about it would steer clear of smoke signals. When

they headed towards 'em, he knowed they was on the dodge."
He nodded. "I like that better'n Glover having sent the 'breed
on ahead with either the repeaters or the money to buy 'em.
Even if Glover could trust the feller that much, it'd've cost him
one hell of a pile of money."

"Between thirty and sixty dollars apiece, depending on
which kind of rifle they handed out," Dusty agreed. "One gang
couldn't afford an outlay like that, but a town drawing money
from a lot of outlaws could."

"Thing I don't see is how these folks at the town got friendly
enough with Ten Bears to make the deal," drawled the Kid.
"He's always been one for counting coup on the white brother
first and talking a long second."

"You're saying they couldn't have done it?" Edge queried.

"Not after what I saw out there," corrected the Kid. "I'm
only wondering how it was done."

"The U.S. Army's thinking of going to learn the answer to
that," Edge remarked, watching the Kid as he spoke.

"Happen you try, Colonel," drawled the dark-faced cowhand, "the *Kweharehnuh*'ll make whoever goes wish they
hadn't."

"The column would be adequately supported," Edge pointed
out. "I think the Indians would find cannon and Gatling guns a
match for their repeaters."

"You don't reckon they'd be *loco* enough to lock horns with
your column head-on, now do you, Colonel?" the Kid countered. "Those fellers'll be crossing Ten Bears's home range,
which he knows like they'll not get the chance to learn. Maybe
you'd get the *Kweharehnuh* in the end, but it'd cost you plenty
of lives. And that's not counting how the news'd go with the
folks on the reservations."

"How do you mean?" Edge wanted to know.

"You take after the *Kweharehnuh* 'n' get licked, which could
happen with them toting repeaters, and every badhat or restless
buck on the reservation'll be headed for the Palo Duro to take
cards. Them folks might even hand out guns to 'em to hold the
Army out of the town. That happens, and we might's well

never had the peace talks at Fort Sorrel. Because, Colonel, you're likely to get the whole blasted Comanche Nation cutting in."

Going by the glance Howard darted at Edge, the Kid had been confirming points already made. For his part, the officer was surprised to hear such logic from one so young. Edge decided that the stories of the Ysabel Kid's Indian savvy he had heard might be true. Certainly the Kid had just expressed the arguments set out by several experienced Indian-fighters who had been consulted by the governor.

"What's the answer, would you say, Lon?" Howard inquired.

"Send somebody in to see if the town's there and find out just how far they could go to support the *Kweharehnuh*," the Kid answered without hesitation.

"When would be the best time to move against the *Kweharehnuh*, discounting the town and its supply of weapons?"

"Middle of autumn, Colonel. When the braves're back from the winter-food gathering and've started to make medicine. Send in good men then, and you might get the band without too much fighting. I figure you've got to fetch them in. 'S long's they're out, it'll always tempt bucks on the reservations to go and join them."

"That's how the Army sees it, Kid," Edge admitted. "So we want to know in time to get things set up ready."

"Whoever you send in there's not going to have an easy time," Waco commented. "If it's a peace officer, he's likely to get recognized. There's maybe owlhoots from all over Texas there."

"That's why I won't let Jules or the other Ranger captains send in their men," Howard said grimly. "I don't have to explain. We can all remember what happened in Prairie Dog."

For a moment, Dusty's face clouded at the painful memory produced by the governor's words. Sent to investigate complaints from the citizens of the town that had been called Prairie Dog—but now bore another, less complimentary name—his younger brother, Danny, had been exposed as a member of the Texas Rangers and murdered.[8]

"We could go," Waco offered eagerly. "Ain't none of us's held a law badge in Texas. Faking up reward posters'd be easy enough done."

"*Too* easy, boy," Dusty drawled. "It'd take a whole heap more than just sticking made-up names on wanted dodgers to get us accepted. Whoever's running the town's no fool. And I don't reckon he's a soft-shell do-gooder trying to prove that all every owlhoot's needing is a second chance to turn him into a honest man. Which means him, and the folks in it with him, are doing it for money. Jules's heard they take a cut of the loot from everybody who arrives."

"So we're not going?" said the Kid, sounding disappointed.

"*We*'re not," Dusty answered and stood up. Crossing to the sidepiece, he returned and laid a copy of the *Texas State Gazette* on the table before the cowhands. Tapping an item with his forefinger, he went on, "These *hombres* are."

Looking down, the Kid and Waco read the article indicated by Dusty.

U.S. Army Paymaster Robbed
$100,000.00 *Haul for Gang*

Two weeks ago, three men robbed U.S. Army Paymaster, Colonel Stafford J. Klegg, of one hundred thousand dollars in bills and gold. The money, payment for remounts and the Fort Sorrel garrison, was taken following an ambush in which Colonel Klegg, Sergeant Magoon and the six-man escort had been shot and killed.

Questioned by our correspondent regarding the small size of the escort, Colonel Edge of the Adjutant General's Department replied, 'The delivery had been kept a secret, even from the escort. It was decided that sending more men might arouse unwanted suspicions. Other deliveries have been made in the

8. Told in *A Town Called Yellowdog*.

same manner. All the escort were veterans with considerable line service.'

Colonel Edge also stated that news of the robbery had not been released earlier so as to increase the chances of apprehending the culprits.

Captain Jules Murat, commanding Company G, Texas Rangers, has been working in conjunction with the Adjutant General's Department in the investigation. Displaying the kind of efficiency we have come to expect of this officer, Captain Murat has already uncovered details of the evil plot behind the robbery. According to a woman of ill repute with whom he had been associating, Sergeant Magoon had discovered the true nature of his assignment and formed an alliance with the robbers. If so, it appears that he received his just deserts when his companions-in-crime double-crossed him and murdered him along with the rest of the escort.

Captain Murat says that the men concerned have been identified as:

EDWARD JASON CAXTON; in his mid-twenties, around five foot six in height, sturdily built, blond-haired, gray-eyed, reasonably handsome, may be wearing cowhand clothes and carries matched white-handled Colt Civilian Model Peacemakers in cross-draw holsters. Is said to be exceptionally fast with them.

MATTHEW "BOY" CAXTON; half-brother to the above. Six foot two, blue-eyed, blond, well-built, not more than eighteen years of age. Wears cowhand clothes, and two staghorn-handled 1860 Army Colts in tied-down holsters. Can draw and shoot very fast.

ALVIN "COMANCHE" BLOOD: six foot tall, lean, black-haired, with reddish-brown eyes, dark-faced. Wears buckskin shirt, Levi's and Comanche moccasins, is usually armed with a Colt Dragoon, in a low cavalry twist-hand draw holster and an ivory-hilted bowie knife. Is very dangerous when roused.

A reward of $10,000.00 has been offered by the Army for the apprehension of each of the above-named men. Captain

Murat warns that they are armed, desperate and should be approached with caution. He hopes to make an early arrest.

"So that's how we're going to—" Waco began, having read the story.

"Try this one first," Dusty suggested and indicated another item of news.

Protests Over Army Beef Contract

Already vigorous protests are being lodged against a contract to deliver beef to the Army and Navy in New Orleans having been awarded to General "Ole Devil" Hardin's OD Connected ranch. Captain Miffin Kennedy, Captain Dick King and Shangai Pierce each claims that his ranch would be better situated to make the deliveries.

Tempers were high at a recent meeting between Captain Dusty Fog of the OD Connected and the opposing ranchers. Governor Stanton Howard has intervened and is gathering the affected parties in San Antonio de Bexar for a conference to work out an equitable solution.

As the first consignment of cattle is required for shipment at Brownsville, Captain Fog will be sending his ranch's floating outfit to deliver it. He says his men will accompany the cattle to New Orleans in order to study the problems of delivery by sea.

"Damn it!" Waco yelped, looking up from the newspaper. "I thought I'd got what was happening, but now—"

"I didn't know we was dickering for a beef contract from the Army, Dusty," the Kid remarked as the youngster's words trailed off. "But you sure's hell don't get me going on no boat. They're trouble. It was boats that brought you blasted white folks to our country."

"What do you reckon now, boy?" Dusty inquired, watching Waco.

"You, Lon 'n' me're them three miscreants who robbed the

Paymaster and made wolf bait out of poor ole Paddy Magoon," Waco replied. "It'll be Mark who goes as 'Dusty Fog' to meet them riled-up ranchers in San Antone, while the rest of the floating outfit're hard to work driving cattle along to Brownsville and riding the boat some folks's so scared of to New Orleans."

Surprise flickered on Edge's face at the rapid way in which the blond youngster had reached the correct conclusion. When the idea of sending in the floating outfit had been suggested, Dusty had wisely insisted on careful preparations and precautions. In addition to providing a covering story in the newspaper, he had thought up the scheme to divert attention from the similarity of the trio of "wanted men" to himself, the Kid and Waco. There had been numerous occasions in the past when people had mistaken Mark Counter for Dusty. The handsome blond giant looked like the kind of man people expected Dusty to be.[9] So, with the backing of the three "protesting" ranchers, he would pose as Dusty in San Antonio. Clearly Waco understood all that.

"Anybody talks about the way you tote your guns, you can say you're copying Dusty Fog," the Kid remarked. "Folks mostly think about a rifle, not my handgun. But it's sure lucky we haven't given the boy his—Ow!"

A sharp kick to the Kid's shin, delivered by Dusty, prevented him from finishing his reference to a pair of staghorn-handled, engraved Colt Artillery Peacemakers which the floating outfit had purchased as a birthday present for the youngster.

"What haven't you given me?" demanded Waco suspiciously.

"A rawhiding for leading Lon astray," Dusty lied. "What do you pair reckon to the notion of being owlhoots?"

"It could be dangerous," warned the governor. "There'll be a price on your heads, and it's high enough to arouse plenty of interest."

9. Mark Counter's part in the floating outfit is recorded in their other stories.

"Damned if you look worth ten thousand simoleons, boy," the Kid scoffed. "Happen I shoot him, Governor, can I have the reward money in gold? I don't trust that paper stuff."

"Now *me*," countered the young blond. "I never figured *you* was worth ten *cents*. It'll be a sure-enough pleasure not to have that blasted white goat of your'n tromping on my heels."

In their work, which sometimes consisted of helping friends of Ole Devil Hardin out of difficulties, the floating outfit occasionally needed to keep secret their connection with the ranch. So each of them had one well-trained horse in his mount which did not bear the spread's brand. While the Kid's stallion carried no brand, it was such a distinguishable animal that he would be unable to use it. Having seen the OD Connected's wrangler—one of the few people who could handle the white with reasonable safety—at the corral, the youngster had deduced that the trio would be riding their unmarked animals.

"We'll need some money to tote along, Dusty," the Kid said, acting as if Waco was beneath the dignity of a reply.

"And we'll have it," Dusty answered. "Near on a hundred thousand dollars, in new bills and gold shared between us."

"That much?" Waco ejaculated.

"We're not playing for penny-ante stakes, boy," Dusty warned. "The town boss'll expect us to show him a fair sum. And remember this, from the moment we leave here, we're the Caxton brothers and Alvin 'Comanche' Blood. We'll have to fix up our story and all tell it the same way. A feller smart enough to organize that town'll not be easy to fool. We make mistakes and we'll be staying there permanent."

"There's a rider coming at a fair lick, Dusty," the Kid remarked. "You gents expecting company?"

"Not that I know of," Howard replied.

Ten minutes later, a tall, gangling man stood at the table. He was dressed like a cowhand and was a sergeant in Murat's Ranger company. From all the signs, he had ridden hard and he wasted no time in getting down to business.

"Cap'n Jules figured you should know, Cap'n Dusty. Toby Siddons and all five of his gang've been brought in dead for the reward, up to Paducah, Cottle County. Sheriff up there's tele-graphed and asked if he can pay on 'em."

"Did Jules agree?" asked Howard.

"Not straight off," Sergeant Sid Jethcup admitted. "He thought Sheriff Butterfield's name sounded a mite familiar and checked. That's the third bunch of dead owlhoots that's been brought in to him for the bounty on 'em. So Cap'n Jules sent off word that he'd have to be sure it was the Siddons gang, seeing's how he'd got told they was down in San Luis Potosi."

"What'd the sheriff say to that, Sid?" Dusty inquired, guess-ing there must be something more for Jules Murat to send his sergeant. Going by Jethcup's attitude, it was of a sensational nature.

"Damned if Butterfield didn't wire straight back and say we could send a man along to identify them if we was so minded," the sergeant replied. "Allowed the bodies'd keep a while, see-ing's the feller who brought them in'd had them embalmed."

"Whee-dogie!" breathed Waco. "It sounds like them fellers in Hell don't just take a share of the loot, they go the whole hawg, grab the lot and whatever bounty's on the owlhoot's head. I'm starting to think this chore could be a mite dangerous, Dusty."

5

WE'VE GOT TO GET OUT OF SIGHT

Dressed and armed as described in the *Texas State Gazette*, their faces bearing a ten-days-old growth of whiskers, Dusty Fog, the Ysabel Kid and Waco sat their unbranded horses—a *grulla*, a blue roan and a black-and-white *tobiano*, each a gelding—studying the terrain that lay beyond the distant Tierra Blanca Creek. They were selecting the places from which scouts employed by the citizens of Hell might be keeping watch.

In view of the news brought by Sergeant Jethcup, Dusty had insisted upon a slight variation to their plans. The trio had visited the town of Paducah to see what could be learned. While there, they had acted in a manner that had established their characters in the eyes of the customers of the Anvil Saloon. Then, as Dusty had arranged, they had escaped "arrest" by Sheriff Butterfield, Jethcup and another Ranger. The latter had been sent along, ostensibly to identify the dead outlaws, but really to help establish Dusty's party and to check up on the local peace officers.

At the saloon, before being compelled to take a hurried departure, the trio had seen the burly, somber-looking man who had brought in the embalmed bodies of the Siddons gang. They had also discovered that the sheriff kept pigeons, which had struck them as an unusual hobby unless the birds served another purpose.

Although a posse had been formed and set out from Paducah after them, it had not carried out its duties with any great show of determination. When night had fallen, in accordance with Dusty's plan for such a contingency, the Kid had contacted Jethcup secretly and been informed of the latest developments.

Doing so had not been difficult for a man trained as a *Pehnane* brave. Finding a place of concealment at sundown, the Kid had watched the posse, following the trio's tracks, halt and make camp. Later, he had moved closer on foot. When Jethcup had left the camp—under the pretense of going to answer the call of nature—the Kid had joined him. Hidden by bushes, holding their voices down to whispers, they had been able to talk unheard and unseen by the rest of the posse.

According to the sergeant, Butterfield had done all he could to delay the pursuit. Which suggested that the overweight sheriff was in cahoots with the people of Hell. Before Jethcup had gone to meet the Kid, Butterfield had been warning him that the "Caxtons" and "Comanche Blood" would soon be outside Cottle County and hinting that the posse had no legal right to keep after them once that happened. Jethcup had gone on to state that, going by the way they acted, the sheriff and the bounty hunter—who went by the name of Orville Hatchet—had not been fooled by hints the trio had dropped at the saloon about heading for the Rio Grande. Being satisfied as to their ultimate destination, the two men had been determined that they should escape to reach it.[1]

---

1. That had puzzled the Kid, until Dusty had explained why the following day. If the trio had been arrested by the posse, their loot would have to be

To provide the posse—and the Rangers—with an excuse to turn back, the Kid had stampeded their horses during the night. As Jethcup and his companion had been riding horses borrowed from the livery barn in Paducah, they suffered no loss through his action. Later, they could come out without the posse and "lose" the trio's trail in a way that would arouse no suspicion.

Although the pursuit had been effectively halted, the trio had known they would face other difficulties before they reached Hell. If their suspicions should prove correct, Sheriff Butterfield would dispatch a pigeon carrying a message about them on his return to Paducah. As the bird could travel faster than their horses, the people who ran Hell would learn of their coming long before they could hope to arrive.

By riding west along the White River for two days, then swinging to the north, Dusty, the Kid and Waco hoped to slip past the watchers who would be sent to locate them and reach the town unescorted. Doing so might annoy the men behind the outlaws' town, but it would also impress them.

"What do you reckon, boy?" asked the Kid, as he completed his examination of the land ahead.

"I'd say up on that hill's looks like a gal's tit, alongside the nipple," Waco replied. "Or over to the east, top of that peak's stands higher than the rest of 'em. Them scouts could see a hell of a ways from either."

"They're the most likely looking places, Brother Matt," Dusty agreed, it having been decided that they would use their assumed names at all times to lessen the danger of a mistake. "Let's hear from the heathen, though."

"Can't be me he's meaning," grunted the Kid when Waco looked at him expectantly. "I ain't no heathen, no matter what low company I keep."

"Don't you never go taking no vote on that," Waco warned.

---

returned to the Army and the reward shared with the other men involved in their capture. By letting them get through to Hell, Butterfield and Hatchet could expect to make far more money.

"And quit hedging. If you can't see that far, come on out and say so like a man."

"There's another hill, back of them two a couple of miles's they could be using," the Kid said, after telling Waco what he thought of him. "Can't say to anywhere else right now, though."

"I'd seen it," Waco declared. "Didn't say nothing, 'cause I was testing you-all."

"How much farther can we go, you reckon, without them seeing us?" Dusty wanted to know, giving Waco a glare that silenced him.

"Maybe's far as the Tierra Blanca," estimated the Kid. "To make sure, we'll keep off the skyline as much's we can. Once we're over, though, we'll have to do most of our traveling by night."

"How do we find the town happen we do that, Comanch'?" Waco inquired.

"In the day, while we're hid up, we'll look for the chimney smoke," the Kid explained. "What do you reckon, Ed?"

"Seems about right to me," Dusty admitted. "Let's get moving."

Sundown found them on the edge of the Tierra Blanca Creek. Crossing it, they halted on the northern bank. Being in wooded country, the Kid announced that they could light a fire without the risk of its smoke or flames being seen. Doing so, they made coffee and cooked the last of the raw food they had brought with them. Then they pushed on through the darkness.

When the first gray light of dawn crept into the eastern skyline, the Kid selected a draw in which they could camp through the hours of daylight. They tended to their horses before making a meal on some pemmican and jerked meat carried as emergency rations. As a precaution against being located and surprised, one of them kept watch while the other two relaxed and slept near the horses.

All through the day, with the help of a pair of field glasses acquired by Dusty from a Yankee officer during the war, the man on guard searched for *Kweharehnuh* warriors, the scouts put out by the people of Hell, or any hint of the town's position. Night fell without them having been disturbed, but neither had they seen anything to help guide them to their destination.

Another night's riding commenced as the sun disappeared beyond the western rims. It proved fortunate that night that Waco had accompanied the rest of the floating outfit in their campaign to prevent General Marcus and his accomplices from provoking a war between the United States and Mexico.[2] During those wild days south of the Rio Grande, he had developed considerable skill in the art of silent horse movement. It was put to good use when the Kid, returning from scouting ahead, announced that they must go within half a mile of a bunch of resting *Kweharehnuh* braves. The nature of the surrounding terrain precluded their making a longer detour.

There followed a very tense fifteen minutes or so as the Kid, Waco and Dusty, moving in single file, had slipped by the sleeping warriors. They passed downwind of the camp, to prevent the Indians' horses from catching their scent and raising the alarm. Doing so meant that they had to remain constantly alert, ready to stop their own mounts from smelling the *Kweharehnuhs'* animals and betraying their presence.

Walking with each foot testing the nature of the ground before coming down upon it, leading and keeping one's horse quiet, with at least twenty hostile *Kweharehnuh* brave-hearts close enough to detect any undue amount of sound, was a testing experience for the blond youngster. He felt sweat soaking the back of his shirt and wondered if his companions were experiencing similar emotions. Despite his normally exuberant nature and unquestionable courage, Waco was unable to hold down a sigh of relief when the Kid finally declared that they could mount up and ride.

Although he never mentioned the subject, Waco felt sure that he heard a matching response by Dusty to the Kid's words.

On traveled the trio, alert for any warning sounds and carrying their Winchesters ready for use. As dawn drew near, the

2. Told in *The Peacemakers*.

Kid ranged ahead once more. He returned with disquieting news.

"From what I can see, there's no place around for us to hide in," the dark-featured cowhand said grimly. "Not close enough for us to reach afore it's full light, anyways."

"Except—?" Dusty queried, having detected an inflection in the other's voice that hinted at a not-too-palatable possibility.

"Except down at the bottom of a dry wash we should hit afore it gets light enough to be seen from them high places."

"So what's up with us using it?" demanded Waco.

"The sides're's steep as hell," explained the Kid. "Not straight down, but close enough to it."

"Let's take a look at it, Comanch'," Dusty drawled. "We've got to get out of sight. If the feller sees us, he'll let those bucks know that we're here."

Advancing across the gradually lightening range, the three young men came to the edge of a deep, wide dry wash. One glance was all any of them needed to tell that there was no easy point of descent within visual distance. Nor did they have sufficient time to conduct an extensive search. It would only be a matter of five minutes at most before the high points came into view. When that happened, any lookout who was there would be able to see them.

"Hell's fire!" growled the Kid, pointing to the edge of the wash. "A grizzly come along this way late on yesterday afternoon."

While Dusty could not detect the tracks which had led the Kid to draw that conclusion, he felt certain that the other had made no mistake. Which only added to their difficulties. A thick coating of trees and bushes at the bottom of the wash would offer the trio all the shelter and concealment they required, if they could get down. Unfortunately, it would present the same qualities to any predatory, dangerous animal seeking for a place to den up.

There were, Dusty knew, few more dangerous creatures in the Lone Star State than a Texas flatheaded grizzly bear. More than that, *Ursus texensis texensis,* like the other subdivisions of its species, was known to favor such locations as a resting place after a night's roaming in search of food.

Going down into the wash, if the bear should be in occupation, would almost certainly provoke an attack. Neither the Winchester Model '66 nor the '73, with respectively weak and inadequate twenty-eight- and forty-grain powder loads, rated as an ideal tool to stop a charging grizzly at close quarters.

"Well," said Waco, having reached similar conclusions to Dusty and being aware of the need to take cover quickly, "ain't but the one way to find out if he's down there." He paused briefly and raised his eyes to the sky. "Lord, happen there's a bear down there and you can't help a miserable sinner like me, don't you go helping him."

Before the other two could object, the youngster had guided his horse to the edge. For a moment, the *tobiano* hesitated, but Waco's capable handling had won its trust and confidence. So, in response to his signals, it went over. Thrusting out its front legs and tucking the hind limbs under its body, the gelding started to slide down the incline.

With the threat of an attack being made by a grizzly bear when he reached the bottom, Waco had not booted his rifle. Gripping it at the wrist of the butt in his right hand, he did his best to help the horse make the descent. Shoving his feet forward until they were level with the *tobiano*'s shoulders, he tilted his torso to the rear so that the small of his back rested on the bedroll lashed to his cantle. He held out the rifle and raised his reins-filled left hand as an aid to maintaining his and the gelding's balance.

On completing the descent, amid a swirl of dust and a miniature avalanche of dislodged rocks, Waco kicked up with his right leg. Allowing the reins to fall, he sprang clear of the gelding. Landing with his left hand closing upon the Winchester's foregrip, he started to throw the butt to his shoulder. There was a sudden rustling among the bushes, then a covey of prairie chickens burst out and winged hurriedly along the wash. Making an effort of will, the youngster refrained from shooting at them. He grinned sheepishly and hoped that his *amigos* had not noticed his involuntary action in aiming at the birds' position. Lowering the rifle, he turned and waved a cheery hand at them.

Knowing that the birds would not have been in the wash if a bear or other dangerous animal was present, Dusty and the Kid made their descent. Each of them hoped that Waco had not seen him whip up his Winchester as the birds made their noisy appearance. Deciding that attack was the best form of defense, the small Texan gave the youngster no opportunity to comment if he had observed their hasty, unnecessary actions.

"Blasted young fool!" Dusty growled as he reined in his *grulla* and glared at the unabashed blond. "You could've got into a bad fix coming down thataways."

"Which's why I did it," Waco replied. "You pair're getting too old 'n' stiff in the joints for fancy foot-stepping should you've got jumped."

"Boy!" Dusty ejaculated. "There's the blister-end of a shovel just waiting to be ridden when we get back to the OD Connected."

"Matt Caxton's not likely to be going there," Waco pointed out. "Anyways, we're down here safe 'n' all our buttons fastened."

That was the essential and vital point. They were now safely hidden from any lookouts who might have been posted. After some more good-natured abuse, which Waco regarded as being high praise and complete approval of his behavior, the trio set about what had become their usual routine. Saddles and bridles were removed, hobbles fixed and the horses allowed to drink at the small stream that trickled along the center of the wash. Leaving the animals to graze, Dusty, the Kid and Waco studied their surroundings.

Finding a place up which they could climb when night fell, they settled down to rest. Once again the man on guard searched for a concentration of smoke columns to guide them to the town, without doing so. That night, they passed unchallenged between the nearest pair of high points they had selected as lookout places. Dawn found them secure in the cover offered by an extensive clump of post oaks, on a slope that allowed them a good view of the land ahead, to the east or the west.

Hoping that they would locate the town that day, Waco volunteered to take the first spell on watch. He had only just reached his position when he gave a low whistle that caused the other two to join him.

"Smoke," the youngster said laconically. "Up on top of that knob there."

"Just the one fire and made for signaling," decided the Kid, studying the density of the column that rose from the most distant of the points he had picked back beyond the Tierra Blanca Creek. "Only I can't see anybody for him to be signaling."

"Keep watching, boy," Dusty ordered. "I don't reckon it's us he's seen and's sending up the smoke for. So I want to know who it is."

Although Waco continued his vigil for two hours, constantly sweeping from east to west and back with the field glasses, he saw no reason for the smoke signal. Then, just as the Kid came to relieve him, he halted the movement of the glasses and stared hard at the knob.

"There's a feller coming down, L—Comanch'!" the blond announced.

"Try looking off to the east," suggested the Kid and returned to wake Dusty.

"We've hit pay dirt!" Waco enthused as his companions came up. "There's four fellers coming to meet that *hombre* from the knob."

Taking the glasses from the youngster, Dusty watched the meeting that took place. The lookout—assuming that was his purpose for being in the area—was a tall, lean, plainly dressed Mexican and the others, four unshaven North Americans. Although they were a long way from the trio's hiding place, Dusty could make out a few details. Whatever the Mexican was saying apparently did not meet with the quartet's approval. After some talk and gesticulation, they yielded to his demands.

"Well, what do you know about that?" Dusty breathed. "The Mexican's making them hand over their gunbelts."

"And rifles," the Kid went on. "Them folk who run Hell don't take chances. Their man pulls the owlhoots' teeth afore he takes them in."

Having disarmed the four men, the Mexican led them off in a westerly direction. They went by the post oaks at a distance of around a mile and were clearly unaware of being observed by the three young Texans.

"That settles one thing," Dusty stated. "We're going to have to find the town instead of meeting one of their scouts. I'll be damned if I'll go there with my guns across another man's saddle."

Going by their expressions, the Kid and Waco were in complete agreement with Dusty. The day before, they had discussed changing their arrangements if they did not find the town in the next twenty-four hours. Having witnessed the scene that had just taken place, they no longer intended to let themselves be seen by a scout and guided to Hell, if doing it meant being deprived of their weapons.

"We should be able to get a notion of where the town lies by watching 'em," Waco suggested. "It must be a fair ways off, though, if we still can't see their smoke."

"They'd likely not want to meet the owlhoots too close to town," the Kid pointed out. "Give me the glasses, Dusty. I'll—"

"Try watching that you get the names right'd be a good thing," Waco interrupted, delighted that the Kid had for once fallen into error.

"Go grab some sleep, you blasted paleface!" snorted the Kid.

"It'd be best, Brother Matt," Dusty agreed. "Watch 'em as far as you can, Comanch'. Only mind that there's likely to be another of the scouts on the knob."

"I'll mind it," promised the Kid.

Keeping the possibility of a second lookout in mind, the Kid remained in the trees as he watched the departing men. He picked out landmarks that would allow him to follow their route even in the dark. After they had disappeared, he concentrated on a fruitless search for the town's smoke.

In the middle of the afternoon, the scout returned. He was riding a different horse, which suggested that he had delivered the four men to Hell and obtained a fresh mount. It also implied that the town could not be too far away. Yet the Texans still could not detect any hint of it.

"I'm damned if I know what to make of it," Dusty declared as they left the post oaks in the darkness. "We'll go after those fellers as far as we can. Then we'll stop until it's light enough to let you follow their trail, Comanch'. It'll mean moving by daylight, but that's a chance we'll have to take."

"We've not seen any sign of the *Kweharehnuh* for the last two days," the Kid replied. "Could be we're by them and the town's scouts. We ought to make it."

Shortly after midnight, the Kid brought his roan to a halt and his signal caused the other two to do the same. Peering through the darkness, Dusty and Waco could see him sitting with his head cocked to one side as if he was straining his ears to catch some very faint sound.

"What's up, Comanch'?" Waco inquired, when the Kid allowed them to come to his side.

"I'm damned if this chore's not sending me into a tizz," the Kid answered. "I could've sworn I just heard a piano."

"Where?" Dusty demanded.

"Downwind someplace. A long ways off."

"Lordy lord!" Dusty groaned, slapping his thigh in exasperation. "What've we been using for brains these last couple of days?"

"Huh?" grunted the Kid.

"We've not been making a fire during the day so's there'd be no smoke rising to give us away," Dusty elaborated. "And the folks at Hell do the same. Keep moving down into the wind, Comanch', and I'll bet you'll hear that piano again. Then we go to wherever it's being played and we'll be in Hell."

6

I'LL START BY TAKING
YOUR GUNS

By order of the Civic Council, the lighting of fires in the vicinity of the city limits is strictly prohibited during the hours of daylight.

ANY PERSON FAILING TO COMPLY WITH THIS WILL BE SHOT

Signed: Simeon B. Lampart, Mayor.

"Right friendly way to greet folks," commented the Ysabel Kid dryly, indicating the sign. It was one of many similar warnings they had seen since their arrival at Hell.

With the Kid lounging afork the roan to his left and Waco astride the *tobiano* on his right, Dusty Fog rode at a leisurely pace along the town's main—in fact only—street toward the large, plank-built livery barn. No smoke rose from any chimney, which was not surprising if the penalty for disobeying the notices was enforced.

"Makes a feller wonder if it was worthwhile coming," Waco

went on and favored the dark cowhand with a scowl. "You and your blasted piano."

"Them signs show you was right about why we didn't see the smoke during the day, Ed," the Kid remarked, ignoring the blond. "How do we play it now we've got here?"

"Any way the cards fall," Dusty decided. "And we'll start by letting them come to us."

Finding the town had not been too difficult, although not quite so easy as Dusty had suggested the previous night. Riding into the wind, the Kid and, soon after, his companions had heard the faint jangling of a piano. There had been other sounds to tell them that people—and not Indians—were ahead. At first the trio had been puzzled by the absence of glowing lights to go with the sounds of revelry. Passing through an area of dense woodland, they had learned the reason. Surrounded by the trees and erected in the bottom of an enormous basinlike crater, Hell was effectively concealed until one was almost on top of it.

Although there had been considerable activity—in fact, the place had the atmosphere of a Kansas railroad town at the height of the trail drive season—Dusty had decided that they would put off their arrival until morning. He had wanted to form a better idea of what they were riding into. It had also struck the trio as making good sense to conduct their entrance when they had rested and were fully alert.

Seen from the edge of the trees and by daylight, Hell had looked much the same as any other small cow-country town. Maybe a mite more prosperous than most, but giving no hint of its true nature and purpose. There did not appear to be a church or school. On the slope down which the Texans had made their entrance was a graveyard that seemed too large for the size of the town. To the rear of the livery barn, situated at the extreme western end of the street, four large, adobe-walled corrals held a number of horses.

While approaching, the trio had noticed that, apart from those along the street, all the town's buildings had been constructed of adobe many years before and more recently repaired. Wooden planks appeared to be *de rigueur* for the premises flanking the main thoroughfare. It offered much the usual selection of businesses and trades to be found in any town of comparable size. Two of the learned professions were represented by shingles advertising respectively a doctor and a lawyer. Noticeable omissions were the normally ubiquitous stagecoach depot, law enforcement offices, jailhouse and bank.

The largest building in town—as might have been expected —with a size even exceeding that of the livery barn, was the two-story Honest Man Saloon. On its upper front verandah rail it had a bullet-pocked nameboard that was devoid of the usual descriptive illustration favored by similar establishments.

Flanking the saloon, if somewhat overshadowed by it, were the premises of Doctor Ludwig Connolly and Simeon Lampart, attorney-at-law. The latter was a good-sized, one-floor building of sturdy construction, with thick iron bars at the left front window that bore the inscription MAYOR'S OFFICE. Facing the Honest Man, almost matching it in length if not height, the undertaker's establishment must have had a sobering effect upon revelers with a price on their heads, or a hangman's rope awaiting them if they should be captured. Only a town with a high mortality rate could support such a large concern.

On reaching the double doors of the barn without being challenged, or even addressed, by such of the citizens as they had seen, the trio dismounted. Leading their horses inside, Dusty read the words "Ivan Basmanov, Prop." painted above the front doors. Entering, they found only four stalls empty and none of them adjacent to the others. Overhead, a hayloft stretched halfway across the stable portion of the building, being reached by a ladder in the center of the frontal supports. The cooing of pigeons in the loft came to their ears as they continued to examine their surroundings. Two doors in each side wall gave access to an office, tack-, fodder- and storerooms. Opposite the front entrance, an equally large pair of doors were open to show two of the adobe corrals' gates.

Hinges creaked and a big, bulky man came from what appeared to be the barn's business office. Sullen-featured, with a heavy, drooping moustache, he wore a good-quality gray shirt, Levi's pants and low-heeled Wellington-leg boots. Slanting down to his right thigh hung a gunbelt carrying an ivory-handled Remington 1861 Army revolver. It was the rig of a fast man with a gun. A flicker of surprise showed on his face as he looked from the newcomers to the otherwise deserted barn.

"Who brought you in?" demanded the man in a hard, guttural voice.

"Our hosses," Dusty replied. "So now we'd like to bed them down comfortable and let them rest."

"But—but—!" the man spluttered.

"Are you that Ivan Basmanov Prop. *hombre*, who's got his name on the wall outside?" Dusty asked.

"I am."

"Then you're the feller's can say whether we can leave them or not."

"I am also the head of the Civic Regulators," Basmanov growled. "Which of our guides brought you into town?"

Letting the reins slip from his fingers, Dusty moved away from the *grulla* and faced Basmanov. Releasing their horses, the Kid and Waco fanned out on either side of the small Texan.

"Can't rightly say any of them did, mister," Dusty answered. "We come in together and without help."

"You reached here without being stopped by the *Kweharehnuh,* or seen by our lookouts?" The barn's proprietor almost yelped out the words.

"Is it supposed to be difficult?" Dusty countered and let a harder note creep into his voice. "Can we put up our horses or not?"

For a moment Basmanov made no reply. He seemed to be weighing up his chances of taking a firm line against the trio. If so, he must have concluded that the odds were not in his favor. The three young men had positioned themselves in a manner that made it impossible for even the fastest hand with a gun to deal with them simultaneously.

Not only that, but Basmanov noticed a coolly confident attitude about the small Texan, except that Dusty no longer gave an impression of being small. There stood a *big* man and one fully competent in all matters *pistolero,* or the barn's owner missed his guess. In all probability, he would not even require the backing of his watchful, proddy-looking companions to deal with Basmanov.

"Put your horses up, if you want to," the owner muttered, darting a glance at the hayloft. Then he sucked in a breath as if steeling himself to continue. "The price is ten dollars a night, or fifty the week, for a stall. It's seven or thirty if you want to put them in the corrals."

"Each, or for the lot?" asked Waco coldly.

"Each!" Basmanov answered.

"That's sort of high, ain't it?" Waco challenged.

"This's no ordinary town, Brother Matt," Dusty pointed out, concealing his pleasure at the way in which the youngster had made the correct response to permit his answer. "Fellers like us have to pay high for what we'll get here."

"That's true," affirmed Basmanov, with an air of relief.

"We'll take a stall each for a week as starters, mister," Dusty went on, returning to the *grulla,* opening his saddlebag and extracting payment for the three animals' accommodation.

"My men aren't around yet," Basmanov commented, slightly louder than was necessary, as he accepted the money. "If you don't mind making a start on your horses, I'll go and fetch them."

"For what we're paying—!" Waco began, bristling with indignation.

"We can do the gent a li'l favor," Dusty interrupted. "Let's make a start."

Although he had taken no part in the conversation, the Kid had not been idle. His eyes and ears had continued to work, the latter gathering information that might prove of use later. Basmanov returned to his office and closed the door. Looking pointedly at the hayloft, the Kid raised his right forefinger in a quick point and then vertically as if indicating the number one. Nodding to show they understood, Dusty and the youngster selected stalls and led in their horses. While taking care of the animals, the trio discussed their plans for celebrating and Dusty warned the other two about taking too many drinks.

Basmanov still had not returned by the time the trio had off-saddled and attended to the feeding of their horses. While they did not mention the matter, each of them assumed that he had left through another door in his office and was reporting their arrival to the mayor. Each of them stood outside his horse's stall, waiting for it to finish eating. The sound of approaching footsteps and voices, one a woman's, reached their ears. It seemed unlikely that the proprietor's "Regulators" would announce their coming in such a manner, but instead of taking chances, the trio turned toward the front doors.

Accompanied by four young men, a small, petite, shapely and beautiful brunette entered. Dressed in a top hat, with a long, flowing silk securing band, riding habit and boots, she looked to be in her early twenties and seemed to enjoy being the center of the quartet's attention. The riding gloves she wore concealed her marital status. Whatever it might be, going by her companions, she showed mighty poor judgment of character or a misplaced faith in human nature.

All the quartet dressed well, like cowhands after being paid off from a trail drive. Their guns hung in fast-draw holsters and they exhibited a kind of wolf-cautious meanness that screamed a warning to eyes that knew the West. Even more than his companions, that applied to the tallest newcomer.

The swarthily handsome features of Ben Columbo had been displayed prominently on wanted posters outside most Texas law enforcement offices. He had committed a number of robberies, always killing his male victims and doing much worse to any woman unfortunate enough to fall into his hands.

Although Dusty could not place them, two of Columbo's companions probably had prices on their heads. He harbored no such doubts about the third. The last time they had met, Joey Pinter was a member of Smoky Hill Thompson's gang and Dusty had been the marshal of Mulrooney, Kansas. Luckily for the success of the trio's mission, rumor claimed that Pinter had branched out on his own recently. Dusty hoped it was true. He had no wish for Thompson, an old friend, to be in Hell, as that might complicate matters. Recalling how he had rough-handled Pinter at their last meeting, Dusty knew that the other would have neither forgotten nor forgiven him.

Everything depended on how effectively the beard served to disguise Dusty.

Becoming aware of the trio's presence, the new arrivals stopped talking. All of them looked hard at Dusty, Waco and the Kid. As yet, Pinter showed no hint of recognition.

"You are strangers," the brunette challenged, her voice holding just a touch of a foreign accent that tended to enhance her obvious charms. "Has my husband seen you?"

"Depends on which of these gents he is, ma'am," Dusty replied.

"None of them. He is the mayor of Hell," the woman explained. "But if he has not seen you, why are you wearing those guns?"

"I didn't know we was supposed to check them in, ma'am," Dusty said, watching the quartet studying his party. "Anyways, these gents're wearing their'n."

"But yes," agreed the brunette. "My husband has given them permission to do so. It is the ruling of the Civic Council that no visitor may wear a gun without being given permission. Surely your guide explained that to you?"

"No, ma'am," Dusty drawled, growing increasingly aware of the scrutiny to which Pinter was subjecting him. "We didn't bother with no guide to get here. Still, if them's the rules, we'll play along. Let's go and see the mayor, Brother Matt, Comanch'."

A sensation of cold annoyance bit at Columbo as he thought back to how he had been compelled, by the threat of lurking *Kweharehnuh* warriors, to hand over his weapons. That he had submitted to such an indignity and the small, insignificant stranger had avoided it aroused his anger. He knew how Giselle Lampart regarded such matters and suspected a threat to his position as her favorite escort.

"It's not that easy, *hombre*," Columbo declared, stepping

away from the woman. "You don't walk around heeled until *after* Mayor Lampart says so."

"Is that the for-real legal law?" Waco inquired, lounging with his left shoulder against the gatepost of the *tobiano*'s stall.

"It is here in Hell," Columbo confirmed and, attracting one of his companions' attention, gave a nod that sent him moving toward the young blond.

"Are you the town's duly-sworn and appointed peace officers?" Dusty asked.

"You might say that," answered Columbo. "Which being so, I'll start by taking your guns."

"Ma'am," Dusty said, addressing the brunette but keeping his gaze on the men, "would you mind waiting outside?"

"But why?" Giselle Lampart smiled.

"If Columbo tries to take my guns, I'm going to stop him," Dusty explained in a matter-of-fact tone. "And I'd hate to shed his blood before a beautiful and gracious lady."

"Gallantly said, sir!" Giselle applauded, knowing her actions would act as a goad to Columbo.

"Just go wait by your hoss, Giselle," Columbo ordered, cheeks turning red. "This won't take but a minute."

"My!" the brunette sighed. "I feel just like a lady from the days of King Arthur, with the knights jousting for my favors."

With that, Giselle strolled to where a dainty palomino gelding stood in a stall. Her whole attitude was one of complete unconcern and suggested that such incidents had become commonplace in her daily life. Reaching the gate, she turned to watch the men with an air of eager anticipation.

"All right, short stuff," Columbo snarled menacingly. "Hand over the guns and nobody'll get hurt."

"If you want 'em, you'll have to come and take 'em," Dusty warned. "Only, happen that's your notion, fill your hand before you start. Because if you try, I'll see you don't get the chance to rape another girl."

"You've just got yourself killed, you short-growed son of a bitch!" Columbo spat out and flickered a glance to his right.

"Watch the 'breed, Joey. You keep the kid out of it, Heck. Leave short stuff to me, Topple."

About to obey, Pinter became aware of the change that had apparently come over Dusty. In some way, the small Texan appeared to have gained size, bulk—and an identity that showed through the beard and the trail dirt.

Like most men who had locked horns with and been bested by Dusty Fog, Pinter had ceased to think of him in mere feet and inches. Instead, he regarded the small Texan as a *very* big, tough and capable fighting man. A man such like the bearded blond giant who loomed so menacingly before them.

Exactly like him, in fact!

"Watch him, Ben!" Pinter barked, commencing his draw. "He's—!"

Due to his surprise and haste to deliver the warning, Pinter had made an unfortunate selection of words. Catching the urgency in his voice as he said, "Watch him," Columbo did not wait to hear the rest of the message. Already as tense as a spring under compression, Columbo needed little stimulation to trigger him into action. Even as Pinter tried to identify Dusty, Columbo's right hand started to grab for its gun's fancy pearl butt.

Since coming to Hell, Giselle Lampart had witnessed a number of gunfights and even provoked a few of them. So she considered herself to be a connoisseur of such matters. In her opinion—and it was the reason why she had shown him so much attention—Ben Columbo was the fastest man with a gun she had ever seen. It seemed most unlikely that his small adversary could hope to survive the encounter.

Crossing so fast that the eye could barely follow their movements, Dusty's hands closed on the bone handles of his Colts. Half a second later, the guns had left their holsters, been cocked, turned outward, had the triggers depressed and roared so close together that the two detonations could not be detected as separate sounds. At almost the same instant, a .45 of an inch hole opened in the center of Pinter's forehead and a second bullet caught Columbo in the center of the chest.

Having come to a halt some twenty feet from Waco, Heck heard Pinter's shout and started his draw. Thrusting himself away from the gate, the young blond sent his right hand dipping to the off-side Army Colt. Flowing swiftly from its contour-fitting holster, the gun lined and bellowed. Hit over the left eye, Heck went down with his weapon still not clear of the holster.

Having decided that his help would not be needed, Topple stood with his thumbs hooked into his gunbelt. At the sight of Columbo reeling backward and Pinter's lifeless body spinning around, he snatched free his right hand with the intention of rectifying his mistake. Alert for such a possibility, Dusty also realized that the young outlaw possessed sufficient skill to pose a very real threat to his existence.

Cocking his Colts as they rose on the recoils' kick, Dusty swung their barrels to the right. Even as Topple's revolver started to lift in the small Texan's direction, two 250-grain bullets passed over it and into the outlaw's torso. Flung from his feet, Topple dropped his gun and crashed to the floor.

Although he had taken a serious wound, Columbo neither fell nor dropped his Colt. Bringing his bullet-propelled retreat to a halt, he tried to lift and aim his weapon. Almost of its own volition, Dusty's right-hand Colt cocked, passed beneath his extended left arm and turned toward the vicious young killer. Again flame spurted from the muzzle and lead struck Columbo, still without knocking him down. Turning his left-hand Colt and elevating it to eye level, Dusty took the split second needed for a rough alignment of the sights. He squeezed the trigger and the hammer fell. The top of Columbo's head seemed to burst open as the bullet drove up through the handsome face and out of his skull. Stumbling backward, he struck the wall by the door and collapsed.

Once again Dusty thumb-cocked the Colts as their barrels lifted to the thrust of the recoil. Spinning to the left, he pointed his guns at the men who appeared through the door of the tackroom.

"Stay put until I know who you are and where you stand!" Dusty commanded.

"Which's my sentiments all along the trail," Waco went on, turning right to cover another pair of townsmen who came out of Basmanov's office.

Satisfied that his *amigos* could attend to the new arrivals, the Kid let them get on with it. Twisting out his old Colt, he tilted its barrel toward the floor of the hayloft.

"And tell that feller's was stamping around up there to come down, *pronto,*" the Kid continued. "Else I'll send something up's'll make him wish he'd been more fairyfooted."

"You are right, Ivan," boomed the man who stood behind the barn's owner at the tackroom's door. Stepping by Basmanov, he walked toward Dusty. "They *are* remarkable young men. Gentlemen, please put up your guns. I'm Mayor Lampart and I extend you a cordial welcome to the town of Hell."

7

ONE TENTH OF YOUR LOOT

The mayor of Hell was a rubbery, blocky man of middle height, jovial-faced and with a pencil-line moustache over full lips. Clad in a well-cut gray Eastern suit, a diamond stickpin glowing on his silk cravat, he exuded an air of disarming amiability like a professional politician.

At a word from Lampart, Basmanov ordered the man to come down from the hayloft. The other new arrivals crowded forward to look at the four bodies. As a sign of his good faith, Dusty holstered his Colts.

"I'm right sorry I had to do that in front of your good lady, sir," the small Texan stated, indicating the dead outlaws. "Only you can't let that kind push you around."

"I suppose not," Lampart replied and gave his wife a glance. It was the first sign he had made of being aware of her presence. "Giselle will survive it. Won't you, my dove?"

"I will," agreed the brunette, displaying neither distress nor concern over having seen her four companions shot down. "But I don't think Ben will be so lucky."

"His death was only a matter of time," Lampart said philosophically. "A most unstable young man, with a number of objectionable traits, I always found him. And whom, may I ask, do I have the pleasure of addressing?"

"Didn't ole Lard-Guts Butterfield's pigeon get here to say we was coming?" Waco inquired, having holstered his Colt and strolled to Dusty's side.

"You know about *that*?" Lampart demanded, and Basmanov let out a low exclamation in a barbaric-sounding foreign language.

"Brother Ed figured it out," Waco explained, in a tone which implied that, with his "brother" doing the figuring, it must be so. "He allowed ole Lard-Guts'd send word's soon's he got back to Paducah and'd soaked his aching feet-bones in hot water."

"Huh?" grunted the mayor, looking puzzled.

"They do reckon doing it's good for aching feet-bones like he'd have." Waco grinned.

"I—I'm afraid I don't understand," Lampart told Dusty in his pompous East Coast accent.

"Two Rangers tried to jump us in Paducah, but we got the drop on them," Dusty elaborated. "Sheriff had to get up a posse and come after us. We figured he'd take kind to having an excuse to stop afore he caught us, so Comanch' here went back the first night out and give him one."

"How?" Giselle asked, staring at Dusty with considerable interest.

"He ran off all their hosses, ma'am," Waco answered. "Serves 'em right, for shame, fetching along that undertaker when they was chasing us."

"Undertaker?" the brunette gasped, swiveling her gaze at her husband.

"If he warn't, he sure dressed like one," Waco told her. "Big, hungry-looking jasper. That gun he toted, though, he could maybe drum up some business if there wasn't any."

While Dusty had said that the trio should try to impress the people of Hell by deducing Butterfield's connection with the town, he had also decided that they should pretend that they did not tie Hatchet in with it.

"You ran off Orv Hatchet's horse?" Giselle gurgled delightedly. "Oh, dear. What I would give to have seen his face."

"You know the gent, ma'am?" Dusty asked.

"You made a shrewd assumption about the sheriff, Mr. Caxton," Lampart interrupted, silencing his wife with a glare. "Now, if you gentlemen will accompany me to my office, I will acquaint you with certain matters pertaining to the running of our community."

"How about those four?" Dusty asked, nodding to the corpses.

"How about them?" Basmanov challenged.

"There's ten thousand dollars on Columbo's head," Dusty replied. "Pinter's worth another five and I'd say there's a reward on the other two."

"So?" growled Basmanov.

"So it's a right pity we're out here and got no way of toting them someplace's we could turn 'em in," Dusty drawled. "Only they'd not keep above ground long enough in this heat."

"That's true," Lampart agreed. "So we will accommodate them in our boothill. Leave these gentlemen of the Regulators to attend to that."

"It's your town, Mr. Mayor," Dusty answered. "Get your gear, boys. We're ready when you are, sir."

A small crowd had gathered at the front doors, being kept outside by the man from the hayloft and some of the Regulators. These latter had the appearance of prosperous businessmen. All wore guns, but did not give the impression of being experts in their use.

Taking his wife's arm, Lampart glanced at the front doors and suggested that they leave by the side entrance. With their saddles and bridles slung over a shoulder and saddlebags dangling over the other arm, Dusty, the Kid and Waco accompanied the couple from the building. While leaving, Lampart acted as if he were watching for somebody. If that was so, the expected parties did not make an appearance. Looking relieved, Lampart led the way along the rear of the buildings.

As the party was passing the Honest Man Saloon, the center of its rear doors opened. A statuesque, beautiful blond woman stepped out to confront them. From the looks of her, she had not long been out of bed. Her face had no makeup and the hair was held back with a blue ribbon. One naked, shapely leg emerged provocatively through the front of her blue satin robe and it was open sufficiently low to suggest that it came close to being her only garment.

"Who was it, Simmy?" the blonde asked, in a relaxed, comradely manner that implied she made her living entertaining men.

"Ben Columbo, Joey Pinter, Heck Smith and Topple," the mayor replied.

"I figured somebody'd get around to them," the blonde said calmly, looking at Dusty. "Did you take Columbo out?"

"He sure did, ma'am," Waco enthused. "Along of Pinter 'n' Topple. Getting a regular hawg that ways, Brother Ed is. Didn't leave but that Smith *hombre* to li'l me."

"If you burned down Heck Smith, you'd best watch out for his brothers. One of them's a limping, scar-faced runt," the blonde warned. "The other two look like Heck, only older, dirtier and meaner."

"I'll mind it, ma'am," Waco promised, ogling the woman's richly endowed frame with frank, juvenile admiration.

"You're new here," the blonde hinted, ignoring the youngster and directing the words to Dusty.

"This is Edward and Matthew Caxton, and Alvin Blood, Emma," the mayor introduced. "Gentlemen, may I present Miss Emma Nene, the owner of the Honest Man."

"Right pleased to know you, ma'am," Dusty said.

"We've been expecting you," Emma Nene declared. "Hey! Seeing how you boys made wolf bait of them four lameheaded yacks, the drinks are on me tonight."

"Then we'll be in there, a-drinking free, regular 'n' plentiful, ma'am," Waco assured her. " 'Cause we done got every last blasted one of 'em."

"Shall we take these gentlemen to your office, Simeon?" Giselle suggested, her voice and attitude showing that she did not like the blonde.

"Of course," Lampart agreed. "If you'll excuse us, Emma?"

"Why not," the blonde answered. "The shooting woke me up, but I reckon I can get to sleep again. Don't you boys forget to come around tonight, mind."

"Ma'am," Waco declared fervently, keeping his gaze fixed on the valley between the hillocks of her breasts, "you just couldn't keep us away."

Walking on, Dusty was conscious of the blonde's eyes following him. The party turned along the alley separating the saloon from what was apparently the Lamparts' home as well as his place of business. The front door opened into a pleasantly decorated hall. To the left, a sign on the door in the center of the wall announced "Mayor's Office" and at the right was the entrance to Lampart's second room in which, apparently, he carried out his duties as attorney-at-law. Excusing herself, with a dazzling smile at Dusty, Giselle disappeared through a curtain-draped opening leading to the rear half of the building. Lampart opened up the mayor's chambers and waved the Texans to enter.

As Dusty passed through the doorway, he noticed the thickness of the interior wall. He concluded that, if those on the outside were equally sturdy, the room would be secure from unwanted visitors. That view was increased by the stout timbers of the door and heavily barred windows. The room itself proved to be a comfortable, but functional, place of business. In its center, a large desk faced the door. On its otherwise empty top, an ivory-handled Colt Civilian Peacemaker lay conveniently placed for the right hand of anybody who sat behind the desk. The reason for the cocked revolver and sturdy fittings might be found in the steel-bound oak boxes that formed a line along two of the walls.

While his guests were setting down their saddles and freeing the moneybags, Lampart drew three chairs to the front of the desk. He waved the trio to sit down and went to occupy the chair behind the desk but kept his right hand well away from the revolver.

"Now, gentlemen," Lampart said, producing a box of cigars from the right side drawer and offering it to Dusty, "you will understand that, as mayor of this somewhat special community, I must ask questions which might sound impolite."

"Ask ahead," Dusty authorized, accepting a cigar. He opened the left bag and took a copy of the *Texas State Gazette* from it. "This'll tell you the parts Sheriff Butterfield couldn't get on his message."

While Lampart examined the paper, Dusty, the Kid and Waco lit up their cigars. After a short time, the mayor raised his eyes and nodded.

"This clears up some of the details, but there are others which require further clarification."

"Fire them at us," offered Dusty.

"Since bringing Hell into being, I have, naturally, gained considerable knowledge of outlaws in Texas, New Mexico and the Indian Nations. Yet I have never heard any of your names mentioned."

"That figures. Matt, Comanch' and I've never pulled a robbery afore this one. But it was too good a chance to miss."

"You must have been fortunate to have met this Sergeant Magoon," Lampart remarked, tapping the paper with his forefinger.

"Not all the way," Dusty objected. "Sure, it was lucky meeting him at the right time. But we'd knowed him afore when we joined the Cavalry. Fact being, we'd done one of those payroll deliveries, afore they got wise to the boy's real age and talked about heaving him out. We all quit afore they could do it. Then one night we met Magoon in a saloon. He was drunk and talking mean about the Army, 'cause they'd passed him over for top sergeant. While he was bellyaching about it, he let enough slip for me to figure he was on one of the escorts. We got him more liquor and talked him 'round to our way of thinking. After that, it was easy. We knew where, when and how to hit."

"And Magoon?"

"Once a talker, allus a talker's how I see it. Happen we'd given him a share, he'd've got stinking drunk and bawled it to the world what he'd done. So we dropped him."

"Only the bastard'd already done some lip-flapping," Waco put in indignantly. "That's how the Rangers got onto us so quick."

"It's possible," Lampart said noncommittally. "How did you know about Hell?"

"Man learns more than soldiering in the Army," Dusty replied. "Was a feller who'd been on the dodge and he told us about it. So, soon's we heard the Rangers knowed us, we came on up here."

"But how did you avoid the Indians and our scouts, and find the town?"

"Comanch' was raised Injun," Waco answered. "He brought us through's easy's falling off a log."

"Not all that easy, boy," Dusty objected. "Fact being, we had some luck in doing it. We traveled by night all the time until we found the tracks of shod horses. Allowed they must be coming here and followed them in."

"What made you suspect Butterfield?" Lampart wanted to know.

"He dresses a heap too well for a John Law in a one-hoss county," Dusty replied. "Saw the pigeons on the way in and found out who they belonged to. The rest was easy. Somebody was paying him good, and it wasn't the citizens of Cottle County. So it near on had to be you folks in Hell, having him pass the word about anything's happened or owlhoots headed your way."

"That's shrewd thinking," Lampart praised.

"Are you satisfied with us now?" Dusty inquired.

"I am, although I may ask you to supply further details or to clear up a few points later."

"That's all right with us," Dusty declared.

"Then there is only one thing more to be settled," Lampart announced. "The matter of payment for the benefits we offer you."

"How much'd that come to?" Waco asked suspiciously.

"One tenth of your loot," Lampart said, with the air of expecting to hear protests.

"A *tenth*!" Waco yelped, acting his part with customary skill.

"That's a fair price," Dusty drawled.

"Fair!" Waco spat back. "Hell, Brother Ed, that's—"

"Your brother is aware of the advantages, young man," Lampart said calmly. "If I know the Army, much of the paper money is in new, easily traced bills."

"Yeah," the youngster mumbled. "It is!"

"So there is nowhere in Texas, or even in the whole country, where you can chance spending it for some considerable time to come," Lampart enlarged. "If you tried, you'd bring the law down on your heads. One tenth is a small price to pay for your safety, and that is what you get for your money. Not only safety. Here you can find girls, gambling, drinking, clothing. Everything in fact that you committed the robbery to get. And without needing to watch over your shoulder while you're enjoying them."

"And when the money's gone?" Dusty asked.

"You will be faced with the same solution to that as would await you anywhere else," Lampart replied. "Work for, or steal, some more. Our guides will take you out by the *Kweharehnuh* so that you can do it. Occasionally, we are in a position to suggest further—employment—to men we can trust to come back."

"You're saying we can stay here, whooping it up, as long's our money lasts out," drawled the Kid. "Then we get told to leave?"

"Of course we don't tell you to leave," objected Lampart. "Unfortunately, supplies cost us more than they would in an ordinary town. So the chances of obtaining charity are correspondingly smaller. And no man of spirit likes to live on handouts, does he?"

"Way you put it, the deal sounds reasonable to me," commented the Kid. "Do we go in on the pot, Ed?"

"We go in," Dusty confirmed. "Count out ten thousand dollars and give it to his honor, Brother Matt."

"You say so, Brother Ed," Waco muttered. "Lend me a hand, Comanch'."

"Where can we bed down, sir?" Dusty said as his companions started to count out wads of new bills.

"At the hotel," the mayor suggested. "You'll find it at the other end of the street to the livery barn. There's sure to be at least two empty rooms. But the prices are high."

"Same's at the barn!" grunted Waco, stopping counting.

"And for the same reason," Dusty pointed out. "These folks here have a whole slew of expenses other towns don't."

"That's true," agreed Lampart, eyeing Dusty in a calculating manner. "If you wish, gentlemen, you may leave the bulk of your money here. In one of those boxes, to which you alone will have the keys. You can, of course, draw it out as and when you need it."

"That's a smart notion," Dusty declared, silencing Waco's protest before it could be made. With the youngster scowling in a convincingly suspicious manner, he went on, "Hold back five hundred for each of us, Comanch', and put the rest in one of the boxes."

"You trust me?" Lampart smiled.

"Why shouldn't I?" countered Dusty. "You don't need to bother robbing us. Sooner or later, you or one of the other folks'll get most of our money without going to that much trouble."

"How do you mean?" Waco growled.

"Who else do we spend it with while we're here?" Dusty asked. " 'Sides which, setting up this place cost too much and running it's too profitable for the folks to want it spoiling that way."

"As I have said before, Mr. Caxton," Lampart declared, "you are a most perceptive young man. Taken with your gun savvy, that makes a formidable combination."

"Comes in handy to have it on your side, sir," Dusty remarked. "Which box do we use?"

With the payment made, the remainder of the money was placed in one of the boxes. Dusty pocketed his five hundred dollars and the keys. Going to the door, Lampart opened it and his wife entered carrying a tray.

"Mr. Caxton and his friends will be staying, my dove," the mayor said.

"Good," Giselle answered, pouring out cups of coffee.

While drinking and making idle conversation, they heard the front door open. Going to investigate, Lampart returned with two of the men who had been in the barn. He introduced them as Manny Goldberg, the owner of the hotel, and Jean le Blanc, the barber. Middle-sized and Gallic-looking, le Blanc started to talk.

"I have seen Pinter's gang and they are not concerned with avenging his death. Money is short with them and they are considering leaving; have been wanting to for the past few days, but he wouldn't go. Topple's leader is more relieved than angry as he was getting ambitious and, with Columbo's backing, might have taken over the gang."

"That leaves Columbo's bunch," Dusty drawled.

"They are the Smith brothers," le Blanc replied. "At the moment, all three are at Dolly's whorehouse and too drunk to cause you any trouble. But you must walk warily in their presence, *mes braves.*"

"They can walk warily 'round us," Waco snorted truculently.

"How does the town stand on it, happen we have to take their toes up, Mr. Lampart?" Dusty wanted to know.

"We let our visitors settle such matters amongst themselves," the mayor replied. "Beyond the city limits for preference. There's a hollow in which duels can be fought without endangering civic property or innocent bystanders."

"Happen they want it that way, we'll go there with them," Dusty said. "But the first move'll come from them. You hear me, Comanch', Brother Matt?"

"I hear," grunted the Kid.

"You, Brother Matt?" Dusty demanded, a grimmer timbre creeping into his voice.

"All right," Waco answered in a grudgingly resigned tone. "I hear you."

Interested eyes studied the trio as they left the mayor's house and walked along the street to the hotel, but nobody interfered with them in any way. They had been told by Goldberg to go and ask for rooms, while le Blanc had put the facilities of his shop and bathhouse at their services. Walking along the center of the street, a logical precaution considering what had happened at the livery barn and the presence of Heck Smith's brothers in town, they were able to talk without the risk of being overheard.

"Lampart's interested in you-all, Brother Ed," Waco drawled.

"Let's hope he stays that way," the Kid went on, for the plan was that they should gain the confidence of the town's boss.

"Happen he does," Dusty warned, "you pair might have to watch how you go."

"Why?" Waco asked.

"He could figure I'll be more use to him—and safe—with you both dead," Dusty explained.

8
IT WAS ME HE WANTED
SAVING

*"I saw a big-pig Yankee marshal a-coming down the street,
Got two big sixguns in his hands 'n' looks fierce enough to
eat."*

Sitting in a cubicle of the barber's bathhouse, the Ysabel Kid
raised his pleasant tenor voice in a song guaranteed to start a
fight with peace officers anywhere north of the Mason-Dixon
line. As he sang, he soaped his lean brown torso with lather
raised on a washcloth and let the heat of a tub full of water
soothe him after the long journey. Close by, his gunbelt lay
across the seat of the chair, which also held a towel and his
newly bought clothes. His old garments lay on the floor where
he had dropped them as he undressed.

On their arrival at the hotel, Dusty, the Kid and Waco had
been allocated quarters. Dusty would occupy a small single
room and his companions share another with two double beds.
The building had offered a good standard of comfort and clean-

liness, which was not surprising considering that the manage-
ment charged three times the normal tariff.

With their saddles and rifles locked away, the trio had set off
to buy new clothes and freshen up their appearances. The bathroom section of the barber's premises had only two cubicles, so
the Kid had allowed his companions to make use of them first.
With Dusty and Waco finished and gone into the front half of
the building, the Kid had taken his turn in a hot bath.

"Now big-pig Yankee stay away, stay right away from me,
I'm just one li'l Texas boy 'n' scared as I can be."

Having rendered the chorus, the Kid prepared to give out the
second verse. He heard a soft, stealthy footfall outside the cubicle and its door began to inch open. Even as he opened his
mouth to call out that it was occupied, shots thundered from
the front section of the building.

Like the hotel, the barbershop had furnishings and fittings
worthy of any city's high-rent district. It offered two comfortable, well-padded leather swivel chairs, white towels and cloths.
On a shelf in front of a large mirror stood bottles of lotions,
hair tonics, patent medicines and other products of the tonso-
rial arts.

Lounging at ease in the right-hand chair, Dusty allowed le
Blanc to work on his head with combs and scissors. The barber
carried out his task with a deft touch. Incompetence at his
trade had not been the reason why he had settled and gone into
business in Hell. Waco was in the second chair, with le Blanc's
tall, lean young assistant trimming his hair.

Although Dusty was seated with his back to the door, the big
mirror allowed him to keep watch on it. With the type of cus-
tomer he catered to, le Blanc must have been compelled to have
such a fitting installed. No man with a price on his head took to
the notion of having people come up behind him unless he had
the means to keep an eye on them.

All the time the scissors were clicking, Dusty kept the door
under observation. That was partly caution, but also because of

the interest le Blanc and the assistant showed in what was going on outside. Ever since Dusty and Waco had taken their seats, the two barbers had repeatedly glanced through the window at the far side of the street.

"You wish the beard removed, *M'sieur* Caxton?" le Blanc inquired as he was putting the finishing touches to Dusty's hair.

"Trim it up a mite is all," the small Texan replied. "I've always found the gals go for a feller with hair on his face. They want to know if it tickles when he kisses them."

"That is a very good reason." Le Blanc smiled, throwing another look at the window and stiffening slightly. He laid his left hand on the back of the chair. "I will make it so that the ladies fall in love with you at first sight."

At that moment, two men walked into the shop. Tall, lean, the first looked like an older, dirtier and meaner version of the late Heck Smith; he moved to his left. The other was smaller, with a long scar twisting his right cheek. As he stepped to his right, he exhibited a noticeable limp. Even without seeing their hands dropping toward holstered revolvers, Dusty had decided that they must be the dead man's brothers. Nor did it call for any deep thought to realize that they had come to take revenge for the killing of their kinsman and gang's leader.

The man who entered the Kid's cubicle had a sufficiently strong family resemblance to Heck Smith for there to be no need to swap introductions. Tall, young, hard-eyed, he was already drawing his Army Colt. Glancing first at the dirty buckskins on the floor, he swiveled his eyes to the figure in the bath. Indignant at the invasion of his privacy, the Kid knew who the man must be and why he had come. Things looked desperate for the Indian-dark cowhand, but that brief interval while the intruder checked his identity gave him all the respite he needed.

Before the man could slant the revolver his way, the Kid acted with typical *Pehnane* speed. Swinging up the soapy washcloth, he flung it so that it hit and wrapped wetly around Smith's face. Letting out a startled, muffled yelp, the man grabbed at the cloth with his empty left hand in an attempt to restore his obliterated vision.

Bringing down the hand that had flung the cloth, the Kid used it to help him rise and drop over the edge of the bath. Landing on the floor, he rolled across his old clothes to the chair. Gripping the front leg with his left hand to hold the chair steady, he folded the fingers of his right fist about the ivory hilt of the bowie knife. Looking over his shoulder, he took aim and plucked the great knife from its sheath. Then he swung his right arm parallel to the floor, releasing his hold on the weapon at the appropriate moment.

The knife hissed through the air as the would-be killer tore the soaking cloth from his features. Vision returned too late to save him. Flying on a horizontal plane, the clip point spiked between two of his ribs. The weight, balance and design of the weapon—brought to perfection at the instigation of a master knife-fighter—caused it to drive on until it impaled his heart. Letting his gun fall, he clutched ineffectively at where the hilt rose from his torso. Then he stumbled and blundered helplessly out of the cubicle.

Coming to his feet, as naked as the day he was born, the Kid jerked the Dragoon Colt from its holster. Cocking it, he made for the door. He heard voices from the front of the building. Realizing that he could not go there in his current state of undress, he returned and draped a towel about his waist.

Bad though the position might appear, Dusty knew that it was not entirely hopeless for Waco or himself. Their gunbelts were hanging with their hats on the sets of wapiti horns fixed to the wall for that purpose. If the Smith brothers had been more observant, they might have noticed that both the belts had something missing. Each of their prospective victims, did the brothers but know it, was nursing his right hand Colt under the long cloth that the barber had draped around his neck to protect his new clothing. All that remained for the OD Connected men to do was spring from the chairs, turn and face their respective assailants—if they could do it before the outlaws' guns came out and threw lead into them.

About to shove himself from his seat, Dusty felt it starting to

move. Gripping the back of the chair, le Blanc tugged sharply
at it. Instead of trying to jump, Dusty gambled on a hunch and
allowed himself to be carried around. Sure enough, the barber
halted the chair as its occupant faced Smith.

Shock twisted briefly at the tall outlaw's face as he took in
the sight. He opened his mouth to speak. Then the cloth covering Dusty from the neck down formed a pyramid. Flame burst
from its apex and a bullet twirled across the room into the
man's head. All expression left his face and his mouth dangled
open without words leaving it. Reeling backward, he collided
with the wall and slid down it until he sat in a heap on the
floor.

If anything, Waco had been slightly better prepared than
Dusty for the pair's arrival. From his seat, he had been able to
see the door and out of the left-hand window. With his attention drawn that way by the assistant barber's behavior, he had
observed two men crossing the street at an angle that would
bring them to the door of the shop. At least, he had assumed
that to be their destination when he had noticed the taller's
resemblance to Heck Smith and the other's scarred face.

There had not been time for Waco to warn Dusty of the
danger. However, the youngster assumed that his "brother"
was equally alert to its possibility. So, like Dusty, Waco was
preparing to leap from his seat when the assistant barber
started to swing it around.

Seeing that le Blanc had treated Dusty the same way, Waco
formed rapid conclusions from the actions of the barbers. It
seemed that the two townsmen intended to help their customers escape from the guntrap. Yet in his eagerness to do so, the
assistant had put too much force into his pull on the back of
Waco's chair. The youngster knew that it was turning too fast
to halt when he faced Heck Smith's limping brother.

With Waco, to think was to act. Ramming his shoulders
against the back of the chair, he used them to thrust himself
sideways and roll off it. The smallest Smith proved to be faster
than any of his brothers. Out flashed his revolver and lined at

the blond cowhand's chair. Smith was still trying to correct his aim in the light of Waco's actions when the gun crashed. Lead winged above Waco and embedded itself in the back of the seat he had just deserted.

Tearing off the barber's cloth as he fell, Waco landed on his left side and continued to roll. As his back came to rest on the floor, he stabbed forward the long-barreled Army Colt. Already cocked, it roared and missed. Across lashed his left hand, its heel catching the spur of the Colt's hammer and carrying the mechanism to fully cocked, while his forefinger held back the trigger. On being released, the hammer flew forward and set off another load. Three times Waco repeated the process.

Fanning the hammer offered the fastest known method of emptying the cylinder of a single-action revolver, but had never been noted for accuracy. During the one and a half seconds taken by Waco to get off the shots, the method proved accurate enough. Although scattered about his body, all four bullets struck Smith. Dropping his smoking gun, so that it fired and sent a bullet into the floor, he pitched headlong across the room and crumpled lifeless in a corner.

Snatching off the smoldering white cloth, which had been ignited by the Peacemaker's muzzleblast, Dusty tossed it aside and stepped from the chair. While treading on it to put out the fire, he looked to where Waco was rising. "Are you all right, boy?" Dusty asked.

"He missed," the youngster replied. "Hey! There's three of 'em. Maybe the other's gone—"

"Hell, yes!" Dusty spat out and darted to the door that gave access to the bathroom.

Going through, with Waco on his heels, Dusty almost tripped over the body of the Kid's victim. Dragoon in hand, the Indian-dark cowhand stepped cautiously out of the cubicle. The weapon lined at them, then lowered.

"Figured you'd be all right," the Kid remarked calmly. "Only I didn't aim to take no chances was I wrong."

"Damned if he ain't gone back to the war whoops, Brother

Ed." Waco grinned, eyeing the towel that formed the Kid's only item of clothing. "That sure is one fancy li'l breechcloth."

"He'll send all them sweet li'l *naivis*[1] into a tizz happen he wears it at a Give-Away dance," Dusty agreed, watching the Kid retrieve his bowie knife.

"I *allus* did," declared the Kid and stalked with what dignity he could muster into the cubicle. "Why'n't you blasted pale-faces go leave a man to take his bath in peace?"

Returning to the barbershop portion of the building, the Texans found le Blanc and his assistant examining the bodies.

"They cashed in?" Dusty inquired.

"I've never seen anybody more cashed in," le Blanc answered cheerfully.

"Toby Siddons ought to be grateful to you, Mr. Caxton," the assistant went on, looking at Waco in a worried manner. "Limpy Smith shot him in the back two weeks ago."

"It's nice to know we've shot somebody and won't have another bunch coming after us," Waco replied. "Wonder if Toby'll set up the drinks for us, Brother Ed?"

"It's not likely," the assistant warned. "Toby's dead and buried in our boothill. His gang left just after the funeral to see if they could raise some more money."

From the way in which he spoke, the assistant was acting like a man trying to stop another thinking about a mistake he had recently made. Despite having certain suspicions, Waco wanted to convince le Blanc that he suspected nothing about having been treated in a different manner to Dusty.

"Anyways, *gracias, amigo,*" the youngster said to the assistant. "You sure saved my hide. Only, should it happen again, don't shove the chair so hard. You near on spun me all the way 'round instead of towards him."

"I—I'm sorry," the assistant said, exhibiting signs of alarm.

"Shuckens. You've got no call to be, seeing's you saved my life," Waco assured him. "Likely you was's surprised's Brother

---

1. *Naivi:* an adolescent Comanche girl.

Ed 'n' me when they come busting in. But you acted for the best and I'm right grateful."

Several people, including Lampart and Basmanov, had heard the shooting and come to investigate. As at the livery barn, a couple of townsmen stood at the door and kept the curious onlookers outside the shop.

"There's another of them," the mayor announced, glancing at the bodies. "He might have gone after Mr. Blood."

"He did," Waco admitted. "Had he asked, I could've told him not to. Ole Comanch's a mite touchy who he shares his bath with."

"Mr. Blood isn't injured?" Lampart inquired.

"Nope." Waco grinned. "But he's sure a sight to see, with that li'l ole towel wrapped around him."

While the mayor was talking with Waco, Dusty watched Basmanov examine the two corpses. To the small Texan, it seemed that the owner of the livery barn looked a mite relieved at discovering that both had been killed almost instantaneously and so would have been unable to do any talking before they died.

"I never thought they'd come after you so soon, Mr. Caxton," Lampart remarked to Dusty.

"Or me," growled Waco. "After we was told about them being stinking drunk."

"Easy, boy," Dusty ordered. "They must've got sobered up when they heard what had happened—"

"They didn't hear about it from Manny and me!" le Blanc declared.

"If they had, you wouldn't've saved us the way you did, sir," Dusty replied soothingly and saw Basmanov dart a scowling glance at the barber. "Or they maybe wasn't's drunk as they made out. Would there be anybody else likely to take this up for them, Mr. Lampart?"

"I shouldn't think so," the mayor answered. "They weren't the most popular or likable of our visitors. And in view of what's happened since you came, there'll be second thoughts before *anybody* decides to go up against you gentlemen. By the way, Ed—if I may dispense with formality—?"

"Feel free, sir. It's your town."

"It's remiss of me not to have done so earlier, but my wife and I are giving a dinner party for the gang leaders tonight at the hotel and we would like to offer you an invitation to attend."

"Just me?"

"Meaning no disrespect to your brother and Mr. Blood, it is only for the gang's *leaders,*" Lampart apologized. "Much as I would enjoy your company, gentlemen, I can't invite you without asking along all the other visitors."

"Well," Dusty began hesitantly, "that being the case, I don't—"

"Aw. You go on and go to it, Brother Ed," Waco suggested, his attitude hinting that he would not be averse to being away from his "elder brother" with a celebration in the offing. "Comanch' and me's not much for them fancy, sitting-down polite dinners. And, anyways, that blond gal's setting up free drinks for us tonight at the saloon."

"Mind you don't have too many of them," Dusty ordered bluntly. Then he turned to Lampart and continued, "I'd be right honored to come, sir. Only I'd maybe best get these whiskers trimmed decent first."

"No sooner said than done, *mon ami,*" le Blanc announced, darting a triumphant grin at the scowling Basmanov. Swinging on his heel, the barn's owner stalked from the room and the barber went on, waving to his chairs, "If you and your brother will sit down, we'll attend to you. This time there shouldn't be any interruptions."

"How do you read the sign on what happened in there, D—Ed?" the Kid asked half an hour later as he, Dusty and Waco strolled toward the hotel. "Way I see it, the barber and his louse figured the Smiths'd be coming and saved your lives when they did."

"Likely that's what Lampart told them to do," Dusty replied. "Only, was I you pair, I'd not count on it happening while I'm not with you tonight. It was me he wanted saving."

"But le Blanc's boy twirled 'Brother Matt' there around—" the Kid objected, recalling the conversation that had taken place, while he was having his hair cut and beard trimmed, discussing the shooting at length.

"And damned near twirled me too far," Waco interrupted. "Way I see it, there's not much goes on in Hell that Lampart doesn't get to hear about. You can bet he knowed the Smiths was sober enough to be figuring on coming after us. If he'd wanted us all dead, he'd've passed the word to let them get us. And he'd've warned us happen he'd wanted all three of us alive."

"I'm with you so far," admitted the Kid.

"Instead, he must've told le Blanc to keep watch and save just Brother Ed. They figured to let you take your chance, Comanch'; and to let Smith get me, but make it look like they'd tried to save me. If I'd've took lead, you'd likely've reckoned it was through the young feller spooking and turning the chair too hard."

"That's about the size of it," Dusty conceded.

"Just leave us have that young yahoo off somewheres quiet for a spell," suggested the Kid, sounding as mild and innocent as was humanly possible. "We'll soon know if your figuring's right or not."

"Leave it be," Dusty advised. "We'll let them believe we're thinking the way they want us to. I reckon that Lampart's looking for backing against that Basmanov *hombre*. If so, given a mite of luck, I'll get him thinking that three of us're better than one. If we can get close to him, we can learn all there is to know about this town and how to bust it wide open."

"We know one thing now," Waco said soberly. "They kill off fellers with rewards on their heads and get the bodies out to towns where they can collect the bounties."

"We'd figured that much afore we got to Paducah," commented the Kid.

"And we know for sure now," Waco insisted. "Toby Siddons

was back-shot in town and buried here, 'cording to the barber's louse. It'd be mighty interesting to try opening up some more of those graves in boothill."

"Don't try doing it tonight," Dusty ordered. "And watch how you go, boys. Basmanov might get somebody else to try and make wolf bait of us, to stop us tying in with Lampart."

9

I WAS SAWING MY WIFE
IN HALF

Wearing his freshly cleaned black Stetson, a frilly-bosomed white silk shirt, black string tie, gray town-fashion trousers tucked neatly into shining Wellington-leg boots and a Colt-laden gunbelt, Dusty Fog strolled into the hotel's dining room. The time was just after ten o'clock in the evening of his first day at Hell. As the mayor had explained in a note that had been delivered to the small Texan, due to the rule prohibiting the lighting of fires during the hours of daylight, the dinner could not be prepared and served any earlier.

That afternoon, Dusty, the Ysabel Kid and Waco had made an extensive examination of the town and its surroundings. To avoid arousing suspicions as to their motives—cowhands being notorious for their dislike of walking—Dusty had given a reason publicly for their perambulations. While enjoying an excellent cold lunch at the hotel, he had announced in loud tones that he and his *amigos* would be taking a stroll that afternoon. So, happen any of Columbo's, Pinter's, Topple's or the Smith brothers' friends had the notion, the trio would be ready and available to accept objections.

The challenge had not been taken up. So Dusty, the Kid and Waco had conducted an enlightening survey of the area. Passing through the graveyard, they had located Toby Siddons's "grave" and studied headboards bearing the names of other outlaws. Half a dozen Mexicans and Chinese coolies had been digging holes to accommodate Columbo, Pinter, Topple and the Smith brothers. Walking on, Dusty had wondered if the men killed by himself and his *amigos* would occupy the graves. Or if the other corpses whose names appeared on the headboards were really buried there.

Sixty or more adobe buildings were scattered around the wooden establishments on the street. Some were used by outlaws who probably objected to paying the hotel's high prices, or had been unable to obtain rooms in it. Others housed the Chinese and Mexicans who were employed to carry out various menial tasks in the town. The Kid had guessed that the latter were once slaves owned by the *Kweharehnuh* and traded, or given, to the citizens of Hell.

The discovery of six large wagons parked in three of the buildings had led the trio to make a closer scrutiny of the livery barn's corrals. They had found that a number of the horses were of a type bred for heavy haulage work. That had helped to explain how the town obtained its supplies.

One building in particular had aroused Dusty's interest. Situated about two hundred yards to the rear of the mayor's residence, it conveyed a similar impression of sturdiness. Small, cubic in shape, in an exceptional state of repair, its adobe walls had a single stoutly made oak door, secured, like the heavily shuttered window, with double padlocks. Although Dusty had noticed the building while accompanying the Lamparts from the livery barn, he had not been aware of the full implications. The door and window were at the rear, and on a bench under a shady porch, two Mexicans armed with shotguns kept watch on them. All the trio had wondered why the place should require a guard, and Dusty had resolved to find out as soon as possible.

Ever curious, Waco had asked why the original settlers had selected such an inhospitable region for their home. The Kid had suggested that they were Spanish colonists. Adobe was a building material with lasting qualities, and apart from various repairs that had been carried out recently, the houses looked to be of considerable age. Going by the absence of a church, normally the first thing erected by the priest-ridden Spanish colonists, Dusty had concluded that the settlers had been nonbelievers driven by religious persecution to take refuge in the Palo Duro country.

Returning to the hotel at the conclusion of their inspection, the trio had exchanged gossip with le Blanc in the barroom. Then they had gone to their rooms, where they had rested and tidied up ready for the night's celebrations. Before coming downstairs, Dusty had given Waco and the Kid instructions as to how they were to act when they arrived at the saloon. By doing so, they would help him to convince Lampart that they too would be of the greatest use to him.

Like his equally duded-up companions, Dusty now sported a neatly trimmed chinbeard and moustache which he hoped would continue to serve as a disguise. Looking around the crowd of guests, he saw nobody whom he recognized from other towns and wondered if it would be mutual. Some of the male faces appeared to be familiar, but only because he had seen them on wanted posters. Others belonged to townsmen who had been at the livery barn that morning.

To Dusty, it was obvious that the citizens had started to form into two factions. Those who supported Lampart stood slightly apart from Basmanov's group. Although the mayor seemed to have the largest number on his side, Dusty guessed that some of them would be fence-sitting and waiting for a definite show of strength before declaring on his behalf. Having the backing of the acknowledged fastest gun in town would be tremendously in Lampart's favor. Which probably accounted for the way the mayor left his companion on seeing the small Texan arrive in the dining room.

Although Dusty had devised an excuse for wearing his guns, he soon discovered that there would be no need for him to make it. Every man in the room, with the exception of Lampart, carried at least one revolver on his person.

"Ah, Edward!" the mayor greeted, coming over and extending his right hand. "Let me introduce you to the other guests before my wife gets here." He indicated a tall, handsome Mexican in an excellently tailored charro costume and wearing a low-hanging 1860 Army Colt with a set of decorative Tiffany grips. "This is Don Miguel Santiago. You already know Jean here. These are Doctor Connolly, our medical practitioner, and our undertaker, Emmet Youseman."

"I hope you can guess which of us is which," boomed the big, red-faced, cheerful man in the loud check suit. "In case you can't, I'm *not* the doctor."

There was, Dusty decided, good cause for the comment. Tall, cadaverous and dressed in sober black, Doctor Connolly fitted the popular conception of an undertaker far better than the hearty, extroverted Youseman.

"It's looking the way I do that made me settle here," the undertaker went on jovially, shaking hands with the small Texan. "Fellers I get here don't have kinfolks to object. I reckon Doc helps my business. When a wounded feller sees him, he figures he's so close to the grave that he might's well go the whole hog and get into it."

"It's no matter for levity," Connolly declared in a high, dry voice and turned to walk away without acknowledging Lampart's introduction.

"Don't pay him no never-mind, Ed," Youseman advised. "He's riled because you boys gave me all the trade instead of him."

"I'll mind it, happen I have to shoot anybody else," Dusty promised. "Only I've always been taught that any man who's acting bad enough for me to draw down on him is acting bad enough to be killed for it."

Even as he finished speaking, Dusty realized that his words had come during a lull in the general conversation. Not that he regretted them, for he realized that such a flat statement might do some good.

With the casual ease of an experienced host, Lampart steered Dusty onward and rattled off other introductions. Nine of the men, like Santiago, could be found prominently—if not honorably—mentioned in the "Bible Two," the Texas Rangers' annually published list of fugitives and wanted persons, which most peace officers in the Lone Star State read far more regularly than the original Bible. Wary eyes studied Dusty, but the greetings and handshakes were cordial until he reached the man who stood by Basmanov. Tall, handsome, well-dressed, he had a pearl-handled Colt Artillery Peacemaker in a fast-draw holster tied to his right thigh.

"And Andy Glover," Lampart concluded.

"You're the *hombre* who dropped Ben Columbo, huh?" Glover growled, keeping his right hand at his side. "Ben was real fast."

"Sure," Dusty conceded. "There was only one thing wrong. Just the once, he wasn't fast enough."

"Can't say I've heard your name," Glover said sullenly, conscious that every eye had turned toward him and the small Texan.

"I've heard yours," Dusty answered. "Seen it on wanted posters, too. That's the difference between us, *Mr.* Glover. I've been too smart to get myself wanted until the stakes were worth it."

"They say you robbed an Army paymaster," Glover gritted, not caring for the chuckles that greeted "Caxton" 's response. "I've never known the bluebellies sent their money about thataways."

"Happen a secret gets known to too many folks, it stops being a secret," Dusty countered. "I just happened to have been in a position to get to know. That's how me and the boys managed to pull it off, *mister*. We knew where, when and how to do it."

"And you're still on the dodge."

"So're you, *mister*. Only I'm willing to bet that I brought in more money with that one robbery than you and your bunch were toting when you hit Hell."

More laughter rose from the majority of the guests. It was common knowledge that, due to the Rangers' continual harassment, Glover's gang had been compelled to leave behind most of their loot. The bank robbery at Wichita Falls had been their last throw of the dice and had failed to come anywhere near their expectations in the amount of money it had produced. Dull red flooded into Glover's cheeks, but he had noted "Caxton" 's repeated use of the word "mister." No Texan said it after being introduced, unless he wished to show that he did not like the person he addressed it to.

"I see that you prefer the cross-draw, *señor*," Santiago remarked. "The same as Dusty Fog."

"Why, sure," Dusty agreed, wondering if there might be some hidden meaning behind the Mexican's words. "Fog's real fast, they do tell. So I figured the way he totes his guns must be something to do with it. That's why I wear them like I do."

"Makes you fast, huh?" Glover muttered sullenly.

"Ben Columbo, Joey Pinter and Topple likely wondered that self-same thing, *mister*," Dusty drawled, looking straight at the big outlaw. "They learned. If *anybody* feels so inclined to find out, I'm willing to step out onto the street and accommodate them."

Gently spoken the words had been, but everybody present knew that they put the gauntlet straight into Glover's teeth. The remainder of the guests began to draw farther away, waiting silently to see what developed. Despite being the host, Lampart made no attempt to intervene. Nor did Basmanov, in his capacity as head of the Civic Regulators, do anything to try to keep the peace.

Almost thirty seconds ticked away, although they seemed to drag by for Glover. Much as he wanted to, the tall gang leader could not look away from his challenger. The *big* blond Texan's gray eyes held his own and appeared to be boring through and reading his innermost thoughts.

One thought beat at Glover. Before him stood the man who had simultaneously outdrawn and outshot Columbo and Joey Pinter, killing Topple an instant later. That put him into a class of *pistolero* skill to which Glover could not hope to aspire. Yet if Glover backed down, he was finished in Hell. The story would be all around the town by morning and might even lose him the control he had previously exerted over the men in his gang.

Although determined to stand up against any man who tried to ride him, a good way to stay alive in such company, Dusty did not particularly want to kill Glover. So, having asserted himself, he sought for a way in which he might avoid taking the affair to a fatal conclusion. Sensing that Glover wanted to back off, Dusty saw an opportunity to let him do so. It had a certain amount of risk to the small Texan, but he felt sure that other issues swayed it in his favor.

Giselle Lampart stood at the open door, looking into the room. Jewelry sparkled at her fingers, wrists and neck, while the dress she wore leaned more to daring than decorous. Turning his back on Glover, Dusty swept off his Stetson with his left hand and walked toward the brunette.

"Good evening, ma'am," the small Texan greeted, his whole attitude suggesting that he regarded the incident with Glover closed. "My thanks for your kind invitation."

Sucking in a deep breath of mingled anger and relief, Glover glared after the departing Texan. The outlaw's right hand hooked talonlike over its revolver's butt, almost quivering with anticipation as he tried to decide whether to draw or not. Common sense, and a knowledge of the other guests' feelings, supplied him with the answer. If he started to pull the gun, one of his rivals might warn "Caxton." In fact, somebody was certain to do it, for Glover's action would endanger Giselle Lampart. Given the slightest hint of what Glover was planning, "Caxton" would turn to deal with the situation. Glover could not forget the *big* Texan's earlier comment on how he would treat any man who made him draw.

"Come and sit down, Andy," Basmanov said in a loud voice. "We don't want any unpleasantness."

Never had the Russian barn owner's voice sounded so delightful to Glover. Yet the outlaw could sense a tinge of disappointment in it. Refusing to let that disturb him, he swung on his heel and walked with Basmanov to the long table that had been laid for the dinner.

"It looks as if nobody feels inclined to find out, Edward," Giselle remarked with a mischievous smile. "You may escort me to the table. I've had you placed next to Simmy and myself so that I will have a handsome man on each side of me."

The tension had oozed away with the entrance of the brunette and Glover's retreat. Talk rose again and there was a general movement in the direction of the table. Guided by Giselle, Dusty went to the end of the table presided over by her husband. On the other end, Basmanov stood scowling from Dusty to the mayor. Going by the knowing looks thrown at him from various gang leaders, Dusty sensed that he was being awarded a place of honor. Perhaps the last time the Lamparts had given a dinner, Ben Columbo had occupied it. Dusty refused to let that thought worry him. To his left were Giselle and her husband, with Santiago on his right and le Blanc facing him across the table.

Moving with well-trained precision, Goldberg's Mexican waiters started to serve the meal. The food and wine proved to be of excellent quality, which did not surprise Dusty in the light of what he had already seen around the hotel. Soon conversations were being carried on and laughter rolled out. Although apparently at ease, Dusty remained constantly alert. Carefully he guided the talk in his group to the presence of the town in the Palo Duro.

"That was Simeon's doing," le Blanc declared. "Why not tell Ed how it happened, Simmy?"

"There's not much to tell," the mayor replied, in a mock depreciatory tone, and went on in a matter-of-fact manner.

"The first time the *Kweharehnuh* saw me, I was sawing my wife in half."

"Huh?" Dusty grunted, genuinely startled.

"That's right, Ed," Giselle confirmed. "And it wasn't the first time. He'd done it to me twice a night for years."

"You're a magician!" Dusty ejaculated, staring at Lampart with a growing understanding.

"One of the best, if I say so myself," the mayor agreed. "A most useful talent, I've always found it. And never more so than that night. We, the present citizens of Hell, were on a wagon train making its way down from the railroad in Kansas to Santa Fe. Our scout rode in to say that we were surrounded by Indians and they would attack our camp at dawn. We wouldn't have stood a chance in a fight, so I decided to try something else. Luckily I had all my props along. So Giselle and I put on our entire performance by fire- and lamplight. Of all my extensive repertoire, sawing Giselle in half went down the best. Ten Bears had never seen anything like it."

"Or me, the way I dressed for the act," Giselle put in, eyeing Dusty in a teasing manner.

"The whole band came down to watch," Lampart continued. "Next day, instead of attacking, they brought the medicine woman to see and, I suspect, explain the miracle. When she couldn't, Ten Bears decided that I must have extra powerful medicine and made me his blood brother. After that, getting permission for us to make our homes here was easy."

"Don't you want to know *why* we chose to settle here, Ed?" asked Youseman, sitting between the mayor and the barber.

"I figure that, happen he reckons it's my business, Mr. Lampart'll tell me about it," Dusty replied, guessing that no further information would be forthcoming right then.

"I always feel so immodest when I talk about it," Lampart remarked, placing a hand over his glass as the wine waiter offered to fill it. "No more for me, thank you."

"If a man's done something as smart as starting this town, I don't see why he needs be that way about telling it," Dusty praised. "Fact is, the only modest fellers I've ever met are that way because they've never done anything and don't have any other choice." He looked up and shook his head at the wine waiter. "I'll pass this deal, *amigo.*"

"You don't drink much, Edward," Giselle commented. "Aren't you enjoying yourself with us?"

"I'm having a right fine time, ma'am," Dusty answered. "Only I figure a man who has to pour liquor down his throat to enjoy himself doesn't have much to enjoy."

"You object to people drinking, *señor?*" Santiago inquired, but in a polite and friendly manner.

"I object to *me* drinking," Dusty corrected, hoping that somebody would take the bait. "What other fellers do is none of my never-mind."

"From the way your brother talks," Lampart put in, just as Dusty had hoped, "I don't think he shares your views."

"Matt talks better than he drinks," Dusty replied, taking the chance to impress the mayor with the Kid's and Waco's sterling qualities and the fact that they would be of use to him. "They're good kids, him and Comanch' both. As loyal as they come and they always do just what I tell them. Tell you what, gents, I said they should stay sober tonight. And I'll bet a thousand dollars they're that way if we go along to the saloon when we're through here."

"With Emma handing out the free drinks?" Le Blanc laughed. "You have much faith in them, *mon ami.*"

"Enough to make it five thousand dollars they'll still be sober," Dusty offered, watching Lampart out of the corner of his eye and seeing him give a quick confirmatory nod to the barber.

"You are on, *mon brave,*" le Blanc declared, thrusting his right hand across the table. "Who will hold the stakes?"

"Anybody who suits you," Dusty said indifferently. "I don't care who I get the money off."

"You are so sure of winning, then, Edward?" Giselle asked.

"So sure that I'd go up to ten thousand simoleons on it," Dusty declared, apparently addressing le Blanc, but actually watching the mayor's reaction.

"Not with me." Le Blanc chuckled as he received a negative

headshake from Lampart. "Against such confidence, I almost wish I had not made the wager."

"Call it off, you feel that way," offered Dusty. "I know those boys and you-all don't."

"No," the barber decided, after another glance in the mayor's direction had told him what to do. "We shook hands on it, so the bet is on. Besides, I too have faith. In Emma's hospitality and persuasive powers. We will see what happens when we get to the Honest Man. But who holds the stakes?"

"Mr. Lampart'll suit me fine," Dusty stated. "That way, he can put your money straight into my box in his office after I've won."

10
IF YOU WASN'T WEARING
THEM GUNS

"Ed Caxton!" Emma Nene said accusingly, bearing down on Dusty as he entered the Honest Man Saloon with Lampart, le Blanc and Santiago. "What have you told those two boys of yours?"

With the dinner at an end, the party had started to split up and go their separate ways. First to leave had been Basmanov's faction, including the scowling, still angry Glover. Dusty had noticed that two of the men who had been with the Russian earlier stayed behind. Others, whom the small Texan had marked down as fence-sitters, showed a more open friendship toward Lampart. Already, it seemed, the fact that the mayor was apparently winning the support of "Ed Caxton" was bringing its rewards.

There had been some after-dinner talk, then the men had decided to make their way to the saloon. Clearly Lampart had no intention of allowing his rival to make friendly advances toward Dusty and intended to reduce the chances of a success-

ful attempt to assassinate the small Texan. The mayor had
asked Dusty, along with le Blanc and Santiago, to be his guests
at the saloon after they all had escorted Giselle home.

For all the deficiencies of its signboard, the Honest Man Saloon came up to the high standard set by the rest of the town.
On a dais at the left side of the room, the piano that had guided
Dusty, the Kid and Waco to Hell combined with three guitars,
two violins and a trumpet to beat out a lively dance rhythm.
Before the dais was a space left clear for dancing. At the moment of Dusty's arrival it was hidden behind a wall of laughing,
cheering Mexicans, members of Santiago's gang. Several pretty,
shapely girls, white, Mexican and Chinese, in no more scanty
attire than would be seen at a saloon in a normal town, mingled
with the sixty or so male customers. Behind the bar counter,
two Mexicans and a burly, heavily moustached white man
served drinks from the extensive range of bottles gracing the
shelves of the rear wall. Mexican waiters glided about carrying
trays. Two tiger-decorated faro layouts, a chuck-a-luck table, a
wheel of fortune and three poker games catered to the visitors
who wished to gamble. At each end of the bar, a flight of stairs
led up to the first floor.

Clearly Emma Nene did not apply the almost sedate clothing
standards to herself. She wore a flame-colored dress with an
extreme décolleté which left no doubt that all under it was flesh
and blood, and which clung to her magnificently feminine body
like a second skin. Its hem extended to her feet, but was slit up
the left side to the level of her hip. One leg, made more sensual
by a covering of black silk, showed through the slit in a tantalizing manner. Her eyes held a puzzled, yet admiring, expression as she addressed the small Texan.

"How do you mean, ma'am?" Dusty answered, although he
could guess.

"I thought they'd be drinking me dry, seeing that I offered to
pay and going by the way they talked," Emma elaborated. "Instead, they've only had a couple of whiskies apiece and won't
take any more."

"Oh, no!" le Blanc groaned.

"Something wrong, Jean?" the blonde asked.

"It would seem that I have lost five thousand dollars," the barber replied. "Ed bet me that his friends would still be sober when we arrived."

"They're that, sure enough," Emma admitted. "Are you fellers going to stand here all night, or come over and buy a girl a drink?"

"It'll be my pleasure to buy one for you, ma'am," Dusty declared.

"Hey, Brother Ed!" Waco whooped, coming up with his left arm hooked around the waist of a pretty, red-haired girl. "This here's Red and she reckons I'm the best-looking feller she knows."

"She shows right good taste, boy." Dusty grinned. "Where's Comanch'?"

"Whooping up a storm over there with a right sweet li'l *señorita,*" the youngster replied, waving a hand to the dancefloor. "And me all this time thinking all he knowed was wardances 'n' hoedowns."

As the party made their way to the bar, Dusty looked through the gap in the Mexican crowd. Beyond them, the Kid and a vivacious girl of Latin blood were giving a spirited rendering of a *paso doble.* From the sounds let out by the onlookers, even Santiago's gang were impressed by the Indian-dark Texan's part in the performance.

"He sure dances pretty," Dusty drawled. "How're things going, boy?"

"Couldn't be better," Waco enthused and nodded to the blonde. "Soon's Miss Emma seed we wasn't wanting to drink, she called up Red and Juanita to see after us. This's sure one friendly li'l town."

"Looks that way," Dusty admitted. "Go have your fun, boy. Only keep minding what I told you."

"Don't I always?" Waco grinned. "Come on, Red gal. Let's go buck the tiger for a whirl."

"You were right, Ed," Lampart said, watching Waco depart

with an air of calculating appraisal. "It's fortunate that they survived the Smiths' treacherous attack."

"Right fortunate," Dusty agreed. "Three sets of guns're better than one comes a fuss."

"Do they *always* do as you tell them, Ed?" Emma inquired, signaling to the white bartender.

"They've found life's a whole heap easier if they do," Dusty answered.

"Mr. Caxton's money is no good tonight, Hubert," Emma informed her employee. "Set the drinks up over at my table." She smiled at the men. "It's not ladylike to stand guzzling at the bar. Do you insist on other people doing everything you tell them, Ed?"

"Depends on who they are," Dusty declared. "I can take orders just as easy as giving them, provided I think the man doing the giving's smarter than me."

Although Dusty spoke to the blonde, his words had been directed at Lampart and he knew that the mayor was taking them in.

"Such as who, for instance, *mon ami*?" le Blanc challenged.

"Like I said, *anybody* who's smarter than me," Dusty countered, and looked around. "This's some place you've got here, ma'am."

"Why, thank you, kind sir." Emma smiled, and led the way to a table on the right side of the room.

"Yes, sir," Dusty said, as if half to himself. "I'd surely admire to be the man who made this whole town possible."

"You'll be making me blush next," Lampart warned, but he could not hide the pleasure he felt at the praise. "Sit down. This is Emma's private table and reserved for the guests she says can share it with her."

"Take the end seat, Ed," the blonde offered. "You're our guest of honor tonight, and deserve to be for ridding Hell of a bunch of murderous rats."

Sitting down, Dusty watched the other men take their places. Emma seated herself around the corner from him and Lampart sat opposite to her with his back to the wall.

"Pup-Tent Dorset's bucking the tiger, Miss Emma," the bartender said *sotto voce* as he set down a tray of drinks. "He's losing heavy and getting riled."

"Is Glover here?" the blonde asked, turning to glance around the room.

"Come in with Basmanov," Hubert answered. "They got a bunch up in one of the rooms for a game of poker."

"Did Dorset talk to Glover before they went up?" Lampart put in.

"Him and Styles Homburg went over to ask for some money, what I could see of it," Hubert replied. "They talked for a spell over by the stairs. Funny thing, though, Glover made 'em hand over their guns afore he gave them a stake."

"Dorset and Homburg are always poor losers," Emma commented, after the bartender had returned to his duties. "Oho! They're coming over here now."

Turning his head, Dusty studied the two men who were approaching from the faro layout to which Waco had taken the saloon girl. Pup-Tent Dorset was slightly over medium height, moustached, with a stocky, powerful build. He was dressed in plain range clothes, and his gunbelt's holster was empty. Bigger, bulkier, Styles Homburg looked like a sedate traveling salesman in a brown town suit. He too appeared to be unarmed.

After studying Dorset and Homburg, Dusty darted a quick glance around the room. The dance had ended and the Kid was taking Juanita through the laughing, applauding Mexicans to join Waco at the faro table. From his friends, the small Texan turned his attention to locating possible enemies. At the bar, standing clear of the other customers, he located the remainder of the Glover gang. Tommy Eel, tall, slim and tough-looking, leaned by the shorter, heavier, surly-featured Saw Cowper. Each of them had a revolver holstered at his right side.

"Hi, boys," Emma greeted, in her professionally cordial manner, as the two outlaws came to a halt at her table. "Can I help you?"

"Not you," Dorset replied and pointed at Lampart. "Him. We want some money from you, *hombre*."

"In that case, I would suggest you go and ask Mr. Glover," the mayor advised. "He holds the only keys to your gang's box."

"And you know just how little's in it," Homburg growled. "Not enough for us to have another week here. So we reckon you should ought to do something about it."

"You can hardly blame me for your extravagances," Lampart pointed out. "I warned you on the day you arrived that this was an expensive town."

"And took a tenth of our loot," Dorset spat out. "So we figure we're entitled to some of it back."

"I don't, in fact can't, see it that way," Lampart protested, aware that he was the focal point of much attention.

Silence had fallen on the room. The band had stopped playing, conversations ceased and various games of chance were temporarily forgotten as the customers and employees turned their gaze to Emma's table.

"What's that mean?" demanded Dorset.

"I told you when you first arrived that it was a donation to the Civic Improvement Fund," Lampart explained. "If I hand some of your donation back, I'll be expected to do the same with everybody who asks."

"We said we wanted to borrow—" Dorset began.

"And meant you wanted a gift," the mayor interrupted. "Where could you get money to repay me?"

"We'd maybe win it, was the games in here straight," Dorset answered, seeing that the crowd sympathized with Lampart's point and hoping to turn them in his and Homburg's favor.

"Are you sore losers trying to say my games aren't honest?" Emma challenged indignantly.

"*Your* games?" Dorset sneered. "Word has it you don't but run this place all cozy and loving for Lampart. And him with a nice, sweet li'l wife, for shame."

Wood squeaked against wood as Dusty sent his chair skidding back. Coming to his feet, he faced the two men.

"Was you wanting to stay healthy," the small Texan drawled,

"you'd best say 'Sorry we lied about you, ma'am' and then get the hell out of here."

"Wha—?" Dorset began.

"You got business with Mr. Lampart, that's fine," Dusty continued. "Only some'd say you've picked a poor time to come doing it. It stops being fine when you start mean-mouthing and lie-spouting about a for-real lady. So I'm telling you to wear out some bootleather walking away."

"Lampart's hired your gun, huh?" Homburg almost shouted, recollecting the orders Glover had given regarding the pair's behavior.

"If Glover told you that, he's as big a liar as you pair," Dusty countered. "And I'm getting quick-sick of seeing your faces."

"You're the feller who dropped Ben Columbo, ain't you?" said Dorset. "That makes you a real big man."

"Talking pretty won't make me like you," Dusty warned.

"Could be you wouldn't be so big," Dorset declared, "if you wasn't wearing them guns."

"Now there's an interesting thought," Dusty answered, starting to unfasten the pigging thongs which held the tips of his holsters to his legs. "You figure happen I was to take them off, you could make me eat crow?"

For a moment, Dorset stood dumbfounded by the unexpected turn of events. He was uncertain of what he should do next. Then he realized what a chance was being presented to him and he nodded eagerly.

"That's just what I think!"

"And now you got all these good folks wondering if it be true," Dusty continued as he unbuckled and laid his gunbelt on the table. "So we're just natural' going to have to find out."

"You fixing to take on me or Styles?" Dorset grinned.

"You, him, or both," Dusty confirmed. "Call it any way you've a mind."

"I reckon I'll be enough," Dorset declared, the grin fading away. "Come ahead, short stuff. This I'm going to enjoy."

Clenching his fists, Dusty adopted the kind of stance favored by the professional pugilists of the day. At least, he positioned his hands and arms in the conventional manner. His feet formed a T position, the right pointing to the front and, a shoulders' width away, the left directed outward. By bending his knees slightly, he distributed his weight evenly on the balls of his feet.

Throwing a grin at Homburg, Dorset moved toward Dusty. An experienced fistfighter, the outlaw watched Dusty's hands for a hint of how he planned to attack. At the same time, Dorset stabbed his right at the blond's face. Weaving his torso aside and letting the blow hiss by his head, Dusty swung his left foot around and up.

Concentrating on Dusty's hands, Dorset was taken by surprise by the kick. Caught in the groin, he might have counted himself fortunate in that Dusty had not been able to build up full power while making the attack. As it was, pain caused him to double over and retreat. Gliding closer, Dusty hooked his knotted left fist into the outlaw's descending face. Lifted upright, Dorset was wide open for the continuation of his small assailant's assault. Hearing footsteps approaching from his rear, Dusty hurled across his right hand. Hard knuckles landed on the side of Dorset's jaw, sending him spinning and reeling back to the faro table he had recently quit. Landing on it, he scattered markers, coppers, money and cards in all directions.[1]

Even as Dusty knocked Dorset away, he felt himself gripped by the shoulders from behind. Giving a lifting heave, Homburg hurled the small Texan toward the bar. At first Dusty could do nothing to halt himself as the savage propulsion caused him to turn in Homburg's direction and run backward. So far, the big outlaw had not followed him, which proved to be a foolish omission. Waiting until he had regained control of his equilibrium, Dusty seemed to tumble backward. A concerted gasp rose as he went down, mingling with Homburg's yell of tri-

1. A more detailed description of a faro game is given in *Rangeland Hercules.*

umph. Then the man started to rush forward, with the intention of stomping Dusty into the floorboards.

Spitting out a mouthful of blood, Dorset sank until his left knee touched the floor. His right hand went to and started to draw a knife from its sheath in the top of his right boot. The blade came clear, but its owner was given no chance to use it. Powerful fingers clamped onto his right wrist and the scruff of his neck. Then his trapped arm was twisted behind his back and he felt himself being dragged until he leaned facedown on the table once more.

Unlike the majority of the crowd, the Kid felt no concern over the sight of Dusty toppling backward. He was aware that the small Texan possessed considerable acrobatic agility. In part, it had been developed as a precaution against injury if he should be thrown when taking the bedsprings out of bad horses' bellies. It had also served him well while receiving instruction in the fighting skills that did so much to offset his lack of inches when dealing with larger, heavier men. Down in the Rio Hondo, working as Ole Devil Hardin's personal servant, lived a small man thought by many to be Chinese. While undeniably Oriental, Tommy Okasi insisted that he came from some place called Nippon. To Dusty, he had handed on the secrets— all but unknown at that period outside Japan—of *jujitsu* and *karate*. Learning how to fall had been an important and vital lesson. So the Kid expected Dusty to avert the danger of the stomping, probably in a spectacular manner. He was not disappointed.

Breaking his fall on his shoulders as Tommy Okasi had taught him, Dusty rolled into a ball. Then, with a surging thrust, he uncoiled and catapulted back to his feet. The action took Homburg by surprise, just as the kick had Dorset, and he was granted as little opportunity to recover. Ducking under Homburg's belatedly grabbing hands, Dusty wrapped his arms around the outlaw's thighs, just above the knees. Drawing the legs together, Dusty exerted all his not inconsiderable strength and straightened up. He lifted Homburg from the floor, heaving the man backward. Flatfooted and with his legs still not parted, Homburg hit the floorboards with an impact that knocked him breathless and witless.

Bounding after the man, Dusty sprang into the air. Tilting back until his body was horizontal, he hurled the soles of his boots full into the center of Homburg's chest. Hurtling across the room, the outlaw crashed through the batwing doors. He barely touched the sidewalk while crossing it and sprawled facedown on to the hard-packed surface of the street.

Maintaining his twin grips, Waco kept up the pressure on Dorset's trapped arm until the hand opened and released the knife. With that accomplished, the youngster transferred his other hand to the outlaw's collar, jerked him erect and thrust him away.

"Go pick on Broth—" the youngster began.

Catching his balance, Dorset spun around and hurled a punch to the side of Waco's head. Twirling on his heel, the youngster landed back-down on the table. Instead of turning to Dusty, the outlaw leapt closer to the young blond. Grabbing hold of Waco's throat, Dorset hauled him up and started to choke him.

At the bar, Eel and Cowper had been watching the developments with a growing sense of alarm. When they saw Dusty leap up and kick Homburg backward, while Waco was disarming Dorset, the pair knew that they must help carry out their boss's orders. They also decided that bare-handed tactics were not for them. Moving away from the bar, they started to reach for their guns.

Instantly a menacing figure seemed to just appear in front of them. It wore a gray shirt, string tie, town trousers and Indian moccasins, the white man's attire being topped by the savage features of a Comanche warrior on the lookout for a coup-counting.

Having been certain that Dusty could deal with Homburg, the Kid had kept the other two members of the Glover gang under observation. When they made their move, he stepped in fully ready to counter it.

"I ain't like Ed 'n' Matt, so I don't waste time with fool

fistfighting," the Kid warned, and the Dragoon in his right hand seemed to vibrate with homicidal eagerness. "You want to side your *amigos,* shed your guns and go to it. But happen your pleasure's shooting, I'll be right willing to oblige."

Although partially dazed by the blow he had received, Waco threw off its effects fast. Placing his palms together, he thrust them up between Dorset's arms. Snapping the hands apart, he knocked the fingers from his throat. Then he bunched his left fist, dropped his shoulder behind it and ripped a straight-arm punch to the center of Dorset's face. Nostrils spurting blood, the outlaw blundered backward across the room.

Landing from his leaping high kick, Dusty turned and saw Waco's predicament. Before the small Texan could go to his *amigo*'s assistance, Waco escaped and put Dorset into retreat. As Dorset came toward him, still going backward, Dusty interlaced his fingers. Looking like a baseball batter swinging for a home run, Dusty pivoted and smashed his hands into the man's kidney region. Agony contorted Dorset's features as the blow arrived. He arched his back and stumbled helplessly in the direction from which he had come. Leaping to meet him, Waco hurled a power-packed right cross. With a solid "Whap!" the youngster's knuckles struck Dorset's temple. The outlaw pitched sideways and slid several feet before coming to a stop.

"How do you want it?" the Kid demanded as Dorset's limp body came to a halt. "Now's the time to say."

"Pup-Tent and Styles called the play," Eel replied. "It's none of our fuss, feller."

Glover stood with Basmanov and others of the poker game on the right-side set of stairs. Glaring furiously at the scene, the gang leader advanced a couple of steps below his companions. Drawing his revolver, he started to line it at the small Texan.

11
HE'S GOT A FORTUNE
STASHED AWAY

The crash of a shot sounded over the excited chatter that had followed the unexpected ending of the fight. On the stairs, Glover heard the eerie sound of a close-passing bullet, felt its wind on his face and gave a startled yelp. Jerking back in an involuntary motion, he sat down hard. Across the room, at Emma Nene's private table, smoke curled from the barrel of Santiago's Colt.

"What is the betting that I won't miss a second time?" asked the *bandido,* taking a more deliberate aim as he cocked the revolver's hammer.

Fright flickered on Glover's face, for he knew that his life had never been in greater danger. If anybody offered to bet, the Mexican would not hesitate to shoot. For a moment, Glover thought of trying to turn his weapon on Santiago. Yet doing so would avail him but little. Even if he should be successful, the *bandido*'s men would kill him. Covered by "Comanche Blood" 's Dragoon, Eel and Cowper would be unable to back his play. Nor could he count on help from Basmanov's party. That had been made plain to him during the poker game. As the Russian had warned, Glover's future in Hell depended upon how the plan worked that had been hatched between them after leaving the hotel. From what Glover had seen since coming downstairs, it had been a miserable failure.

"Easy there, Mig!" Glover said, trying to keep his voice firm and friendly. He dropped his gun. "What was I to think when I come down and see the Caxtons beating up one of my boys and Blood there holding the others back with a gun?"

"Put up your gun, *amigo*," Dusty agreed, going to the table and picking up his belt. "Man's right about the way it looked. Trouble being, things aren't always how they look." Once more, silence had come to the room, and its occupants listened to his words with rapt attention. "No, sir. Take when them two yacks of his came over. Way they talked and acted, it could've looked like I'd been hired by Mr. Lampart to stop folks getting their right and fair money out of his office."

"That was the impression they tried to give," Santiago confirmed.

"Some's say they was lucky, them two, that their boss'd taken their guns away—" Dusty went on.

"I could see they was getting riled over losing at faro," Glover interrupted, standing up. "So I did it for the best."

"Why, sure," Dusty agreed. "It looks that way. Only you could've got them both killed, doing it."

"How?" Glover growled.

"Would Ben Columbo or Joey Pinter've taken off their guns to deal with them?" Dusty challenged. "And if I hadn't, when I concluded to stop them mean-mouthing Miss Emma with their lies about her and her games, folks might've seen it wrong. They might start to figure—'specially was somebody to put it into their heads"—his eyes flickered briefly at Basmanov— "that I was working for Mr. Lampart and the other gents with money in his care could wind up dead when they wanted it back."

A startled exclamation in his native tongue broke from Basmanov as he heard Dusty exposing his plot. Not only exposing it, but doing so in such a manner that nothing could be salvaged from it.

Glover had been willing to sacrifice Dorset and Homburg in the interests of raising mistrust against the mayor. Far from the most intelligent of men, the pair had been persuaded to hand over their guns and then provoke a fight with "Ed Caxton." There had been a chance that he would grandstand, to impress Lampart and Emma Nene, by agreeing to fight bare-handed. The conspirators, however, had felt it more likely that he would shoot his challengers down regardless of them being unarmed. If Eel and Cowper had been able to avenge their companions by killing "Caxton," all well and good. If not, Basmanov would be able to circulate the kind of rumor that the small Texan had suggested.

They had not achieved their ends; the whole affair had gone wrong. Worse than that. Basmanov sensed that the *big* dangerous newcomer suspected his part in the scheme.

"Put that blasted hand-cannon away, Comanch'," Dusty commanded, having completed the buckling on of his belt and secured its holsters to his legs while apparently addressing Glover but really speaking to the crowd, "Those two fellers only want to tend to their *amigos'* hurts."

"Yo!" answered the Kid and obeyed.

"Do it," Glover said as Eel and Cowper glanced at him. "You'd best have Doc Connolly see to them; they could be hurt bad."

"Hank," Dusty called, to a gang leader who wore the clothes favored by professional gamblers. "Just to straighten out any doubts them two yacks might have stirred up, will you check over that faro layout."

"I've done it every night," the man replied. "It's like all the games in here, as straight as Emma's beautiful."

"You saying things like that about the lady, I reckon I'd best ask you to show Mr. Glover and his boys what to look for in a crooked game." Dusty grinned. "Fancy-talking competition like yours I can do without. Course, they might not want to take your word on it."

"Hank knows what he's talking about and what he's said's good enough for us," Glover growled, picking up and holstering his revolver. "Pup-Tent and Styles was allus poor losers. So I took their guns off 'em, to stop them making trouble if their luck stayed bad."

"Like I said, they was lucky you did it," Dusty drawled. "Only, happen they come mean-mouthing or spreading lies about Emma again, I'll not waste effort fistfighting. And that goes whether *they're* wearing guns or not."

"That Dorset *hombre*'s got a real hard head," Waco went on, alternately rubbing his right hand's knuckles and working its fingers. "Happen we lock horns again, I'll be inclined to hit him with a teensy bit of lead 'stead of my dainty li'l fist."

"We'll mind it," Glover promised sullenly. "Come on, Tommy, Saw. Let's get the boys to the doctor's."

"Hey, you musicians!" Emma called. "Earn your pay. Come on, fellers, you'll put me in the poorhouse, sitting on your hands instead of buying or playing."

Taking their cue from the blonde, the band started to play a lively tune. Girls and waiters set about stimulating the activities that had been brought to a halt by the trouble. By the time Glover, Eel and Cowper had carried Dorset from the room, it reverberated with the sound of revelry.

"Where-at's Emmet Youseman?" Dusty inquired. "Don't tell me he's undertaking at this hour of the night?"

"I shouldn't think so," Lampart answered, looking a touch furtive.

"He didn't strike me as a feller who'd miss the chance to bend an elbow in good company," Dusty remarked, flickering a glance at Waco.

"Most likely he's doing some undertaking at the cathouse," le Blanc remarked. "Only with live customers."

"Where's Red got to?" Waco whooped and the girl ran up. Scooping her in his left arm, he kissed her. "I thought you'd backed out, gal."

"What on?" Emma demanded.

"Why, I've bet her that I've got more hair on my chest than she has," the youngster explained. "And, happen it's all right with you, Miss Emma, I was figuring on taking her out for a whiles to show for most."

"I told you that Red was your gal," Emma reminded him. "Run along and get your bet settled."

"You heard the boss lady, Red, gal." Waco grinned. "Let's go."

"What it is to be young." Emma smiled, almost wistfully, watching Waco and the girl making for a side door.

"Aren't you going to fix Ed up with a girl, Emma?" le Blanc asked.

"I already have," the blonde stated. "Come on, let's set the paying customers a good example. Sit down and get happy."

"Let's do that," Dusty agreed. "I sure hope that gal of mine's a blonde."

"You know," Emma replied, "she just might be at that."

Although the party sat down and resumed their conversation, the subject of the motives behind the fight received no discussion. In fact, to Dusty it seemed that Lampart was trying to avoid it. The mayor kept the others laughing with a flow of rude stories. When he ran out, he offered to demonstrate a few of the tricks he had learned as a stage magician.

"You're not sawing me in half," Emma warned.

"Spoilsport." Lampart chuckled. "Get me a couple of decks of cards, I may be able to baffle you."

Dusty had to admit that Lampart was a skilled performer. Handling the cards with deft professionalism, he kept his audience baffled. Emma had been asked to sing a song and was on her way to oblige, while Lampart concluded his show by demonstrating how to shuffle a deck of cards in each hand, when Glover returned.

"Look, Simmy, I don't want to bother you," the outlaw said as he came to the table, "but I need some money to pay Doc Connolly. The boys aren't the only ones who lost tonight."

"Very well," Lampart replied.

"I wasn't fixing to ask," Dusty drawled, "but seeing's you've got to open your office, I'll come and get myself a stake. There's a diamond bracelet down to the jewelry store that'd just do fine for a birthday present."

"Who for?" le Blanc smiled.

"Not my mother, you can count on that." Dusty grinned back.

"You know the rules, Andy," Lampart said. "I have to have a member of the Civic Regulators with me if I open the office after dark."

"Mr. Basmanov's upstairs," Dusty hinted.

"So he is," agreed Lampart. "Why should he sit gambling and carousing when I've got to work? Ask him if he'll come with us, will you please, Jean?"

"With the greatest of pleasure," Le Blanc responded and went to do so.

By the time a scowling Basmanov had arrived, Emma was coming to the end of her somewhat ribald song. Acknowledging the applause, she left the dais and walked back to her table. On being told that Dusty would be leaving, she extracted his promise to return as soon as possible.

"Tommy'll have to come along," Glover said, indicating Eel standing on the sidewalk as the men emerged from the saloon. "He's got the other key to our box."

"That's all right with me," Lampart comfirmed, but he caught Dusty's eye and shook his head briefly. "Where's Mr. Cowper?"

"Down to the doctor's," Glover replied. "You stove in three of Styles Homburg's ribs when you jumped up and kicked him, Ed."

"Feller who taught me to do it allowed that could happen," Dusty answered disinterestedly. "How's the other one?"

"Still unconscious," Eel put in. "His head's broke, the doctor says."

"They called the play," Dusty reminded the outlaws.

"Nobody's gainsaying it," Glover grunted.

Approaching the mayor's house, Dusty saw a glint of light

showing through a crack in the curtains at the window of the mayor's office. He recollected his host having mentioned that the room was kept illuminated all night as a precaution against attempted thefts.

Unlocking the front door, Lampart allowed the other men to precede him into the hall. A lamp hung in the center of the ceiling, throwing its light over the party. Closing the door, the mayor went to his office.

"Come in, Andy," he said, turning another key. "You'll have to wait until I've dealt with these gentlemen, Ed."

"That's all right with me, sir," Dusty drawled. "Just so long as I can get to the jewelry shop before it closes."

"You'll do that easy enough," Basmanov said, in a more friendly voice than he had previously employed. "He stays open until daybreak. Fellers get generous to Emma and her girls late on. You don't need me in there, do you, Simmy?"

"No," the mayor replied, but Dusty thought he detected an undercurrent of worry in the one word. "I'll handle things."

"What do you think of Simmy?" the Russian inquired as he and Dusty stood in the hall after the other three had disappeared behind the door of the office.

"I like him fine," Dusty replied. "He's a good man. Smart, too."

"What with his cut from you fellers' loot, and the saloon's takings—he owns it, not Emma, you know." Basmanov went on. "He's got a fortune stashed away."

"It says right in the Good Book that the laborer's worthy of his hire," Dusty pointed out. "Which I don't reckon any of you fellers who live here's wives need to take in washing to help buy your bacon and beans."

"I admit it's profitable," the Russian replied. "But some are making more than the others."

"Drop those guns!"

Muffled by the thickness of the walls and door, Lampart's shouted words came to Dusty's ears. They were followed by four shots which sounded as a very rapid roll of detonations.

"What the hell!" Basmanov spat out in Russian, leaping toward the door.

About to follow him, Dusty became aware of another factor entering the game. The front door flew open and Cowper burst in with a revolver held ready for use. At the sight of Basmanov, he seemed to hesitate. That cost him his life. Dusty's left hand had already commenced its movement toward his right side. Steel rasped on leather, being all but drowned as the off-side Colt came from its holster, lined and crashed.

With his mouth opening to yell something, Cowper received a bullet between his eyes. Back snapped his head, while his feet continued to advance. The latter left the floor and the former struck it with a shattering thud that the outlaw did not feel.

"Watch that one!" Dusty barked, springing by Basmanov.

On trying the office's door, Dusty found it to be locked. Although he had kicked an entrance into a room on occasion, he doubted if he could do so with that sturdy door. Bare feet slapped on the floor at the rear of the passage. Clad in a robe donned hurriedly after leaving her bed, Giselle darted in. Skidding to a halt, she stared from the smoking Colt in Dusty's hand to the body lying half in and half out of the front door.

"What's—?" the brunette began.

"Do you have a key for this door?" Dusty demanded.

"No," Giselle answered, with surprising calm under the circumstances. "But why should—?"

"There's no other way out of it?" Dusty interrupted.

"Of course not!" Giselle declared. "What is happening, Edward?"

"There's been some shooting in the office," Basmanov explained. "We want to get in to investigate."

"You could try breaking down the door," Giselle suggested, still not displaying any concern for her husband's safety.

"You'd best get some of the Regulators at the windows before we try it," Dusty told the Russian. "But if they've got Mr. Lampart alive, we're in trouble."

At that moment, the lock clicked and the door opened. Instantly Dusty pushed Giselle along the passage with his right hand and lined the Colt with his left. Holding the revolver from his desk, Lampart stood in the doorway. Fear showed on his face as he found himself staring down the barrel of Dusty's gun.

"Hey!" Lampart yelped feebly.

"Are you all right, Mr. Lampart?" Dusty asked, lowering the revolver.

"Yes," the mayor confirmed and looked relieved. He stepped back, pointing with his empty hand. "I'm afraid I had to kill them both."

Entering the office and holstering his Colt, Dusty looked around. Gripping a revolver in his right fist, Glover sprawled on his back. Blood oozed from the two holes in his chest. Eel hung facedown along the line of boxes to the left of his boss, his gun on the floor and his back a gory mess where two bullets had burst out. Going closer, Dusty noticed that the hammer of each dead man's revolver was still at the down position and Glover's forefinger extended along the outside of the triggerguard. Two padlock keys lay in front of a box.

Allowing Basmanov and Dusty to make their examination of the office, Lampart went to his desk. He flopped into his chair and laid the revolver in its usual place. Walking over, Dusty leaned on the desk to place a hand upon the mayor's shoulder. At the same time, his other hand rested on the cold metal of Lampart's Colt.

"Are you all right, sir?" Dusty asked gently.

"Y-yes," Lampart answered. "I had to do it, Ivan, Ed."

"Likely you did, sir," Dusty drawled. "Best tell us all that happened."

"We came in and I did as I always do when somebody is drawing out money, sat behind the desk here. They went to their box, then turned and drew their guns. I had to start shooting. It was them or me."

"You did the right thing, sir," Dusty declared. "Don't you reckon so, Mr. Basmanov?"

"Yes!" grunted the Russian. "But why would they try it?"

"They were almost out of money, 'cording to what was said

at the saloon," Dusty pointed out. "Taken with their *amigo* coming busting in at the front door, when he was supposed to be along at the doctor's place with them hurt fellers, I'd say it all points to them figuring on robbing Mr. Lampart."

"I suppose so," Basmanov admitted sullenly, aware that several people had arrived and were listening.

So was Dusty. Figuring that some of the arrivals would be outlaws, he went on. "And not just Mr. Lampart. Had they got away with it, they'd've emptied all our boxes to take with them."

"Without the keys?" Basmanov asked, trying to salvage something from the death of Glover.

"Why not?" challenged Dusty. "They likely aimed to keep Mr. Lampart quiet while they bust the locks. It could be done without too much noise. Quietly enough not to be heard outside, anyways."

Seeing that, for the time being at any rate, he could not use the incident in his campaign to unseat the mayor, Basmanov raised no further objections. Instead, he set about his duty as head of the Regulators and attended to the removal of the bodies.

Waco and the Kid had both been among the crowd, but having satisfied themselves that Dusty was safe, they returned to the waiting girls. Listening to Red warning the young blond that she "wouldn't go walking 'round no more creepy ole graveyards," Dusty grinned. Clearly Waco had been trying to solve one of the mysteries that puzzled the trio. Then, seeing the possessive manner in which the girls clung to his companions' arms, he realized what was happening. Lampart was keeping "Matt Caxton" and "Comanche Blood" under observation in a way that would be unlikely to arouse their suspicion.

Having taken some money from his party's box, Dusty called at the jeweler's store and purchased the best diamond bracelet in his extensive stock. Then he went back to the saloon. Although Emma came straight over to ask what had happened and if he was hurt, Dusty did not find the opportunity to hand over his present until just before the place closed.

"For your birthday," Dusty whispered, slipping the bracelet into her hand as they watched the other customers leaving.

"My—?" Emma gasped.

"This year's, or last's, whichever's closest," Dusty explained.

"Why thank you, Ed!" the blonde purred. "My, you did dirty your shirt in the fight. You can't wear it until it's been washed."

"You want for me to change it down here?"

"Of course not. Come upstairs and I'll show you where you can do it."

Going upstairs and to the rear of the building, Emma escorted him into the bedroom section of her quarters.

"Take it off and I'll have my maid wash it," the blonde offered.

Removing his tie, Dusty peeled off the shirt. Emma took it from him and left the room. She returned empty-handed and her eyes roamed over his powerfully developed bare torso.

"Oh, my!" she said, reaching behind her and unhooking her dress. "Haven't I made a mistake? You can't walk out of here without a shirt."

"What'll I do, then?" Dusty inquired.

The dress slid away. All Emma wore under it was a pair of black silk tights.

"Can't you think of anything?" she asked.

"You know," Dusty replied, "I just might be able to at that."

12
THEY WON'T TOUCH THAT BUILDING

"Whooee!" enthused the Kid as he and his companions exercised their horses on the fringe of the wooded country that surrounded the vast hollow that held the town of Hell. "Ole Mark'd sure enjoy being here. Who won that bet, boy?"

"You mind your own blasted business!" the youngster ordered indignantly. "Way your bed was a-creaking and a-groaning last night Red and me didn't hardly get any sleep."

"What Juanita and me heard through the wall, you pair wasn't doing much of that sleeping anyways," countered the Kid. "Which I'm right grateful to you for the loan of your room, Ed."

"Emma and me figured you might's well use it, seeing I'd paid for it and wouldn't be," Dusty answered. "So she sent her maid along with the key. Did you pair learn anything from the gals?"

"Only that I've got more hair on my chest than she has." Waco grinned, then became more serious. "They don't know anything much. Only that some gangs go and come back and others just come the once."

"We already had that figured out," Dusty said.

"I was fixing to take a *pasear* round the back of the undertaker's afore I went to bed," the Kid stated. "But those gals wouldn't go leave us long enough and I didn't take to the notion of climbing that fence back of the shop with Juanita hanging on my shirttail."

"It can't be helped," Dusty said philosophically. "They didn't leave me on my lonesome, either."

"I talked to a couple of fellers who saw Columbo's bunch being planted," Waco remarked. "Can't say's I claim to know sic 'em about undertakering, but I don't reckon there'd've been time for ole Happy Youseman to've embalmed them afore he put them under."

"I wonder if anybody saw them in the coffins?" Dusty replied.

"Maybe they've planted those *hombres* and don't aim to claim the bounty," the Kid suggested. "Just to still the talk." He shook his head. "If there's been any talk, I haven't heard it. And Columbo 'n' Pinter both're worth a damned sight more in reward money than Toby Siddons was."

"When I asked, they reckoned Youseman was at the hawgranch," Dusty pointed out. "It could be."

"Did Glover try to stick the mayor up, you reckon, Brother Matt?" Waco inquired, changing the subject.

"Could be," Dusty replied. "Couple of the Regulators found their horses, saddled and ready for traveling, around the back of the houses."

"Was Basmanov in on it?" the Kid wanted to know.

"He may have known they planned something like it, suggested that they tried it even," Dusty answered. "But I don't reckon he was expecting it last night, or he wouldn't've come with us."

"Maybe Glover just meant to collect his money from the box, then rob one of the other townsmen afore they lit out," Waco suggested, selecting the true reason although he would never know it. "With that cocked Colt on Lampart's desk, they'd know better than try it against him."

"You'd figure they would," Dusty agreed. Then he gave his companions a warning about that particular weapon, concluding, "It's just a notion I've got, but keep it in mind. It could help keep you alive."

"We'll not forget," the Kid promised. "Did you learn anything from Emma?"

"Nothing to help us," Dusty admitted. "But I got the feeling she wanted to tell me something. Could be she's got notions of how she'd rate around town with us three backing her play, only she's not sure how I stand with Lampart."

"Talking about him," Waco drawled, "his missus's headed this way."

"I'd a notion she might," Dusty replied. "They made sure we couldn't get together and talk in private last night and it looks like they figure to keep on doing it."

Giselle's arrival, riding her dainty palomino, brought the trio's discussion to an end. However, they had managed to exchange some information—mostly negative—and more important, Dusty had had the opportunity to warn his *amigos* about the revolver that always lay cocked and ready for use on Lampart's desk.

"I wish I'd known you meant to come riding, Edward," Giselle said. "I do enjoy taking Goldie here out, but Simmy prefers I have an escort."

"We'll keep it in mind, ma'am," Dusty declared.

Clearly Lampart did not intend letting Basmanov make an attempt to win "Ed Caxton"'s friendship. On returning from their ride, the trio found the mayor and le Blanc waiting at the stable with an invitation for them to go to lunch. The Russian watched them go, scowling and brooding, but made no comment and did not try to interfere.

Playing on Lampart's eagerness to impress him and his companions, and win their approbation, Dusty led him to talk about the town. The mayor had great pride in the community, or rather in his part in founding it. So he needed little prompting to divulge details of its history.

From what Lampart told them, Dusty, the Kid and Waco began to realize that the wagon train had been of a somewhat unusual nature. With the exception of the Lamparts and Orville Hatchet, their scout, every person on it had been a fugitive from justice. It had been Lampart who gathered them and arranged what should have been a safe passage to Mexico. Wishing to avoid coming into contact with peace officers, they had swung east of the regular route and so found themselves in danger of being massacred by the *Kweharehnuh*. The trio had already heard how that peril was averted and turned to Lampart's advantage. Beyond mentioning how he had possessed contacts who put him in touch with a prime selection of fugitives, Lampart had refused to give further information in le Blanc's presence.

The rest of the day passed quietly. In the afternoon, Hatchet returned from "buying supplies" in Paducah. Showing a lack of tact, Giselle told him that "Comanche Blood" was responsible for the loss of his horse when he had been riding with the posse. No trouble came from the remark, for Hatchet claimed he knew who had done it and why.

Dusty and his *amigos* found no opportunity to hold a private discussion that day. The Lamparts kept them occupied until sundown, then Emma and the girls took over. Once again Dusty shared the blonde's bed. While she made passionate love to him, he sensed she wanted to take him into her confidence on some matter. However, they separated next morning without her doing so. He wondered if he should encourage her, or if he would be better employed in keeping Lampart satisfied with his loyalty. There was a chance that Emma had been told to learn his real feelings and report them to the mayor.

Due to the ruling about fires, the town tended to do most of its business at night. Consequently most of its residents and visitors slept late in the mornings. Dusty, the Kid and Waco were no exception to the rule.

Picking Giselle up at noon, the trio escorted her on a ride

around the area. They were repaid by information when she mentioned that Hatchet had already left town to collect more supplies, and did not need an explanation of what that meant. On their return they were invited to take a belated lunch with the Lamparts. As they were alone, the mayor expanded on the histories of the people who inhabited Hell.

Youseman had been a surgeon and Connolly's partner carrying out experimental research on the subject of longevity. Needing corpses to work on, they had dealt with New York body snatchers. Then they had graduated to killing healthy people to obtain fresh blood, tissues and organs for their experiments. The law had got wind of their activities, causing them to flee for their lives. They had been able to produce sufficient money to buy places on Lampart's wagon train.

Le Blanc had been a fashionable barber in New York until he had fallen in love with the beautiful wife of an elderly millionaire. Not until he had killed her husband did he discover that she loved another man and had merely been using him. He had murdered the couple in jealous rage, but was cool enough to carry off a large sum of money and a valuable collection of jewelry they had obtained to use as a start to their new life. With no other avenue of escape open to him, le Blanc had been willing to accept Lampart's offer of transportation.

Goldberg and the jeweler had been prominent Wall Street brokers, manipulating the stock market for their mutual advantage. After they had organized a slump that ruined thousands of investors, they had been exposed by a Pinkerton agent planted in their office. Needing a safe haven for themselves and their ill-gotten gains, they had snapped up Lampart's offer of providing it.

Driven from Russia because of his political activities, Basmanov had soon been up to his old tricks in the United States. Along with other anarchist agitators, he had formed a society whose aims had been to overthrow the government and take control in the "interests" of the people. They had extorted money from immigrants, and their funds had been further swelled by donations from various "liberal" associations. Unfortunately, one of their number had planted a bomb on a bridge, wrecking a train with a heavy loss of lives and drawing unwanted attention to their activities. Sensing the net tightening about him, Basmanov had betrayed his companions and absconded with their not-inconsiderable funds. He too had been drawn into Lampart's band of escaping criminals.

None of the other citizens had more savory backgrounds, their activities covering everything from white-slaving to drug smuggling and mass murder. One thing they all had in common: they were rich enough to pay their way and live in comfort—providing the forces of law and order did not find them.

From acquainting his audience with the unworthy natures of his fellow citizens, Lampart went on to impress them with his own brilliance. On winning the confidence of the *Kweharehnuh* and hearing about the ruined village deep in the Palo Duro country, he had seen its possibilities. After some argument, he had brought the other travelers around to his way of thinking. They had become persuaded that not only would they be safer than in Mexico, but they could also make their accumulated money earn more while awaiting the day when it would be safe for them to show their faces in public again.

Between them, the travelers had possessed the finances needed to rebuild the town. Owing to his part in a bloody racial conflict, the owner of the Chinese laundry was wanted by the law. However, he was an influential member of his tong and brought in coolies to help with the work of building. As the Kid had guessed, the Mexican peons were slaves purchased from the *Kweharehnuh*. When all was ready, Hatchet had passed the word around the outlaw trails of what the town had to offer. The news could not have been better timed. It had come just after the Rangers were reformed and they were striking hard, closing down many hideouts used by the gangs.

From the beginning, Lampart had insisted on offering the visitors a high standard of service. Not only were the food and drinks of top quality, but the gambling games at the saloon were scrupulously honest. Considering that some of the players would be crooked gamblers capable of detecting any cheating method or device, the latter had been a wise precaution.

The high standard served a dual purpose, Lampart told the Texans. Scouts were posted to meet and check on the men who came to Hell, disarming them before guiding them in. That was to safeguard against protests when the outlaws learned they must hand over one tenth of their total loot if they wanted to stay. Lampart could point out the excellent amenities, and explain how much they cost, as an excuse for taking the money. Secondly, the quality went toward justifying the increased prices charged in the town. He stated that, after their first visit, none of the outlaws had raised objections to paying to the Civic Improvement Fund when they came again.

That, apparently, was as far as the mayor intended to go on the subject of the visitors. Guessing that they would not hear about the fate of the dead outlaws, the Kid had asked about Ten Bears's reaction to having white men passing through his territory. Lampart admitted that, at first, the chief had not been keen on the idea. A further display of magic, backed by the offer of a repeating rifle and ammunition for every brave in the band, had brought him to a more amenable frame of mind.

"Could be a mite risky giving all them bucks rifles and shells," Waco warned. "They might figure, having 'em, their medicine's stronger than your'n."

"I made sure they know they'll only have luck as long as they use the guns to help me," Lampart replied. "And I only hand out fifty rounds a month to each man. I had one bit of good fortune. A warbonnet chief called Kills Something was getting restless. He borrowed bullets from other men to arm a war party. They ambushed a patrol, but something went wrong and he was killed. His party had used up a whole lot of ammunition, with precious little but dead and wounded to show for it. That's quietened the others down. They know there's no more bullets for them until the next new moon."

"That's fine as long as you don't disappoint them when the time comes," Waco said, catching the Kid's eye and wondering what he thought about having, inadvertently, helped Lampart to keep control of the *Kweharehnuh.*

"I can," Lampart claimed. "The shack behind the house is filled with ammunition, and they know it."

"Maybe they'll figure on helping themselves afore the new moon," Waco went on. "Comanch' allows that *Nemenuh* brave-hearts can sneak a man's hoss from under him on a dark night, and him not know until he tries to ride off on it. Be they close to that good, they'd get by them fellers you've got guarding it."

"They won't touch that building," Lampart declared, with an air of self-satisfied confidence. "I've made sure of that."

"How?" asked the Kid.

"In two ways. I've had photographs of Ten Bears and the medicine woman taken. They think I've captured their souls and they'll be damned if I destroy the pictures. So they use their influence to keep the braves in hand."

"Which's only one way," Dusty hinted.

"When the first of the guns and ammunition arrived, I called a meeting with Ten Bears and his men," Lampart obliged. "I warned them that I'd put a curse on the whole consignment which would kill any man who tried to steal from me or harm my friends. Then I gave them a practical demonstration. I placed a keg of powder out in the center of a large, bare patch of sand, stood fifty yards from it and told any brave who thought I was lying to try to fetch it back. Two took the challenge and the keg blew up when they reached it." He paused and finished, "Before they had even touched it at that."

"You had a feller hid out and he put a bullet into it," Waco guessed, knowing that the mayor wanted them to try to explain how he had worked the trick.

"Unless it had been fired from so far away that the man could barely see the keg, much less hit it," Lampart replied, "they would have heard the shot."

"You couldn't've run a fuse out to the keg," the Kid decided. "The braves'd've known what you was up to when you lit it."

"True enough, Comanche." Lampart grinned. "What do you think, Ed?"

"You used a wire fuse and a 'magnetic' battery to set the keg off," the small Texan stated, watching the mayor's face register mingled annoyance and admiration at his summation. "I've heard tell of such, but never seen one used."

"The Indians hadn't even heard tell of it," Lampart announced. "On the night before the meeting, I'd buried the wire and smoothed away all traces of it. Next day, while Giselle performed a special 'medicine' dance around the box holding the battery, I carried the keg out to the wire."

"The Indians were all watching me," the brunette remarked. "And if you'd seen what I was wearing, you'd know why."

"It distracted them all right," Lampart agreed. "None of them saw me find the wire and connect it to the detonator in the bottom of the keg. Then I came back, joined Giselle and we both made some 'medicine' while I coupled up the other end to the battery. Misdirecting the audience is the basic part of a magician's trade. I got the braves to take up my challenge and set off the keg when they reached it. You can imagine what kind of effect that made."

"Near enough," Dusty agreed. "But there's more to it, isn't there?"

"A little. I had Giselle do another dance around a second keg and let the Indians see me take it into the shack. Ten Bears and his braves believe it will explode if anybody tries to take it. And it will."

"Now you've lost me," Dusty admitted, guessing what was implied but hoping to gain more information.

"I've got that keg wired up to a battery in my desk," Lampart explained, indicating the left side drawer. "The moment one of my guards raises the alarm, Giselle or I come in here and touch it off."

"You've sure got it all worked out slicker'n a hawg greased down for cooking," the Kid praised inelegantly.

"Yes, sir," Waco agreed, then grinned. "No offense, sir, and with all respect, ma'am, I'd sure admire to see you do that medicine dance."

"You'll have your chance in six days," Giselle promised. "I do it every time the braves come in to draw their ammunition. We have to take the medicine off and put it back on again. And Ten Bears likes to see me do it."

"He's not alone in that," Waco declared, playing "Matt Caxton" to the limit.

"Aren't you interested in how Emma comes to be here, Ed?" Giselle inquired, making it plain that she wanted the subject changing.

"I figure she'd tell me, was I to ask," Dusty replied.

"Don't let my wife worry you, Edward," Lampart said soothingly. "There's not much to tell. We knew Emma from our theater days, and when I decided to open the saloon, I sent for her to come and run it. She agreed and has proved capable and efficient. There are no wanted posters out on her, or any murky secrets."

"I never thought there was," Dusty stated. "But she's sure one hell of a woman, if you'll pardon the word, ma'am, and we get along just fine."

"Lord!" Lampart barked, looking at the clock on the dining-room wall. "Is that the time? I've got to go to a meeting of the Civic Council. Basmanov's trying to get the 'no fires' rule canceled again. Do you think it would be a good thing to let him, Ed?"

"Nope," Dusty declared, aware of that answer being expected. "You get all this town's smoke rising and somebody might figure out it's here. Somebody we none of us want to see, like a cavalry patrol."

"They're likely to be out in strength, seeing's one of their patrols got jumped," the Kid went on. "Maybe even strong enough to push through this far. Was I you, I'd stand firm against having fires during the day."

"Rest assured that I will," the mayor promised. "I must go now."

"We better drift down the barn, boys," Dusty remarked. "Time we've bedded the horses down, it'll be coming up toward dinner. Juanita and Red won't like it happen you pair's late to the Honest Man."

13

IT'S OUR TOWN NOW, ED

"Nice neighborly sort of folks hereabouts, Ed," the Kid commented as the trio walked behind the street's buildings toward the livery barn. "One or another of them, they've done just about every meanness 'cept hoss-stealing."

"Bet some of them's even done that, but they're ashamed to admit it," Waco went on. "Not even their mothers could like 'em."

"That's the way Lampart wants us to think," Dusty admitted. "Then we'll not be likely to throw in our hands with anybody else."

"He made Emma out clean enough, though," Waco remarked. "You reckon it's the truth he told, Brother Ed?"

"I reckon so," Dusty decided. "He allows I've got a fond feeling for her and doesn't want to chance lying 'case I learn the truth."

"He's one smart son of a bitch," drawled the Kid. "Way he's

played things, I can see how he's got Ten Bears and the medicine woman eating out of his hand."

"We'll either have to bust up his medicine, or get rid of that ammunition before we pull out," Dusty declared. "Only, right now, I don't see how we're going to do either. So we'll keep playing along with him and watch our chance."

"You reckon he trusts us all along the line now, Ed?" the Kid inquired.

"I'd say he's close to it," Dusty replied. "At least, he's letting us walk around without anybody hanging onto our shirttails."

When the trio reached the barn, they found it deserted except for Pigeons, the custodian of the town's winged messengers. Apparently Basmanov had already left to attend the meeting of the Civic Council. Being one of the Russian's supporters, Pigeons exhibited a distinct lack of cordiality and did not offer to help them with their work.

Having fed and done everything necessary for their horses' well-being, Dusty and his companions returned to the hotel. There they found Red and Juanita waiting, demanding the dinner treat that had been promised to them. Leaving the Kid and Waco to deal with the girls, Dusty went to his own room. Unlocking the door, he went in and slammed to a halt.

"What the hell—?" he growled, hurriedly closing the door.

Smiling at his surprise, Giselle rose from his bed. A long cloak was draped over a chair and Dusty could understand why she had worn it. All she had on was a most abbreviated white doeskin copy of an Indian girl's costume. In two pieces, it covered so little of her that its use on a stage would have resulted in the authorities closing down the theater. Dusty had to admit that the brunette, small though she might be, had a body perfectly developed to complement the outfit. Looking at her, he could see that she had not been boasting when she claimed that she had held the Indians' attention while her husband had made his preparations to fool them.

"With Simmy at the Council meeting," Giselle remarked, gliding toward Dusty in an undulating, sensual manner, "I thought I'd come and show you my medicine dance costume."

"You made a poor thought, ma'am," Dusty answered, noticing that she halted well clear of his arms' reach.

"Don't you like me?" Giselle challenged, placing her hands on her head and rotating slowly to let him study her gorgeously molded little body from all sides. "I am beautiful, aren't I? Don't you think so?"

"You'll get no argument from me on that, ma'am," Dusty admitted. "Any man would, *Mrs.* Lampart."

"But the fact that I am married bothers you."

"What bothers me most is you're married to a man I admire and respect. Which being so, I reckon you'd best get covered over and head for home."

"After I picked your lock to get in to see you?" Giselle pouted, but still kept her distance. "You're sure that's what you want?"

"I've never been surer," Dusty stated. "I'm going to see the boys, ma'am, and I'd be truly grateful if you'll be gone when I get back."

Leaving the room, Dusty shut the door. He went to his companions' quarters and found them getting ready, helped by the girls, for the evening's round of entertainment. With Red and Juanita present, he could not discuss Giselle's visit. When he returned to his room, he found that the brunette had gone.

That evening, on entering the saloon, Dusty went to where Lampart was sitting in solitary state at Emma's private table.

"I don't know whether to be riled or flattered," the small Texan announced as he sat down.

"That went straight by me." Lampart smiled.

"You sent your wife along to my room to try me out," Dusty elaborated. "That could've riled me up some, except that I reckoned you must trust me enough to know she'd be safe."

"And you fully justified my faith in you," the mayor praised, then the arrival of Youseman and le Blanc brought the conversation to an end.

During the evening, Dusty noticed an increased air of hostility between Basmanov's supporters and Lampart's clique. That told the small Texan why the mayor had been so loquacious at lunch and had sent Giselle to test his loyalty. Unless Dusty missed his guess, Lampart intended to lock horns with the Russian and settle who would control the town, so wanted to be sure of having "Ed Caxton"'s backing in the showdown.

Nothing was said on the subject until Emma mentioned it indirectly. It was after the saloon had closed for the night and she lay in bed with Dusty's arms around her.

"That was one stormy Council meeting this afternoon, Ed," the blonde remarked as they separated from a kiss.

"Was, huh?" Dusty replied, feeling her snuggling closer to him. "Is Basmanov still pushing to get that 'no fires' ruling changed?"

"That's only part of it," Emma answered, and kissed him with fiery passion. Drawing back her face, she went on, "Mostly he's trying to make Simmy share out the Civic Improvement Fund instead of holding it all at his place."

"Does Simmy do that?"

"He does. Even some of his own crowd aren't too happy about it."

Having delivered the information, Emma started to make love. Dusty had never known her so insistent, or eager to give herself to him. After a time they lay side by side on their backs and the blonde spoke again.

"I bet Simmy's got well over half a million dollars stashed away, Ed, what with the Fund, the profits from the saloon and his share in the other—"

"What other?" Dusty demanded as the words trailed off.

"Connolly and Youseman have found a way of embalming bodies so they'll keep long enough to be sent out of the Palo Duro and the bounty collected on them."

"The hell you say!" Dusty growled, simulating surprise as he sat up and stared at the blonde through the darkness.

"It's true," Emma insisted. "That's why Youseman wasn't in the saloon the night you first came in. They were treating the bodies of those fellers you'd shot. I got the story from Youseman one night when he was drunk. What they do, I mean; it was before you got here. Him and Connolly found out how to do it at Simmy's suggestion. He fixed up the rest. Hatchet takes the bodies out to one of the towns where the sheriff's in cahoots with them. They had to take Basmanov in with them when he found out about it. None of them care much for that."

"And nobody else knows?"

"Nobody. Youseman was so drunk that he's forgotten he told me. They put the bodies in trick coffins, so anybody who wants can see them. Then, when the lid's screwed on, the bottom opens to drop the corpse into the basement, the empty box is buried and the body sent out."

"That's the sort of neat planning I'd expect from Simmy," Dusty drawled.

"Is that all it means to you?" Emma asked, sitting up.

"What else should it mean?" Dusty countered.

"There's ten thousand dollars on each of your heads," the blonde reminded him, and slid closer to wrap her arms around him.

"Simmy's my friend," Dusty pointed out.

"He was Ben Columbo's friend too," Emma warned, sagging back to the pillow and drawing him with her. "There's still an empty coffin in his grave."

"Simmy needs me and the boys' guns," Dusty began, being stopped by her lips crushing against his mouth and tongue slipping between his teeth.

"The time will come when he doesn't," the blonde cautioned at the completion of the kiss. Her hands roamed over Dusty's body. "What a waste it would be, Ed. Embalming you, I mean."

"I'll have something to say afore they get the chance to do it," Dusty threatened.

"So will I," Emma promised, and pressed her lips lightly to his. Then she whispered, "Ed. Over half a million is a lot of money."

There the matter came to an end. Clearly waiting for Dusty to make a comment, Emma said no more. He made no response, other than returning her caresses, until sleep claimed them both. The exertions of their lovemaking caused them to be late out of bed next morning. In fact, it was way past noon before they had eaten breakfast and dressed to go downstairs. They found Waco and the Kid in the barroom, although Red and Juanita were no longer in evidence.

"You pair expecting a war?" Dusty inquired, nodding to the Winchester in the Kid's right hand.

"Nope," Waco replied. "Last night my Red gal got saying how she just loves turkey. So Comanch's fixing to go out and shoot one for her."

"There's a gentleman for you," Emma praised. "The boys take after you, Ed."

"They couldn't pick a better ex—" Dusty began, then stopped to stare as the side door opened and Giselle ran in. "What's up, Mrs. Lampart?"

"It's Basmanov," the brunette replied. She was wearing her usual style of clothing and looked concerned. "He's lit the fire in his office stove and Simmy's going down there to make him put it out."

"Could be he'll need help," Dusty barked. "Let's go, boys."

"I'll see to Mrs. Lampart," Emma remarked, catching hold of the brunette's right arm in a firm rather than gentle grip. "Leave her to me, Ed."

"Gracias, querida," Dusty drawled. "Don't you fret none, ma'am, we'll see Simmy comes back safe."

Giselle had obviously wasted no time in bringing the news. Leaving the saloon by the rear door, the three Texans saw Lampart halfway along the back of Doctor Connolly's premises. Hearing their footsteps, he turned to face them.

"What—How—?" the mayor gasped, showing surprise and relief.

"Your lady told us what's happening," Dusty explained. "We concluded that you'd need some help."

"I do," Lampart admitted, and indicated the white-handled revolver thrust into his waistband. "After the way Basmanov took on at yesterday's meeting, I'm sure this is his way of calling me out for a showdown."

"He'll have friends along," Dusty declared, not offering to walk on.

"It's possible," the mayor admitted. "Pigeons will be there. Probably Diebitch, the blacksmith, Rossi, his usual clique."

"Then we're going to play it smart," Dusty decided. "I don't reckon they've seen us yet. So you and me'll go along the street, bold as all get-out, right through the front door."

"Just the two of us?"

"Matt and Comanch'll be around when we need them."

Leaving his companions, Dusty accompanied the mayor at a leisurely pace through an alley to the street. Already the smoke rising from the barn's chimney had attracted considerable attention. Men and women pointed it out to each other. Then they turned their gaze to Dusty and Lampart. Only le Blanc offered to help. Carrying a twin-barreled shotgun, he ran from his shop.

"It's come, then, Simmy?" the barber greeted.

"As you say, Jean," Lampart confirmed. "It's come."

"Don't walk so fast," Dusty advised. "Diebitch's watching us from the front door, so we'll be expected. Leave them sweat it out a whiles—and let my boys get into place before we go in."

"I don't see Matt or Comanche," Lampart reported worriedly, glancing in passing along the alley that separated the barn from its next-door neighbor.

"It's lucky Diebitch's ducked back in," Dusty growled. "You'd've give the whole snap away. They're around. You can count on it."

Walking on, the three men stepped through the open front doors of the barn. With le Blanc to his left and Lampart at the right, Dusty studied his surroundings. Basmanov and the slim, vicious-looking Diebitch confronted the trio, but there was no sign of any other members of the Russian's faction.

"You know the penalty for lighting a fire between dawn and sundown, Ivan?" Lampart challenged.

"I do," Basmanov admitted. "And you'll pay it. You and one of your magic tricks lit the stove."

"Now, who'll believe that?" Lampart asked.

"I reckon they'll believe whichever of us comes out of it alive." Basmanov grinned. "Only you wouldn't have the guts to face me man to man."

"Wouldn't I?" countered Lampart.

"You've brought le Blanc and Caxton along," the Russian pointed out.

"Only to see fair doings," Dusty drawled. "If Mr. Diebitch'll back off, me and Jean'll leave you gents settle this between you."

"That suits me," Diebitch stated fervently and moved aside.

"And me," Lampart declared. "Go and wait by the doors, gentlemen."

"To show I don't want no edge," Basmanov said, when Dusty and le Blanc had obeyed. "I'll ask you to count to five, Mr. Caxton. We'll draw when you get there."

"Go ahead, Ed," Lampart commanded.

"One!" Dusty said. "Two!"

Down drove Basmanov's right hand, closing about the butt of his gun. At the same moment, he saw a mocking smile playing on Lampart's lips. It was the expression of a man who had outbluffed a bluffer.

As soon as Basmanov moved, the mayor whipped out his own revolver. Although it had an ivory handle, it proved to be a snub-nosed British Webley Bulldog and not the Colt Peacemaker from the top of his desk. Twice the weapon crashed, with a speed that was only possible by trigger pressure—as opposed to fanning the hammer—when using a self-cocking, double-action mechanism. Although he had started his draw slightly after the Russian, Lampart had about six inches less barrel to get clear. That made all the difference. His bullets tore into Basmanov's chest before the other's gun could point at him.

"Get them!" Diebitch screamed, grabbing for the revolver he wore.

Throwing up his shotgun, le Blanc cut loose from waist level. Seven of the nine buckshot balls that belched from the right-hand tube found their mark and flung Diebitch lifeless from his feet.

While Dusty had agreed to take a passive role, he had been under no delusions regarding Basmanov's sense of fair play. So he had been prepared for treachery and knew instinctively where it would come from. Sure enough, Pigeons loomed into sight from behind the hay bales at the front of the loft and started to swing a shotgun to his shoulder. Even as Lampart's Webley spoke, Dusty's hands crossed with their usual speed. The small Texan took the extra split second needed to raise his right-hand weapon to eye level and take aim. He shot the only way he dared in the circumstances, for an instant kill. Passing Pigeons's rising shotgun, the .45 bullet winged into his head.

Big and bulky, the blacksmith had also risen from concealment in the loft. The ambush had been planned. That was obvious from the way the man took aim at and shot le Blanc, although he did so too late to save Diebitch. In echo to the blacksmith's revolver, Dusty's left-hand Colt lined and barked. Hit in the body, Pigeons's companion screamed, spun around, toppled over the bales and crashed to the floor below.

In the tackroom, Rossi and another man gripped their revolvers and waited to cut in on the fight that would determine who ran Hell. So interested were they in what was going on between Basmanov and Lampart that they failed to notice the face that peered in through the window. On seeing the Russian's bid fail, Rossi prepared to throw open the door leading into the stable.

Having reached the barn undetected, Waco saw enough through the window to know that he must act fast. Kicking open the outside door as he had learned to do from Dusty, he plunged into the tackroom. The two men heard the crash and spun around with their weapons thrusting in the youngster's direction. Left, right, left, right, flame erupted from the muzzles of Waco's Army Colts. Rossi died instantly, a bullet severing his jugular vein. Hit in the shoulder, the second man dropped his gun and stumbled into the stable. Being unarmed did not save him. Turning fast, Lampart shot him in the head.

While that was happening, the Kid raced in through the back doors. Bounding along the gap between two lots of stalls, he appeared before another pair of Basmanov's supporters as they came from one of the storerooms. Seeing the dark-faced savage, they forgot their intention of shooting Lampart and tried to turn their guns on the Kid. Lead hissed by him, calling for an immediate response. Working his Winchester's lever at its fastest possible speed, he poured out eight bullets in an arc that encompassed the two men's torsos. Both went down, torn to dollrags by the tempest of flying lead.

No more men appeared. The bloody battle for mastery of the town had come to an end. Horses squealed, snorted, reared and kicked at their stalls in fright as the acrid powder smoke wafted away.

"See to the horses—Comanch', Matt," Dusty ordered, having to make an effort to prevent himself from using their real names. Looking at le Blanc, he went on, "Jean's cashed in."

"He's been avenged," Lampart answered, and started to go around Basmanov's party to check on their condition. "And he'll have plenty of company; they're all dead too."

People came pouring into the barn. Outlaws went to help the Kid and Waco calm down the horses. Townsmen studied the bodies and exchanged glances. Those who had supported Lampart showed their satisfaction. On other faces, anxiety and concern left their marks. Those were the emotions of Basmanov's less active partisans, who wondered what the future held for them on account of it. Already the fence-sitters were beaming their approval at the mayor. However, Lampart ignored all of them. After ordering the jeweler to put out the fire in the office's stove and directing Youseman to give le Blanc the best possible funeral, he apologized to such outlaws as were present for disturbing their horses. Then he called the three Texans to him, thanked them for their support and asked them to accompany him to his home.

On the street, the men found Giselle, Red, Juanita and Emma waiting. The blonde held a bottle of champagne and declared that the victory called for a celebration. Giving his agreement, Lampart took them to his house and established them comfortably in the sitting room. With the drinks served and toasts to their continued success drunk, Dusty decided to obtain some information.

"How did you know when to set the fire off, Simmy?" the small Texan asked. "If you'd done it too early, we might none of us been around to back your play."

"I waited until I saw Comanche and Matt taking the young ladies back to the saloon. Emma's maid had already drawn the curtains in her bedroom, which meant you and she were up and about. So I made my arrangements, knowing your brother and Comanche would be waiting for you."

"How'd you get in and light the fire?" Waco inquired. "You couldn't've just touched her off and got out—somebody'd likely've seen you."

"It's a trick I learned, making a fire start at a given moment. I won't say more than that—a magician is under oath not to divulge the nature of his secrets. I went there, picked the office because it was empty, made my arrangements and came back to await results."

"You knew Basmanov'd see the smoke and guess what your game was," Dusty drawled. "But you counted on him wanting a showdown, gathering his stoutest sidekicks and waiting for you to come."

"That's true," Lampart admitted. "I also knew that, with you helping me, I had the edge. None of them could even come close to matching your gun skill."

"That's for sure," Waco put in. "They didn't have the sense to watch the outside windows."

"All went off perfectly," Lampart declared, showing no hint of regret over le Blanc's death. "It's my town now."

"*Your* town, Simmy?" Dusty queried, seeing Emma throw him a glance pregnant with meaning.

"That wasn't what I meant," Lampart amended. "It's *our* town now, Ed."

"I said you could count on Simmy to do the right thing, Ed," Emma remarked.

14
TAKE YOUR CLAWS
OFF MY MAN

In all his eventful young life, Dusty Fog had never received a shock to equal that which greeted him as he entered the mayor's office toward sundown on the day after the gun battle. Fortunately, Lampart had his back to the door and did not see the small Texan's reaction to the sight of the woman who was placing a bulky set of saddlebags into one of the deposit boxes. Straightening up and closing the lid, she stared in Dusty's direction. At first surprise played on her strikingly beautiful features, to be replaced almost immediately by an expression that denoted understanding.

Black hair flowed from beneath the brim of a gray Stetson hat with a band decorated by silver conchas. She wore a fringed buckskin jacket, open down its front to exhibit a dark gray shirt tucked into figure-hugging black riding breeches. High-heeled boots with spurs attached graced her feet. The clothes served to display a body every bit as voluptuously curvaceous as Emma Nene's. Emphasizing the full contours of her hips, a gunbelt slanted down with the tip of the holster tied to her magnificently molded right thigh. In the holster, carefully positioned to facilitate a fast draw, rode what looked like a wooden-handled Colt Model 1851 Navy revolver.

Without the need for closer examination, Dusty knew the woman's gun to be a five-shot copy of the Navy Colt manufactured by the now-defunct Manhattan Firearms Company. Going by her display of emotion on his arrival, she could identify him despite his clothes, the beard and moustache. She had been a blonde on their two previous meetings, but Dusty found no difficulty in recognizing the famous lady outlaw, Belle Starr.

"Ed!" Belle greeted, her voice a pleasant, warmly inviting Southern drawl. "I just might have known I'd find you here, after all the things I've been reading about you-all in the *Texas State Gazette*."

"You know each other?" Lampart inquired, bringing his gaze from its contemplation of Belle's physique.

There was a hint of suspicion in the mayor's voice, and Dusty could figure out what had caused it. Lampart had not forgotten how "Ed Caxton" had claimed to have led a law-abiding life until committing the robbery that had resulted in him fleeing for safety to Hell. So Lampart was wondering how he could have made the acquaintance of such a prominent member of outlaw society.

"Why, sure," Dusty agreed, thinking fast. "It was while we were with the Army up in the Indian Nations. Me and the boys got sent with a patrol to search for Miss Belle at her pappy's place."

"Why, they just did me the biggest favor in my whole life," Belle went on. "The three of them were sent to search the barn and Comanche found my hiding place. But Ed said for me to be covered up again and they never let on where I was to that mean old officer."

In view of her close relationship with Mark Counter,[1] Dusty

1. How that relationship began, developed and finally ended is told in the "Bounty on Belle Starr's Scalp" episode of *Troubled Range, The Bad*

had not expected Belle to betray him. She had recognized him immediately, recollected the story of the robbery in the newspapers and guessed what was happening. No matter why she had come to Hell, it seemed that she was willing to play along with the small Texan's game.

"You paid us back in Dallas," Dusty pointed out, feeling that so short an acquaintance would not account for her recognizing him. "If you hadn't loaned me that five hundred dollars, I might've had to kill some of the gambling man's sidekicks to stop them pestering me for it."

"I had my money's worth," Belle claimed, darting an arch smile at Lampart. She, too, felt that the situation needed a little expanding. "Ed's quite a man, you know, Simmy. Although I don't suppose you *could* know, not that way."

"I suppose not," Lampart agreed stiffly, and looked at Dusty. "Miss Starr—"

"I've already said you can call me Belle," the girl interrupted.

"Belle has just arrived, Ed," the mayor went on. "I've explained the rules of the town and she agrees to them."

"That figures," Dusty drawled, glancing at the girl's gunbelt. "Did you have trouble getting here, Belle?"

"None. But I was just a teensy mite worried when the guide said I'd have to hand over my guns. He was telling the truth about me getting them back after I'd talked to the mayor."

"Why'd you need to come?" Dusty challenged, knowing some such comment would be expected by Lampart.

"Belle had heard of our community," the mayor injected, just a shade too quickly. "And with the Indian Nations being somewhat disturbed—"

"*Disturbed!*" Belle ejaculated. "Land-sakes-a-mercy, Ed, it's hotter than a two-dollar pistol up there right now. So I concluded I'd better stay away from home for a spell. Of course I'd heard of Hell and decided to take a look at it."

Bunch, Rangeland Hercules, the "Lady Known as Belle" episode of *The Hard Riders* and *Guns in the Night.*

"Seeing's how Belle's such an old friend of mine," Dusty remarked to the mayor, "I reckon we can forget her contribution to the Civic Improvement Fund."

"Well, I admit a twentieth of my money does seem a lot," Belle purred, glancing at the stack of bills that lay alongside the white-handled Peacemaker on the desk. "But I shouldn't have any special favors. It just wouldn't be fitting, Ed."

"A *twentieth's* a whole heap of money," Dusty said coldly. "Has Simmy introduced you to his wife, Belle?"

"I was going to, after we'd concluded our business," the mayor declared, with an annoyed glare at the small Texan.

"If she's busy, it can wait her convenience, Simmy." Belle smiled. "Why don't you show me to the hotel, Ed? I'm just dying to hear all about that robbery you and the boys pulled."

Although he threw a scowl at Dusty, Lampart raised no objections. Belle locked her box and dropped the keys into a jacket pocket. Then she and Dusty left the office. Giselle peered around the curtain at the back end of the hall, but withdrew without coming to be introduced. On emerging from the mayor's house, Dusty became aware of somebody watching him. Looking at the saloon, he saw two of the girls standing on the first floor's verandah. They were displaying considerable interest in Belle and himself. Even as he watched, one of them darted into the building. Dusty did not need much thought to figure out where she was going. So he concluded that he had better get Belle off the street before Emma came to investigate.

"What's the game, Dusty?" Belle asked as he started her moving away from the saloon. "I nearly had a fit when you walked in. Luckily I remembered that story in the paper and came up with the right answer—or some of it."

"Thanks for not saying who I am," Dusty replied. "I hoped you wouldn't."

"Now, play fair with me," Belle suggested. "I'm here on business and I'd like to know where I—"

"Mr. Caxton," called a voice, and Dusty saw the jeweler waddling across the street in his direction. "I was hoping to see you. I've had the clasp on that necklace repaired and it's ready for you."

"Gracias," Dusty answered. "I'll come around later and—"

"Now, who would you be buying a necklace for, Ed?" Belle challenged, a merry gleam dancing in her eyes. "Come on. I'm dying to see it."

"Maybe you should go and get a room at the hotel," Dusty told her.

"There's time for that later," Belle insisted. "Come on."

So far, Dusty observed as he made for the jeweler's shop, Emma had not made an appearance. The delay would allow her time to do so before he could get Belle inside the hotel. So, in the interests of peace and quiet, he figured he had best take the lady outlaw out of the blonde's sight. They entered the shop without Emma having emerged from the Honest Man. Passing around the end of the counter, the owner disappeared into a back room. He seemed to take an exceptionally long time before he returned carrying a magnificent diamond necklace. Dusty could hear significant sounds from the street, but hoped he might be wrong about their meaning. From what he could see through the window, he doubted if he was.

"My!" Belle breathed, laying a hand on Dusty's sleeve. "Now isn't that the sweetest li'l ole trinket you ever did see?"

The front door flew open and a furious feminine voice hissed, "Take your claws off my man!"

Turning with the speed of a wildcat preparing to defend itself, Belle confronted Emma. The blonde was dressed ready for her night's work, and a couple of rings with sizable stones flashed on her fingers. Ignoring the people who gathered behind her, Emma looked Belle over from head to toe. The saloon girls had spread the word, and a number of men and women waited to see what would develop.

"Easy, Emma," Dusty said soothingly. "I was just taking Miss Starr down to the hotel."

"Why, Ed," Belle purred. "You've never called me 'Miss Starr' before."

Annoyance bit at Dusty. Instead of Belle letting him handle

things, she seemed set on provoking trouble. Dull red flooded into Emma's cheeks, and she bunched her right hand to form a capable-looking fist.

"He won't do it ag—!" the blonde began, drawing back her arm.

Out flashed Belle's Manhattan, its hammer clicking back and muzzle pointing at Emma's heaving bosom. Poised to attack, the protruding stone of a ring glinting evilly on her clenched fist, the blonde stood very still.

"You try to ram that blazer into my face," Belle threatened, "and I'll put a window in your apples."

"I can soon enough take the rings off!" Emma spat back, making a move as if to do so.

"Please, ladies," the jeweler implored. "No fighting in here."

"Let it drop, both of you!" Dusty ordered.

"If *you* say so, Ed," Belle replied. "What do folks do for entertainment around here, Mr. Jewelry Man?"

"G-go to the Honest Man Saloon," the shop's owner replied.

"You put your face inside it," Emma promised grimly, "and I'll throw you right back out."

"Will you be there tonight, Ed?" Belle inquired.

"That won't matter to you," Emma declared before Dusty could reply. "What I said goes. If you show your face in my place tonight, gun or no gun, I'll make you wish you'd hid in some other brothel instead of coming here."

"That's big talk for a fat old harridan," Belle jeered, conscious that the exchange had an audience. "I'll be there tonight. Without my gun and, to give you a chance, wearing moccasins. That'll make us even, for all your blazers and long talons."

With that, Belle holstered the Manhattan and pushed by Emma to leave the building. For a moment, the blonde appeared to be on the verge of hurling herself after the lady outlaw. Then, glancing at her rings and fingernails, Emma stalked out of the door. She did not even look at Dusty before departing.

"Whoo!" ejaculated the jeweler, and ran the tip of his tongue across his lips. "It should be something to see at the Honest Man tonight, Mr. Caxton."

"Likely," Dusty admitted absently, wondering why Belle had taken such an attitude.

"How about the necklace?" the man asked as Dusty turned from the counter.

"I reckon I'd best take it with me," the small Texan decided, thinking that it might prove useful as a peace offering to Emma.

Apparently practically everybody in town shared the jeweler's summation. Dusty had never seen such a crowd as he found in the Honest Man Saloon on his arrival at nine o'clock. There were people present he would never have expected to find in a saloon. Giselle sat with Lampart at Emma's table. Other townsmen had also brought their wives. The madam of the brothel was there, accompanied by her whole staff. So far, neither Emma nor Belle had made an appearance. Dusty figured that they soon would.

Despite his efforts, Dusty had failed to change either of their minds. Although delighted with the necklace, Emma had stated the only way she would forget the incident was if Belle made a public apology and never entered the saloon. Due to the interest her arrival had aroused, Dusty could not manage to get Belle alone for more than a few seconds. Asked to let the matter drop, she had declared herself willing to do so—if Emma invited her into the Honest Man.

Consulting the Kid and Waco, Dusty had finally decided to leave the women to settle the issue themselves. From what Mark had told them, Belle could take care of herself. She had also fixed it so that Emma would be unable to wear the dangerous rings and most likely had to cut short her nails. So both should escape serious damage. Waco had warned that the town would deeply resent any interference that halted the fight. Already, the trio suspected, Lampart was seeking a way to remove them. There was no point in giving him a weapon with which to turn the population against them.

"Mig Santiago will be annoyed to have missed this," Giselle remarked, after Dusty had sat down and exchanged greetings.

Any comment the small Texan might have considered making on the subject of the Mexican's departure, under pressure from his financially embarrassed gang, went unsaid. The low hum of conversation died away around the room. Every head swung to stare at Belle as she strolled through the batwing doors.

True to her promise, the lady outlaw had left off her gunbelt and boots. Missing, too, were the Stetson and her jacket. She made an attractive picture in her moccasins, riding breeches as tight as a second skin, shirt with its sleeves rolled up and hands covered by thin black leather gloves.

Posted to keep watch for Belle, a girl on the balcony darted away. When Emma came slinking gracefully down the stairs, the way in which she was clothed threatened to overshadow the black-haired beauty's appearance. The blonde wore nothing but a brief, lace-trimmed white bodice, black silk tights and high-heeled slippers with pom-poms on the toes. Showing her unadorned hands, she drew on a pair of white gloves. Then, in a silence that could almost be felt, she advanced to the center of the area in front of the bar, which had been cleared of tables and chairs to make room for the anticipated battle.

"I'll set up drinks all round after I've handed her her needings, folks," Belle announced, moving toward Emma like a great cat stalking its prey.

"*If* she licks me," the blonde countered, "I'll give drinks to the house all night."

That was all the conversation carried out. Warily the two gorgeous creatures circled each other. Suddenly Belle whipped her arm right back and swung her open palm in a roundhouse slap to Emma's left cheek. It cracked with a sharp, vicious sound, snapping the blonde's head around and bringing an involuntary squeak of pain. For all that, Emma responded almost immediately by whipping out first one hand, then the other. The explosive smacks of her palms against Belle's face rang out loud. Eager to follow up her advantage, the blonde crowded forward with arms flailing. Bewildered by the onslaught, Belle was forced to retreat. Excited yells rose from the crowd. Men and women came to their feet, moving to form a wall of humanity around the open space in which the girls were tangling.

Desperate to halt the stinging punishment, Belle suddenly entwined her fingers into Emma's blond tresses. She backed off a long stride, hauling the saloonkeeper's head down and throwing up her knee. An experienced barroom brawler, Emma had known what to expect. Swiftly she folded her arms in front of her face and Belle's knee struck them. Although the blonde had saved herself from serious damage, the impact snapped her erect. Belle had retained her hold on Emma's hair, so the pain caused by the halting of her head's upward movement ripped into the blonde. Letting out a screech, Emma sank both hands deep into Belle's free-flowing black hair. She jerked and twisted at the ensnared locks with deliberate fury, only to have Belle reply in a similar manner.

Lurching from side to side, their heads bobbing and shaking with the violence they put into the hair-yanking, the girls also staggered back and forward a few steps at a time. They clung determinedly to each other's hair, looking as if they desired to hand-scalp each other. Forehead to forehead, they panted and grunted, striving all the time to retain their balance on widespread legs.

It could not last. With a final wrench bringing squeaks of agony, almost as if by mutual consent, they jerked free their hands and went into a clinch. For a few seconds they tussled on their feet. Then Belle managed to twist away and drag Emma over her buttocks. Turning a somersault, the blonde went to the floor. However, she had clung onto Belle and the outlaw followed her. Curling over in midair, Belle lit down on her back.

Rolling over swiftly, Emma writhed until her open thighs made an arch over Belle's head and her knees held the outlaw's arms pinned to the floor. Bending forward, the blonde thrust her fingers onto the trapped girl's bust. With the pain knifing into her, Belle supported herself on her bent left leg, and, lifting her rump from the unyielding planks, jerked her right knee

hard against the top of the blonde's forward-tilted skull. The
blow caused Emma to remove her fingers from the sensitive
region and lurch away.

Snatching her arms from beneath Emma's knees, Belle rolled
into a sitting position. She turned just in time to meet the
blonde's diving attack. Bust to bust, fingers again ripping at
hair, they pitched full-length on the floor. Belle's legs were
doubled under her, but she managed to writhe them free. A
sudden heave brought the outlaw on top, both hands tugging
outward at hanks of blond hair. Shrieking in torment, Emma
tried to bow her body upward. Her left hand lost its grip on
Belle's hair. Scrabbling for a fresh hold, she grasped the open
neck of Belle's shirt. A fresh surge of pain from the tortured
locks of hair caused Emma to wrench savagely at the garment.
Buttons popped and, dragged out of Belle's breeches, the shirt
split open down its front.

Angered by the damage to her clothing, Belle released the
hair. Wriggling until her right knee rammed against Emma's
abdomen, she sought for revenge. Drawn down around her
right bicep, the shirt did not entangle her arms sufficiently to
inconvenience her. Laying her right hand on Emma's face, she
pressed the blonde's head to the floor. Greedily the outlaw's left
fist clamped on the front of the bodice, tugging and pulling
until the flimsy material came apart from décolleté to waist.

Almost unseated by Emma's furious struggles, Belle advanced to sit astride her shoulders. Transferring her hand to the
side of the blonde's head, she drew back the other fist ready to
pound Emma's face. At the table, Dusty wondered if he should
intervene. To do so might bring about his death, for the wildly
excited crowd would expect to see the fight through to a deci-
sive victory for one or the other girl. Yet, held down in such a
way, Emma might suffer serious damage at the hands of her
enraged rival. Before he could reach a decision, Dusty saw
Emma was shouting something. Although the noisy acclaim of
the spectators prevented the small Texan from catching the
words, Belle obviously heard them.

Instead of pummeling the blonde's face to a bloody ruin, the outlaw's fist held back. Like a flash, Emma braced her feet and head against the floor. Up curved her body, with a force that flung Belle forward and away from her. Rolling onto her stomach as Belle landed facedown, Emma plunged onto the outlaw's back. For several seconds, the blonde remained on top. With her thighs squirming to hold down Belle's legs, the blonde hooked her left arm under and around the other's throat while her right alternately punched the trapped head and tore away the remains of the shirt.

Screeching and struggling with the strength of rage-filled desperation, Belle contrived to roll onto her right side. The arm was still about her neck and the blonde's legs, the knees showing whitely through the ruptured silk of the tights, straddled her hips. While Belle's right arm attempted to drag Emma away by the hair, her left fingers raked ineffectively at the blonde's ribs to complete the destruction and removal of the bodice.

Oblivious of her naked torso, Emma fought on. So did Belle. Losing her chokehold, the blonde allowed the outlaw to reach a sitting position. Then, sitting up herself, she wrapped her legs in a scissor grip about Belle's bare midsection. Gasping as the crushing pressure bit at her, Belle clawed at Emma's upper leg in a futile effort at escaping. Tilting sideways and resting on her left elbow, the saloonkeeper slammed her clenched right hand into the center of the outlaw's face. Blood trickled from Belle's nostrils. Mouthing croaks of pain, Belle took her hands from Emma's right leg. She put them to better use by grabbing hold of and crushing at the blonde's jutting bare right breast. Emma's scream rang out loud. Lifting her right leg, she shoved up with the left to try to dislodge her tormentress. Such was Belle's relief at the end of the scissors that she released her own hold and rolled away.

Dragging themselves to their feet, the girls stood for a moment to regain something of their energy. Then they rushed at each other with fists flying. Wildly propelled knuckles impacted on faces, busts, stomachs, or missed as chance dictated. Coming in close to try to minimize the punishment being inflicted, they went into a mindless tangle of primitive, unscientific wrestling. Arms, legs, elbows, hands and feet were used indiscriminately and teeth brought into play. Emma was barefooted, her tights in ribbons, while Belle had lost one moccasin and her other leg showed where the breeches' seam had split. Six times they made their feet and went down, while the crowd screamed itself hoarse, encouraging them to further efforts.

On the seventh time of rising, the girls clutched at one another's throats and held on with a choking grip. Reddish blotches showed around their fingers as the digits gouged into sweat-soddened flesh. Guttural sounds broke from them. Although fairly evenly matched, Emma had a slight weight advantage. Not much, but enough in their present condition. Slowly she bore Belle backward, but without causing the other to let go.

In an attempt to free herself, Belle slid her legs between Emma's spread-apart feet and lowered her rump to the floor. And found she had made a serious mistake. She was sitting with the back almost touching the dais on which, at other times, the band played. Before she could rectify the situation, Belle was trapped. Spreading open her thighs, Emma lunged to kneel on the dais and crush Belle against it.

Realizing the consequences of failure, Belle put all her strength into a desperate effort. Bracing her shoulders against the dais, she thrust forward. Finding herself being tilted off balance, the blonde tried to spring to the rear. Landing awkwardly, she sat down hard. Lurching upright, Belle swung around her right leg. The sole of the bare foot slammed against the side of Emma's jaw. As she fell backward, Belle stumbled away.

Sobbing with exhaustion, the outlaw turned to defend herself. She saw Emma lying supine, right leg bent, right hand clasped on her forehead and left arm stretched out limply. Calling on her last dregs of energy, Belle returned to the blonde's side. Standing astride the motionless figure, Belle folded her legs until her rump came to rest on Emma's bosom. She had the blonde at her mercy, arms trapped beneath her knees, but waited to regather her strength. Then she felt two hands beneath her armpits, lifting her. For a moment, she tried to struggle and twisted her head to see who was holding her.

"For God's sake, Belle," Dusty Fog said, dragging her from the unconscious blonde. "Leave Emma be. She's licked."

"T-take-me-hotel!" Belle croaked back. "D-damn it. Take me. I've won and it's due to me."

15
WE HAD TO KNOW
WHO'S BOSS

"I hope you haven't got the wrong idea, Dusty," Belle Starr remarked as she stood with her back to him and, wincing a little, donned a flimsy nightgown. "Because only one man has ever shared my bed."

"So Mark told me," Dusty replied. "What the hell did you fight Emma for?"

As soon as Dusty had seen Emma was beaten, he had left the table and prevented Belle from inflicting further punishment. Nobody had objected, being more concerned with reaping the full benefits of the blonde's defeat. Deeply puzzled by the lady outlaw's behavior, he had escorted her to the hotel. She had clearly made arrangements for her return. A hip bath, filled with warm water, stood in the corner of her room, and she had used it to wash away the dirt, sawdust and sweat of the fight. Powdered witch-hazel leaves had stopped the bleeding from her nose and other minor abrasions. Although she had a mouse under her left eye and a mottling of bruises, she did not appear to have suffered any serious damage.

"For two reasons," Belle said, sitting on the edge of the bed. "I don't take to blond calico cats mean-mouthing me. And I wanted a chance for a long, private talk with you." She gingerly touched her swollen, discolored left eye. "If I'd known how tough that girl of yours was, I'd've picked an easier way of doing it."

"She's not my gal," Dusty corrected. "Except that she figures 'Ed Caxton' might be able to help her against Mayor Lampart."

"Does she?" Belle said, with some interest. "And why is 'Ed Caxton' here?"

"I could ask you the same thing. Day comes when the Indian Nations gets so 'disturbed' Belle Starr has to run out, I'll start voting Republican."

"Considering what I went through tonight, just to be all on our lonesome with you, *Ed* honey, I think *you* should answer me first."

"All right," Dusty drawled, not offering to leave the chair he had occupied since entering the room. "Me and the boys came here to find out all we could about this town, so that the governor can figure out a way to close it down."

"I thought that's about what it would be," Belle admitted. "From all I've heard, you've been busy since you got here. Word has it that you're Lampart's right-hand gun."

"I've made myself useful," Dusty said, with an expression of distaste. "So far, everybody I've had to kill've been fellers who deserved it."

"You're going to break Lampart before you leave," Belle commented, as a statement and not a question.

"If I can," Dusty agreed, and told her all he had learned since coming to Hell.

Belle sat and listened without interruption all through Dusty's lengthy recital of the town's history. Relying on Mark Counter's assessment of her character, the small Texan held back no aspect of the citizens' and the mayor's infamy. Revul-

sion flickered on her bruised features as she heard of how men
had been murdered for the bounty on their heads. Then he
mentioned one last thing, an item that he figured would seal her
hatred of Lampart.

"Lordy lord!" the lady outlaw ejaculated. "You mean
he's actually given repeaters and ammunition to the
Kweharehnuh?"

"I wouldn't lie to you, Belle," Dusty declared.

"Lands-sakes-a-mercy!" the girl gasped, shutting her eyes
and visualizing what could result from the mayor's actions.
"They're a prime set of scum, the people here. But I do declare
that Lampart's the worst of them all."

"Out and away the worst," Dusty confirmed.

"I'm right pleased that I was asked to come here and help
rob him," Belle announced.

Almost ten seconds ticked by before Dusty spoke. From
along the street came the sounds of celebration. If the noise was
anything to go by, the crowd were enjoying to the full the free
liquor brought to them by Belle's victory over Emma.

"So that's why you're here," Dusty breathed. "Who sent for
you?"

"I didn't have time to find out before your sweet honey
called me for a showdown," Belle replied, a faint smile playing
n her lips.

"You don't know?"

"I had this offer, through a man I can trust, to come here for
the job. I was given a thousand dollars traveling money and
half a hundred-dollar bill. Whoever wanted me here would
show me the other half and we could make our deal. It seemed
worth looking into, so I came along. I'd heard about having to
hand over a tenth of the loot, so I fetched along around fifteen
thousand dollars."

"That's a heap of cash money—"

"I'm not a two-bit thief," Belle pointed out. "So I'd be ex-
pected to have plenty. Anyways, all but three thousand of it's
Confederate States currency. And I did get a reduction from
Simmy."

"So I noticed." Dusty grinned. "Mark always said you could charm a bird down off a tree, had you a mind to."

"It saves waving a gun ar—" Belle began.

"What's up?" Dusty whispered as the girl stopped speaking and adopted an attitude of listening.

"Somebody's just come and's listening outside the door!" Belle answered, just as quietly. "Quick. Strip to the waist. Stay sat and lift your legs so's I can pull your boots off."

Swiftly, Dusty unbuckled and removed his gunbelt. Then, while Belle drew off first one boot and the other, he divested himself of tie, shirt and undershirt. Having completed her part of the undressing, Belle rose, threw back the covers and climbed into bed. Drawing his right-hand Colt, Dusty tiptoed across the room. Looking at what should have been a continuous strip of lamplight glowing between the floor and the bottom of the door, he made out the dark blobs caused by the listener's feet. Turning the key, he unlocked and threw open the door in practically one motion.

"What the—?" Dusty spat out as a figure clad in a hooded cape almost fell through the door into his arms.

"Let me in, Ed!" Emma Nene begged, *sotto voce* but urgently. "Quick. I'm not here to make trouble."

Having already seen the thing she gripped in her right hand, Dusty knew that the blonde was speaking the truth. So he withdrew and allowed her to dart by. Glancing along the lamp-illuminated passage to make sure they had not been observed, Dusty closed and relocked the door.

"I didn't think you could make it before morning, after the licking I handed you." Belle smiled, sitting up and swinging her legs from the bed. "Do you have the other half of the bill?"

Thrusting back the hood, Emma allowed her cloak to fall open. Under it, she wore the nightgown that Dusty had come to know so well during his stay in Hell. Like Belle, the blonde had bathed and attended to her injuries. Emma's top lip was swollen and her right eye resembled a Blue Point oyster peeping out of its shell. Walking to the bed as if Dusty did not exist, she held out the half of a hundred-dollar bill that had told him that she had come on a peaceful visit. It had also given him food for speculation, in view of what Belle had said.

"Here's mine," the blonde said. "Where's yours?"

Taking down her gunbelt from where it hung around the post at the head of the bed, Belle produced the other half of the bill from a secret pocket. She handed it to Dusty and told Emma to do the same.

"They match," the small Texan affirmed, placing the edges together. "Now will somebody tell me what the hell it's all about?"

"Your sweet honey had me come here to help rob the mayor, Ed," Belle replied, and repeated what she had already told him so that Emma would not suspect they had discussed the matter.

"How do *you* stand on it, Ed?" the blonde inquired, having scanned his face worriedly all through the story.

"You-all gave me half a million good reasons for not trusting Simmy, Emma gal," Dusty drawled, and saw relief replace the anxiety on her face. "But, knowing who she was and why she'd come, why in hell did you pick that fight with Belle?"

"I didn't know for sure, until it was too late," Emma insisted. "By the time I did, there were folks listening. What would they have thought, knowing *me*, if I'd done nothing after coming on some stray tail-peddler pawing at my man? And what's more important, Simmy would have got suspicious if he'd heard I let her get away with it, even knowing she was Belle Starr. He's smart enough to start guessing I'd got a reason for keeping friendly with her."

"You could've let Belle know—" Dusty began.

"She did," the lady outlaw commented dryly. "Just as soon as I got her held down and primed for plucking, she squealed out that she'd got the other half of the bill. Then, when I held back from whomping her even uglier than she is, she cut a rusty and bucked me off."

"You could've broke it off easy enough," Dusty pointed out, recollecting the incident. "All one of you had to do was make out she was licked."

"Which one?" Emma countered. "I didn't aim to and she sure as hell wouldn't."

"She's right, Ed," Belle went on. "After it'd got that far, we had to know who's boss."

"It was your fault!" the blonde hissed, glaring at Belle. "You didn't have to come to my place. I'd've come and seen you later."

"Not that it would have stopped me coming, but I still didn't know how you tied in with me," the lady outlaw answered. "How would it have looked to whoever had sent for me if I'd shown as such a fraidy-cat that I let a fat, blowsy calico queen back me down?"

"Just because you got lucky—!" the blonde spat, clenching her hands.

"Are you pair going to quit mean-mouthing each other and get down to horse-trading?" Dusty growled, sounding his most savage. "Because, happen you start hair-yanking again, I'm going to chill both of your milk *pronto,* and I won't do it gentle. I'm not missing my chance of a cut in a half-million-dollar pot because two blasted she-males don't like each other."

"Don't get riled, Ed!" Belle yelped, in well-simulated anxiety, knowing that his outburst was directed mainly at the blonde. "I'm sorry for what I said, Emma. If you'll say the same, we'll forget our quarrels."

"You're no tail-peddler," Emma apologized, and sat down on the end of the bed. "It's over as far as I'm concerned."

"Let's hope you both mean it," Dusty said, swinging his left leg over the back of the chair and settling astride its seat. "Now I like you pair fine, and it's sure pleasing to a man's ego to have you fighting over him. But there's a time and a place for it. You can snatch each other baldheaded, or bite off your apples so you're both flat-chested once this chore's over. Until then, you'll stay peaceable."

"We'll mind it, Ed," Belle promised, seeing that the blonde was taking the warning very much to heart. "Now I'd like to hear what kind of game I'm getting dealt into."

"Simmy keeps all his money, packed in flour sacks in case he has to load up and get out in a hurry, in a cellar under his office," the blonde explained. "It's got a secret, trick door that only two people know how to open."

"You're one of them?"

"No, Belle."

"Forcing Simmy to open up won't be easy," Dusty warned, thinking furiously of how he could turn the unexpected situation to his advantage. "He's one tough *hombre* no matter how he acts and talks."

"We won't have to force him," Emma corrected. "Giselle's going to open up for us."

"His *wife*?" Belle ejaculated.

"And *my* half sister," the blonde elaborated. "She doesn't like the way he uses her and she's sick to the guts of being buried alive in this godforsaken hellhole. Only she's like me, she hates going hungry. That's why we've figured this deal out."

"Why send for me?" Belle wanted to know. "There're dozens of men in and out here all the time who could have helped you."

"Do you know why I don't have a picture on my sign board?" Emma countered. "Because you can't get a painting of something that doesn't exist."

"Gracias," Dusty drawled.

"Somehow, the Lord knows how, I get the feeling I can trust you, Ed. But you hadn't come when I sent for Belle. I needed somebody with brains enough to help me set things up, and with enough knowledge to get us away after we'd pulled the robbery. I'd always heard you're a square shooter, Belle, so I got in touch with you."

"Then why make the big play for me?" Dusty asked.

"We decided we could use a few real good guns to back us up if things went wrong," Emma admitted frankly. "Giselle was set on bringing in Ben Columbo and his riffraff. I was sure relieved when you boys made wolf bait of them all, Ed. And after I'd watched you for a spell, I believed we could count on you, Matt and Comanche."

"I get a notion this's *not* going to work out as easy as it looks from the top," Belle remarked. "Way I see it, we'll need a wagon to tote away all that much money—"

"The saloon could use some supplies," Emma told her. "And Ed owns the livery barn. Its last owner left it to him in his will."

"It was Simmy's idea I should have the place," Dusty explained. "For helping him gun down its old owner and his sidekicks."

"And if I know Simmy," Emma went on, "he's already figuring out ways to get you boys killed and take it back. That's the wagon, and a reason for wanting it, fixed up, Belle."

"There's a right good way we could pull it off tomorrow, happen you girls're up to it," Dusty drawled.

"Tomor—!" Emma gasped, darting an inquiring glance at the lady outlaw.

"I'm up to it if you are, Emma," Belle declared, and the blonde nodded.

"How many of your crowd can you trust, Emma?" Dusty inquired. "I mean trust all the way. With your life, because that's what's at stake if you're wrong about any one of them."

"Hubert's the only man of 'em. Simmy hired all the others. Then there's Red, Juanita and four more of the girls. But—"

"That'll be enough, way I plan it," Dusty insisted, and went on with a comment in keeping with the character he was playing in Hell. "We don't want to have to cut the pot too many ways, now, do we?"

"If we use them," Emma announced grimly, "they're in for their share."

"Why not? It's big enough." Dusty smiled, sensing that the blonde was sincere and liking her for it.

"What's this idea of yours, Ed?" Belle inquired.

Instead of answering, the small Texan cocked his head in the direction of the window. The sounds of revelry still rolled unabated from the Honest Man Saloon.

"You sure packed them in tonight, Emma gal," Dusty finally said.

"Just about everybody in town. I've never drawn such a crowd," the blonde answered, and threw a grin at the lady outlaw. "If we wasn't figuring to be gone by night, I'd near on suggest that you and I lock horns again tomorrow, Belle."

"Now, it's funny you-all coming out and saying that," Dusty put in, and something about the way he spoke drew the girls' eyes to his face. "I was just going to say you should do it."

Silence followed the small Texan's words, lasting for several seconds as Belle and Emma digested the implication behind the soft-spoken but significant words. Involuntarily, two sets of female fingers fluttered to bruised faces. Then the girls looked at each other and Dusty could see the speculation in both sets of features.

"You mean you want us to put on another catfight to get everybody in my place watching us," Emma guessed. "Then your boys, Hubert and my girls go with Giselle, load up the wagon with Simmy's money and pull out?"

"Something like that," Dusty agreed.

"And what happens to us when he finds out the money's gone?" the blonde demanded. "He'll figure who must have taken it and how."

"I've got a way around *that*," Dusty assured her. "Time he knows about it, we'll have a good head start on him. Only the fight's not going to take place at the saloon. You're going to have it out at that hollow on the other side of town from Simmy's place."

"I think I noticed it on the way in," Belle remarked, nodding in satisfaction. "Anybody out there won't be able to see Simmy's house for the other buildings in between. You've hit it, Ed."

Emma did not join in the lady outlaw's paean of congratulation. Having been longer than Belle in Hell, the blonde knew that the hollow in question was the area set aside beyond the town limits, so that visitors could settle disagreements without endangering lives or civic property—using guns.

16
I'LL BRING 'EM BACK TAMED

Leaving his saddled *grulla* standing ground-hitched by its dangling reins, Dusty Fog looked around. With the time wanting ten minutes before four in the afternoon, almost everybody in the town had already gathered at the hollow. They were all eagerly awaiting a continuation of the events that had so excited them in the Honest Man Saloon the night before. A glance toward Hell told Dusty that he had been correct about the invisibility of the mayor's house from the hollow. If careful planning and attention to detail could command success, the small Texan hoped that his work in the town called Hell would soon be at an end.

At first, on learning where he wished the clash to take place, Emma had vehemently refused to take part in it. Even Belle had been startled on being told of the purpose to which the hollow was usually put. Patiently, Dusty had elaborated on his plan and the girls had admitted that it could work. So they had discussed it at length, amending and improving, until all had

felt sure that it stood a better than average chance of suc-
ceeding. Despite facing the prospect of another confrontation,
the girls had parted on friendly terms. So much so that Emma
had not raised a single objection to "Ed" remaining in Belle's
room for the rest of the night.

"I don't want to be a hog, Belle," the blonde had claimed
cheerfully. "And if you feel like lovemaking tonight, I'll near
on be willing to admit you're a tougher gal than me."

Not that Emma had needed to worry about such an eventu-
ality, although the reason for Belle abstaining from "lovemaking" had nothing to do with her current physical condition. As
the lady outlaw had told Dusty earlier, only one man had
shared her bed—and Mark Counter was the small Texan's
amigo. So Dusty had slept on the floor, which had been his
intention all along.

Rising somewhat earlier in the morning than had become his
habit since arriving in Hell, Dusty had left Belle and gone to
find his companions. On wakening the Kid and Juanita, he
discovered that Emma had wasted no time the previous night.

On her return to the saloon, slipping in by a rear entrance as
unnoticed as she had left, Emma had waited until the place was
closing and sent her maid to collect the Kid, Waco and the
trusted members of her staff. After satisfying herself that they
were all sober enough to understand what she was saying, she
had told them of "Ed Caxton" 's plan. Sharing Giselle's antipa-
thy toward the town, Hubert and the girls had stated their
eagerness to leave, especially as they would do so with a sizable
stake for their futures. Before they had gone to their respective
beds, they had all known the parts they would play in the
robbery. Always something of a madcap, Red had been particularly pleased with the role she was selected to play.

Leaving his *amigos* to dress, Dusty had visited the livery
barn and given orders for a wagon to be prepared. To lull any
suspicions the bleary-eyed hostlers might have felt, Dusty had
explained that the previous night's celebrations had depleted
the saloon's stocks to such an extent that there was some urgency in obtaining a fresh supply of liquor.

That had paved the way for the next stage of the operation. Returning to the hotel, Dusty had escorted Belle to lunch in the crowded dining room. Before the meal had ended, Emma stormed in. Give the girls their due, they had put on quite a performance. Screaming insults at each other, they had seemed on the verge of coming to blows. When Dusty had intervened, Belle had warned Emma that she intended to settle the matter permanently. Instantly the blonde had flung out a challenge to meet Belle at the hollow. Amid a low mutter of excited comment from the eavesdropping occupants of the room, the lady outlaw had taken up the challenge. Mockingly saying that Emma would need time to settle her affairs, Belle had suggested they meet at four o'clock. Agreeing, Emma had stalked away.

So, at ten minutes to four, the scene was set, the audience assembled and waiting for the arrival of the principal performers in the drama. Soon after lunch, the Kid had brought word that Emma had contacted Giselle and the little brunette was ready to play her part. On visiting the barn, Dusty had found the wagon provisioned for the journey, its team hitched up, but the whole staff already on their way to the hollow so as to make sure of a good view of the proceedings. When Dusty had left in the wake of the crowd, Hell had had the appearance of a ghost town.

Elbowing his way arrogantly through the crowd, Dusty found Lampart in the forefront. The small Texan now had a part to play, one which would make a tremendous difference to the success of the plan. Glancing around and seeing a couple of the Honest Man's gamblers taking bets among the crowd, he believed he knew how to handle things.

"Hey, Simmy," Dusty greeted. "Where's Giselle?"

"She's decided not to come," the mayor replied. "Had too much to drink last night and's feeling the effects."

"Sounded like you sure had a time." Dusty grinned.

"Yes," said Lampart coldly. "And all free."

"Why worry? You'll get it back and more, way they'll be drinking and talking after this. It's a pity we can't get some betting on it."

"Can't we?" Lampart asked.

"Hell. Who's going to bet against Belle in a shoot-out?"

"You're sure she'll win?"

"I'd say it's a foregone conclusion."

"I wouldn't," Lampart answered. "Emma's a damned good shot."

"You tricky ole son," Dusty drawled admiringly. "Hell, though, you've made one li'l mistake. Emma might be able to shoot, but I'm betting she can't lick Belle to the draw."

"Damn it!" the mayor ejaculated. "You're right. If—There's a way out."

"There'd best be," Dusty drawled. " 'Cause Belle's coming now."

Carrying her coat and hat, Belle walked through the crowd. She was dressed in a shirt, Levi's pants and moccasins, with her gunbelt strapped on. Behind her, ground-hitched by Dusty's *grulla,* stood her powerful bay gelding. Hooves drummed, and Emma, clothed in the same way as Belle but with a Navy Colt thrust into her waistband, rode up. Dismounting, she dropped her reins and followed the lady outlaw through the gap that had opened in the crowd.

"Hi, Ed, honey," Belle greeted, then jerked her head in the blonde's direction. "Your fat slack-puller's not backed out."

"I sure hope you got all you wanted last night, tail-peddler!" Emma replied. "Because it was your last night in this world."

"Yeah?" Belle hissed, crouching slightly and hooking her right hand over the Manhattan. "Well—"

"Ladies!" Lampart barked, and the girls looked at him. "I thought this was supposed to be a fair fight?"

Concealing his grin of elation, Dusty watched the mayor do just what the plan called for. When Belle insisted that she would not have it any other way than fair, Lampart pointed out her advantage in a draw-and-shoot affair. Then he suggested that they fight as in a formal duel.

"You'll stand back to back, each holding her gun," Lampart enlarged. "Then I'll give the word. You each step off six strides, turn and start shooting."

"That's all right with me!" Belle declared.

"Anyway'll do me just so I can get a bead on her," Emma went on.

Going into the center of the hollow, the girls stood back to back. Looking around, Dusty was satisfied that none of the crowd had eyes for anything other than Emma and Belle. Across at the other side of the circle, Waco stood between Red and a Chinese girl from the brothel. The size of the crowd caused the girl to press against his side. That too was what Dusty wanted to happen.

"If you're ready, ladies," Lampart said, from the rim of the hollow, and on receiving answers in the affirmative, continued, "Start when I reach three. One! Two!—"

Having made a circle of the town to make sure that all was clear, the Ysabel Kid returned to the livery barn. Hubert sat on the box of the wagon and, at the Kid's nod, started the team moving. By the time they had reached Lampart's house, Juanita and the other girls were already inside.

"Move it, all of you!" the Kid ordered, looking in at the rear door.

"We already have," Giselle answered, indicating the pile of bulging flour sacks on the floor. "Get them loaded while I pick the locks on the deposit boxes. There's no sense in leaving their contents behind."

"Nope." The Kid grinned, thinking of how the losses would affect the town and its citizens. "There sure ain't."

"What about the guards at the shack there, Comanche?" Hubert inquired, darting a worried glance at the adobe building and remembering the men who usually stood watch over it.

"They've gone to see the fight like everybody else," drawled the Kid. "Go help the gals. I'll make sure nobody comes around asking what we're at."

Sweating girls, unused to strenuous activity, darted to and fro, fetching and dumping sacks of money into the wagon. While they did so, Giselle put to use her ability as a lock-picker to unfasten the boxes in which various gang leaders had left

their loot for safe keeping. Working swiftly, the girls emptied
each box in turn and the brunette locked it up again. All the
time, the Kid's party were conscious of a continuous rumble of
noise reminiscent of the crowd's reaction to the previous night's
fight at the saloon.

"We've got it all," Giselle announced at last, hurrying out of
the house.

"Don't forget that key," warned the Kid.

"I won't," the brunette replied. She closed the door and left
the key on the outside but did not lock it. "I've left a note
telling Simmy that I'll be down at the saloon until dinnertime."

"Will he figure anything suspicious about that?" the Kid
demanded, watching the girls boarding the wagon. "You and
Emma never acted friendly."

"It's all right," Giselle insisted. "Before Simmy left for the
hollow, I told him that I meant to take over the saloon if Emma
was killed. He'll think that's what I'm doing."

"It'll maybe buy us some more time, then," drawled the Kid.
"Get aboard, ma'am, so's we can be going."

With all the women in the rear of the wagon and its canopy's
flaps closed, the Kid leapt astride his roan. Hubert set the team
into motion, swinging them away from the street. As they
reached the top of the slope, the Kid looked back to make sure
they had not been observed and followed.

"Three!" Lampart finished and the crowd waited in silent
expectation.

Instead of stepping straight off, Belle addressed Emma over
her shoulder. Her words carried to the spectators' ears.

"Hey, slack-puller. You're lucky I'm going to kill you. After
last night, Ed wouldn't waste his time bedding with a fat old
whore like you."

Letting out a shrill shriek of what sounded like genuine rage,
Emma hurled her revolver aside. She twirled around, left hand
shooting forward to catch hold of Belle's right shoulder. With a
jerk, the blonde swung the lady outlaw to face her and delivered a slap with the other hand. There was no faking with the

blow. It impacted on Belle's cheek, sending her reeling and, in part, causing her to drop the Manhattan.

Landing on one knee, Belle saw Emma rushing at her. With a yell, the lady outlaw plunged upward, diving to tackle the blonde about the waist. Down they went, rolling and thrashing on the ground in a brawl every bit as wild as the one they had put up the previous night.

Although the crowd had come to witness a gunfight, none of them raised objections at the way things had turned out. Prudence and caution had caused them to stay on the edge of the hollow when lead might start flying. Once Belle and Emma discarded their firearms and resumed the kind of fighting that had entertained the onlookers at the Honest Man, the crowd began to move forward. Throwing a grin at Red, Waco contrived to keep the Chinese prostitute at his other side.

Walking to the waiting horses, Dusty watched the people moving down into the hollow. Lampart was going with them. Despite his gamblers having money wagered on the result, he could not resist the temptation to sample once more the erotic delight of watching two beautiful women embroiled in primitive conflict. Everything was still going as the small Texan had planned.

Dusty had realized from the beginning that a gunfight, even if its result could be faked, would not last for long enough to let the robbery be carried out and the wagon disappear over the rim of the crater. So he had told the two girls how to act. Belle's reference to Emma as a slack-puller—which, like tail-peddler, meant a whore of the cheapest variety—and comment about the previous night had been sufficient to bring the blonde's reaction without arousing the spectators' suspicions.

"Come on, Lon!" Dusty thought. "Get things moving!"

If the Kid and his party had set to work as soon as possible, they ought to be coming into view soon. The longer the delay, the greater chance of something going wrong. Lampart might become aware of the ammunition guards' presence in the crowd and order them to return to their post.

There was the wagon now!

Good for Lon and Hubert. They had remembered their orders and hidden the girls in the back of the wagon. Trust Lon to restrain any urge the bartender might show toward making the team go faster. If anybody should happen to see the wagon ascending the slope, there was nothing about it to hint at a hurried, illicit departure. However, the leisurely pace also had its disadvantages.

While Belle and Emma were aware that they must keep their fight going for long enough to let the wagon's party escape undetected, things could go wrong. In the heat and excitement of the tangle, tempers might easily be lost and one or the other knock her opponent unconscious. So far, from all Dusty could see and hear, they were carrying out their assignment in a satisfactory manner.

At last, after what seemed a far longer period than it had actually taken, the wagon disappeared among the trees. With a long exhalation of relief, Dusty hung Belle's jacket and hat—handed into his keeping by the lady outlaw before going out to take up the dueling position—on her saddle. Vaulting afork his *grulla,* he gathered up the other horses' reins and set the three animals into motion. Riding onto the slope, he caused a hurried scattering of spectators anxious to avoid being ridden down. On reaching the front of the crowd, he saw that he had not come too soon.

With fingers interlaced in matted, sodden, disheveled hair, Belle and Emma knelt clinging weakly to each other. Their shirts had gone and they looked to be close to collapsing through sheer exhaustion. Leaping from his saddle, Dusty stalked forward. Silence fell over the crowd as they watched and wondered what the small Texan planned to do. Reaching the girls, he bent and gripped their back hair in his hands. Drawing the heads apart, he snapped them together with a hard, crisp click.

"What the hell?" Lampart barked as Dusty released the girls' hair and they crumpled in a heap at his feet.

"If these two bitches wanted to shoot it out, it was fine with me," Dusty replied, bending again and lifting Belle from

Emma. Holding the lady outlaw in his arms, he continued his explanation while walking toward the horses. "That way, I'd've been shut of one or the other. I'll be damned if I'm going to have them keep cat-clawing each other over me. Neither's fit to bed with when she's through fighting."

"But what are you planning to do with them?" Lampart insisted, watching Dusty heave Belle belly-down across her saddle.

"I'm going to take 'em off aways, just me and them," Dusty explained and went to collect Emma. With the blonde draped limply over her horse's back, he went on. "Comes night, I'll bring 'em back tamed."

"But—But—!" Lampart spluttered, wondering how he could turn the small Texan's actions to his own advantage.

Slowly Dusty walked over and retrieved Belle's Manhattan. A low mutter rose from the crowd, querulous in its timbre if not out-and-out hostile. Straightening up, he stuck the revolver into his waistband. Hooking his thumbs into the gunbelt, he swung around and left a descent of silence where his eyes had passed over.

"Anybody who objects can step right out and say so," Dusty declared. "Only he'd best come to do it with a gun in his hand."

There was no reply. Everybody present knew "Ed Caxton" as the feller who had simultaneously outdrawn two of the fastest gunhands Hell had ever seen, then made wolf bait of a slew of other bad *hombres* who had crossed his trail. If any member of the crowd should accept the challenge, that man would die almost as soon as he mentioned his intentions. In every male mind—except possibly Lampart's—lurked the same summation. They had seen a mighty enjoyable catfight. One which, way the contestants had been looking during the last few seconds, would have tamely ended in a draw through them both fainting from exhaustion.

So why get killed over it having been stopped?

"Ed Caxton" sounded like he aimed to keep both girls around. One thing was for sure if he did, they would be unlikely to grow friendlier. So, for all his proposed "taming," there was always the chance that they would lock horns again. In which case, the wisest thing for every man present to do was let that big Texan tote them off, stay alive himself and wait to see what the future held.

Seeing that he had made his point, Dusty mounted his *grulla*. He rode up the slope, leading the two horses and their inert burdens. Lampart watched him go, thinking fast.

"Didn't some of you fellers have money bet on who won?" the mayor inquired as Dusty rode over the edge of the top of the hollow.

At the words, Waco gave Red a nudge with his hip to warn her that she must play her part. Excitement glinted in her eyes. Springing by the youngster, she confronted the Chinese girl.

"You quit a-pawing my feller, you slit-eyed whore!" Red shrieked.

"What you speak, round-eye calico?" the Chinese girl spat back, for there was no love lost between the prostitutes and Emma's employees.

"I'll show you what I speak!" Red promised, conscious of being watched by both factions.

Ducking her head, Red leapt at and butted the Oriental in the chest. Reeling backwards, the girl sat down. Another of the brothel's contingent made as if to attack Red. That did it. Already brought to a pitch of wild excitement by the fight between Belle and Emma, the two factions needed no more urging. Squeals and yells rose, then that section of the crowd exploded into a multiple tangle of hair-pulling, fist-swinging, screeching females.

"You started th—!" the brothel's bouncer began, moving toward Waco.

Before the words ended, the blond youngster's fist took the man under the jaw and knocked him from his feet. Like the ripples spread by throwing a stone into a pond, the fight developed until it engulfed every member of the crowd. Even Goldberg's plump, pompous wife joined in, mixing it as gamely as any saloon girl with her husband's partner's younger, prettier spouse.

A good ten minutes went by before Waco found himself close to Red. In that period, the fight had become general and a matter of attacking the nearest person of the same sex. Red sat astride Mrs. Goldberg and the jeweler's wife, pounding indiscriminately at both while they continued to settle old scores. Grabbing the girl by the hair, Waco hauled her bodily clear of the mêlée. When she tried to turn on him, he first slapped, then shook her into a more pacific frame of mind.

"That's better," Waco growled, carrying her up the slope. "I'll take you back to the saloon and you can get into something you can travel in."

"Wh—When do we g-go?" Red gasped, brushing away her tears.

"After I've done a li'l job for Du—Ed," Waco replied.

Fortunately, Red's exertions had left her in no state to think clearly. So she did not notice the blond youngster's mistake. Clinging to him, she pressed her bruised, scratched face against his shoulder.

"What's the li'l job?" the girl asked. "Is it important?"

"Enough," Waco answered.

The blond did not explain how if he succeeded in his "li'l job" he would most likely save the lives of many people—or that the penalty for failure was even more likely to be death.

17
MISS NENE, MEET CAPTAIN DUSTY FOG

"Howdy, Simmy," Waco greeted, strolling along the sidewalk to where the mayor was unlocking his front door in a decidedly furtive manner.

Lampart looked anything but his usual, neat, immaculate self. Unable to slip away before the general brawl had entrapped him, he had been compelled to fight back until he had dropped to the ground and feigned unconsciousness. By the time he had finally escaped, leaving the battle still raging, he had lost his hat, jacket and cravat. His torn shirt looked as if it had been walked on—and had. It had been his hope to reach his home without anybody seeing him, for he knew there would be those who wanted to know why he had done nothing to end the conflict. Although the street was clear, that blasted blond youngster had come through the alley and surprised him.

"How did you get here?" the mayor demanded ungraciously.

"Same's you. I got out soon's I could."

"So it seems," Lampart growled, glaring at Waco's unmarked features and all too aware of his own injuries. "What do you want?"

"Some money out of our box."

"Can't it wait?"

"Sure. Happen you don't mind the chance of the saloon getting damaged."

"Huh?" grunted the mayor.

"I sure's hell don't aim to stay away from it," Waco explained. "And there could be them's reckons Red 'n' me's to blame for that ruckus at the hollow. So I conclude buying drinks good 'n' regular ought to change their minds. Talked to your lady down there, and she claims I've got a right smart notion."

"My wife's at the saloon?"

"Why sure. Taking on like she owns it."

That figured to anybody who knew Giselle, the mayor mused. From what she had been saying when she had heard about the gunfight, his wife had expected her half sister to be killed. So she had not waited to hear the result before going to assert her control of the saloon. One thing was for sure. No matter who ran the Honest Man, its profits—and losses—descended on Lampart. What young "Caxton" said was true, too. After a night without a drink being sold—although many were consumed—due to that blond bitch's boastful stupidity, Lampart had no desire to incur further losses.

"Come in and get what you need," the mayor ordered, wanting to get off the street as quickly as he could.

With which sentiment Waco heartily concurred. Nobody had seen him meet the mayor. Even Red was unaware that he had, having gone to her room to change ready for their departure. That made the blond youngster's task just that much safer.

"I allus got the notion Ma Goldberg and that fancy young wife of the jeweler's didn't cotton to each other," Waco commented cheerily as Lampart took him inside and locked the front door. "They sure was whomping each other all ways when I lit out."

"She always blamed Melissa for Goldberg getting caught

out," the mayor answered, opening up his office. "I should have one of the Regulators here—"

"You've got one," Waco pointed out. "Me. You made me one after we'd got rid of ole Basmanov's bunch for you."

"Of course," Lampart grunted and waved his hand toward the boxes. "Help yourself."

"Gracias," the youngster drawled, walking by the desk. Scooping the Colt from it, he turned and threw down on the mayor. "Only I've changed my mind."

"You've done what?" Lampart spat, staring at the Peacemaker as it lined on his chest.

"Changed my mind," Waco repeated, thumb-cocking the revolver. "So, if you'll open up that drawer with the 'magnetic' battery in it, I'll touch off your ammunition supply and head for home."

"Home? With a price on your head!"

"Shuckens, that's not worrying me one li'l bit."

"Do you reckon that the Army will forget what you've done just because you've got rid of my ammunition?" Lampart sneered.

"Just what have I done?" Waco countered.

"Helped to kill a colonel, sergeant and six men," the mayor reminded him.

"You shouldn't believe all you read in the newspapers, Mr. Mayor," the blond youngster drawled. "Those fellers're no closer to heaven—or hell, I'd say in Paddy Magoon's case— than down to the OD Connected."

"The—?" Lampart gulped.

"The OD Connected. That's our spread. Me, the Ysabel Kid —and Dusty Fog's."

"Dusty Fog?" croaked Lampart.

"Yes, sir, Mr. Mayor," Waco confirmed. "My 'Brother' Ed's Dusty Fog. Now open that drawer, or I'll do it myself."

"Can you?" Lampart challenged.

"I can give it a whirl. This room's pretty thick-walled. I could burst the desk open without making enough noise to be heard outside of 'em."

"You've a point," Lampart admitted sullenly, hanging his head in dejected fashion. He walked around and sat behind his desk. Without looking at Waco, he opened the required drawer with his left hand. "Here you are."

For all his beaten aspect, Lampart was grinning inwardly. In addition to having been a successful stage illusionist, he was also a skilled maker of magical tricks and gadgets. Being aware of the type of people with whom he would be dealing, he had put his inventive genius to work in Hell. Not only had he fitted a secret door to the cellar which held his wealth, but he had equipped the desk with a protective mechanism. The latter had already proved its worth.

On their last night alive, Glover and Eel had not meant to return to Hell. So their use as a future source of revenue had ended. They had not attempted to draw their guns until he had shouted the unnecessary warning—and by that time it was too late. In fact, he had even been compelled to pull out Eel's weapon to make his story ring true. Fortunately, Cowper had been close enough to the building to hear the shots. Rushing in to investigate, holding his gun, naturally, he had died at "Ed Caxton" 's hand.

Except that the *big* Texan was not "Ed Caxton," if the blond youngster was telling the truth. He was Dusty Fog and he had come with his two companions to destroy Hell.

Which raised the question of why Fog had sent the young blond to handle the dangerous task of blowing up the *Kweharehnuh*'s reserve ammunition supply.

Most likely the blond had asked to do so, as a means of winning acclaim and, probably, higher financial rewards. Judging the Rio Hondo gun wizard by his own standards, Lampart decided that Dusty Fog would be only too pleased to let another man take the risk. Whatever had happened, the blond was going to pay for the rash, impetuous offer with his life.

Still keeping his head bowed, so that no hint of his true feelings would flash a warning to his victim, Lampart rubbed his left foot against the inner support leg of his desk. A click sounded and a section of the desk's top hinged up close to his left hand. Out of the hole exposed by the section rose a block of wood. On top of the block rested the ivory-handled Webley Bulldog that had taken Basmanov's, Glover's and Eel's lives. Scooping up the weapon, he lifted his eyes to Waco's face and a mocking smile twisted at his lips.

Ever since organizing the escape of so many badly wanted criminals, Lampart had felt a growing sense of his own brilliance. He had brought Hell into being, arranging for it to become the lucrative proposition that it now was. With each achievement, he had grown more certain that no lesser man could equal his superlative genius, or defeat him in a match of wits.

Fog and his companions might think they were clever, but Lampart would teach them differently. There was no need for haste, not even in dealing with that impetuous young fool who stood before him. He wanted to see the other's expression on pulling the Peacemaker's trigger when only a dull, dry click rewarded the gesture. The appearance of the Bulldog would have been a severe shock, but the failure of the Colt would be even worse.

So Lampart moved in an almost leisurely manner—and paid the penalty.

Instead of trying to fire the useless Peacemaker, Waco had drawn his left-hand Army Colt as soon as the section of the desk began to move. Flame ripped from the eight-inch barrel as the Webley was lifted from its resting place. Hit in the head, Lampart slammed back. Tipping over under his weight, the chair deposited him on the floor. The Webley slid unfired from his lifeless left hand.

"Dusty was right," the youngster breathed, placing the Peacemaker on the desk and darting to the window that overlooked the street. "Knowing about that old plough handle did help to save my life."

Even before Dusty had touched the revolver and found it was too cold to have been fired, he had suspected that some other weapon was responsible for Glover's and Eel's deaths. The shots had been fired too quickly for a single action even being fanned. Which meant that the mayor had another firearm. It was not on his person, so it must have been concealed in the desk. Confirmation for the suspicion had come from the examination of the bodies. If Glover had been pointing his revolver at Lampart, his forefinger would have been in the triggerguard. A man with the outlaw's experience, however, would have known better than to place his finger on the trigger until the barrel had left the holster and was pointing away from him.[1]

Having heard Dusty's warning, Waco had turned his own thoughts to the matter and come up with further conclusions. One clue had come from Dusty's description of Lampart's ambidextrous card manipulation. Considering that, the youngster had decided the mayor had used his left hand when firing the hideaway gun. The cocked Peacemaker would be there to distract his victim. Carried a stage further, Waco had decided it was unlikely that the Colt would fire. It would be too easily available to an enemy—as his own actions had proved—for a *hombre* as smart and tricky as the mayor to chance having it capable of being turned on him with live ammunition in the cylinders.

So Waco had never intended trying to defend himself with the borrowed Colt. Instead, he had gambled on his own ambidextrous ability and had won.

Looking along the street, the youngster decided that the shot had not been heard. He returned his Colt to its holster as he went to the desk. Taking hold of Lampart's body, he dragged it to a corner so that it could not be seen from either window. With that done, he went to examine the contents of the open drawer. A sigh of relief burst unbidden from his lips. The "magnetic" battery was there, coupled up and ready for operation. It was one of the portable variety designed to supply an electric current for use with a mobile telegraph station. Bent had one just like it at his place in the Indian Nations, and ever

1. Why is told in *The Fast Gun*.

curious about unusual things, Waco had learned how it was worked.

On Waco throwing the activating switch, there was a deep roaring bellow from behind the house. The adobe shack disintegrated in a sheet of flame and billowing black smoke. Even in the mayor's office, Waco could feel the blast and concussion of the explosion shake the house. Glass shattered as windows broke and he heard shouts of alarm rising. Darting from the office, he locked its door and pocketed the key. Then he sprinted through the living quarters. Giselle had followed Dusty's orders to the letter—trust ole Lon to see to that. Going out he found the key in place in the rear door. He turned, removed and pocketed it. Then, as the first of the people attracted by the commotion appeared, he began to shake at the door.

"What happened, Matt?" demanded an outlaw whose face carried marks from the battle at the hollow.

"I'm damned if I know," the youngster replied. "That blasted bullet-shack just son-of-a-bitching went up."

"Where's Lampart?" the jeweler demanded, looking around. "I've warned him that this might happen, keeping that blasted fuse wired up."

"Door's locked," Waco replied. "Somebody'd best go around the front."

Men dashed to do so, returning with the news—which did not surprise Waco—that there was no sign of the mayor or his wife.

"I'll tell you one thing," Waco yelled. "I'm not waiting around to find out where he is. When the *Kweharehnuh* hear there's no bullets coming to 'em, they're going to get mean. Comes that happening, I figure to be long gone."

With that, he pushed through the crowd and headed for the livery barn. Red was waiting, dressed in Levi's pants, a blouse and dainty hat.

"What hap—?" the girl began.

"Don't talk, mount up and ride," Waco interrupted, indicating the horses that stood saddled and ready. "We've got some miles to cover afore we catch up with the others."

Three days later, the united party made camp a few miles north of the Swisher Creek's junction with the Prairie Dog Fork of the Red River. They had come that far without difficulty, other than that suffered by Belle and Emma. Although each claimed that she had held herself in check all through the second fight, both now had two blackened eyes and so many additional bruises that they could not ride their horses.

On being questioned about the explosion, Waco had told the truth without revealing his companions' true identity. He had said that he considered his actions were for the best. Destroying the ammunition would cause even the outlaws whose boxes had been looted to be more concerned with fleeing from the Palo Duro than in pursuing their party. Giselle had taken the news of her widowhood calmly, declaring that she was relieved to know that she need never worry about Simmy tracking her down.

Waco's summation had proved correct, for nobody had come after them. They had seen one group of *Kweharehnuh* warriors, who had ridden by without stopping. Indicating a distant column of smoke, the Kid had guessed that it rose from the Antelopes' village and was calling the various parties of braves in for a conference about the destruction of their ammunition.

A couple of the town's guides had approached the party. On hearing what had happened in Hell and discovering that their presence was unwelcome, they had ridden away. When last seen, they had been heading east as fast as their horses would carry them.

After supper, while Waco was hoorawing the Kid for having forgotten the excuse which it had been arranged that Giselle would use to prevent her husband suspecting she had left town, Dusty asked Belle and Emma to join him for a stroll. They were in safe country at last and the time had come for certain matters to be settled. Once out of earshot of the others, the blonde raised the very subject that Dusty had meant to introduce.

"When do we share out the loot, Ed?" Emma asked.

"That's what I asked you both out here to talk about," Dusty admitted.

"What's to talk about?" Emma demanded. "We just sit around the fire and go 'one for you,' 'one for you,' 'one for you' until it's all split up even."

"Not quite," Dusty objected. "You stop going 'one for you' when you, Belle and Giselle have fifty thousand apiece and the girls and Hubert have ten thousand each."

"There's well over half a million in the pot, Ed," Emma said coldly. "I'd say you and your boys're taking a kind of selfish split."

"Not when you consider we've got to share it with all the banks it came from," Dusty countered.

"B-banks—" Emma spluttered and swung to the lady outlaw. "Do you know what the hell he's talking about?"

"Yes," Belle replied. "I think I do. He's giving us a reward for helping him finish off a chore."

"Now I don't know what the hell *you*'re talking about," Emma groaned. "Unless you're in cahoots—"

"You might say we are." Belle smiled. "And before you start something we'll both of us regret, I reckon I should introduce you to this feller you've been fighting me for."

"Intro—!" Emma yelped. "I know who he i—"

"Miss Nene, meet Captain Dusty Fog," Belle interrupted.

"Is—" the blonde finished, then her mouth trailed open and she stared at the *big* Texan. "D-did she say *Dusty Fog*?"

"That's what she said," Dusty confirmed.

"Then you're not Ed—you've been using me!"

"No more than you were willing to use me," Dusty pointed out, studying the play of emotions on the blonde's face. "I was sent by the governor to close Hell down, and with you folks' help, I've done it. Now this's my deal. You-all take the cut I've just offered and go with Belle. She'll see you safe through the Indian Nations to Kansas. And you've got my word that I'll not say a thing about you being part of the town."

"It's a good offer, Emma," Belle remarked. "And seeing that we've no other choice, I reckon we'd best take it."

"You're not Ed Caxton!" the blonde breathed, eyes fixed on Dusty and showing no sign that she had heard the lady outlaw. "You're—I've slept with Dusty Fog!"

"Stop your bragging just because you've done something I haven't," Belle suggested with a smile.

"You mean that you and E—D—nothing happened last night?" Emma gasped, showing she had heard Belle's last comment.

"Dusty slept on the floor like a perfect gentleman," Belle declared. "How about it, Emma, do we take Dusty's offer? If not, I took a lot of lumps for nothing."

"I reckon fifty thousand dollars ought to make up for them," Emma replied. "You're calling the play, E—D—Captain Fog."

ARIADNE PAPPA ... ...ent
of Gree...

THE SUSPECTS

WIN RANDOLPH, star professor
GILLIAN RANDOLPH, Win's wildly jealous wife
BENNIE THOMPSON, night watchman with
a secret crush
ARIADNE'S FAMILY, strangely unconcerned
about her disappearance

THE SLEUTH

ANTONIA NIELSEN, adapting her academic
research techniques to the real world of detection

The
ARIADNE
CLUE

One of the most spellbinding
mystery thrillers of the year.

The
ARIADNE
CLUE

CAROL CLEMEAU

BALLANTINE BOOKS • NEW YORK

To my Father and Mother

Library of Congress Catalog Card Number: 82-10359

ISBN 0-345-30736-4

This edition published by arrangement with Charles Scribner's Sons

Manufactured in the United States of America

First Ballantine Books Edition: October 1983

Contents

In Greek legend, the Cretan king Minos offended the god of the sea by refusing to sacrifice to him a beautiful white bull. In revenge the god caused Minos' queen, Pasiphaë, to fall in love with the bull and conceive by it a monstrous offspring called the Minotaur. The half-human creature was imprisoned in a maze called the Labyrinth, where it fed upon youths and maidens that Minos forced his subject city Athens to supply.

The Athenian prince Theseus appeared one day at Minos' palace and quickly won the heart of the king's elder daughter, Ariadne. The princess gave him a ball of thread, or clew, which he was to tie to the doorpost of the Labyrinth when he entered and unwind behind him as he went in search of the Minotaur in its depths. After slaying the monster, he could retrace his steps to the entrance with the help of the thread.

The scheme worked: the hero emerged victorious from the Labyrinth, carried off the princess who had saved his life and enhanced his reputation, and sailed away into the Aegean sunset. Unfortunately, however, he abandoned Ariadne halfway back to Athens; the legend says he "forgot" her.

Although Ariadne's fate after Theseus left her is variously described, all versions agree that her younger sister, Phaedra, later married the ungrateful prince, to his bitter sorrow. But that is another story.

1. Now that April's Here

WHY HAD SHE SAID NO?

She stared unseeing at the manicured expanses of green—a green, at this time of year, so implausible as to suggest Astroturf rather than living grass—and saw instead the lush greens of the Mesara in April, green of lemon and orange groves and wild grasses starred with white flowers.

Why *had* she said no?

She heard the slap of her own sandals on the poured-concrete walkways that crisscrossed the campus and remembered the smell of hot stone above Kato Zakro. Living too, that stone—alive with the pungency of thyme and the upbeating heat of a Cretan summer.

She stopped abstractedly at one of the chrome and fiberglass kiosks that announced "Coming Events of Interest to the University Community." The poster for the Aegean Gold exhibition was simple but effective: the famous Mask of Agamemnon on a black ground, and below it in simple black letters on a wide band of gold, the words AEGEAN GOLD. *University Museum, April 15–June 3*. That was all, but such was the genius of the nameless Mycenaean artist that no more was needed to compel the attention of the passerby. Golden eyelids closed in death, lean golden aristocratic nose, thin severe lips of gold—perhaps,

1

thought Antonia, it was the tension between the austerity of that ancient face and the barbaric splendor of the material that gave the thing such power.

Reluctantly, Antonia tore her attention away from the poster and looked around as if to remind herself where she was.

She was a couple of hundred yards from her destination, the Humanities Building. She was surrounded by the artificially gentled slopes of an urban university campus on the East Coast, by clouds of dogwood and great spraying fountains of forsythia, by carpets of crocus and violets. The temperature, quite remarkably for early April, was already well into the seventies even though it was only eight-thirty.

Perhaps it wasn't too late even now to say yes.

It was almost two months since the girl had invited Antonia to spend the summer with her in Crete, among her uncountable uncles and cousins and great-aunts. The invitation was awkward and abrupt, as lacking in social grace as Ariadne herself and as fiercely sincere.

"I thought," the girl said gruffly, "we could hike around from village to village—they're scattered all over the island, my people. Can't afford anything else, and they wouldn't mind putting you up too. If you're interested."

Antonia had hesitated, searching for words that would express both the firm refusal that was necessary and warm appreciation, words that would be something more than polite clichés. Ariadne was not a person to be dismissed with a cliché.

But as Antonia groped for the right phrase, the girl spoke again. "Phaistos," she said, "and Ayia Triadha. Gournia. Zakro." Her voice, no longer gruff with shyness, caressed the harsh old names as if they were the names of lovers. Yet Antonia knew Ariadne had never seen the palaces and shops and country houses of Minoan Crete, except in her imagination and in books.

"And Knossos, of course." Here the young voice had seemed to falter momentarily, but it grew strong and resonant again as she concluded, "It might be kind of a *different* way of seeing the island, for you I mean. For me it's the *only* way—the only way I can afford."

Antonia had declined, of course. The litany of ancient

Minoan sites kindled her imagination almost as much as it did Ariadne's. The prospect of spending the summer in a series of Greek farmhouses, far from putting her off, as the girl seemed to fear, was a powerful inducement. Even the prospect of tramping the baked hillsides and subtropical plains of Crete in July didn't deter her. She had done it once, as a graduate student, and she could do it again.

She had declined, quite simply, because she didn't believe in close teacher-student friendships, neither in their desirability nor even in their possibility.

But now—two months later and less than three weeks from the end of the spring semester—she was less certain.

In those two months, her odd relationship with the Greek girl had changed subtly. The distance that Antonia had always maintained between herself and her students remained. Neither called the other by her first name; they never saw each other except in Antonia's office. Their talk was exclusively of what Antonia's colleagues would have called "professional matters."

Yet their conversations, Antonia thought wryly, would hardly have passed muster as "professional" in some quarters. They had never so much as alluded to the academic job market, the latest issue of the *American Journal of Philology*, or the contacts they had made or failed to make at last December's American Philological Association convention. Oddest of all, they had never once talked about Ariadne's dissertation. The girl herself never brought the matter up, and Antonia steered clear of it, thinking that perhaps it was taboo, graduate students being notoriously touchy on the subject of half-finished doctoral theses.

But they had discussed the tangled question of Euripides' attitude toward women, the curious mixture of sympathy and horror with which he portrays his terrible heroines. Once Ariadne had put forth a strikingly original interpretation of the *Iliad* that had so impressed Antonia that she urged her to think seriously about working it up and publishing. Astoundingly, Ariadne had only shrugged. Once they had talked of Michael Ventris' decipherment of the Mycenaean-Minoan syllabary in the fifties, and of the electrifying moment when the young Englishman announced to the world of scholarship, "The language is Greek!" Characteristically, Ariadne's dark eyes had shone with excitement as she repeated in a whisper, " *'The lan-*

guage is Greek!' Those were my people, Miss Nielsen,
and until Ventris we weren't even sure they were Greek!"
You might have thought someone had accused her ancestors of having tails or being ignorant of fire and language.

Yes, passionate intensity and a profoundly personal involvement with her subject were very definitely Ariadne's
mode. No doubt the approach had its limitations. It
wouldn't always be easy for her to maintain either tolerance or the scholarly "objectivity" so dear to the academic
heart. But by God she was refreshing after the cold-blood-
ed careerists and intellectual file clerks who littered the
groves of academe nowadays.

From these few conversations with Ariadne, conversations unrelieved by anything so social as even a cup of
coffee, Antonia had had more "intellectual stimulation"
(as her colleagues would, without enthusiasm, have called
it) than from five years of desultory chatting around the
coffee urn in the faculty lounge.

An unconventional relationship. And yet it was on
grounds of convention, of what was not or should not be
done, that she had rejected the girl's invitation. Was she
perhaps becoming as careful, as conventional, as fearful
of even the pettiest risks as her colleagues, as her students,
for that matter? And what on earth would she be risking
anyway? Convention no longer militated against student-
faculty relationships of any kind at all, let alone one as
devoid of sexual overtones as hers and Ariadne's. No, the
barrier was strictly of her own erecting, based on a vague
feeling that there would be less trouble, less friction, less
confusion of roles if she kept her distance from her students, all her students.

But now, as she looked around her once more at the
neat, artfully landscaped campus, Antonia was struck by
its resemblance to the lives of its denizens. Attractive,
intelligently planned, without violent contrasts of incon-
sistencies, it was a landscape in which change was permitted only in the form of long gentle dips and rises duly
graded and turfed and mowed, a landscape without crags
and without chasms.

She thought again of the summer five years ago when
she had hiked through Crete, of the eye-searing glare of
whitewashed walls against cerulean sea, the rugged lime-
stone gorges and precipices of the south, the crushing heat

of the wind that comes in from Libya. Violent, unmodulated, uncompromising country—and suddenly she felt all the pettiness and timidity of her refusal to go there with Ariadne.

Moreover, there were no emotional encumbrances at the moment. There had been a man, but both he and the brief regret that lingered after him were gone now, leaving behind only the pleasant sense that she was absolutely free to do as she liked—to go to Crete with Ariadne, for instance.

It was what she wanted, it was what she would do, and she would tell Ariadne at twelve-thirty.

Spring fever, with Antonia, often took the form of wanderlust. She had never been really comfortable with the enforced immobility of the academic year, short though it was. But her restlessness always became particularly acute at just about this point in second semester: three more weeks of classes, exams and grading for another two weeks after that, and through it all morale—hers and everyone else's—at low ebb.

But now that something had been decided, now that there was a definite terminus to her presence on campus—what had Ariadne said? May twentieth, something like that—the flowery blandness of the place didn't seem nearly so depressing.

Not only were leaves and grass showing signs of awakening; even the students seemed to have taken a new lease on life, at least temporarily, until exams began and term papers fell due. Young shoulders were held a little straighter under the green khaki straps of book bags, and there was a jaunty swing to the long coltish legs instead of the despairing trudge of recent months. Frisbees, as well as birdsong, were in the air: one of them sliced across Antonia's path just east of Everett Hall, narrowly missing her nose. A few hours hence, if the thermometer continued its present trend, large numbers of luscious young bodies would be draped in various degrees of near nudity over every available square yard of grass on campus.

The one incongruous element in this idyllic scene was the media people. Even before the warm spell, Antonia had noticed an occasional photographer lugging equipment up the steps of the museum or crouching in odd corners to get dramatic angle shots of its façade. But now, only eight days before the much-publicized opening of the Aegean Gold exhibition, the photographers were everywhere. One of them, a shaggy youth in jeans, waylaid Antonia herself as she rounded the corner of the Humanities Building. She was passing between him and an Aegean Gold poster tacked to the trunk of a maple tree, and his idea seemed to be to catch the poster, the tree's bark, Antonia's emerald-green dress, and a chunk of abnormally blue sky in a single offbeat composition. This she deduced from the fact that he was lying on the grass, awkwardly supported on his left hip and elbow, squinting up at her through his lens. She obliged by gazing for a moment at the poster with what she hoped was the proper professional intentness, then flashed him a thoroughly unprofessorial grin and continued on her way.

"Dynamite shot, Miss!" he called after her. "Thanks a lot!" Antonia waved back at him without turning around.

As she started up the steps of the Humanities Building, a stocky figure erupted from the main entrance and plunged down the steps, almost colliding with her. It was Tommy Wakowski, one of the Classics graduate students, and he was probably due at a class on the opposite side of campus in three minutes. He usually was.

"Oh, hi, Miss Nielsen," he panted. "Sorry if I—say, do you happen to know where I could find Ariadne? I need to borrow her Teubner Bacchylides."

"Sorry, Tommy, I don't know where she is right now. She has an appointment with me at twelve-thirty, though. I'll tell her you're looking for her."

"Thanks, Miss Nielsen. She sure is hard to find sometimes, Ariadne. Well, see ya." And he resumed his headlong flight across campus, careening off several fellow students who had the poor judgment to cross his path.

Antonia entered the building. The atmosphere was already stuffy; by noon it would be intolerable, especially in the tiny airless faculty offices. She headed toward hers with the pleasant sense that she was within two classes and one appointment of a spring weekend. Let Buildings and Grounds do their worst: Professor Nielsen would be sunbathing on her balcony this afternoon, thank you, sublimely indifferent to the temperature inside the Humanities Building.

And after that, a shopping expedition for something to wear to the Aegean Gold opening. Something long and fluid and white to set off the new tan that by then should be coming along nicely.

And after *that,* the Randolphs' dinner party. There would be Gillian, of course. But there was no point in speculating about the potential for trouble from that quarter. One dealt with Gillian when and as necessary, not according to some premeditated strategy that would almost certainly turn out to be irrelevant or worse. Forget her, in short, until the time came.

That still left all of Saturday and most of Sunday to work on the article she had hoped to send off to *The Classical Journal* no later than January. The demands of her job had, as usual, made it nearly impossible to find time for writing. But slowly the pages had accumulated, and now the work was tantalizingly close to completion. What remained to do was mostly fun, and she was looking forward to it.

She would talk to Ariadne after her last class, tell her she wanted to go to Crete with her after all. They would spend a delightful half hour making plans for the trip, maybe even call the travel agency and get it started on Antonia's tickets.

All in all a full, well-balanced, thoroughly satisfying weekend.

It would be two hours, almost to the minute, before it all began to fall apart.

2. The Boots of Miss Lilly

Her nine and ten o'clock classes—the end of Antonia's teaching week—prolonged her sense that life was flowing along pretty much as usual. In Greek Drama in Translation she lectured on the discovery of the *Dyskolos* papyrus in 1957. Her students, predictably, were excited by the resurrection of a comedy two thousand years old and bored by the play's text. Her advanced Greek class, equally predictably, was sluggish. It is difficult at the best of times to get emotionally involved with the aorist subjunctive, nor is Thucydides commonly an undergraduate's favorite author. And when to the difficulties of morphology, syntax, and content are added the enticements of a gorgeous spring day, the first of the year—suffice it to say that Greek 406 that Friday morning was not one of Antonia's most memorable pedagogical experiences.

It was therefore with a business-as-usual sort of feeling, neither especially high nor especially low, that Antonia headed for the lounge after her last class.

The faculty lounge on the second floor of the Humanities Building, at 10:55 on a Friday morning, was always well patronized. Professors who still had one or more classes to teach would stop to refill their coffee mugs on their way to eleven o'clocks, while those who were through for the day were beginning to drift in to confirm their sense that the weekend had indeed arrived at last.

On this particular Friday, however, the lounge was doing an unusually brisk business. Small clusters of professors and teaching assistants spilled out into the hall, some waiting to get in and some, steaming mugs in hand, moving unhurriedly on an outward-bound course. The crowd was denser, the conversation noticeably less desultory than usual, though it was some time before Antonia was able to make out the cause of the excitement.

The only concrete indication that anything out of the ordinary was going on was the unwonted presence of Miss Lilly. The Humanities Building was on the opposite side of campus from her customary haunts, but there she sat, enthroned upon the less disreputable of the lounge's two sofas, surrounded by senior faculty and one or two of the more enterprising T.A.'s. It became clear to Antonia, as she made her tortuous way through the crowd toward the coffee urn, that Miss Lilly was somehow the center of the excitement.

Emma Lilly was, almost literally, a landmark on campus. During freshman orientation tours she was regularly pointed out to bewildered newcomers as one of the sights worth noting. ("On your left is Everett Hall, the last of the original buildings. Over there is Armistead Quad, where May Day festivities are held. And *that* is Miss Lilly.") She had been at the university longer than many of the buildings and before half the faculty was born.

Her impending retirement, at the end of the current semester, was viewed with regret throughout the university. In her own fiefdom, the University Museum, it was regarded as a major catastrophe. Various schemes had been put forward, only half in jest, for circumventing the retirement regulations. They ranged from petitioning for a special dispensation from the governor to falsifying Miss Lilly's birth certificate.

The mood behind these proposals, a mood that in some instances bordered on panic, was based upon the simple fact that Miss Lilly knew more about the history, the administration, and the contents of the University Museum than any other living individual. Her official title might be assistant to the director, but in practice she combined the functions of *genius loci*, data-retrieval system, and platoon sergeant.

Peering over the shoulders of the colleagues who crowded around her, Antonia thought Miss Lilly was looking a little haggard, but it was hard to be sure at such a distance. For the moment she concentrated on reaching the coffee urn.

"What *is* going on around here?" she said to the backs of the last two men standing between her and the coffee.

The two men turned to her in unison.

"You have not heard the news of Mademoiselle Lilly?" inquired Gatineau of Romance Languages.

"It's simply incredible, Antonia!" exclaimed Atwood of English.

"Nil admirari," said Antonia. "May I *please* have a cup of coffee before I faint at your feet?"

Atwood appropriated her mug and began to fill it from the urn while Gatineau explained, gesticulating gracefully with a slice of coffee cake.

"It is the museum, *chère collègue*. It has been—how does one say these days—torn off? The Aegean Gold has been . . ."

'Torn—you mean stolen?" she gasped. "But that's impossible."

"Afraid not," said Atwood, handing back her mug. "Not the entire collection, of course, but some pretty choice pieces, I gather."

"One says," Gatineau added with a flourish of coffee cake, "that the chancellor is telephoning to some Greek government official in Athens at this very moment. I should not," he added with feeling, "like to be in the boots of the chancellor just now."

Nor the boots of poor Miss Lilly, for that matter, thought Antonia. She moved away from Gatineau and Atwood with a vague smile, instinctively searching for someone in her own department, someone who might feel as she did about the loss of such a treasure. But there was not a classicist anywhere in sight, except for Win Randolph on the far fringes of the crowd, and he seemed to be about to leave. There was no hope of reaching him, but she caught his eye and he smiled at her—rather wanly, she thought—but then disappeared from her view.

She decided to try Miss Lilly, who could be counted

upon to have a more accurate view of the facts of the case
than anyone else in the room. But approaching Miss Lilly
was no simple matter, surrounded as she was by a close-
packed throng, all talking at once and none of them inclined to yield his hard-won vantage point to Antonia.

She persevered, insinuating herself into the crevices that
occasionally opened between two earnestly discoursing
colleagues, her coffee sloshing precariously in its mug.
Snatches of conversation assailed her ears from every side.

Morrisroe of Art History was saying, "There's a good
deal of popular appeal in this sort of exhibition, of course—
what I call the King Tut mentality—but the really *significant* thing . . ."

A short dark teaching assistant who kept running his
fingers self-consciously through his hair was holding forth
to an admiring circle: ". . . right there the day they un-
crated. I was supposed to be helping with inventory in the
storeroom, but that stuff pulled me in like a magnet.
Looked like Fort Knox around there for a while—crowns
and goblets and necklaces and these teacup-like things—
wow! That little guy from the National Museum in Athens
was hopping around like a cricket for fear we'd put a dent
in his Precious. And the director, well, he was playing it
cool and suave as usual, but you could tell that stuff was
blowing his mind too. I mean it was like . . ."

It was a relief to come upon Win Randolph, closer now,
making, like herself, slow progress toward Miss Lilly's
sofa. Apparently he had not left the lounge as Antonia
had supposed; he had plunged into the crowd as she had,
but from the opposite side of the room.

"Well, well, Antonia, what do you make of our little
mystery? Isn't often we get such a brouhaha around here
before lunchtime, eh?" He grasped her elbow protectively.
It was typical of Win to offer superfluous guidance to
women who hadn't asked for it.

Win Randolph was a young looking forty-two with a
carefully maintained physique and an elegantly flaring
moustache that reminded some coeds of Faulkner and others of their father. He did not discourage either reaction.
Though he was not tall, his body was compact and well
proportioned and did full justice to the professorial tweeds
and corduroys he affected. Antonia sometimes wondered,
in fact, if the popular-professor persona was conscious or

unconscious with him. It was so complete as to constitute almost a parody of itself, right down to the suede elbow patches and the painstakingly mellowed pipe. At any rate, whether contrived or not, the pose worked—worked, that is, if what you were after was popularity with your students.

And with your colleagues for that matter, she added to herself with scrupulous fairness. He *was* well liked among the faculty. And there had been a time when she herself— well, thank heaven *that* had come to nothing, anyway. He had simply been extremely kind to her when she first arrived at the university five years ago, fresh out of graduate school and slightly bewildered at the prospect of her first job, had helped her find an apartment and a used car, had shoved her office furniture around until the arrangement pleased her, had introduced her to a lot of her new colleagues outside the department. He had, in short, immeasurably eased for her the passage from graduate student to professor. It would have taken longer and been more painful without him, and Antonia had been—still was— grateful.

She was slightly less grateful for his present assistance. Together they were making even slower progress through the crowd than Antonia could have made alone. And Win's excited chatter about the burglary was more irritating than enlightening.

". . . business about the Shaft Grave daggers, old girl?" he was saying.

"Good Lord!" she exclaimed, "are *they* gone?" She must have put more force into the words than she realized, because all around her the talking stopped for an instant and a dozen heads turned to stare at her. She grinned apologetically but took advantage of the slight disarrangement in the solid phalanxes around her to forge ahead once more in the direction of Miss Lilly's sofa.

Few ancient artifacts had more of what Morrisroe of Art History had just contemptuously dismissed as "popular appeal" than the famous Shaft Grave daggers, the exquisite inlaid blades that lay for thirty-four centuries in the tombs of the lords of Mycenae: golden lions and hunting leopards, silver waterfowl and tiny huntsmen with figure-eight shields—all the motifs dearest to the hearts of the Bronze Age warrior-barons, picked out in enamel and precious metals. Antonia had always had a particular fondness for these beautiful little blades, their points and cutting edges gnawed away by time and oxidation but their inlaid blades as fresh as the day they were put to rest for all eternity with the forefathers of Agamemnon.

Then suddenly, before Win could reply to Antonia's stunned question, someone stepped aside and she was standing in front of Miss Lilly.

Miss Lilly appeared to be in, or to have recently recovered from, a state of shock. Several hairs in the white chignon were actually out of place, and there was a barely perceptible tremor in the hand that held the coffee cup. But her voice, though it sounded tired, was calm and steady.

"No, my dear," she was saying to a girl Antonia recognized as one of the English department's T.A.'s, "I'm afraid it wasn't a bit like *Topkapi*. Our arrangements, I regret to say, are rather primitive. No invisible-light screens or ultrasonic waves or anything like that. I've been begging the board for a more up-to-date security system for years, but of course they're very expensive and I got nowhere. Now that the worst has happened, I daresay we'll get something quite grand."

"So the thief wouldn't have had to lower himself melodramatically from the ceiling on a steel cable, like Michael Caine?" asked another *Topkapi* fan.

"Oh dear no," said Miss Lilly. "In fact, on this particular night—last night, that is, though it seems longer ago somehow—it appears that all the thief had to do was open the door, walk in, and help himself." The white chignon quivered with indignation.

"But surely your night watchman—" objected Morrisroe of Art History, "what's his name? Thompson—"

"Our night watchman, Bennie Thompson, is a most reliable young man," said Miss Lilly firmly. "It appears that he was simply in another part of the building when it happened. It's a big place, of course, and he can't be everywhere at once. Also, our alarm system, such as it is, was never activated, goodness knows why, so Bennie had no reason to think anything was wrong in that workroom. When he finally got there, in the normal course of his rounds, he realized that some of the Aegean Gold was missing and called the police at once."

"Miss Lilly," asked Antonia, "what about the daggers, the Shaft Grave daggers? Were they . . . ?"

"Ah, Antonia, there you are!" There was just the slightest suggestion of relief in Miss Lilly's voice. Here at least was someone who would take a properly serious view of the situation.

"It's an odd business, really," Miss Lilly continued. "I was telling Mr. Greenfield about it just a few minutes ago. This thief, for the most part, took pretty much what one would expect—several gold cups and goblets, a silver jug, quite a lot of gold jewelry, a diadem—in short, what was most portable and most obviously valuable. But there are two rather curious exceptions. One is a large ceramic jar from Knossos, decorated with typical Minoan reliefs of bulls' heads and double axes. It isn't a particularly attractive piece, though of course it's of great historical interest. But to the layman's eye it must be rather unappealing, covered with cracks and patches and crude faded pictures. Even more to the point, it's quite heavy and bulky—it stands nearly three feet tall. If, as we assume, the thief packed the smaller gold and silver objects inside it to leave his hands free, it must have weighed close to fifty pounds when he walked out of the museum with it."

"He was taking quite a risk, too, wasn't he?" asked the English T.A. "I mean, he could hardly conceal it under his coat, could he? He must have been conspicuous as a dinosaur, walking around with a thing like that."

"But the daggers, Miss Lilly," Antonia urged gently.

"I'm just coming to them, dear. They are the second exception I mentioned. But in this case, the odd thing is that the thief *didn't* take them!"

Antonia breathed a sigh of relief.

"What he did take," Miss Lilly went on, "was a *reproduction* of the most famous of all the daggers, the Lion Hunt Blade from Mycenae. The originals, of course, have mostly lost their gold hilts, and the bronze blades are badly corroded after three and a half millennia. But the lovely inlays are in perfect condition, and they are among the most popular of Bronze Age artifacts. Students, collectors, the general public, archaeologists, and art historians—everyone finds them irresistible."

"Yet this thief of yours," Morrisroe cut in, "somehow contrived to resist them, and took a more or less worthless modern copy instead. Plain gross ignorance is the answer to that little puzzle, I should think."

"Perhaps, Mr. Morrisroe," said Miss Lilly, "though I would hardly call the copy worthless. It's meticulously accurate, of course, and beautifully executed, and I daresay it could be sold to some unscrupulous collector for several hundred dollars. But you're right that any one of the originals would bring many times that from the same collector. But what is puzzling is this: why would a thief, so amazingly ignorant as not to realize that a collection of ancient blades, corroded and hiltless though they are, is a hundred times more valuable than a flashy modern reproduction—why would such an uninformed thief go to all the trouble and risk of carrying off a great heavy jar that only the most discriminating collector would be interested in?"

"I see what Miss Lilly means," said Antonia thoughtfully. "A thief smart enough, and determined enough, to steal the Knossos jar should have been smart enough to pocket a handful of knives that were just as valuable and a lot easier to fence . . ."

"And a thief dumb enough to pass over the daggers should have been too dumb to bother with the jar!" the dark teaching assistant who had witnessed the uncrating finished triumphantly.

"Precisely," said Miss Lilly.

"But surely this is all a bit academic," put in Win Randolph. "With all the publicity this exhibition has been getting, there must be thousands, tens of thousands of people who would recognize the stolen objects. We've been bombarded with pictures of them in newspapers, magazines, television for weeks now. Surely these things won't get very far before someone spots them."

"Yes, that's what the police are saying too," said Miss Lilly without much enthusiasm. "They're quite optimistic, in fact. Or so they say."

"You yourself are *not* optimistic, then?"

Words, for the first time in anyone's memory, failed Miss Lilly. But the faculty rallied around and plied her with reassurances, expressions of confidence in detectives and insurance investigators, and encouraging anecdotes about previous art thefts. By the time Antonia slipped quietly away, Miss Lilly was looking considerably less ravaged by the morning's ordeal.

Antonia herself, as she walked back through the deserted corridors to her office, tried to sort out a confused set of reactions. Concern for the lost Aegean Gold and sympathy for Miss Lilly and the other museum officials struggled with a skeptical sense of the improbability of the situation. Odds and ends of irreplaceable ancient gold just lying about loose in a workshop somewhere in the bowels of a great museum? A security guard who didn't happen to notice that someone was stealing them? There was a certain musical-comedy implausibility to the whole thing when you stopped to think about it.

Then she remembered her twelve-thirty appointment with Ariadne and abruptly ceased to think of the museum burglary as a Sigmund Romberg absurdity. Her last thought before she opened her office door was: *I must break this gently to Ariadne. She won't have heard, and she'll be terribly upset.*

Antonia waited until almost one o'clock, but the girl never appeared. Antonia thereupon packed up her briefcase and departed, silently cursing the irresponsibility of graduate students and wondering whether a summer in Crete with a representative of the scatterbrained younger generation was really what she yearned for after all.

A few minutes later she left campus with her colleague Barry Greenfield of the English department. The halcyon weather had inspired him to ask her to share a picnic lunch and a bike tour through Mill Creek Park. An afternoon or evening with Barry was always pleasant, and on such a beautiful day irresistible. She had decided her shopping and sunbathing could wait and accepted gladly.

It was therefore by a margin of about four minutes that she missed the arrival of Detective Lieutenant Steven Caracci, who was annoyed to find that most of the faculty had already left and were not expected back on campus before Monday morning.

He was investigating the museum burglary, of course, and it appeared that he had particularly wanted to question Professor Antonia Nielsen.

3. Missing Gold, Missing Girl

FOUR HOURS OF BIKING THROUGH CLOUDS OF DOGWOOD and forsythia, drinking red wine, and eating Barry's chicken sandwiches put Ariadne's small dereliction into perspective. By the time Barry deposited her at her apartment around five, she felt pleasantly tired, but distinctly more mellow.

She was due at the Randolphs for dinner at eight and was looking forward to it. There would be talk of the unseasonable weather, no doubt, but there would also be the burglary to analyze and speculate about, and surely even the dullness of an academic dinner party couldn't kill *that* as a topic of conversation. She just hoped Gillian would be all right.

She took a long hot shower that left her feeling marvelously relaxed and buoyant. Her big Afghan hound, Nike, laid her muzzle against the crack under the bathroom door and kept watch until Antonia reappeared. The dog also found hot showers soothing, provided that she herself was not required to get wet while admiring the sound of them.

Antonia emerged, her long caramel-colored hair still

17

piled haphazardly on top of her head, just as the doorbell rang. Nike gave her single sharp the-doorbell-is-ringing bark, and together they went to answer it.

It is not recorded which of them was more startled, Antonia at the identification card in the detective's palm, or he at the tall figure in flowing caftan and high-piled hair. Only Nike seemed unabashed at the situation, sniffing politely at the lieutenant's ankle and retreating to the spot before the fireplace where she customarily presided over company gatherings.

"Miss—ah, Professor—Nielsen?"

"Yes?"

"It's about this burglary at the museum, Miss Nielsen. May I . . . ?"

"Of course. Sorry. But I don't quite see . . ."

"Thanks." He closed the door behind him and moved toward an armchair near the fireplace, giving Nike a brief but knowledgeable rub behind the ear before he sat down. The silky plume of Nike's tail moved once in acknowledgment of this tribute, and she gazed adoringly at him throughout the remainder of his stay. Here, clearly, was a man worth cultivating.

"Can I offer you a drink, Lieutenant, or would that be against regulations?"

"No, Ma'am, thanks anyway. Though strictly speaking I am off duty. I missed you this afternoon at the university, and I was passing not too far from here on my way home, so I thought I'd give you another try."

"Of course I'll be glad to help any way I can, but I really don't have a great deal to do with the museum. Surely you aren't going to question the entire university faculty? So, why me?"

"It isn't exactly you we're interested in, Miss Nielsen. It's a student of yours, Ariadne Pappas."

"Ariadne? But why on earth . . . ? She's not really a student of mine. I had her in a seminar once a couple of years ago, that's all."

"Several of your colleagues mentioned that Miss Pappas is in the habit of coming to your office rather frequently." A faint smile stirred briefly behind Caracci's professional impassivity as he added, " 'Mother confessor' was the expression one of them used to describe you."

"That," said Antonia, "is an exaggeration. Or rather,

it's inaccurate. It's true that she's taken to stopping by my office this year—she had an appointment with me this afternoon, in fact. But our conversations are hardly what I'd call confessional. In glaring contrast to most of her contemporaries, Ariadne rarely talks about herself."

"What does she talk about then?"

"Her work. Or rather the subject of her work."

"I'm afraid I don't quite see the difference."

"Well, Lieutenant, what most academics talk about is their work—what *I*'m researching, what *I*'ve published, what *I*'m trying to accomplish. When she talks at all, Ariadne talks about antiquity. What the Greeks or Romans or Minoans thought and wrote and achieved. I think the Mediterranean world of two or three thousand years ago is a good deal more alive, more real to her than this campus or her fellow students or the academic profession. It borders on the neurotic, in fact, this reverence of hers for things classical. But I still don't see why you're interested in Ariadne."

"As you may know, Professor Nielsen, Miss Pappas has been working part-time at the museum. I understand that several graduate students were hired a few months ago, to free some of the regular staff for work on this exhibition of, ah, Aegean Gold." He pronounced it *Eegian*, knowing he had probably got it wrong.

Antonia did not smile at his gaffe. "I'm sorry," she said, "but I still don't see . . ."

"The stolen objects had been left overnight in a kind of workroom or large office where the student employees have their desks. There seems to be some evidence that Miss Pappas was working late last night in that room. She didn't come to work this afternoon, and no one we've been able to locate so far has seen her since she left the museum at regular closing time yesterday."

"Lieutenant," Antonia burst out indignantly, "if you are implying—"

Ignoring the interruption, Caracci went on imperturbably. "You say the girl had an appointment with you this afternoon Did she keep it?"

"No," said Antonia reluctantly.

"And what was the purpose of this appointment? Since she's not in any of your classes at present . . ."

"That's right. I don't know why she bothered to make

an appointment, actually. It was unusual. Normally she just drops in when she happens to be in the building. I don't think she has many friends, and she's probably lonely. But yesterday she stopped by on the way to her job and asked if she could see me today at twelve-thirty."

"But she never showed up."

"No. But really, Lieutenant—"

"I know, Miss Nielsen, I know." Caracci's voice sounded a little weary. "This student couldn't possibly be involved in the burglary, she isn't the type, et cetera." He held up a restraining hand as Antonia opened her mouth to protest once more.

"Miss Nielsen, we're not accusing your student of anything. As a matter of fact I don't see her as a very promising suspect myself. From what the museum people have told us, she's conscientious, reliable, responsible—everything you could ask for in an employee. But the fact remains that she was with those objects last night, the night of the burglary, she failed to show up for work and for an appointment today, and she can't be located now. There's probably some explanation, but you can't expect us to ignore all that simply because her friends assure us she's not the type to steal things."

"No, of course not, Lieutenant. Sorry if I sounded defensive." Antonia was feeling slightly foolish. Why on earth had she leaped to the defense of Ariadne, who presumably needed no defending?

"Don't apologize, Miss Nielsen. Most people, especially the innocent ones, get a little uptight at the idea of themselves or their friends being questioned by the police. But we do need to talk to Miss Pappas."

At this point Nike rose with great dignity from her spot before the fireplace, padded over to Caracci's chair, and laid her muzzle suggestively across his knee. He rubbed absently behind her ear as Antonia too stood up.

"Sure you won't change your mind about that drink, Lieutenant? I'm going to make myself one."

"No, thanks," said Caracci, "I'll be leaving in just a minute. But you go right ahead." By the time Antonia returned, highball in hand, the expression on the Afghan's face was one of blissful and oblivious idiocy. Antonia smiled at the two of them.

"Well, Lieutenant," she said, "you seem to have made

quite an impression on old Nike. She's a pushover for anyone who knows how to rub ears properly."

"Yes, Ma'am. Dogs do seem to like me as a rule. Well—" He straightened up in his chair with a back-to-business air and Nike collapsed on his shoes with a contented sigh. "About the Pappas girl. Do you have any idea where she might be?"

"I'm afraid I can't help you much there." Antonia glanced at her watch. "At six o'clock on a Friday evening, I suppose she would normally be in her apartment. But presumably you've covered that."

"Yes, Ma'am. Of course we'll try again later."

"Well, she could be working in the library. She's up against a dissertation deadline in about four weeks. And I think she has a family living somewhere in the city."

"A mother and a sister. We've talked to them too. They weren't exactly cordial, but they claim they haven't seen her for several weeks. They're supposed to let us know if she shows up there."

"As I said, I have the impression that Ariadne doesn't have many friends, but she must have a few, and I suppose she could be with one of them. I can't give you any specific names, unfortunately. Wait—I think she had a roommate last year. The girl moved out some time ago, but I believe they may still see each other occasionally. The dean of graduate students could track down her name for you, I expect."

"Well, every little bit helps," said Caracci with as little enthusiasm as originality.

"You've talked to Professor Randolph? He's directing Ariadne's dissertation—probably meets with her once a month or so. I suppose he knows her as well as anyone on the faculty, though as you can see that isn't saying a whole lot."

"Yes, I talked to him just before coming here. He wasn't able to tell me much either. He gives pretty much the same picture of this girl as you do—hardworking, lonely, uncommunicative, a bit screwy on the subject of antiquity."

Antonia winced at the last of his adjectives. It could be a direct quote from Win Randolph for all she knew, Win being somewhat given to sarcastic hyperbole where students were concerned.

" 'Screwy' is putting it rather strongly, Lieutenant," she said, trying not to sound offended. "Ariadne doesn't distort realities, ancient or modern. In fact, in some ways she's a very hardheaded practical person. I suspect she's had to be, to survive at all. It's only on this one point that she—I guess you could say she overidentifies. I know, I know," she added in response to the disapproving expression that was coming over Caracci's face, "that sounds like psychiatric jargon. But it's the right word for Ariadne's relationship with the ancient world. She functions very well as a twentieth-century American student. But her deepest loyalties, and all the bottled-up enthusiasm one senses in her—they go to her remote ancestors. She speaks of the streets and gates and markets of Athens and Knossos as you or I might speak of Wall Street or Central Park. They have an uncanny kind of *reality* for her that I can't really describe. You'll see what I mean when you meet her."

"Yes. Well, that's exactly what I'm trying to do, Miss Nielsen, meet her."

"You may find Ariadne a disappointment when she *does* turn up. You can't be as certain as I am that she had nothing to do with the burglary, I suppose. But as for her noticing anything fishy going on around the museum—well, I'm doubtful. She isn't very alert to people and things around her. More than once she's passed me on campus without speaking or seeming to notice I was there. It's not intentional, I'm quite sure—when she sees me, she's always very cordial. But there are times when her mind is just—elsewhere."

"But from your description of her, I should think any threat, any suspicion of a threat, to the museum's treasures would be the one thing she *would* be alert to."

Antonia was startled at his perception. He hadn't seemed to be listening so closely to what she had told him of Ariadne. Apparently he understood the girl better than she had given him credit for.

"Point for you, Lieutenant," she conceded. "If there was anything of that sort to be noticed, Ariadne probably would have noticed it. But isn't it hoping for rather a lot— a squint-eyed stranger skulking about the museum, I mean?"

"Yes, Ma'am." For the first time Caracci grinned. "We

don't get too many of those types nowadays. It'd make our job too easy, I expect." He moved toward the door, escorted by the still-hopeful Nike. "But sometimes a small thing, something less melodramatic than your squint-eyed stranger—you'd be surprised what people can remember sometimes if you prod their memory a bit."

"I suppose so. Although it doesn't seem to have worked that way in my case," she added ruefully.

"Don't worry about it, Miss Nielsen. We'll talk to her when she turns up." He gave Nike's silky head a farewell pat at the door.

After he had gone, Antonia gulped the last of her watery Scotch and for a few moments stared unseeing out the window at the darkening street below. Nike came silently up behind her, leaned companionably against her right thigh, and looked out too.

"I don't like it, old girl," Antonia mused, "I don't like it. Ariadne Pappas, of all people, vanishing like a magician's rabbit just when—oh, it's preposterous."

And she disappeared into the bedroom to dress for Gillian Randolph's party. Nike remained at the window, gazing at the shifting patterns of lights from the traffic below.

4. "They Never Get Any Older!"

THE SALAD GREENS WERE VERY CRISP, THE CRUST OF the quiche Lorraine very flaky, the white wine superbly dry. Gillian herself, as usual on such occasions, was in her element. Though she was not a beautiful woman, few men were aware of the fact. She was wearing one of the fluid jersey dresses that she collected so assiduously and that softened her rather angular figure. This particular specimen was black, which had the additional advantage of setting off the masses of dark red hair draped elegantly about her head. The sleek mahogany coils in turn distracted one's attention from her long equine face.

Antonia, on more than one previous occasion, had found herself neglecting her own food as she gazed hypnotically at Gillian's hands. Once again they were transforming the most mundane of tasks into a kind of ballet, the long slender fingers gliding deftly among silver and porcelain, lifting a slice of quiche, transferring salad from bowl to plate.

Her voice rose gaily above the flatter American intonations of her guests, its accent carefully preserved from her days as a scholarship student at Cambridge's Girton College. Win, on the other hand, took little part in the conversation. Antonia had long suspected that he deliberately effaced himself in favor of his wife at such affairs, preferring to let her exercise her social gifts as fully as possible. She had few enough opportunities to do so, as Win had once ruefully remarked to Antonia. The least he could do was let her make the most of them.

She was making the most of them now. Antonia had rarely seen her so vivacious. The combination of the wine, the company, and the excitement of the museum burglary seemed to have left her even more exhilarated than usual. She turned now to Roy Sandler, the Classics chairman, and inquired:

"I suppose the Aegean Gold exhibition will have to be postponed now, won't it? What a pity!"

"No, as a matter of fact our unsinkable Miss Lilly assures me that 'The Show Will Go On.' I even suspect, though I didn't say so to her, that the burglary may actually give the exhibition a certain *succès de scandale.*"

"Hardly the sort of publicity to appeal to poor Miss Lilly," observed Renée Gatineau sympathetically.

"No, of course not," said Sandler. "Still, if it brings in a few extra dollars . . ."

"Perhaps they could be applied toward her new security system for the museum," suggested Pierre Gatineau. "There would be in that a certain poetic justice."

"There would indeed," said Sandler, "but I'm afraid poetic justice isn't exactly what the financial administration of this institution is famous for."

"Well," said his wife, Martha, "at least the Faculty Women's Club won't have to reschedule its Spring Outing. We've persuaded Professor Morrisroe to give us a lecture tour of the exhibition, you know. And after what I've been through trying to get the whole thing organized . . ."

Martha Sandler, a plump and motherly woman in her early fifties, was as renowned for her nonstop tongue as for her kindly and sympathetic heart. Her husband, after thirty years of practice, had become adept at spotting her monologues in their early stages. He seemed to sense one approaching now, and with the kindest of intentions moved to forestall it.

Turning to his host, he asked, "It's odd about the Pappas girl, isn't it, Win? What do you make of the cops' interest in her?"

Win, who had been gazing at the centerpiece, looked startled. "I didn't make anything of it," he said irritably. "Just assumed they were covering the whole museum staff, I suppose."

"I'm not so sure," said Sandler. "When they talked to me, they seemed pretty interested in her financial situation."

"Nonsense!" snorted Win. "Ariadne Pappas swiping ancient artifacts to pay her grocery bills—now *there* is a deduction worthy of our local gendarmerie! If you ask me," he added abruptly, "the whole thing is nothing but an outbreak of *febris vernalis* among our clean-limbed young seekers after wisdom. In short, a student prank."

"Oh, come on, Win, surely you don't . . ."

"I mean it. I fully expect to wake up one morning and find Clytemnestra's diadem gracing the brazen brow of President Higgenbotham's statue in the Quad."

"What is *febris varn*—what he said?" inquired Martha Sandler.

"It means spring fever," Antonia replied. "Or so he imagines. But I'm afraid there's more to it than that, Win. The police really *are* interested in Ariadne—they grilled me about her too."

Gillian had temporarily withdrawn from the conversation to dispense second helpings and refill wine glasses, not forgetting her own. When she spoke now there was an odd metallic edge to her voice that Win and Antonia recognized instantly.

"Quite a lot of people seem to find this Ariadne Pappas a very—*interesting* girl. Up from the slums and all that. Smoldering Mediterranean eyes too, I shouldn't wonder."

Win muttered, "Now, Gillian, don't start . . ."

Roy Sandler managed a fair show of casual heartiness as he said, "Really, Gillian, have you ever actually met the girl? She's hardly the femme fatale type."

"Possibly not," said Gillian, "but I have yet to meet an American student who wasn't irresponsible, self-centered, and . . ."

"That's true," put in Antonia, "of a good many of them. But Ariadne's a different breed entirely. She's conscientious and responsible to a fault."

But Gillian was not to be placated. "Well, *I* don't call
it responsible behavior when a girl rings up at . . ."

Win interrupted her with greater urgency this time:
"Gillian, *please* . . ."

Taking his turn in the attempt to pour oil on the ruffled
waters, Pierre Gatineau said, "While I cannot agree with
Win that the burglary itself was a student prank, still there
may be something in the idea of spring fever. The campus
was delicious this afternoon, with the—" he turned to his
wife, Renée "—*cornouiller?*"

"Dogwood, *chéri,*"

"Yes, dogwood. And the daffodils and the student girls
in their swim costumes. This girl, this Ariadne—perhaps
she also has succumbed to the *ambience* and simply departed for the weekend?"

But his efforts too were doomed to failure. At the mention of sunbathing coeds, Gillian's face took on an expression of triumphant disapproval. The moral depravity of
Ariadne Pappas and her kind had obviously been dem-
onstrated to *her* satisfaction. She said nothing, however,
but collected a few dinner plates and disappeared into the
kitchen with them.

While she was gone, her guests tried halfheartedly to
sustain some semblance of general conversation, but their
embarrassment was painfully obvious. After a few minutes, under cover of clearing away the remaining dishes,
Antonia followed Gillian into the kitchen.

She was standing at the sink, making a rather uncon-
vincing show of scraping and rinsing the dinner plates. A
half-empty highball glass stood nearby on the Formica
countertop. Gillian glanced up as the kitchen door swung
closed behind Antonia, then turned back to her drink. She
spoke over the rim of her glass while Antonia set her
offering of plates and salad bowls on the counter.

"I daresay you all think I'm making a spectacle of myself, don't you? P'raps you're right, too. But what you
don't know is what it's like . . ." She paused for another
gulp of the rapidly diminishing highball, ". . . what it's
like, sitting in this bloody house with practically nothing
to do, knowing that your husband is being exposed day
after day, year after year, to hundreds of attractive girls
who never get any older." She seemed pleased with the

phrase, because she repeated it with heavy dramatic emphasis. *"They never get any older."*

At least, thought Antonia, she left out the bits about being exiled three thousand miles from home, and childless. When Gillian brought all her big guns to bear simultaneously, she could be quite impossible.

"Really, Gillian," she said, "aren't you being a bit melodramatic? Win, as you well know, is devoted to you. And Roy is quite right about Ariadne Pappas—she's just not a likely candidate for the role of homewrecker."

"No?" Gillian's voice was almost arch. She had reached, Antonia judged, the game-playing stage where the contest was more of wits than emotions. Gillian was right about herself in one respect: she was an idle, aimless woman, bored to distraction, and a lively argument would probably give her a good deal of satisfaction. Even one designed to demonstrate her husband's infidelity.

"No," said Antonia firmly, "and you must stop this. You're beginning to sound like something out of Albee."

"You mean Martha, I suppose. The one with the emotional maturity of a twelve year old."

"Exactly. And it isn't worthy of you." She hurried on before Gillian could reply. "Look, I sympathize with what you said about American students. I get pretty turned off by them myself at times But this Pappas girl really is different. I'm not sure she's interested in men of any kind, let alone married ones nearly twice her age. She's so wrapped up in her work she's hardly aware of anyone, of either sex. And as for Win, if he were going to philander—which I doubt—it wouldn't be with Ariadne."

"Why not? I suppose you're going to tell me she's plain and frumpy."

"No, not frumpy." How to describe Ariadne to one who had never seen her? The "Mediterranean" eyes did indeed "smolder," in Gillian's words—though almost certainly not for Gillian's husband. And the sweep of black hair, though it needed a little shaping and a lot of brushing—no, "mousy" was definitely not the word for it either.

Finally, Antonia said, "It's just that she makes it so obvious, so blatantly obvious, that she's not interested—not in sex, not in anything outside her work—that most men would be instantly repelled, I think."

"But even a girl like that—so keen on her work and

all—they've been thrown together so much. Win's her dissertation director, he's *part* of her work."

"You mustn't think in terms of a British tutorial, Gillian. The relationship between student and dissertation director here is often pretty tenuous. Some directors, with a student as independent as Ariadne, might not meet her more than two or three times all year. With Win and Ariadne, I don't know, I suppose they get together about once a month. And that's hardly enough to wear down resistance as massive as hers."

There were other and more compelling reasons why the girl could not possibly be interested in Win Randolph, though they could hardly be conveyed to Gillian. One had only to look at them to see the impossibility—at Win's loose-limbed casual elegance, every inch of him the conventional tweed-and-suede professor, and at Ariadne with her tense lean figure like a coiled whip. . . .

"Well," Gillian interrupted her thoughts, "they've obviously been seeing a good deal more of each other than *that!*" The note of triumphant self-vindication had returned to her voice, and she pulled a piece of paper from her apron pocket and waved it under Antonia's nose.

"I found this in the pocket of his winter coat yesterday morning. And you needn't fancy I was prying, either. With the weather so warm, he'd worn just a light jacket to the office, and I thought I could get the coat cleaned before it turned cold again. I was just emptying the pockets to take it to the cleaner." She thrust the paper at Antonia.

"Really, Gillian, I don't want . . ."

"Go on, read it. You'll see what I mean." The distant note of hysteria was creeping into her voice again, and Antonia was reluctant to aggravate her. She took the note.

Dear Win,
   If you keep pressuring me like this, I will have no choice but to tell someone what is going on. You seem to think I couldn't go on without you, but if I have to I will.
   Can't you see how much this means to me—much more than it possibly can to you? I am doing this for love, however it may look to other people.

*Please stop by Thursday night so that we can settle
things once and for all.*

Ariadne

"What I see," said Antonia, handing back the note, "is
that she calls him Win, as most of the doctoral students
do—graduate students of both sexes. He encourages it,
Gillian, and it's not uncommon these days anyway. But
more importantly, I see an overwrought girl in the final
throes of writing her dissertation, who has probably had
a chapter criticized or even rejected outright and has overreacted. It's a well-known syndrome. Knowing both Ariadne and Win, I emphatically do not see in it what you
apparently do. The men Ariadne Pappas gets passionately
involved with, Gillian, have been dead for three thousand
years."

"But that peremptory tone, the familiarity of it—it's in-
sufferable. This is the outburst of an exasperated lover,
Antonia, not a student."

It was the outburst, Antonia thought, of a tired, neurotic
student who had probably not had much respect for her
professor to begin with, and by now was in an advanced
state of exhaustion, anxiety, and frustration.

Aloud she said, "I know the state she's in, Gillian, from
the inside as well as the outside. When I was finishing
my dissertation I lost fifteen pounds, shouted at my director, had nightmares about him—in short, acted thoroughly
unbalanced. And I've seen Ariadne, and she's been looking haggard and anxious for the last few weeks. It's a
very difficult time for a student, Gillian. Try to understand."

Before Gillian could reply, Win came through the
swinging door into the kitchen. "Gillian's feeling a little
upset right now, Win," said Antonia. "I think she should
lie down for a while. You and I could serve the dessert
and coffee, couldn't we?"

"Yes, of course, but . . ." He turned anxiously to his
wife. "What is it, Gillian? Surely you're not upset about
this wretched Pappas girl?"

"My feelings are hardly the issue," retorted Gillian,
brandishing Ariadne's note. "The question is, how serious
are *you* two?"

Even though half the note was concealed by Gillian's

long fingers, Win seemed to recognize it and relax. "So that's where it was—I'd been wondering where it had gotten to. But I don't see why that note should upset you, Gillian."

"That's funny, Antonia has the same problem. She can't see what it has to do with me either. You both seem to think I'm blind, deaf, and dumb. *Very* dumb, apparently."

"Darling, let's discuss it later. Antonia's right, you ought to rest for a bit." He put his arm around Gillian's shoulders and started toward the kitchen's second door, which opened into a back stairway to the upper floor of the house, but Gillian twisted away from him.

"I don't want to rest," she whispered, her long equine face suddenly contorted with fury. "What I want is for you to keep your *hands* off those bloody little . . . bloody little . . ."

Gillian had kept her voice low to avoid being overheard by guests in the next room. But Antonia recognized the tone. She and Win and a handful of others had heard it just once before.

About nine months before, in fact, at a Fourth of July picnic given by the Sandlers. Gillian had come upon Win talking and laughing with an attractive blond graduate student in an out-of-the-way corner of the garden. Antonia, to her chagrin, had been standing nearby and could not avoid witnessing the whole incident. It must, she assumed, have been the culmination of a long period of tension, frustration, and suppressed anger between Win and Gillian, but that climactic moment was all she or anyone else saw, and to the startled onlookers it appeared as sudden and savage as a flash flood.

So shocking had the scene been, both in its ugliness and in its incongruity with the decorous little academic picnic, that Antonia could remember only isolated fragments of it with any clarity.

Gillian, in the same low-pitched but vicious tone she was using now, calling the bewildered student a bloody little bitch.

Gillian's long pale fingers around the girl's throat.

Gillian's expression, a mixture of relief and baffled fury as Win pulled her off and led her unresisting to their car.

It had been several weeks before Gillian had appeared in public again. Antonia was one of the few who knew that this temporary withdrawal was due to more than just mortification at the spectacle she had made of herself.

A few hours after Win had taken her home, Gillian had tried to kill herself.

Both Win and Antonia were painfully aware of the whole episode as they stood now in Gillian's kitchen, embarrassed and baffled. But their dilemma was resolved, suddenly and unexpectedly, by Gillian herself. Though she still stood as if at bay, her back against the refrigerator, the look of animal rage passed from her face as abruptly as it had appeared. When she spoke to her husband again, her voice was stiff and formal but calm.

"I'm sorry, Win. I expect you think I've overreacted. All right, we'll just drop it for the time being. One has to solve one's own problems in one's own way, of course, and I'm afraid I tend to forget that at times. Sorry." She glanced around her kitchen as if reminding herself where she was and what needed to be done next. Plunging into the refrigerator, she extracted from it a chocolate mousse evidently intended as the evening's *pièce de résistance*. Then, with a coolness that was almost arrogant, she said, "Just bring the coffee in for me, would you, Antonia?" And she swept out of the kitchen without a backward glance.

"Think she'll be all right?" said Antonia after a moment.

"I don't know," said Win unhappily as he unplugged the electric coffee pot. "What on earth was in that note to set her off? Something about meeting me to hash out the last chapter of the dissertation? It came—let's see— almost a week ago, and needless to say I didn't memorize the damn thing."

"The tone is a bit intense, that's all. I tried to explain about predoctoral melancholia, but I don't think she bought it."

"She wouldn't, no. People—which by courtesy includes students—are supposed to have stiffer upper lips than that, in Gillian's view." He started for the door, coffee pot in hand. "We'll just have to muddle through the rest of the evening and hope for the best."

With some misgivings Antonia followed him into the dining room.

*   *   *

Shortly before midnight she returned to her apartment, where Nike greeted her sleepily with two slow waves of her tail before dozing off again.

The tensions of the Randolphs' dinner party, coming on top of the physical fatigue of a long afternoon of biking, had left Antonia feeling utterly drained. For a moment she considered the tempting possibility of simply collapsing on the floor beside Nike and losing consciousness until morning. But that, she told herself firmly, would probably mean a backache tomorrow, and besides the dog had to be walked. It was even possible that a stroll on the quiet campus would have a soothing effect.

They set out toward the university campus, Nike trotting briskly ahead with an occasional glance over her shoulder to make sure Antonia hadn't strayed. Nike loved the campus because it was the only place within walking distance of their apartment where she could really stretch her legs, and their walk was the high point of her day.

They took their standard thirty-minute tour, which comprised the library, the physics building, the administration building, and the student center, and ended at the museum. They had almost reached it, and Antonia was about to turn back toward home, when Nike suddenly froze at attention, a warning rumble rising in her throat, legs stiff and muzzle pointing tensely toward the museum.

Assuming that the source of the dog's excitement was a bird or squirrel, Antonia started to pull her back along the path. But then she too noticed something moving in the shadows at the base of the dark mass that was the museum. It was hardly more than a shadow itself, but it was certainly not a small animal. For an instant Antonia wondered if a bear had escaped from the zoo and was prowling the campus. But then the thing rose to its full height—it must have been bending over, looking at something on the ground—and she could see that it was a man. A huge, shapeless figure, but definitely a man, perhaps one of the varsity football players. He moved clumsily but swiftly away, around the museum, till the corner of the building hid him from view.

Nike, who took her responsibilities seriously, continued to grumble discontentedly deep in her throat for a while, but eventually decided the peril had passed and it was safe to return to her detailed examination of the nearby shrubbery. She took Antonia home a few minutes later, without further incident.

5. Night People

ANTONIA SPENT SATURDAY MORNING SHOPPING FOR her Aegean Gold dress. She found it at last, a shimmering cascade of narrow white pleats from neckline to hem. When she stood very still it made her feel like a Doric temple column, and when she moved she thought she looked like an Alpine waterfall. Naturally, a dress that could do all that was not to be resisted, and she bought it.

She devoted two hours in the middle of the day to the beginnings of the tan that the temple-column-waterfall dress clearly called for. By two o'clock she was in her office, putting finishing touches to the overdue article. She spent three blissful hours retouching her prose, verifying a few footnotes, and composing a cover letter to *The Classical Journal* editor. When at last she could find nothing more that seemed to require polishing, she gave the article a quick read-through to judge its overall effect, and was pleased. With a great sense of satisfaction she laid it on the department secretary's desk to be mailed Monday morning. The feeling accompanied her all the way home across the fragrant campus.

When she reached her apartment at five o'clock, there

was a young black man sprawled on the floor outside her door.

He sat there, back to the wall, long legs jacknifed because the corridor was too narrow to allow him to extend them full length, the toes of his battered boots braced against the opposite wall. His head hung limply at a grotesque angle, in the manner of those who fall asleep sitting bolt upright. As Antonia bent down to reassure herself that he really was only sleeping, her long hair must have brushed his cheek, because he leaped up with a startled cry.

He stood before her, one hand on his neck, turning his head stiffly from side to side, looking disoriented but unembarrassed. He was very tall and lean, and had an air of having been carelessly assembled: the various parts of his body, though decently shaped and well proportioned in themselves, gave the impression of having only tenuous connections with one another, as if he might fall apart at any moment.

"Miss Nielsen? My name's Bennie Thompson. I'm a friend of Ariadne Pappas."

Antonia had the door unlocked by now, but she turned at the mention of Ariadne's name. "Have you seen her? Do you know where she is?"

Before Bennie could answer, something dark and shapeless and very large exploded from the apartment door, striking Bennie squarely in the chest and hurling him violently back against the wall of the corridor. He slid slowly down the wall into a sitting position reminiscent of the one he had just quitted.

"Down, Nike! That's enough, get down!" Antonia's voice was stern, but there was a hint of amusement in it. The big Afghan, after giving Bennie's nose one solicitous lick, padded docilely back into the apartment and sat down with a sigh just inside the door.

"Sorry, Mr. Thompson. She probably thought she was protecting my life and limbs. At any rate, she wouldn't have hurt you. If she decided you were dangerous, she'd just sit on your chest pending further instructions. If she chose to regard you as a friend, she'd do the same thing out of pure affection. She must have known you were out here—they're hounds, you know, keen noses and all that. How long *have* you been here, by the way?"

Bennie had struggled to his feet for the second time in three minutes and was massaging one shoulder, which had hit the wall with considerable force. The expression of astonishment and fear that had swept over his face when the dog lunged at him was giving way to one of annoyance. "I dunno. Couple of hours, I guess. I remember now, she barked once when I rang the bell but I fell asleep after that. Forgot there was a dog in there."

Antonia, feeling more secure now that Nike was around, gestured to Bennie Thompson to enter the apartment. He walked in with a nervous glance at the dog and stood uneasily in the middle of Antonia's small living room. She followed him in, closing the door behind her.

"Well, Mr. Thompson," she repeated, "*have* you seen Ariadne?"

"No, Ma'am," he said wearily, "I haven't, not since Wednesday night. I was sort of hoping maybe *you* had. Looks like I come all this way for nothing." He sounded resentful.

"No, wait a minute, Mr. Thompson. Let's not give up quite so fast. You say you saw her Wednesday night. Where?"

"In the museum. I work there, see, night watchman, eleven to seven. That's how I met Ari." With a significant glance at Antonia's comfortable-looking armchair he added, "And that's why I flaked out on your doorstep like that. Afternoons, see, that's when I usually do my sleeping."

Taking the hint and motioning him into a chair, Antonia said, "But what on earth would she be doing in the museum at that hour of the night?" She could hear Bennie draw a deep breath before he answered.

"She's been working there at night a lot lately. Not her regular job for the museum, that's in the afternoon. Something of her own."

"Something of her own. That would be her dissertation, presumably. But why in heaven's name in the museum, and after midnight? Did she ever talk to you about what she was doing?"

"No, Ma'am. But it ain't hard to figure why she was doing it in the museum. It's this apartment she's got. I saw it once, and it's really godawful. Plaster falling off the walls, and roaches, and a filthy bathroom on a different floor. Got so she couldn't stand to be in the place except to sleep. So she comes to work in the afternoon and then leaves for a while and eats and comes back around eleven. She has a key to the side door of the museum so she can let herself in. Then she does her own thing all night and goes home about five or six in the morning and sleeps until noon. Like I said, that's how I come to know her. She has a coffee pot, and I stop by her office a couple times a night and we rap awhile. Helps keep us awake."

"So naturally after the burglary Thursday night Ariadne became a prime suspect. They must have assumed. . ."

"No, Ma'am," Bennie interrupted. "You got it all wrong. The fuzz got no special suspicions of Ariadne, as far as I can see. I never said nothing to them about her hanging around the museum at night. Leastways," he added darkly, "not yet."

"I'm afraid I'm not following you."

Bennie sighed, whether from fatigue or from exasperation at Antonia's obtuseness she couldn't tell. "Ari don't want anyone to know she's spending nights in the museum, see. I don't know why, she ain't hurting nothing, but she's always after me not to talk about it. So I promised her."

"You said nothing about this to the police? They've questioned you too?"

"Yeah, Thursday night after the break-in. I didn't say nothing then, but I can't wait much longer. I come here to see if maybe you knew where I could find her—tell her she's gotta tell the cops about this whatever-it-is or else I will. But it looks like you don't know any more'n me. So . . ."

"But if they *don't* suspect Ariadne, then why . . . ?"

"Look, Professor, what this all adds up to is the fuzz ain't got a clue who ripped off that stuff outa the museum, and I'm the handiest one to pin it on. And that I *don't* need," he finished bitterly. "So all right, I promised Ari I wouldn't blab about her being in the museum at weird hours—but there's limits, dammit."

"In other words, Mr. Thompson," Antonia put in angrily, "not to put too fine a point on it, if Ariadne doesn't show up pretty soon and explain herself to the cops, you'll do it for her. And that, you figure, will put her right at the top of the suspect list. Which at the moment consists of just one name—yours."

"Now hold on, Professor, don't you go making me out some kinda monster or something. I'm trying to do right by Ari, but the fact is she *has* been acting real peculiar lately, and that stuff *did* disappear outa the very same room she's been working in, and she *ain't* been seen since. And maybe all that don't mean nothing and then again maybe it do, but either way it's gonna look a whole lot like withholding information from the cops if I just happen to forget to mention what she's been up to. I ain't exactly on their Forty Top Favorites list already, Professor, and I got no mind to put my head in no noose, even for Ari."

"All right, all right, take it easy, Mr. Thompson. I see what you mean. But you know Ariadne—surely *you* don't think . . ."

"Couple months ago, I would of said no way. But now— I dunno, Professor, I still say something funny's going down in that museum. But Ari and that gold stuff—naw, she never would of done nothing like that. She's a funny chick and she could sure use some extra bread, but she'd never rip off the museum to get it. The stuff in that museum, it's like holy relics or something to her. One night she took me around and showed me some of the stuff they got stored away that nobody ever sees. Old hunks of stone with carving on 'em, mostly, and busted clay pots—millions of busted pots. That junk sure didn't turn *me* on, but you shoulda seen what it did for *her.* Like somebody turned on a big light bulb somewhere inside her skull and it come shining out through those black eyes of hers. That is one fine-looking chick, y'know that, Professor? I never noticed it before that night. She mostly goes around with her head down and a kinda scared look—or maybe just tired—and wearing some grungy old shirt. She looks like a real bear, mosta the time. But that night, with that light bulb behind her eyes and her whole face sorta lit up— Jeez, she was somethin' else!"

He paused for a moment, remembering.

"Naw, she never would of ripped off no museum," he repeated. "But she might be into something—I dunno— something funny."

"Why do you say that?"

"There was this one time—I ain't told the fuzz yet because I would of had to tell them about Ari hanging around there nights—but about a month ago I was making my first round—a little before midnight, that'd be—and I come down to the basement level. When I opened the door into the corridor where Ari's office is, I heard her talking to someone in her room. Couldn't hardly hear her voice, she talks so low, but there was a man in there with her and I could hear *him* loud and clear."

"Could you tell what they were talking about?"

"Naw, not really. I heard the guy say, 'I never asked you for nothing,' something like that. But they musta heard me coming down the hall, because they stopped talking all of a sudden. When I got to Ari's door, it was wide open and I looked in." Bennie paused for a moment, and there was an odd expression on his face.

"Well, Ari was just sitting there at her desk like she always does, with a pencil in her hand and those old yellow papers she uses spread out in front of her. And this dude that'd been hassling her, he was nowhere near her, I mean, he wasn't threatening her or nothing, he was standing halfway across the room beside the big worktable they have in there. When I stuck my head in at the door, he swung around kinda slow like until he was facing me. He didn't say nothing, just looked at me. Man, he was the baddest-looking cat I *ever* saw. He musta weighed two fifty if he weighed a pound, and wasn't none of it fat. I always thought I was pretty tall, but he had two, three inches on me, plus he was twice as wide in every direction.

"But him being so big wasn't what got to me. I seen plenty of big cats before, a lot of 'em are clumsier or dumber than me so they don't worry me none. It was his head. It was like it was bigger'n it shoulda been, even for such a huge dude. And those little tiny eyes—you know what they reminded me of? The eyes on those statues they got in the museum that Ari told me used to be painted but now they're just blank. They look like they're seeing everything—or nothing, you can't tell which. That's how this guy looked, like he was seeing everything I'd ever thought, or maybe he didn't even notice I was there. Man, he was spooky."

"But you're supposed to be responsible for security at the museum. Shouldn't you have thrown this person out or reported him or something? Or at least warned Ariadne not to have visitors in the museum at such hours?"

"Hell, Professor, that's easy to say—now. But it wasn't like she was throwing wild parties down there or something. That was the one and only time she ever had anyone in her office after hours that I know of. You know how she is, so quiet and serious—well, it just didn't seem like a big security risk at the time, that's all. Even if the dude was kinda weird looking."

"Yes, I see what you mean," said Antonia. "But under the circumstances I think you ought to tell the police about him now."

"I dunno," said Bennie sullenly, "Caracci ain't gonna buy it, not from me. He'll most likely think I'm trying to turn the heat offa me and onto Ariadne or the stranger. Might even think I'm making the whole thing up—wouldn't put it past him."

"You know Lieutenant Caracci, then?"

"Yes, Ma'am." The boy's voice was unmistakably bitter now. "Him and me are old—friends. Except he don't exactly trust me."

"Well, you've got to tell him about this unidentified man anyway. If he's simply a friend of Ariadne's, the police will find it out. You and I know, even if they don't, that Ariadne must be innocent. We *don't* know that he is."

"I guess you're right. And if this dude is making some kinda trouble for Ari, or if he's even mixed up in the burglary, then it'd be better for both of us if the cops brought him in, wouldn't it?"

"Exactly. And if you're still worried about the cops' knowing that Ariadne has been working late at night in the museum—and may even have been there Thursday night—look at it this way: it can hardly make her look worse in Caracci's eyes than disappearing like this, on the very day of the burglary. To anyone who knows Ariadne, it's only an unfortunate coincidence, but to the rest of the world—including the police—it's a pretty suspicious circumstance, you know."

"Yeah." Antonia was startled to see a malicious grin spread over Bennie's dark face. "Yeah, that's the way their minds work, all right. That's exackly what they *would* figure, ain't it?" And he emitted a laugh that seemed to combine approximately equal parts of derision, contempt, and disgust. It stopped as abruptly as it had begun.

"Awright, I'll go call the lieutenant. I got a pretty good idea what he's gonna say, but after he's said it he'll have to check it out anyway." Wearily, he uncoiled his awkward length from the depths of the armchair. "And Caracci can't hardly say nothing to me I ain't heard from him before."

Antonia closed and locked the door after Bennie Thompson and gave a reassuring pat to Nike, who had escorted him out civilly but with a certain wariness in her manner. She thought briefly about dinner but decided she couldn't face the prospect of cooking. Instead she got herself a beer out of the refrigerator, carried it back into the living room, and flopped down wearily to try to sort out the puzzling events of the last two days.

What exactly had made Bennie Thompson come to her? Concern for Ariadne? Perhaps, in part. But he himself was apparently a prime suspect in the business of the burglary, which tended to cast some doubt on the purity of his motives in mentioning Ariadne's poverty, her familiarity with the museum, her possession of a key to the side door. Worst of all, it had never occurred to anyone, as far as Antonia knew, that Ariadne was in the habit of spending most of the night in the museum, indeed had quite possibly been there on the very night of the burglary. It had never occurred to anyone, that is, until Bennie suggested it. Had he perhaps come to Antonia to give the story a sort of trial run—if she didn't dismiss it out of hand, he would risk trying it on the police?

Moreover, Bennie had hinted strongly that he had a criminal record and that the police fully expected him to get into trouble again sooner or later. Miss Lilly trusted him, and her judgment was not to be lightly dismissed— but on the other hand, how much could she be expected to know about young delinquents? She had probably hired him on a charitable but naive impulse, without realizing the risks she was taking.

Still Antonia shrank from drawing the obvious and uncharitable conclusion concerning Bennie Thompson. At least if he was somehow trying to frame Ariadne or the stranger, or even just distracting attention from himself, he wasn't being especially clever about it. All the details that told against him had been ingenuously called to her attention by Bennie himself. His connection with the museum, of course, was public knowledge. But no one had had any reason to suppose that he had ever so much as heard of Ariadne Pappas—until he volunteered the information. If the missing girl was under suspicion already, as it appeared she was, why would another suspect, eager to clear himself, gratuitously step forth and associate himself with her? Of course, at the same time he might also be attempting to incriminate her still further, but was it worth the risk? The police would no doubt be interested to know that Ariadne had been spending her nights in the museum, but would they not also be intrigued by Bennie's failure to report this fact to the museum authorities weeks ago? He had, by his own account, turned a blind eye to Ariadne's peculiar behavior. Why? What was in it for him? An occasional cup of coffee and a chat to help pass the dreary hours from midnight to 7:00 A.M.? No doubt— but merely that and nothing more?

And why would he invent a grotesque and sinister figure, glimpsed in the museum at an outrageous hour a few weeks before the break-in—and then deliberately undercut the story's effect by suggesting that the police probably wouldn't believe it? It hadn't occurred to her to question the reality of Bennie's Frankenstein monster, until Bennie himself planted the seed of doubt in her mind.

As she rose stiffly from the armchair in which Bennie had been sitting an hour earlier, Antonia decided that the only conclusion justified by this tangle of guesses, suppositions, and unanswered questions was no conclusion at all. The boy might be on the level, genuinely concerned for Ariadne as well as for his own skin—or he might be playing some far more sinister game, the object of which she could see no point in trying to guess at.

So file Bennie for the moment—she simply didn't have enough data on him yet to make a rational assessment. But what about Ariadne, whom she knew so well? Now that Caracci wasn't around to see her doubt and uncertainty, Antonia had to admit that it really was a bit much— Ariadne and the Aegean Gold missing at the same time, the gold from the very room in the museum where the girl had been secretly working, presumably against all rules and regulations, until dawn.

Yes, a bit much to be pure coincidence. And yet, unlike Caracci, she did know the girl and she had not been ex-aggerating when she told the detective it was unthinkable that Ariadne could have stolen the missing pieces of Ae-gean Gold, poverty or no poverty. Though she hadn't said so to Caracci for fear of seeming to protest too much, in her own mind Antonia was quite certain that the girl would literally starve before she would steal classical artifacts. Perhaps, if Ariadne were desperate enough, she might rob a bank, a liquor store, or a blind beggar, but ancient Greek works of art—never.

So what was the connection between the Aegean Gold and Ariadne—Ariadne, the quintessential loner who seemed to have so little connection with any aspect of the life around her? And yet now suddenly there seemed to be all sorts of connections between Ariadne and other, more or-dinary people. Caracci was scouring the city to find her, Bennie—hypothetically at least—was sticking his neck out to protect her, Gillian was hysterically jealous of her.

Antonia became aware that her thoughts were going around like mice on an exercise wheel, whirling faster and faster but never breaking out of the same monotonous circle. She seemed unable to stop thinking, yet was in-capable of making her thoughts add up to anything definite or useful.

She forced herself to put it all out of her mind for a while and spent the next couple of hours doing humble but necessary chores around the apartment. She fixed her own and Nike's dinner, washed her hair, and wrote a letter. She gave careful consideration to the dust in the corners and decided it wasn't nearly thick enough yet to justify getting out the vacuum cleaner. Shortly before eight she unplugged the phone, sank blissfully into her deepest armchair with a copy of *Northanger Abbey,* and retired from the world until eleven. When at last she closed the book and drifted slowly back to awareness of her sur-roundings, Nike rose from her spot by the fireplace, pad-ded over to lay her muzzle on the arm of Antonia's chair, and gazed soulfully into her mistress's eyes.

Antonia got the message.

* * *

As usual, the University Museum was the terminus of their nightly walk. Nike knew perfectly well it was the signal to go home, but on this occasion the dog made an elaborate pretense of not recognizing the building or its significance. With a glance at Antonia that dared her to object, the big Afghan turned and galloped madly fifty yards in the wrong direction, then fell into a painstaking examination of the foundation planting around the Math Building.

It was a familiar delaying tactic, but Antonia was in no hurry to get home anyway. Though the night air was cool, it was still prematurely springlike with the rich smells of earth and blossom. There was no moon, but the sky was so clear that crowding stars cast a faint glimmer over shrubbery, footpaths, and college buildings. In the serenity of the silent campus, Antonia found that her thoughts were much clearer and less harried than they had been after Bennie Thompson's departure. Instead of chasing each other around in her head to no purpose, they now marshaled themselves under a few simple headings, and stayed put.

Her instinct was to trust Bennie. Even if some self-serving motives were involved, she had the feeling that his concern for Ariadne was genuine. His story of the girl's late nights in the museum had the ring of truth, too: slaving till dawn over her dissertation in a drafty and deserted building—yes, improbable though it might sound to anyone who didn't know her, that was precisely the sort of thing Ariadne would do.

As for the unlovely visitor Bennie claimed she had entertained there one night—suddenly it occurred to Antonia to identify him with the shadowy figure she herself had glimpsed yesterday evening near the museum. She had dismissed him at the time as one of the more massive forms of student fauna: wrestler, varsity linebacker, something like that. But if there was any chance he was the man Bennie had found arguing with Ariadne in the museum workroom—well, she would tell Caracci what she had seen and perhaps he would be able to make something of it.

Caracci. Antonia grinned to herself in the dark, a little ruefully. In her present, more mellow mood she suspected she'd done the man less than justice. He'd caught her off guard, turning up unannounced like that, and she'd been unnecessarily prickly in countering what had seemed like attacks on Ariadne. They weren't attacks, of course, but legitimate and probably quite routine questions. In fact, in retrospect she had to admit that Caracci had been scrupulously fair to Ariadne. Next time, Antonia vowed, she would try to be as fair to him. She even found, somewhat to her own surprise, that she was looking forward to that next time.

Rousing herself from her reverie, Antonia looked around for Nike and was about to whistle her in when a shadowy figure came into view near the museum. Two such apparitions on two successive nights. Antonia felt, were really too much, especially in light of Caracci's assurance that skulking strangers were out of style. The next instant, however, she realized her mistake. This was not the same man but someone shorter and much more lightly built.

Another second and she saw that it was Win Randolph. So much for mysterious skulkers.

But as she was about to call out a greeting to Win, something huge and featureless erupted from the shrubbery behind him and seemed to engulf him. Antonia thought she heard a strangled cry of surprise and fear, but there was no other sound. Her heart pounding, she started toward the two figures struggling together on the ground, calling to Nike as she ran.

The Afghan brushed past her at full speed, a gray blur only a few shades lighter than the starlit dimness. As on the previous night, there was a warning rumble in Nike's throat, though Antonia suspected it was more a gesture of good sportsmanship than a serious challenge to the enemy.

Whatever Nike's intentions, her arrival alone was enough to send the attacker on his way. Few men, even large ones, are inclined to argue with sixty pounds of growling dog. This man, at any rate, was not so inclined. With a muttered curse, he made off around the corner of the museum as on the previous night. Nike was clearly longing to chase him, but Antonia called her back and put her on the leash.

"You all right, Win?" Antonia asked a little breathlessly.

"I think so." Understandably enough, he sounded confused as well as scared. "What the hell hit me, anyway? And what are *you* doing here?"

Antonia explained as Win stood up, dusted himself off, and regained his composure. "Well, then, thanks, Antonia," he said. "*And* Nike." He gave the dog an awkward pat on the shoulder. "I suppose I'd better report this to the campus cops. If some crazed fraternity brother has escaped his keepers, they'll want to know about it."

It wasn't until she and Nike were back in the apartment that Antonia realized she hadn't told Win about his assailant's previous appearance. Assuming that is, that it *was* the same man she'd seen the night before. Just before she went to bed, Antonia added this to her mental list of "Things to Do Tomorrow for Sure."

The only other item on this list was something that had occurred to her on the walk back from campus: "Go Talk to Ariadne's Family."

6. The Labyrinth

THE TWO-BUS, FORTY-FIVE-MINUTE RIDE THROUGH BUSY streets to the north side of the city had, temporarily, the effect Antonia had hoped for. It gave her the illusion of going somewhere, of doing something. By way of rationalizing this rather quixotic foray into alien territory, she kept reminding herself that she had, after all, gotten a bit of information out of Bennie Thompson that he had withheld from Caracci's men. For some reason he had trusted her more than he had the police. Well, perhaps Ariadne's family would feel the same way. She clung to the thought.

Once she was off the bus, the alienness of the district became more and more oppressive. She moved through a welter of blowing newspapers and junk-food wrappers. Most of the shop signs she passed were in Greek: *TAVERNA, ARTOPOEION, FARMAKEION, TAVERNA.*

The address provided by the Student Directory turned out to be neither house nor apartment building but a grimy *taverna*. Faded Greek letters above the door identified it as *O LABYRINTHOS*—The Labyrinth, an odd name for a restaurant.

There was another sign overhanging the sidewalk at right angles to the building, but it was so darkened by age and weather that Antonia had difficulty making out the subject.

48

Painted apparently by an amateur of modest talents, it
portrayed the Minotaur, monstrous offspring of Queen Pasiphaë of Crete and the white bull of Poseidon. Half bull
and half—Antonia, startled, took a closer look and shivered. Was it mere technical incompetence, or had the unknown painter deliberately set the glowering bull's head
on the body of a young child, narrow in the shoulders and
chest and without any suggestion of musculature in the
arms or thighs? The effect, far from being fearsome or
even grotesque, was almost pathetic. The massive beast's
head seemed a cruel burden for the childish body on which
it rested. It reminded her horribly of a five-year-old hydro-
cephalic she had once glimpsed in a hospital corridor.

She stepped into The Labyrinth with some misgivings.
The interior, however, was not particularly forbidding—
nor particularly labyrinthine either. The proprietor was apparently one of those small restaurateurs whose entire
imaginative capital is expended on the invention of a col-
orful name for their establishment, leaving them without
the wherewithal to carry out the theme. In this instance,
Antonia thought, it was probably just as well, if the sign
outside was any indication.

The place was dark and dusty looking, but otherwise
ordinary enough. Most of the bottles behind the bar were
nearly full—*ouzo*, several varieties of *retsína, mavro-
daphne,* and one incongruous fifth of Scotch. They stood
shoulder to shoulder with a small army of *bríkia*, the little
brass pots in which is brewed the powerful coffee of Greece
and Turkey. The leatherette seats of the bar stools were
cracked and torn, with bits of kapok protruding here and
there like mocking tongues. The bar itself was stained and
scarred, but it was still damp from a recent wiping.

No customers were in evidence, and Antonia was about
to investigate a second room that opened off the first,
where sounds of scrubbing seemed to indicate the presence
of an employee. At this moment a beaded curtain rattled
and a woman appeared behind the bar.

She was the kind of woman of whom one immediately
and irresistibly thinks "she must have been beautiful
once." Not, in this case, because she was very old—not
more than forty-five, Antonia judged—and certainly not
because she was aging gracefully. She was, in fact, fat
and slovenly, but she had the indefinable air common to

many fat women of never having cast off the habit of believing herself beautiful. It was in the way she carried the ugly fat on the splendid bones, it was in the arrow-straight Greek nose, it was in the dark eyes that were bitter and defiant now but must once have been invitingly bold.

"Ti thélete, kyría?" she said abruptly. "What you want?"

"Mrs. Pappas?" Taking a barely perceptible movement of the head as a grudging affirmative, Antonia forged ahead. "I'm Antonia Nielsen, one of Ariadne's professors at the university, and I'm a little concerned about her. I suppose you know that she's been missing for several days now, and—"

"You don' want nothing to drink?" The tone was belligerent.

"No, I only—that is, yes, I'll have a glass of wine. *Parakaló.*" Slightly mollified, the woman poured a glass of the most expensive *retsína* and pushed it a very few inches across the bar toward Antonia.

"Look, lady, I don' know nothing about my daughter. I never see her no more, she don' come home once a blue moon. I tol' the cop, I ain' seen her since February. What business it is to you, anyway?"

"Mrs. Pappas, I don't think you quite understand the situation. There's been a burglary at the University Museum where Ariadne works, and she's under suspicion."

The woman gave a contemptuous snort that jiggled her collection of chins. "She never do a thing like that."

So there is a spark of maternal loyalty buried under all that hostility, thought Antonia. Maybe I'm getting to her. "No," she said, "I quite agree. We all think . . . ."

"She ain' got the guts," said the woman with finality.

So much for the maternal-loyalty angle. There was one other possibility, a long shot, but the best Antonia could do on the spur of the moment.

"She could go to prison, Mrs. Pappas. For a long time. And her chances of getting a job afterward . . ."

Far from her being shocked into a more cooperative attitude, Mrs. Pappas' tone grew uglier. "You mean she's gonna leave us on the lurch? *Kalá, kalá!*" And she burst into a torrent of Greek that Antonia couldn't follow in detail but that appeared to contain a high proportion of invective. It was clear that no help was to be expected from

Ariadne's mother, and Antonia reached for her purse, intending to pay for her wine and leave. At a pause in the shrill tirade from behind the bar, she glanced up and realized that the last few words had been directed not at her but at a third person who was now standing in the doorway that connected the two rooms of the small *taverna.*

It was a young woman of twenty or so, dressed inelegantly in denim overalls and a headscarf. Her hands were abnormally clean and red, as if from hot sudsy water, and she was wiping them on a towel that protruded like a saucy tail from one hip pocket. She was evidently the source of the floor-scrubbing noises Antonia had noticed earlier. She listened dispassionately to the finale of Mrs. Pappas' tirade while she finished drying her hands. She had evidently witnessed such outbursts before and seemed neither startled nor embarrassed.

"Sigá, mamá, sigá," she said when her mother paused for breath. "Professor Nielsen is only trying to help Ari." Then, turning to Antonia, "Miss Nielsen, I heard what you said and I appreciate your concern, but Mamá is a little upset and I don't think she cares to talk about it right now. If you'd like to finish your wine, I'll go change my clothes and walk you back to the bus stop. I was going out anyway." And she ushered her mother gently but efficiently back through the bead curtain and up a narrow staircase that apparently led to the family living quarters on the second floor.

Antonia barely had time to finish the bitter *retsína* before the girl returned. The transformation was startling. Gone were the shapeless overalls and grimy bandanna. A simple knit dress, while leaving much to the imagination, hinted strongly that imagination was unlikely to exaggerate the facts. A great mane of black hair, freed from the scarf, fell in glossy masses over her shoulders. The huge dark eyes held a suggestion of mockery and more than a suggestion of determination, perhaps even ruthlessness if the need should arise. The mouth was good natured enough, wide and straight, the lips seeming barely to curve at all.

Yet despite the girl's almost melodramatic good looks, it was a small but incongruous detail that Antonia found most intriguing: a bracelet on the girl's left wrist, of simple design and exquisite workmanship. It was the only jewelry she wore, and perhaps the only piece she owned. It appeared to be made of solid gold.

As they left the *taverna*, Antonia involuntarily glanced up at the faded Minotaur sign. The girl's eyes, following her gaze, darkened as if at a painful memory. But her voice was matter-of-fact.

"We really ought to take that thing down, I suppose. My father painted it just before he died—that'd be almost twelve years now. He wasn't much of an artist, was he? It was kind of a family—joke, I guess you could call it. Mamá always hated it, though. When I was a kid I used to use it for a target: rocks in summer, snowballs in winter. The idea was to hit the bull's nose. I'd give myself ten points for hitting him square on the nose. The other kids would never play that game with me, though. I think they were a little scared of the sign, didn't understand what it meant. Or maybe they *did* understand. Anyway Ari always stopped me before I had a chance to zero in on that nose. She'd get real mad and make me quit." And she smiled with the amused tolerance of the grown woman of twenty for the ten-year-old tomboy she no longer recognizes as a part of herself.

"I take it that your father was something of a student of ancient Greece, then. I suppose that's where Ariadne got her interest in Classics?" It seemed innocuous enough as an opening gambit. Antonia had the impression that the girl was no more anxious than her mother to speculate about Ariadne's present predicament.

"I guess you could say that," the girl answered without enthusiasm. "It was sort of a bond between them, made them quite close in fact." Her tone was elaborately casual, almost bored, but again the little girl was visible behind the woman's self-possession. It wasn't hard to imagine the two sisters, one with a four- or five-year head start on capturing their father's attention by lisping bits of Euripides or Homer, the other feeling helpless anger as she realized she couldn't compete. Wrong tack again. What the hell was the *right* tack with this family, anyway? Antonia tried again.

"I'm sorry if I upset your mother again. I know having the police here must have been difficult enough. But I've been worried about Ariadne, and I thought possibly . . ."

"Don't worry, Professor, you didn't upset her. Nothing upsets Mamá. That's just the way she is about Ari." She paused and glanced at Antonia from under long, straight black eyebrows. She looked as if she were adding up a column of figures in her head.

"You see, Mamá has gotten it into her head that Ari is—well, prosperous. I've tried to explain to her that Ari isn't a professor yet, she's just in training, she doesn't have a real job. Mamá doesn't want to hear about all that. She's convinced herself that Ari has money somewhere that she's not sharing with us, and it nearly drives her mad. I'm afraid Mamá isn't very rational on the subject of money. I guess a lot of poor people aren't."

"Yes, but practically to wish her own daughter dead, in front of a total stranger! I couldn't follow everything she said in Greek, but . . ."

"Yes, Ma'am, that's just about what she was saying all right. My father used to say the Cretans are a violent people, and if Mamá's anything to go by I guess he was right. With her it's just talk, though. Mamá wouldn't actually *do* anything to anyone. Doing things isn't exactly her strong point." The wide straight lips curved in a bitter little smile that seemed to imply that no more family skeletons would be exhibited today.

"But it is true that you haven't seen or heard from Ariadne for some time? And you have no idea where she might have gone?"

"Oh, no, Mamá wasn't exaggerating that part. The last time Ari was here was in February, I think. She came one afternoon to leave a little money with me. She's afraid to mail it for fear Mamá will see the envelope before I do. Mamá isn't very reliable about money, like I said. Once in a while I even stop by Ari's office in the museum to see if she can spare us something. Anyway, that last time she stayed a couple of hours and then left, and we haven't seen her or talked to her since. She didn't say much while she was here either, just that she still thought she could finish up her degree by June and get a regular job in the fall. That's the only thing Mamá's interested in, of course, so that's about all Ari ever talks about when she's here. I really can't tell you any more than that."

"But you do understand what's happened—the burglary at the museum, and your sister's disappearance?"

"Yeah, I saw it on the evening news Friday and the cop explained when he was here." Then, with a smile that rather unpleasantly combined amusement and a kind of perverse satisfaction, she added, "Wherever she is, Ari'll be having a fit right now."

"Why do you say that?"

"You know how she is. She takes all that old stuff so seriously—jewelry and pots and statues, all that antiquity stuff. It'd kill her if any of it got ripped off—and out of her own museum too." Again Antonia heard an undertone of vindictive pleasure in the girl's voice. She seemed as indifferent to her sister's fate as her mother.

Her next words were an embarrassingly apt reply to Antonia's unspoken thought. "Don't get the idea I hate my sister. It isn't that. It's just that she's always been so high and mighty about our precious ancestors and all that. But I don't hate her. I even admire her in a way. At least she's gotten out of this, you have to give her that much. It's more than the rest of us have done." And she glanced bitterly around her at the decaying neighborhood of old apartment houses and dusty shops through which they were walking.

"You're not worried about Ariadne's just vanishing like this?"

"Ari," said the girl with conviction, "can take care of herself. Always has."

"Do you have any idea at all where she might have gone?"

Faced with the girl's unshakable nonchalance, Antonia was beginning to wonder whether she was indeed making mountains out of molehills.

"Not really. But she's done it before. She'll just take off on the bus for a few days, without telling anyone. To do some research, or something."

They had reached the bus stop, and Antonia's bus was approaching. The girl turned to her with an incongruous air of genteel formality, as if they were about to take leave of each other after sipping tea in a Victorian drawing room.

"Miss Nielsen," she said, extending her hand, "I do appreciate your taking such an interest in my sister. But I think perhaps you're exaggerating the seriousness of the situation just a little. I'm sure Ari's all right. It isn't likely we'll hear from her, but if we do I'll certainly let you know."

Across the street from the downtown stop where she had to change to the university bus stood a small pub. Antonia noticed it as she got off the downtown bus and decided to offer herself a drink as compensation for a wasted afternoon. Tomorrow's lecture notes could wait the extra half hour it would take to consume one beer and catch the next westbound bus.

Inside the pub the paneling was very dark and the lighting very dim. As she groped her way toward a booth, Antonia thought she could see a dartboard in one corner, though in that murky atmosphere it was hard to imagine how anyone could play a game without exposing his fellow patrons to the risk of grievous bodily injury.

Fortunately the proprietor's aspirations to authentic Englishness extended also to the serving of a very good imported ale. Antonia had consumed a delicious club sandwich and two ales and was congratulating herself on having salvaged this much at least from her futile expedition, when she saw them.

They had apparently just entered the pub, for the man was hanging their coats on the coatpole attached to the end of their booth, his activity effectively concealing his companion, who had already seated herself. But Antonia recognized him even though his back was turned to her, and when he sat down the woman's head, partially visible over the back of the booth, was familiar too.

Antonia shrank back into the corner of her own booth and hunched over her empty mug, hoping she was invisible in the semidarkness. They were sitting between her and the door. If she left now she would have to pass within a few feet of their booth and they would certainly see and recognize her. She was safe so long as they remained seated with their backs to her. But if she outwaited them there was a chance they would see her when they stood up to leave.

Her decision was hastened by the arrival of the waiter, inquiring whether she would have another mug. She nodded silently.

The girl must have waited at the same stop from which she had seen Antonia off and taken the next bus half an hour later. He would have come into town by the same bus that would take Antonia home, coming of course in the opposite direction. The point at which the two downtown bus routes intersected was an obvious place for a rendezvous, easily reached yet remote from the normal haunts of anyone who knew or cared about either him or her.

Until I went snooping, that is, thought Antonia, feeling both embarrassed and angry.

She made a conscious effort not to hear what they were saying. If it had not been superfluous the gesture would have been self-defeating, like trying not to think about falling asleep when you have insomnia. But fortunately they were sitting side by side, their heads very close together, and speaking very softly. Antonia couldn't hear their words but she couldn't help noticing that their conversation was filled with a certain emotional intensity she found disturbing.

Whatever its subject, the conversation was brief. The man rose abruptly after ten minutes, shrugged his coat on, and departed, leaving his mug half empty on the table. The woman stayed a few minutes longer, then she too stood up to leave.

For a split second, as she turned and reached for her coat, she faced Antonia. That she failed to see Antonia was due not so much to the dimness of the light as to the mental state she was in. That state was painfully obvious.

She had the look of an animal baffled of its prey. The hint of mockery in her dark eyes had hardened to a smoldering fury, the long straight lips were set in a cruel line. Even her hair, an aureole of leaping dark flames about her face, seemed to quiver with anger.

A woman scorned, thought Antonia with more aptness than originality. It looks as if Ariadne's sister has been, as they used to say, scorned. By my dear colleague Win Randolph.

Antonia gave the girl a five-minute head start to reduce the risk of running into her outside, then rose to leave. Halfway to the cashier's desk she nearly collided with a solid-looking figure in a topcoat. It was Caracci.

"What on earth are *you*—" they began in unison. They both laughed.

"Have you got a minute to talk, Miss Nielsen? I could even declare myself off duty and buy you a drink. I was planning to drown my own sorrows anyway."

"Sorry to hear you've got sorrows, Lieutenant, but yes, I'll join you. And thanks."

When he had ordered them a couple of mugs of ale, Antonia said, "This may be less of a coincidence than it looks, Lieutenant. I bet you had the same idea I had, and maybe the same luck. The Pappas women, am I right?"

"Just the mother this time. The daughter was out, so there wasn't anyone to interpret. The way the old girl was carrying on, though, I didn't really need anyone to translate her Greek."

Antonia gave him a sympathetic smile. "I know what you mean. I got exactly the same treatment." She didn't tell him that she had talked to Ariadne's sister, for fear of being drawn into revealing that she had later seen the girl with Win in this very tavern. She wanted more time to think about that, to try to find some innocuous explanation for their being together, before she mentioned it to anyone.

"It was a pretty feeble hope anyway, I suppose," Caracci said. "But I'm not making much progress with this Aegean Gold business and I guess I was grasping at straws." He sounded discouraged.

"Oh lord, the Gold!" Antonia exclaimed.

"Yeah, the Aegean—" Someone had corrected his pronunciation since their previous talk, she noticed.

"No, I mean—I hadn't made the connection until just now, but last night . . ." And she described the attack on Win outside the museum, and her own sighting of what might have been the same man the night before.

Caracci listened intently. By the time she finished, he was looking thoroughly disapproving.

"Are you telling me, Miss Nielsen, that you saw a colleague of yours get mugged last night, got your dog to chase the assailant away, and then calmly went home to bed and forgot the whole thing? That this happened in a place where you had previously noticed a suspicious individual, a place that had been the site of a well-publicized burglary a few days before? And it never occurred to you to mention any of this to the police?"

"Win was going to report it to the campus police. Neither of us associated the attack on him with the break-in at the museum. Surely whoever did that wouldn't be so stupid as to hang around the scene of the crime the next two nights? Win and I both assumed that it was some student, probably drunk, doing one of the silly and incomprehensible things students do under the combined influence of alcohol and spring fever. We thought of it as a *campus* problem, not a matter for the metropolitan police. I also assumed that after Win talked to the campus cops they would pass on to you anything they thought you should know."

"Yeah, they're supposed to." Caracci's moment of indignation seemed to have passed. "Students and spring and chemicals, that's their kind of problem usually. You think maybe this weather's been getting to the kids?"

"I wouldn't be surprised. I know it's been getting to *me*. Friday especially, I was so busy thinking about all the places I'd rather be and the things I'd rather be doing, I could hardly teach. Of course, I stopped short of mugging my colleagues or robbing museums. Lousy lectures are about the closest I ever get to antisocial behavior traceable to spring fever."

"I never thought you liberated professional types would get anything as old-fashioned as spring fever," Caracci grinned. "That's kind of encouraging, in a way."

"Sure we do." Antonia smiled back. "Only of course with us it takes more sophisticated forms. I, for example, was having fantasies about exploring Crete, maybe discovering a whole new Minoan site. Nothing so reactionary as a handsome man on a white horse or a white Honda. That's not permitted to us liberated professional types."

They both laughed, and the subject of the Saturday Night Skulker did not arise again.

7. The Tower

FROM THE NORTHEAST CORNER OF THE OLD BUILDING that housed the University Museum rose a tower. The aesthetic intentions of the Victorian architect who had perpetrated this tower were the subject of endless conjecture and controversy among the wittier elements of the academic community.

There was the Spanish-mission bell tower faction, the Renaissance campanile faction, and the Marxist-oriented faction, which held that the thing was patterned after the smokestacks of a nineteenth-century textile mill. There was even a lunatic fringe that maintained the designer drew his inspiration from a prophetic dream of a rocket gantry.

Whatever its origins, the tower's present function was prosaic enough. Except for its topmost story, it was occupied by the offices of several of the museum's administrative staff. They were the more junior members, expected to take whatever was offered in the way of office space. The tower was well known to be underheated, drafty, and remote from the more active sectors of the museum. It also lacked an elevator. It was nobody's idea of prime office space.

There had been a period, however, just before the new Humanities Building was constructed, when every broom closet and telephone booth on campus was pressed into

service as offices for the humanities faculty. It was a time
they all remembered with distaste, a time of fragmented
departments and long walks to class in every weather.

It was at this unlamented period that Win Randolph and
another classicist had drawn the top floor of the museum
tower. His colleague had departed from the university just
before the completion of the Humanities Building, leaving
Win in sole possession of the dim, low-ceilinged, vaguely
medieval-looking room. When the call at last went forth
for the scattered humanities departments to reassemble
themselves in their new cement-block cubicles, Win refused to move. Five years later he was still holding un-
disputed sway over the only faculty office on campus with
diamond-paned casement windows.

Not surprisingly, a sizable body of legend had grown
up around Randolph's Tower. The gist of it was that the
tower room regularly witnessed scenes of riotous living
unheard of in the antiseptic cubicles of the new Humanities Building. A battered steel storage cabinet was said to
house a respectable array of wines and spirits. A humble
single-burner hotplate was apotheosized, on the lips of the
legend-makers, into the central element of elaborate and
exotic tea ceremonies.

But it was the sagging couch in one of the dimmer
corners of the room that inspired the juiciest episodes in
the Legend of the Tower.

The legend, at this point, split into two distinct branch-
es. According to the first, Win had more than once spent
the night on this couch (alone), after heated marital dis-
putes that terminated in his being locked out of the house
by Gillian.

The second branch was the more popular. It stressed,
predictably enough, the seduction of coeds in numbers that
varied radically from source to source. This subdivision
of the legend was especially rich in variants, some versions insisting, for example, that Win's attentions were not
confined exclusively to students but occasionally extended
to his female colleagues on the faculty.

Knowing Win better than most of his colleagues did,
Antonia had always been quite sure that the juicier seg-
ments of the legend were apocryphal. That he occasionally
offered a cup of coffee to a student was of course quite
possible. And—though all-night bouts of hard work at his

desk were hardly Win's style—it was even conceivable
that he had once or twice fallen asleep on the notorious
couch after working late and spent the night there rather
than drag himself home.

But Win Randolph as wholesale seducer, whether of
coeds or colleagues, in towers or elsewhere—this aspect
of the legend she had never taken seriously. Questions of
moral rectitude and husbandly devotion aside, he was simply not daring enough. But now, as she sat curled up on
her sofa with a sheaf of half-read lecture notes in her lap,
Antonia wondered.

By the time she reached home she had decided that her
instinctive reaction to the interlude in the pub had been
overhasty. She had always been a skeptic on the question
of intuition, feminine or otherwise, and she saw no reason
to become a true believer at this late date. It made no
sense to conclude from one ambiguous incident that Win
Randolph was having an affair with a girl half his age.

On the other hand, if the confrontation in the pub had
not been an amorous adventure—or the terminal episode
of one—then what *had* they been doing there together?
The sister, in conversation with Antonia, had put on an
elaborate show of nonchalance concerning Ariadne's
whereabouts. Was it possible that she was more disturbed
by her sister's disappearance than she had admitted, and
that she had enlisted Win's help in trying to locate her?
But why should she be willing to talk to Win and not to
Antonia? And what could Win have said to make the girl
so furiously angry, if they were discussing her missing
sister?

Reluctantly, Antonia returned to the erotic interpretation
of the scene in the pub. Intuitive it might be, and dis-
tasteful it certainly was, but it seemed to fit the few known
facts better than any other she could think of.

What about Gillian's suspicions concerning Ariadne?
Two nights ago Antonia had thought them ridiculous and
a little pathetic. Had poor Gillian been right, then, or half-
right, barking (unkind metaphor) at the wrong branch of
the right tree?

Antonia turned with relief to the notes, skimming for
continuity through last month's material before settling
down to polish tomorrow's lecture: *Euripides,* she read,
youngest of three great Athenian tragedians. B. during

wars with Persia, d. during wars with Sparta. Wrote 92 plays of which 19 extant plus frgs. Knowledge of lost plays still increasing: papyri. . . .

Monday morning was no worse than other Monday mornings. The usual assortment of students, secretaries, and colleagues paraded in and out of Antonia's office, on the usual errands: I can't understand why I got a B-minus on this exam . . . would you mind signing this . . . have you seen Smedley's article in AJP . . .

The burglary seemed to be losing steam already as a topic of conversation.

Then, just as Antonia was preparing to leave for lunch, Win stuck his head in the door. She had been thankful for his nonappearance during the morning, not knowing how she would react when they did meet. The decision was now taken out of her hands, temporarily at least.

"Thanks again for your deed of derring-do the other night," Win began. "Yours and Nike's, that is. I reported our little fracas to the campus cops, by the way. They seemed less impressed with the peril to my person than I could have wished, but they did promise to look into it. At least it'll keep them constructively occupied and out of trouble for a few days."

The tone of sardonic condescension toward all members of the university community below the rank of full professor was typical of Win Randolph. But beneath the banter Antonia thought she detected a weariness, a kind of heaviness, that was not at all typical. He looked, for once, his full forty-two years, perhaps even a bit more. The battered tweed jacket and rumpled hair failed, this morning, to make him look his usual boyish twenty-five.

"Win," Antonia began abruptly, "is Gillian all right?"

He sank into the steel-and-plastic armchair that was the cubicle's only concession to hospitality. "I don't know," he said unhappily. "She *seems* calm enough now—almost too calm, I'm afraid. Feels she made a fool of herself Friday night, of course."

Antonia made a vague murmur.

"The—other night," he continued with an effort, "she was calm too, after the initial blowup. And yet a few hours later she—but you were there. Of course that was a more violent explosion. . . ."

Indeed it had been. Although the blond coed had showed a quite saintly forbearance after they pulled Gillian off her, it was obvious that the girl had passed through a few moments of stark terror, of genuine—and quite justified—fear for her life. Though not athletic, Gillian was tall and by no means fragile, and she had the added strength of temporary insanity, or what looked a lot like it.

"Which could mean," Win was saying, "one of two things. Either this was a milder . . . attack, or whatever you want to call it—or else it was somehow dammed up before it ran its full course. In which case there may be, God help us, more to come." He stood up painfully. "I'd better be getting home. I may be overreacting, but I'm not really sure I should leave her alone."

He had reached the door. In desperation, Antonia blurted out the question there seemed to be no tactful way of introducing at such a moment.

"Win, before you leave, I—I saw you yesterday talking to Ariadne's sister. I wouldn't have mentioned it except—did you get anything out of her? I went to see her too, and Ariadne might have been a total stranger for all the girl would tell me about her."

Win's voice, as he turned back from the door again, held a trace of annoyance.

"As a matter of fact, Antonia, we weren't discussing Ariadne. She asked me to meet her there to talk over a—personal matter."

Antonia must have looked as embarrassed as she felt, because Win hastily went on.

"Now hold on, Antonia, I didn't mean all *that* personal. The fact is, the wretched girl has been trying to get me to 'exercise some influence,' as she puts it, to get her a job here—preferably as secretary to one of our larger departments. She started in on me the first time we ever met—at Ariadne's desk in the museum. I'd stopped by to return a couple of chapters of her dissertation, as I often do. Since we both work in the same building, it's more convenient. Anyway, her sister was there that day, looking—well, you saw the way she looks. She seemed to take a shine to me. 'Ari's told me so much about you, Professor Randolph,' et cetera. Corny as hell, and of course I didn't fall for it. Not for the first two or three minutes, at least. Next thing I knew, we were having a drink in that same pub where you saw us yesterday, and I was on the brink of earning—at long last—my hitherto undeserved reputation as Lothario-in-residence.''

"Seems a lot of trouble to go to for a typing job," Antonia observed skeptically.

"You don't understand, Antonia. Neither did I, for that matter, not at first. But yesterday—after I'd made it clear that I don't intend to do any more for her—she lost her cool for a few minutes and let me see what she's really after."

"And that is?"

"I hardly know how to put it to one of your enlightened views, Antonia, without giving offense. Her object, in its archaic simplicity and its Neanderthal crudeness, is matrimony."

Antonia refused to rise to the bait. She was remembering the girl's bitter words at the bus stop the day before. *Ari's gotten out of this. It's more than the rest of us have done.* And the occasional little lapses into what she probably thought of as more refined speech: *Mamá doesn't care to talk about it. I do appreciate your interest. . . .* And that beautiful gold bracelet that must have cost several weeks' salary. If she *had* a salary.

"Matrimony," Win went on, "not of course to me, but to one of the dozens of eligible men who would be hanging around her typewriter all day. A graduate student, an instructor . . . who knows? Maybe even one of the lesser deans. A man with a future. That, Antonia, is what was at stake, not a mere 'typing job,' as you so uncharitably put it.''

What was at stake was a whole new life, thought Antonia, remembering the grimy *taverna*. Comfort, security, what used to be called respectability. To someone starting from where the Pappas family had, those things could seem all-important, well worth selling your looks for. Not a very dignified way "out of this," but a lot faster and easier than getting a Ph.D. in nuclear physics, as the feminists would have preferred her to. Or even classical Greek. That had been Ariadne's way. This girl was trying to do it in hers, and Antonia was not disposed to pass judgment on her. But her method was far from subtle—surely trying to seduce Win Randolph was overkill. He would have given her some sort of recommendation for the asking, in all probability. Apparently she hadn't realized that, had imagined the price of entry was higher than it actually was.

"But why yesterday in particular?"

"She'd gotten the idea, from television and perhaps also from that detective, that the university regards her sister as a prime suspect in the museum burglary. She was terrified that this would compromise her job application, here and everywhere else. Kept saying, "Who would ever trust me, after this?""

"What did you tell her?"

"I tried to convince her that her precious application was okay—in actual fact, I suspect it's lying dead in a file somewhere—but she didn't let up. Kept demanding that I talk to someone, make more phone calls, *do* something. Finally I couldn't take any more and told her there was nothing more I could or would do for her. Period. Rather anticlimactic, isn't it, after what you probably imagined you saw yesterday?"

"I'm sorry, Win. You know I didn't mean to spy."

"No, of course not. No harm done. I'll see you tomorrow—or Wednesday more likely. I haven't any classes tomorrow, and I may just loll about the house. Take care."

Watching him go, Antonia remembered the fury on the girl's face. Could the meeting have been as innocent as Win implied?

When Antonia returned from lunch an hour later, Caracci was waiting outside her office, his stocky business-suited figure incongruous among the leggy jean-clad students who hurried past him in the narrow corridor.

She smiled at him. "Didn't expect to see you again so soon, Lieutenant. I'm afraid I haven't any more prowlers, skulkers, or lurkers up my sleeve, if that's what you're hoping for." It was a relief no longer to have any clandestine trysts between Ariadne's sister and dissertation director up her sleeve, either. She unlocked the door and he followed her into the office, where he settled without invitation into the one spare chair.

"Your first one hasn't done much for us so far, Miss Nielsen. We had a man watching the museum last night, and there was nothing to watch. But that's not what I've come about. No further word on the Pappas girl, I suppose." He didn't bother to make it sound like a question, but Antonia shook her head anyway.

"But what I really wanted to talk to you about was this Thompson kid. Bennie Thompson."

"I see." She didn't, but from the not very subtle hints Bennie had dropped concerning his relationship with Caracci, she had a fair idea what to expect.

"I wonder if you do, Miss Nielsen. He finally got around to calling me last night. He says he talked to you Saturday and you were—sympathetic, I think was the word he used. And that's what worries me."

"Now I'm afraid I *don't* see, Lieutenant. You're telling me I shouldn't be sympathetic to Bennie Thompson? I should have thought that was my own business, not a matter fo. police investigation."

"Ordinarily it would be your business, of course. But Bennie isn't exactly an ordinary boy, and I want to be sure you understand what you're getting into."

"I wasn't aware that I was 'getting into' anything, Lieutenant. I've talked to Bennie exactly once, for perhaps an hour. We were both concerned about Ariadne Pappas, who happens to be a mutual friend and who hasn't been seen or heard from for something like four—"

"I know, I know," Caracci cut her short. "And maybe that's all it is, concern for his friend. But I think you should also be aware that—for my money, anyway—Bennie is a prime suspect in this theft business. Even more to the point, he also happens to be a former drug addict."

"But why is that so much to the point, Lieutenant? He's doing very well for himself now, as far as I can see. He's got a steady job, he works hard, he's said to be very reliable—what more could you ask?"

"Nothing—except for the fact that a very valuable collection of objects is missing from his place of employment. Objects that should have been locked up in a safe, but were somehow left lying around loose like pencils and paperclips that particular night. Plus the fact that he just happened to be at the opposite end of the building and two floors up when all that gold was taken. Coincidence? Bad luck? We don't know yet, Miss Nielsen, but we intend to find out."

"I'm sorry, Lieutenant, but to my untutored ear that doesn't exactly sound like an airtight case against the boy."

"I'm not making a case against him, Miss Nielsen. I'm concerned about you, that's all. Even if Bennie had nothing to do with the break-in at the museum, he could be a dangerous friend. I just wanted you to know that. What you do about it is your business, as you say."

"Thanks, Lieutenant. I'll try not to do anything rash. But the one *I'm* concerned about is Ariadne. She's been gone for almost four days now. Isn't there something you can do?"

"Can't do much more than I have, Miss Nielsen. She isn't officially missing, of course—and with a family like hers she isn't likely to be, either. She could be gone four years, let alone four days, and I doubt *they'd* report it."

Her own frustrating encounter with Ariadne's mother and sister still fresh in her mind, Antonia could only agree, silently and glumly, with this assessment of the Pappas family's solidarity.

"In other words, if I want to find Ariadne Pappas I can go and look for her myself." Antonia knew she was being unduly sharp with Caracci, but his imperturbable coolness concerning her student was getting on her nerves.

"No, Ma'am, I wasn't suggesting that. Like I said, we've done everything we can. I doubt you'd have any better luck tracing her on your own—and maybe you don't have quite the resources we have." His voice was calm, without a trace of either condescension or resentment. Unreasonably, Antonia felt her own annoyance increase.

"Sorry, Lieutenant," she said then, in what she hoped was a more cordial tone. "I didn't mean to question your procedures. But I *am* worried about the girl. She's extremely competent academically, but in other ways she gives such an impression of friendlessness, of vulnerability."

"I understand your concern, Ma'am. But if Miss Pappas shows up at her mother's place, or her own apartment, or any hospital in the city, we'll know about it. Most likely, though, she'll just turn up right here at the university in a day or two and wonder what all the fuss is about. Assuming she wasn't involved in the theft. Happens all the time, believe me."

It was only after he had left that the implication of the phrase came home to her. *Any hospital in the city. If she shows up at any hospital in the city, we'll know about it.*

8. Another Labyrinth

THIS DISTURBING TRAIN OF THOUGHT WAS INTERRUPTED by the precipitous entrance of Barry Greenfield. He bounded into Antonia's office unannounced, pointed an accusing forefinger at her nose, and demanded, "Where were *you*, Madam, on the evening of Saturday, April seventh, between the hours of eight and eleven? Or was it the eighth? Anyway, where the hell were you?"

"Saturday," she said thoughtfully. "Ah, yes, Saturday. That was the night I spent with Prince Charles. Or was it—no, definitely the prince. Robert Redford was the Saturday *before.*"

Barry assumed a reproachful expression and flopped into the vacant chair. "Really, Antonia," he said, "your levity is most unseemly. It was a serious question. Couched, it may be, in the typically effervescent Greenfield style, but a serious question nonetheless. You may possibly recall," he added severely, "that I invited you to dinner."

"Oh," she said in a small voice. "Yes. You did, didn't you."

She remembered now. When he had returned her and her bike to her apartment Friday afternoon, he had said something about broiling a steak Saturday for himself and

Marsha—his latest conquest among the graduate students—
and letting Antonia have the bones to gnaw.

Her brief moment of contrition, however, was cut short
by a cackle of delighted laughter from Barry.

"Never mind, old girl. The expression on your face was
compensation enough for one cold T-bone that Marsha and
I had to finish up for you. It was rare—your expression,
that is, not the steak, which was slightly overdone. Associate Professor Antonia Nielsen, M.A., Ph.D., looking
like a kitten that's just been caught in an indiscretion on
the living room carpet."

"I withdraw," retorted Antonia, "any apology that may
have been implied or inferred."

"No, no, my child, you mustn't apologize. We all have
these occasional . . ."

"Oh do shut up, Barry." This was the note on which
their horseplay habitually ended, and implied no rancor
on either side.

An assistant professor of English in his second year of
teaching at the university, Barry Greenfield was already
something of an *enfant terrible* on the faculty. Upon
emerging from the cocoon of graduate school, well-de-
served Ph.D. in hand, he had looked around, taken a deep
breath, and plunged with exuberance into the life so eloquently chronicled in the pages of *Playboy* and *Penthouse*.

In particular, having read somewhere that a man's smile
is one of the first things a woman notices, he had practiced
for weeks to acquire a serviceable basic vocabulary of
smiles: the Smile Friendly, the Smile Confiding, the Smile
Rueful, the Smile Invitational, and (most essential) the
Smile Intimate. What his best friends never had the heart
to tell him was that the entire repertoire resembled nothing
so much as a set of variations on the Grin Boyish.

No matter—by whatever name, the Greenfield smile
worked. It stirred in numerous female undergraduates a
sudden fascination with the intricacies of the eighteenth-
century English novel. It inspired in certain normally mo-
rose departmental secretaries a cheerful willingness to
please that was downright frightening. And it had earned
him a long series of triumphant conquests among the
women graduate students.

This postponed adolescence should have been annoying
in a man almost thirty, but somehow in Barry's case it

wasn't. He had been very busy and very poor during the years when he should have been getting all this out of his system. It seemed to Antonia no more than fair that he should have his fling now, more particularly since he seemed to be causing little grief and a good deal of happiness. He had an amazing knack of leaving few broken hearts, no hard feelings, and a lot of lasting friendships in his wake. Antonia, who was two years older than Barry, had often told him that she was dying to see what he would be like when he grew up. His usual reply was that she would just have to wait and see because he wasn't ready for her yet.

In reality, of course, it was neither his repartee nor the famous smile that attracted Antonia to him. For Barry also possessed certain other qualities, rarely extolled in the pages of *Playboy,* that had made them close friends and that (if the truth were known) accounted for most of his success with women. He was a generous and perceptive man who cared about people he found interesting. Some of these people were women, and Antonia was one of them.

"All right," Barry sighed now, "I abandon the interrogation. But we *were* a bit concerned, especially after we began to hear those rumors about the Saturday Night Skulker. Couldn't reach you by phone, either."

"That's because I'd unplugged it. I'd had a couple of rather trying days and I needed to get away from it all for a while." And she gave a brief account of her first conversation with Caracci, the Randolphs' dinner, and her talk with Bennie Thompson.

"By the time Bennie left," she concluded, "my brain was beginning to crumble around the edges. Ariadne stealing Aegean Gold, Ariadne seducing her thesis director, Ariadne lurking about the museum at three in the morning. . . . I wrestled with all that for a while, trying to make some sense out of it, and then I just forced myself to stop thinking about it for the rest of the evening. I am sorry about your dinner, though."

"Doesn't matter. But this student of yours—she is an enigma, isn't she? Marsha roomed with her, you know, for a short time last year. And from what she's said, Ariadne certainly didn't strike me as the type to get herself involved in burglary and adultery and—well, whatever it is that's going on around here. Whatever type *that* may be."

"I think we can dismiss burglary and adultery from serious consideration. It's this vanishing act that has me worried. But I seem to be the only one who finds it odd. The police, her own family, even Win—they all seem to think there's nothing out of the ordinary in her going off for a few days without telling anyone."

"There's the guard, of course—what's his name? *He* doesn't feel it's so ordinary. Wasn't that why he came to you on Saturday?"

"Bennie Thompson. Well, he *may* be worried about Ariadne, among other things. But that gets us into the question of *his* motives." Reluctantly, wondering if she were betraying some sort of trust, she told Barry about the boy's unsavory past and Caracci's distrust of him.

"But even if he is trying—rather clumsily, it seems to me—to make the girl look suspicious, I doubt he made up that story out of whole cloth. When she comes back, it'll be her word against his, and from what you say I gather Bennie's word doesn't carry a whole lot of weight with the cops." Barry paused. "And that may be your best lead right there, Antonia."

"What do you mean?"

"This office or workroom or whatever it is in the museum. The room where Bennie says Ariadne has been spending her nights, and where the theft occurred, as I understand it."

"What about it? The police have been over it pretty carefully, I assume."

"Yes, but not with Ariadne in mind. They were looking for evidence in connection with the burglary. Now from what you and Marsha have told me about this girl, I get the impression that her work is the most important thing in her life."

"The only important thing, as far as I can see."

"Right. Well then, doesn't it stand to reason that if she's behaving oddly—oddly for *her*, that is—the reason may have something to do with her work? Not her family or her friends, who don't seem to be extremely significant figures in her life, not even the museum theft, but the one thing that *does* matter to her. Her work."

"In other words, something may have gone wrong with

her dissertation." Antonia sounded unconvinced. "It's possible, I suppose. And that probably would be enough to make her act erratically for a while. But surely Win would have said something if it were only the dissertation. He knows I've been worrying about her."

"But what if it isn't her dissertation?"

"But there isn't anything else it could be. The dissertation *is* her work right now."

"She must have job applications outstanding, probably dozens of them."

"Well, yes, but . . ."

"And what about this project she's working on at the museum? What is it they're doing, sorting papyri or something? What if Ariadne has accidentally smashed up an irreplaceable papyrus and aroused the wrath of Miss Lilly?"

"Oh, Barry, for God's sake be serious."

"But I am serious. All right, granted she probably hasn't smashed up any significant quantity of papyrus or dropped much red-figure crockery. My point is, this girl is involved—professionally involved—in more than just a doctoral dissertation. She has a temporary job now; she's looking for a permanent one for next September. That's two potential sources of trouble right there. You know what the academic marketplace is like these days, Antonia, we all do. Every graduate student and untenured faculty member in the country gets the shakes at the very mention of the word *job.*"

"Yes, I suppose you're right,' Antonia said thoughtfully. "And I suppose it's even possible that she's gone stale on the dissertation and turned to something else for a while. I've known graduate students to do that occasionally."

"You mean the old term paper on which one of us scribbled 'with additional research and revisions, this could be a publishable article'?"

"Something like that. Ariadne's the kind who would rather turn to a new project than sit and stare doggedly at something she's too sick of to work at any longer."

"So there's a third possibility for you. Maybe she's just gone somewhere for a few days to do that additional research. Well, my dear, now that I've shed light into the dark places, unraveled the tangled skein, and poured oil upon the troubled waters of your soul, that'll be fifty dollars. Standard consultation fee, rates upon request."

"Your metaphors," Antonia observed tartly, "lack distinction."

When he was gone, though, she admitted to herself that some of his ideas weren't bad.

She did not imagine that he had hit upon the correct explanation of Ariadne's disappearance. The girl might or might not have gone off to do research in another library. She might or might not have suffered a setback in her search for a permanent position, might or might not have had some kind of falling out with her superiors at the museum. That was all speculation.

What mattered was the principle behind the speculation. The principle was, in fact, annoyingly obvious now that Barry had called it to her attention. Look at the girl's work, he had said, look at her professional life. Well, that was precisely what she was going to do. The same restlessness that had led her to The Labyrinth, and her encounter with Ariadne's mother and sister, came over her again.

The police presumably had been through the girl's desk in the museum. But how much would Caracci and his men understand of what they were looking at? Scholarly notes, the rough draft of a research paper, Xeroxed texts in ancient languages with marginal scribbles—what sense could a detective be expected to make of such things?

She glanced at her watch. Four-thirty already. By the time she could get to the museum, it would be within a few minutes of closing. It would have to wait until tomorrow. She packed her briefcase and drove home, feeling vaguely cheated.

She reached her apartment building and rode up in the elevator with a growing sense of oppression and frustration that the closeness of the tiny elevator did nothing to relieve. The feeling was still with her when she stepped out into her own corridor and walked the few yards to her apartment door. But as she groped in her coat pocket for the door key, she had a sudden inspiration. For a few seconds she gazed speculatively at the spot beside the door where Bennie had been lying in wait for her two days ago. Then she rushed into the apartment, brushed past Nike's welcoming gambols, and headed for the bedroom phone.

* * *

The evening passed quickly. The pressures and tensions of the past few days seemed to gather themselves into a bundle of energies and impulses that proceeded to burst forth in all sorts of whimsical directions, like a cluster of skyrockets. It first occurred to her that part of her depressed mood might be attributable to sheer hunger, inasmuch as she had not eaten a really substantial meal in almost three days. So she cooked herself an elaborate stew, with gourmet scraps for Nike and several quarts left over to freeze for some future dinner party.

Thus fortified, she went through her four rooms like the Avenging Angel of Good Housekeeping, dusting off, straightening up, putting away, and throwing out. Nike looked on with an air compounded of bewilderment and disapproval. Under normal circumstances, Antonia's philosophy on the subject was of the once-a-month-if-I-happen-to-think-of-it variety, a philosophy that perfectly coincided with Nike's refined distaste for dust in the air and for the removal of familiar and beloved objects from one place to another. A well-seasoned clutter was Nike's preferred life-style. Now, sensing that circumstances were *not* normal, the dog withdrew to a secluded corner of the bathroom until such time as her associate should return to a more rational view of things.

At ten o'clock Antonia flopped into an armchair expecting to feel pleasantly tired. Finding, however, that she was as restless as before, she evicted Nike from the bathroom and treated herself to a steamy shower. But there was still half an hour to kill. So she corralled the dog and spent the remaining time grooming her, a process that relaxed them both. Nike adored being combed. Her brown-velvet eyes would grow dreamy and remote and she would lean blissfully into the comb, sunk in reveries of her ancestors hunting gazelles along the Nile five thousand years ago.

The ecstasy came to an abrupt end at the stroke of eleven, however. Antonia tossed the comb aside, gave the big Afghan a dismissive whack on the rump, and headed for the coat closet. Nike, with a sigh of regret, shook herself out of her trance and padded hopefully after. Briefly, Antonia considered taking her along, then decided against it. Where she was going, a single wave of that lovely plumed tail might be catastrophic. So she closed the apartment door regretfully but firmly in Nike's face. With a reproachful sigh the dog took up her regular post just inside the door. It had been, from her point of view, a most unorthodox evening.

Antonia had entertained vague apprehensions of staggering blindly through the darkened grounds of the museum, collecting scratches from the shrubbery and perhaps a twisted ankle or two. The reality turned out to be a good deal less Gothic.

The approach to the main façade of the museum complex was through a small garden surrounding a rectangular reflecting pool. Four brick walkways bordered by low hedges led through the garden and up two flights of stairs to the main entrance. Opportunities for tumbling into the pool, stumbling into the hedges, or turning an ankle on the stairs were severely limited, however, inasmuch as the entire area was most efficiently illuminated by a dozen powerful spotlights concealed in the shrubbery and under the eaves of the building itself.

She negotiated the little garden without difficulty but stopped at the foot of the steps that led up to the main entrance. In her excitement, she now realized, she had neglected to tell Bennie where to meet her. The wide front portal, dramatically lighted as it was, looked altogether too public for the sort of cloak-and-dagger operation she had in mind. Oh, come off it, Nielsen, she told herself, and started up the steps.

Somewhere behind her and to her right she heard a low grating sound. Startled, she whirled around and saw a long ribbon of light in the darkest section of the wing enclosing that side of the courtyard. The ribbon slowly widened until it assumed the dimensions of a doorway, most of which was filled by a tall, gangling silhouette. The silhouette hissed her name and beckoned with one hand while holding the door open with the other. She had to take it on faith that the dark shape was Bennie, at least until she was so close to him that escape would have been impossible if it had turned out to be someone more sinister.

It was Bennie, of course. But he yanked her almost violently into the building, and closed and locked the door behind them with such nervous intensity that Antonia was reminded of Caracci's warning not to trust the boy too

far. A bit late to be thinking of that, she told herself, now
that you've got yourself locked up in an unfamiliar building with him in the middle of the night.

His voice was gruff as he said, "Sorry, Professor. But
they got this place staked out, y'know, and I was
afraid . . ."

"They've what? You mean there are cops out there?"

"Yeah, sure. I don't know what they figure is gonna
happen around here *now*, but I told you they didn't trust
me. Or maybe they think Ari might come sneaking back
in the dark of the moon or something. Anyway, they're
out there all right, been there ever since the break-in."

"Well, I suppose there's nothing we can do about it
now. If they saw me come in and if they come in after
us, we'll just have to tell them the truth and hope they'll
buy it. Meanwhile, I may as well get to work. Which way
to the scene of the crime?"

Her flippant tone and optimistic mood were dampened
somewhat by the long trek through the museum's subter-
ranean corridors. The exhibition floors above had been
renovated and modernized several times in the institution's
history, in accordance with changing tastes and notions
about the proper display of art objects and ancient artifacts. Down here, however, little had changed in the
hundred years the museum had been in existence. The
light, which emanated from bare bulbs hanging at widely
spaced intervals from the low ceilings, was dimmer than
it had been outside. The ceilings themselves were a welter
of pipes and heating ducts that writhed over, under, and
around one another. Periodically a group of them would
go snaking off down a side corridor and lose themselves
in the gloom.

The walls had been painted, at some remote period, in
an institutional cream color that had not aged gracefully.
By now it resembled dirty vanilla pudding. Set into the
walls were equally unappetizing metal doors with placards
that flashed past in the half-light as Bennie hurried her
along. She made out a few of them: Associate Curator of
Sculpture, Publications Director, Reproductions Department, Librarian . . .

"Here we are," said Bennie, pulling up outside a door
indistinguishable from the others. In the eerie silence his
voice sounded unnaturally loud. "Workroom," announced

the placard noncommittally. Bennie swung the door open and switched on a bank of fluorescent lights overhead.

"That's Ari's desk over there," he said abruptly. Antonia had the impression that he wanted to dissociate himself as much as possible from her rather unorthodox investigation. A bit late for that, she thought again, though understandable.

"Look, you go and make your rounds or whatever, and I'll do what I can here. Could you come back in half an hour or so and escort me out? I'm not sure I could find that door again, in this heavy twilight."

"Yeah, they got real energy-conscious around here a couple years ago. Okay, you look around in here and I'll come back in about a half hour. Happy hunting, Professor," he added. "I dunno what you figure on finding in here, but between you and the fuzz ain't none of us gonna have no secrets left round here." He laughed sardonically and left, closing the door of the workroom behind him. Antonia could hear his steps for some time. They echoed with abnormal loudness in the deserted building, so that she could follow his progress down the long corridor and around some unseen corner. Finally they died away and she turned to the room.

It was only slightly less depressing than the corridors. Same dirty-vanilla walls, same snaky-looking tangle of pipes infesting the ceiling. But the workroom at least looked inhabited, looked as if purposeful human activities were regularly carried on in it. Each of its four corners was occupied by a large battered desk, one of which Bennie had pointed out as belonging to Ariadne.

Most of the rest of the room was taken up by a huge worktable that appeared to have been beaten with chains and subsequently bathed in acid, several centuries ago. Scratched, scarred, dented, and stained though it was, it stood solid and massive, looking as if nothing short of dynamite could move it. The impression of permanence and indispensability was enhanced by the litter of manuals, papers, and implements that covered most of its surface. There were bottles of adhesive, fixative, varnish, and paint with their attendant brushes and wipe rags.

But most interesting to Antonia was a little army of white cards propped vertically in Lucite holders and ranged in two neat rows in the middle of the great worktable.

Nearby lay a stack of blank cards, an array of lettering pens, and an assortment of India ink bottles.

She stooped a little to read the finished cards.

GOLD BOWL WITH INCISED LINEAR DECORATION, 2800–2500 B.C.? Euboea. 9 cm high.

SILVER CUP WITH TWO HANDLES, 19th C. B.C. Gournia. 8 cm high.

GOLDEN PENDANT WITH APPLIQUÉ AND GRANULATED DECORATION OF TWO HORNETS AND HONEYCOMB. 17th C. B.C. Mallia. 4.6 cm high.

GOLD-HILTED DAGGER, BRONZE BLADE WITH INLAY OF HUNTING LEOPARDS, 15th C. B.C. Pylos. 32 cm long.

BRONZE DAGGER BLADE (HILT LOST) WITH GOLD, SILVER, AND NIELLO INLAY OF A LION HUNT, 16th C. B.C. Shaft Grave V, Mycenae. 23.8 cm long.

GOLD 'TEA-CUP' WITH EMBOSSED DOUBLE SPIRAL DECORATION AND RIBBON HANDLE, 15th C. B.C. Knossos. 3.7 cm high.

GOLD DEATH-MASK, KNOWN AS 'MASK OF AGAMEMNON.' 16th C. B.C. Shaft Grave V, Mycenae. 26 cm high.

GOLD SIGNET RING SHOWING A GODDESS AND RITUAL DANCERS, 15th C. B.C. Tomb near Knossos. 2.6 cm. wide.

The little white rectangles went on and on, enumerating in the cool and telegraphic style of a museum catalogue all the treasures of the Aegean Gold exhibition. It was only after she had read a dozen or so more that Antonia realized the significance of the two ranks of cards. They were all intended, of course, to accompany and identify the hundred-odd pieces contained in the exhibition when it opened in less than five days. But the row on the right, much the shorter of the two, contained descriptions of objects familiar not only to Antonia and her classical colleagues but to every resident of the city who had looked at television or a newspaper during the last four days.

These were the cards that were to have identified the

irreplaceable ancient artifacts that had disappeared from this very room on Thursday night. Antonia read them, too, with a kind of superstitious fervor, as if intense concentration on the details of their dimensions and provenance might somehow bring them back.

GOLD DOUBLE-AXES WITH ENGRAVED DECORATION. C. 1500 B.C., from sacred cave at Arkalochori, Crete. 8 cm wide.

CERAMIC JAR PAINTED WITH BULLS' HEADS AND DOUBLE-AXES. 16th C. B.C. Pseira, Crete. 77 cm high.

RECONSTRUCTION OF THE LION HUNT DAGGER. 37 cm long.

SILVER JUG WITH EMBOSSED ARCADE PATTERN OVER HORIZONTAL FLUTING. 16th C. B.C. Shaft Grave V, Mycenae. 34.5 cm high.

GOLD DIADEM WITH EMBOSSED CRETAN MOTIFS. 16th C. B.C. Shaft Grave III, Mycenae. 65 cm wide.

GOLD EARRINGS WITH GRANULATED CONICAL PENDANT. 14th–13th C. B.C. Knossos. 3.4 cm high.

GOLD SCEPTER WITH CLOISONNÉ ENAMELED GLOBE AND TWO HAWKS. 12th C. B.C. Cyprus. 16.5 cm high.

Antonia shook herself out of the hypnotic fascination exerted by the little cards and reminded herself that she was supposed to be looking for clues to the whereabouts of Ariadne, not the Aegean Gold. And she adamantly refused to believe that there was any connection between the two.

She turned to Ariadne's desk.

The most striking thing about it was the bareness of its surface. A blotter, two sharpened pencils, copies of the Graduate School catalogue, and the Personnel Directory. No photographs, no postcards or silly gag-gifts from friends, none of the personal clutter that normally encumbers a student's desktop. Still another indication of the barrenness of the girl's personal life, or perhaps only a manifestation of the compulsive neatness Antonia remembered from her term papers and exams.

Systematically, from upper left to lower right, she began to go through the drawers of Ariadne's desk.

Exactly thirty-two minutes after he had left it, Bennie reappeared at the door labeled "Workroom." Antonia was half sitting, half leaning against the edge of Ariadne's desk, a sheaf of papers in one hand. Her head was bent above these papers, causing her long hair to fall like a curtain beside her face, concealing its expression from Bennie. She did not look up when he opened the door, nor when he spoke her name.

"Miss Nielsen?" he said again, a little louder.

This time Antonia raised her head and looked at him, and the expression on her face startled Bennie. She looked dazed and gave no sign that she saw, let alone recognized, him. She glanced around distractedly as if trying to remember where she was.

"You all right, Professor?" Bennie's tone hovered somewhere between impatience and anxiety. "Did you . . . ?"

"Yes," she said vaguely. It was not clear which, if either, of his questions she was answering. She stood up then and turned to Ariadne's desk. Its surface was no longer bare but half covered by three piles of legal-size paper. Antonia laid the set she had been reading on top of one of these piles, consolidated it with the other two, and turned to Bennie with the whole bundle in her arms.

"Must go home now." Again she seemed to be speaking to herself as much as to Bennie. Still clutching the papers, she brushed past him and head for the door.

In some bewilderment, Bennie glanced around the room, closed a couple of half-open drawers in Ariadne's desk, switched off the lights, and started after her.

He found himself almost trotting to keep up with her long nervous stride, found himself following rather than leading her through the labyrinth of grimy corridors to the side door by which they had entered the museum.

"Look, Miss Nielsen," he began as he unlocked the door, "I'll call you after I . . ."

But Antonia was gone before he finished the sentence.

Still moving at the same hectic pace, she waved her free hand in farewell without turning around and soon disappeared in the darkness surrounding the floodlit formal garden.

9. The Clew

AT SEVEN-THIRTY THE NEXT MORNING BENNIE appeared at Antonia's door for the second time in three days. He was nearly as groggy as on the previous occasion, but at least this time he was vertical.

When Antonia opened the door she was fully dressed though barefoot, and Nike only waved her tail in dignified acknowledgment of his arrival. The big Afghan stayed at her post in front of the fireplace, perhaps because there was no obvious way of getting from there to the front door.

Not a trace remained of last night's flurry of housekeeping. The living room looked, in fact, as if it had been more recently bombed than cleaned. Overflowing ashtrays, half-empty coffee cups, a couple of empty highball glasses, and Antonia's discarded sandals competed for every square foot of horizontal surface with a welter of books and papers.

At the epicenter of this mess was a small clear space about eighteen inches square, representing the spot where Antonia had been sitting crosslegged on the floor until the doorbell rang. Nearby were the papers from Ariadne's desk.

Antonia herself looked exhausted but no longer dazed.

It was obvious that she was dressed not because she had risen early but because she had never gone to bed. Yet in spite of the shadows under her eyes and the ravaged condition of her hair, there was an air of suppressed excitement about her.

"You found something in that drawer?" Bennie asked.

"*That*, my dear Mr. Thompson, is one of the great understatements of our era." Antonia glanced dubiously around the living room. "You'd better come into the kitchen. There doesn't seem to be anywhere to sit down in here."

The kitchen, though tiny, was in good order and Bennie sank gratefully into one of the two chairs. Nike, having somehow picked her way through the debris in the living room, followed them in and stationed herself suggestively beside a fifty-pound bag of Dog Chow in one corner.

From the sink, where she was rinsing the residue of the night's coffee out of an electric pot, Antonia began, "I had a feeling you'd come here. I seem to remember that I left in rather a hurry last night, and you certainly have a right to an explanation."

"Yeah, I was sorta thinking that myself. But . . ."

"I'm afraid I was in a state of near shock. What I found last night . . ."

"Professor, you're . . ."

"Those papers I found . . ."

Wearily Bennie unwrapped his gangling frame from his chair, stood up, stepped across the narrow space that separated him from Antonia, and grabbed her right wrist. She looked up at him, startled, then followed his gaze down to her hand. It was holding a heaping scoopful of tea that was about to follow its predecessor into the electric coffeepot. She grinned sheepishly and dumped it back into the canister.

"Look, Mr. Thompson, why don't *you* make the coffee while I go take a cold shower and change my clothes. Your workday may be finished, but mine hasn't started yet, and I've got to get myself into some semblance of order. We'll talk when I get back." She left him muttering at the unfamiliar coffeepot.

When Antonia reappeared twenty minutes later in a crisp brown pantsuit, with her long caramel hair brushed and shining and tied with an emerald-green ribbon, she looked thoroughly rehabilitated.

"It probably won't last much beyond noon, but for the time being I feel great," she announced. "How's that coffee coming along?"

Bennie looked up glumly from the mug he was nursing between thick dark hands. "Coffee's lousy," he said. "But then the rest of the day ain't shaping up so great neither. Guess what followed me here from the museum, Professor."

Absorbed as she was in the events of the night just past and the morning she somehow still had to get through, Antonia merely looked blank.

"Fuzz, Professor. Cops. The *po*lice, dig? Think about it real hard, maybe you can figure out what's going through them little tiny minds of theirs. Hell, Professor, they thought they had a burglary on their hands. By now they must be thinking it's a whole goddam conspiracy! Me, Ari, now you—all in it together, that's what they're thinking. Only *I'm* the one that's gonna . . ."

"Hold on, Mr. Thompson. I see what you mean, and I'm sorry I didn't see it before. I'm jeopardizing your job, aren't I? And maybe more than that. I've been so wrapped up in—but it's going to be all right, believe me. When I tell you what—no, let me begin at the beginning."

She poured herself a cup of the lousy coffee, refilled Bennie's mug, and settled herself into the chair opposite his at the small kitchen table.

"Now," she began briskly, "has Ariadne told you what she and the other graduate students have been doing in the museum? What they were *hired* to do, that is?"

"She ain't said much about it, but it has something to do with sorting out some old documents. Sort of an inventory, like."

"That's the general idea, yes. Except that the 'old documents' are ancient papyri, close to two thousand years old. The museum acquired a sizable batch of them last year. They weren't supposed to be anything very sensational, or we wouldn't have gotten them. But the museum didn't have much papyrus, and we thought they'd be useful as teaching materials in our graduate program, if nothing else.

"Nobody really knew what was in the collection. Presumably it had been screened before it left Egypt, I suppose by some sub-sub-underling in the Archaeological Service. I would hate," she grinned maliciously, "to be in that guy's shoes now. He'll be lucky to get a job selling fake scarabs to tourists at the Great Pyramid."

Bennie looked thoroughly mystified.

"Anyway, the papyri arrived in November. Christmas was coming, the Aegean Gold exhibition was coming, the museum staff couldn't handle any more, and someone got the idea of hiring a few graduate students to do a sort of pre-cataloguing job on them. We were delighted, of course—our kids are always hard up for money, and besides the experience could be very valuable for them professionally. So Roy—Professor Sandler, our chairman—handpicked four of our best doctoral candidates, including Ariadne, gave them a crash course in papyrological scripts, and turned them loose shortly before Christmas.

"And that was the last I heard of the project, not being directly involved in it myself. Except for an occasional secondhand report that the kids were starting to grumble about slave labor and so on. It sounded exciting at first—deciphering real honest-to-goodness ancient papyrus. Maybe they thought they'd stumble across the recipe for *tana*-leaf tea or something."

For the first time Bennie grinned knowingly. "Yeah, like in *The Mummy's Curse*. I saw that three times on TV."

"Well, unfortunately your average papyrus isn't quite that exciting. And anyway these kids weren't supposed to read them or date them or try to fill in missing parts. They aren't equipped to do anything that technical. Their instructions were very explicit. They were simply to puzzle out enough of each document to give a one-line description of its general type—marriage contract, death certificate, bill of receipt, or whatever. That's the sort of thing most of the collection was supposed to be. The idea was that when it was finally turned over to a specialist for serious editing it would be in at least some kind of rough order, rather than just a mass of unidentified documents.

"Their instructions were very explicit on one other point, too. Any papyrus they could not decipher, or which seemed to be in any way out of the ordinary, was to be turned over to a designated member of the museum staff for identification." A more somber note crept into Antonia's voice. "And it is those instructions that our friend Ariadne has disobeyed. Blatantly, rashly, magnificently disobeyed."

"You mean she *stole* one of these—papyruses?" Bennie sounded a little confused. "Aw, come off it, Professor, last week it was pots and necklaces she was 'sposed to of ripped off, and now . . ."

"No, no, Ariadne hasn't stolen anything. Not in the sense you mean, at any rate. But she's *found* something— I still can't believe it myself yet, I keep thinking there must be some mistake. Bennie, she has found one of the lost tragedies of Euripides!"

There was a silence of considerable length while Bennie gazed at her as if trying to read the answer to some riddle in her face. Finally he said, "I guess—I guess that's pretty good, huh?"

"Good!" Antonia was almost shrieking. Now that the words were finally out, now that she was no longer the only person in the world to share Ariadne's astounding secret, the dams of scholarly caution and incredulity burst, and all her pent-up delight and exultation came flooding out. She wondered briefly if the little kitchen table would collapse under her if she leaped up on it and did an impromptu cancan. Deciding it probably would, she contented herself with merely shouting at poor bewildered Bennie.

"Good!" she shrieked again. "My dear boy, it's sensational! It's one of the great finds of the century, in a class with the *Dyskolos,* or the Bacchylides papyrus, or —" She stopped abruptly, finally seeing what the expression on Bennie's face meant. He didn't have the foggiest idea what she was talking about.

"I'm sorry," she said more gently, "of course it can't possibly mean as much to a layman. Look, just take my word for it that the manuscript is important in itself. What's important to *us* is what it's going to mean to Ariadne. It's going to be the making of her career, Bennie. It'll mean a really good job, prestige, even fame of a sort. Of course," she added dryly, "the fame is going to look more like notoriety for a while. There'll be a lot of resentment against her, because strictly speaking she had no right to do what she's done."

"What's she done wrong, Professor? She couldn't help finding this papyrus thing, could she? What's wrong with that?"

"Nothing, of course, But having found it and recognized what it is, she was supposed to turn it over to the experts. And she didn't. She had it photographed, transcribed it, edited it, wrote a lengthy introduction—in short, she's very close to having a publishable edition of one of the most dramatic manuscript discoveries of the century."

"And all that gravy shoulda landed on somebody else's plate, right?"

"Right. But the resentment will die down eventually, especially when they see what a solid job she's done. And after that—well, she has an enviable future ahead of her."

"Yeah, I can see that." With meticulous attention to justice, Bennie was apportioning the last of the lousy coffee between their two cups. He was also looking worried.

"All right, Professor," he said, "so Ari's made this great discovery. I dig that. But looks to me like you found something you weren't even looking for. What you *ain't* found is what you *was* looking for. Namely Ari. Far's I can see, we don't know no more'n we did before about where she's got to."

"No, I'm afraid not. But—well, yes, in a way we do know where she is. Or rather where she isn't. Where she *isn't* is in trouble."

"How do you figure that?"

"I think where her career is concerned Ariadne is a very hardheaded, practical person. If her work was going badly, if it was threatened in some way, I can imagine her reacting recklessly. But at a time like this, with the opportunities that will open up to her when this discovery is made public, my guess is that she's being very cautious, very prudent."

"Yeah, maybe." Bennie didn't sound very convinced.

"There'd be idealistic motives as well as practical ones. I strongly suspect that Ariadne sees herself right now—maybe subconsciously—as a sort of divinely appointed guardian to that manuscript. I think she'd take care of herself for *its* sake if for no other reason. Or does that sound too farfetched?"

"No, Ma'am, not for Ari. She *is* kinda weird about stuff

like that, no doubt about it. I just hope trouble ain't come looking for *her.*"

"I don't think it has, Mr. Thompson. But I can tell you who will be in trouble if she doesn't get her body out of this chair and on down to the office in the next twenty-five minutes. In short, I have a nine-thirty class and I've got to get going. Can I give you a lift somewhere?"

"Thanks, Professor, but I'm going the other way. I can catch a bus."

As she saw him out the door, Antonia suddenly remembered the obvious.

"Look, Mr. Thompson, I'll explain all this to Lieutenant Caracci this afternoon. My behavior last night was unorthodox to say the least, and I'll make it clear to him that the initiative was entirely mine and that you went along only very reluctantly. I'll have to tell him what I found, too, and what I think it means. But we mustn't say anything to anyone else about Ariadne's discovery. We've stumbled across something she didn't intend anyone to know about until it was a *fait accompli*—completely finished. I don't know how she'll feel about our knowing about it, but I'm sure she won't want it to go any further."

"No way I'm gonna talk, Professor." He grinned. "Not that I could tell anyone much about it even if I wanted to. It's all Greek to me!"

Antonia sighed ruefully as she closed the door after him. The line was excruciatingly familiar to classicists, and it had been about three hundred years since they found it amusing.

Bennie had not been gone more than ten minutes when the phone rang. Antonia was stuffing lecture notes for the nine-thirty class into her briefcase, trying to remember what the subject of the course was. Trying to get the mental circuits marked "Ariadne" and "Euripides manuscript" to stay in the Off position long enough for her to do her job.

Still thinking about them, she picked up the phone.

"Professor Nielsen? Steve Caracci. I thought you'd want to know we picked up the museum burglar last night. Or one of them. Looks like the character the Thompson kid told us about. Maybe the one who attacked Professor Randolph, too."

The mental circuits whirred and buzzed for a moment, then clicked into place.

"The big man who was talking to Ariadne in the museum that night?"

"Yeah. And it turns out that wasn't so surprising, either."

"What wasn't?" Antonia hoped she didn't sound as disoriented as she felt.

"Him being with the girl like that. Because it turns out this guy we got here is Ariadne Pappas' brother."

10. A Pocketful of Gold

TUESDAY, BLESSEDLY, WAS A ONE-CLASS DAY FOR Antonia, which meant that by eleven o'clock she was free to sit down and try to assimilate Caracci's announcement.

When he called, just as she was leaving for the class, she had all but hung up on him. She managed a hasty "Thanks, Lieutenant, but I'm late for a class. Talk to you later." Then she resolutely thrust his words to the back of her mind and refused to think about them until her lecture was finished.

A ninety-minute lecture is tiring at the best of times. After a sleepless night, and in combination with shock, excitement, and apprehension, it is apt to leave one considerably less than *compos mentis*. For one rather scary moment Antonia found herself entertaining the possibility that everything that had happened in the last twelve hours— her midnight junket to the museum, the Euripides papyrus, Caracci's call—had been some kind of hallucination. But the moment passed. She shook her head ferociously to clear it, and went to fetch a cup of black coffee from the urn in the faculty lounge.

The familiarly execrable brew made everything seem much more down-to-earth, made it seem no more than sensible to go downtown and beard Caracci in his own den for a change. There was some mistake, of course, that was all. The man they had picked up was obviously not Ariadne's brother, for the simple reason that Ariadne didn't have a brother. She had never mentioned a brother. And even if he were somehow related to the strange Pappas clan, that fact wouldn't prove that Ariadne herself had anything to do with the burglary.

The expedition seemed significantly less sensible when Antonia finally stood before the brick and concrete mass of Police Headquarters half an hour later. She thought about having lunch first. She thought about phoning a long-neglected friend in Topeka. She thought she'd better go on in before she lost her nerve.

But Caracci, after she had threaded a maze of institution-colored corridors to his office, didn't seem particularly surprised to see her. He even reached a welcoming hand-shake to her over a desk of battleship-gray steel.

"Afternoon, Professor." He glanced at his watch to check the accuracy of this greeting. "Glad you came. There's a couple things I . . ."

"Look, Lieutenant," Antonia interrupted, "what's this nonsense about Ariadne's brother? She doesn't *have* a brother."

"Yes, Ma'am, so we were led to believe too. But the sister has confirmed it. He's their brother all right. But I got the idea they don't exactly advertise his existence."

"But where . . . how did you . . . ?"

"We went back to the Pappas place yesterday to have another try at questioning the mother and sister. And there he was at the kitchen table eating dinner with 'em, big as life. Or slightly bigger."

"But what makes you so sure he's the thief?"

"He tried to bolt when he saw us, out a window. Since the window happened to be on the second floor, I thought it might be a good idea to try and stop him. Fought like a wild bull, though."

"But that still doesn't . . ."

Caracci's voice went on, patient and implacable, ignoring the interruption. "In his pockets we found a few odds and ends. A couple of earrings that don't match, and a ring, and a thing that looked like a miniature battle-ax about two inches long. Might have been a child's toy, except it was made of solid gold. All the stuff was solid gold, Miss Nielsen."

Antonia had ignored the chair he offered her when she entered, but she sat down now, heavily, feeling suddenly overwhelmed with weariness.

"It isn't a toy, Lieutenant," she said dully. "It's a votive *labrys*, an offering to a war deity. Maybe Pallas Athene herself. They've found a lot of them in Crete. It's also a symbol of the House of Minos, the House of the Double Axe. The Labyrinth."

"Yes, Ma'am." Antonia scarcely heard the note of sympathy in his voice. "That's what Miss Lilly said too. We had her in here this morning to identify the things. Now, Miss Nielsen, I'm sorry but I have to ask you about last . . ."

"Lieutenant, you said on the phone that you'd caught *one* of the museum burglars. Just what was that supposed to mean?"

"Professor Nielsen, try to look at this from our point of view." Caracci sounded a little weary himself now. "This man's sister—*and* her friend Bennie Thompson—are both museum employees. The girl certainly, and Thompson very possibly, are under financial pressure. Miss Pappas has been missing for almost five days. And now there's one new factor, too. This Pappas kid—he's only about eighteen—had stuff from the museum in his pocket all right. What he doesn't have, in my opinion, is the brains to plan or carry out a burglary. My best guess at the moment is that he talked, or forced, his sister into cooperating with him, with or without Thompson's help."

"I suppose he could have held a gun on her, if that's what you mean. But I'm more certain than ever that Ariadne isn't responsible—morally or legally—for the museum theft. I think you were about to ask me what I was doing at the museum last night."

"Yes, Ma'am, I was."

"I was searching Ariadne's desk. I knew you'd probably been through it, but I suddenly got the idea that you people might have missed something, something that only a classicist would be able to recognize as important."

"Really, Miss Nielsen, that's . . ."

"I know, I know, highly irregular. But I did find something—or rather Ariadne did. She's made a once-in-a-lifetime discovery, Lieutenant, a rare and very ancient manuscript that's going to be the making of her career. She'd have to be very stupid, or very impatient, to jeopardize all that—and Ariadne is neither stupid nor impatient. She's worked hard for years, she's had an astounding stroke of luck, the rewards are just around the corner. She'd have to be crazy to get involved in a crime at a time like this, even if she were capable of it under ordinary circumstances."

"All right then, let's say she was forced to cooperate. I still want to find her and talk to her."

With what she regarded as saintly forbearance, Antonia refrained from pointing out that this was precisely what she herself had been trying to do for the better part of a week now. Instead she shifted to a new tack.

"What about her so-called brother? I suppose he denies that Ariadne's involved?"

Caracci shrugged wearily. "I really couldn't tell you what he denies or what he admits, Miss Nielsen. He hasn't spoken six words since we brought him in last night."

"Could I talk to him?"

"No, Ma'am, I'm afraid you couldn't. He's with our tame psychiatrist right now. And I doubt you'd get anything out of him anyway. I doubt even the shrink will get him to talk, and he's pretty good at it, as a rule. But this one, I dunno, I don't see him talking for anyone. If I hadn't heard him say his name last night for the sergeant, I'd be wondering if he *could* talk. What he reminds me of is some kind of wild animal with its foot in a trap, just sitting and waiting, real patient and quiet—and dangerous."

"Very poetic, Lieutenant. Do you always wax so lyrical over your prisoners?"

"No, Ma'am," said Caracci, unbaitable as ever. "This one's different. This one is *real* different."

The neighborhood was quiet and shady, with many old trees and carefully tended shrubs and flowerbeds, a miniature suburbia set down in the heart of the city five blocks from campus. It was also a faculty enclave, and its elderly but comfortable houses were the envy of the younger professors who dreamed of walking to work every morning but who had to settle for a high-rise apartment at the other end of a forty-five-minute bus ride.

The Randolphs' house was distinguishable from its fellows mainly by the neatness of its front sidewalk, which was unencumbered by the strollers, skateboards, and bicycles cluttering the approaches to the other homes on the street. It was not unique in its need of a fresh paint job, but contrived to make its lack of sparkle look like a mark of character rather than shabbiness.

Antonia was thinking of the Randolphs rather than their house as she approached it. She was fairly certain of finding them both at home, but it was anyone's guess what Gillian's mood might be. She had undoubtedly sensed by now that Win was staying home from the office today in order to babysit with his unstable wife, and she was probably resenting it. But if Ariadne was in some kind of serious trouble, Gillian's precious moods would just have to take a back seat for the time being. Antonia squared her shoulders and marched almost defiantly up the Randolphs' sidewalk.

It was Win who answered the doorbell. There was a note of relief in his voice as he said, "Oh, it's you, Antonia," as if he had feared it might be someone—or something—much worse. Even so he made no move to open the screen door and let her in, but stood awkwardly behind it peering out at her. Ignoring his obvious reluctance to talk to her, Antonia pulled the screen door open herself and plunged *in medias res*.

"Win, I'm sorry to barge in like this, but things are starting to look really serious for Ariadne. We've got to find her!"

"All right, all right," Win said, "come on in. But really, Antonia, I've already told you—" He stepped aside to let her pass, then shut the front door behind her.

The living room curtains were closed against the afternoon sun, and it took Antonia's eyes a minute to adjust to the half-light they allowed to filter through. When she could see Win's face clearly at last, it looked haggard and preoccupied. The disappearance of Ariadne Pappas was quite obviously the last thing he had, or wanted to have, on his mind. He seemed in fact to be listening for something, and a few minutes later Antonia caught him glancing up the stairs that led from the living room to the second-floor bedrooms. So it *was* Gillian, she thought. Probably she'd caught them in the middle of a row of some sort. Well, it couldn't be helped.

"Now what's all this about Ariadne?" Win tried for his tut-tut-my-girl-everything's-going-to-be-all-right tone, but it didn't come off very well.

"Her brother's in jail. He was picked up last night with some trinkets from the Aegean Gold exhibition still in his pocket. So of course the police are more convinced than ever that Ariadne is somehow mixed up in the museum burglary. The most charitable interpretation they're prepared to put on the situation is that she may have been forced to . . ."

"Now hold on, Antonia. You've lost me already. You're saying the museum burglar is Ariadne's *brother?*" For the first time he looked as if he was actually listening to her, and listening very intently at that.

"*One* of the burglars, is the way they put it."

"And so the fuzz instantly deduce that Ariadne . . ." He paused for a moment as if contemplating the unsoundable depths of the law's stupidity.

"Exactly. And it's the worst possible time for it, from Ariadne's point of view."

"There's a *good* time to fall under suspicion of theft?"

"No, of course not. But now of all times—Look, Win, has Ariadne said anything to you about a, well, about a discovery she's made?"

The expression on Win's face was memorable but not easy to decipher. In swift succession surprise, annoyance, fear, defensiveness, and resignation flicked across his features like the picture cards that a child riffles with his thumb to produce a primitive movie. But his voice was calm when he spoke.

"I guess she must have changed her mind," he said thoughtfully. "I understood no one else was to know. But yes—to answer your question—she did consult me about it once."

"She didn't change her mind. I came across the manuscript—or rather Ariadne's photographs of it—more or less by accident. I didn't intend to mention it to anyone, but under the circumstances . . ."

"Yes, I see what you mean." Win still looked as if he was thinking hard. "Nice batch of headlines it would make. 'Coed Steals Priceless Ancient Manuscript Plus King's Ransom in Gold.' "

"She hasn't *stolen* the papyrus," Antonia protested.

"No, of course not. But a lot of noses in the profession are going to be sadly out of joint nonetheless. And if she's simultaneously making headlines in connection with the burglary—whew!"

"So what do we do? There must be *some* way of locating her. Could she have gone out of town to do research in another library? Or to talk to a publisher maybe? Or how about a laboratory, to get the papyrus dated? Where's the nearest carbon-14 lab, anyway?"

"I couldn't say, Antonia." His momentary surge of enthusiasm for the Perils of Ariadne seemed to have passed, and once again he sounded bored with the subject. "All of the aforementioned are possibilities, I suppose, but she's said nothing to me about going anywhere to do anything. Really, Antonia, you've got to relax and let our lovable local gumshoes handle this mess. Charmingly inept though they are, they do seem to be making some progress on the burglary, and as for Ariadne . . ." He paused, looking a bit grim. "Ariadne's a lot tougher than she looks, believe me. A *lot* tougher. Ariadne can take care of . . ."

He was interrupted by a faint sound as of someone choking on a drink swallowed too hastily. It came from the direction of the stairs leading up to the second floor, and Antonia was afraid she knew what it meant. As she and Win turned in unison toward the stairway, her suspicion was confirmed.

Gillian stood stiffly on the fourth or fifth step up from the level of the living room, looking down at them and torturing a damp handkerchief with her long fingers. She looked as if she had been crying, but now she was trying to make a smile stay in place on her lips, without much success.

After a moment, she abandoned the pretense of a social smile, and the expression that remained on her face was an unlovely compound of laughter, contempt, and horror. Before Win and Antonia could think of anything to say or do, she spoke. Her voice was hoarse and unsteady, but the words were clear enough.

"Can she, Win? Can she take care of herself? I shouldn't like to bet on it, myself. Then again, she may *take care* of the lot of us. The whole bloody, bloody . . ." Her voice broke and she turned and stumbled up the stairs.

11. Fedra

ANTONIA STOOD AT HER APARTMENT-SIZE ELECTRIC range, staring unseeingly at the hamburger. It had been frying now for twelve and a half minutes, and she had long since forgotten all about it. Nike sat nearby drinking in like some Homeric deity the ambrosial fragrance of the smoking meat. It was beginning to look as if she might get more than the fragrance for dinner, as the charring of the hamburger progressed apace. Nike blessed, not for the first time, the unaccountable fastidiousness of humans in matters of meat.

Antonia had cleared away the cups and saucers and coffeepot she and Bennie Thompson had used eight hours earlier. She was thinking now of the other mess, as yet unreclaimed, that still occupied her living room. On the one hand, she felt guilty about Ariadne's typescript, scattered chaotically over furniture and floor, to say nothing of her own books spread-eagled on the arms of chairs and the corners of tables—hardly appropriate treatment for one of the most exciting manuscript discoveries of the century.

On the other hand—she gazed idly at the smoke that rose in ever-increasing volume from the hamburger—there was a streak of sentimentality in Antonia that resolutely opposed the idea of cleaning up the living room. That clutter of books, papers, and photostats was the visible reminder of a once-in-a-lifetime experience, a night spent alone in the company of a manuscript that only a handful of people had seen for nearly two thousand years. The peculiar mixture of excitement, incredulity, and awe she had felt during the six or seven hours between the time she fled from the museum with Ariadne's papers under her arm and the moment when she opened her door to Bennie—no, that would never come again. And to clear away the clutter that night had left behind would be to distance the memory of it, not to lose it but to put it behind her, to file it away in the past. She wanted to savor it a little longer before she did that.

Since Bennie's appearance on her doorstep at seven-thirty that morning, she had hardly had time to draw a deep breath, let alone to ponder the implications of Ariadne's wonderful discovery. There had been the explanation to Bennie, the morning class, the confrontations with Caracci and the Randolphs, the continuing anxiety about Ariadne herself—not a moment to brood in solitary glee over the tattered sheets of papyrus that would mean so much to their discoverer and to every classicist in the world.

Suddenly she sprang back from the stove, one hand clapped to her right cheek, which had been stung by a spatter from the martyred hamburger. Belatedly she glanced down at her ruined dinner. It was clearly beyond salvaging, and she dumped it into Nike's bowl without regret. Then she took a can of beer from the fridge and carried it into the living room. One armchair had somehow escaped the general inundation there, and Antonia flopped wearily into it to sip and dream.

Ariadne's lengthy introduction to her edition of the papyrus had revealed a streak of romanticism in her that Antonia had not suspected. With surprising warmth of imagination, the girl had traced the manuscript's long history from the heyday of the Roman Empire to the late twentieth century.

Its story began in the second century, around the time of the philosopher–emperor Marcus Aurelius. Somewhere in Upper Egypt a nameless family of Greeks or Hellenized Egyptians had bought a scroll containing some of the tragedies of Euripides. They were not rich people, and the roll on which the plays were transcribed was a modest one—second-grade papyrus, narrow margins, handwriting no more than passable. The purchasers, or their descendants, had not greatly prized their Euripides: in the following century they cut the roll into separate sheets and wrote their household accounts on the blank sides.

By the time their supply of makeshift scratch paper was exhausted, the accounts told a grim tale of the family's decline and fall. Bit by bit cattle, furniture, and slaves were sold off to pay the Emperor's tax collectors, and year by year the taxes grew heavier. Finally—impossible to guess when, even to the century—the house was abandoned, to sink slowly to ruin above the old account sheets and other odds and ends of papyrus. Very likely the last occupants had taken to the roads like thousands of their countrymen, to become vagabonds and worse on the highways of the dying province.

Such was the manuscript's ancient history as Ariadne had pieced it together. It was a plausible account, though not demonstrably true in every detail; ancient history seldom is. But this particular papyrus had an even more tenuous pedigree than most. It had not been unearthed by a legitimate archaeological expedition but had "come into the hands" of the Egyptian government, from which the university had acquired it. This noncommittal phrase very likely meant that the papyri had been discovered by site-robbers who for once had been caught red-handed by the Archaeological Service. In any case, the place and circumstances of the find were unknown and unknowable, except that the Egyptians had passed on to the American purchasers their source's statement that the papyri had all been found together "under a staircase in a ruined house."

Antonia sighed and shook her beer can to see whether it was as empty as it felt. It was. Deciding she was too tired to return to the smoky kitchen for another, she settled deeper into the armchair, closed her eyes, and sank back into her reverie.

Her thoughts turned from the physical survival of the papyrus to the play itself.

It had been known for generations that Euripides wrote such a tragedy. Like many ancient authors, the youngest of Athens' great tragedians left a legacy of titles—works lost but known to have existed—that far outnumbered his surviving works. Often these titles come down to us clad in a few skimpy rags of text—three words quoted by a scholiast, half a dozen mutilated verses from a scrap of papyrus the size of a playing card. These fragments are painstakingly collected, arranged, emended, annotated, and analyzed, published between austere covers of gold-stamped maroon or dark blue, and roundly applauded as the choicest fruits of philological *wissenschaft*. Yet the fact remains that such works, however draped in meticulously edited *fragmenta,* are still for all practical purposes well and truly "lost."

So it was with a strange play of Euripides' middle years called *The Cretans.* It consisted, until Ariadne's papyrus appeared, of twenty verses quoted by Porphyry, fifty more (very fragmentary) preserved on one of the Oxyrhynchus papyri, and another fifty in good condition on a parchment in Berlin.

And that was all that remained of Euripides' version of the horrendous tale of the House of Minos. Sacrilege, perversion, and vengeance—the old legend had offered Euripides a plot as sensational as anything in the "liberated" twentieth-century repertoire. How had he treated it? Three generations of scholars had argued the point, with dubious results. Some said Euripides held the guilty queen responsible for her act, despite the brilliance of the self-defense he wrote for her (preserved in the Berlin fragment). It would not, they argued, be the first time a Sophist-trained playwright had played devil's advocate with such devastating plausibility that the audience was hard put to know whose side he was on.

But other scholars held that the queen's words were intended as valid self-justification, that she was indeed what she claimed to be—scapegoat for an impious and despotic king, a man who had tried to cheat a god more ingeniously cruel than himself, her husband.

Well, they would soon know, Antonia told herself groggily. They would soon know what antiquity's most iconoclastic playwright had made of Queen Pasiphaë. They would soon. . . .

If the phone had rung three minutes later than it did, it probably would have been powerless to wake Antonia. As it was, she heaved herself out of the armchair, staggered blindly down the abbreviated hallway to the kitchen, stumbled over Nike, who had posted herself in the doorway, and scooped up the receiver on the sixth or seventh ring.

The girl's voice was uncharacteristically diffident, almost frightened.

"Miss Nielsen? This is Fedra Pappas. Ariadne's sister?"

In its dazed condition, Antonia's mind produced a surrealistic montage of the following impressions:

Next she'll be telling me she's calling from the palace at Knossos.

It's odd I didn't realize it before, but I'd never been told her name.

Her brother—she's just heard about her brother.

The Princess of Crete, who became Queen of Athens by marrying the man her sister had loved.

It wasn't just a hobby with their father, then, it was an obsession.

As her brain slowly cleared, the girl was saying, ". . . if I could meet you somewhere."

"I'll be glad to see you tomorrow afternoon, Miss Pappas. I have classes in the . . ."

Five minutes later, shuddering under a cold shower, Antonia was trying to remember the Aristophanic polysyllable that meant "unintelligent person (f.) who allows herself to be persuaded too easily; gullible idiot." She couldn't remember the word, but it was obvious that Aristophanes had her in mind when he coined it. She cursed Aristophanes, herself, Fedra Pappas, and, for good measure, the Greek third declension as she climbed into a taxi and headed downtown.

The aspiring English pub was no darker on Tuesday evening than it had been on Sunday afternoon, but at least now the murk seemed less artificial. Two persons of unidentifiable age and sex were actually throwing darts through it, in the general direction of the dartboard. The Pappas girl, as far as Antonia could tell, had not yet arrived. She chose the booth nearest the door and started to sit down on the bench that faced the entrance. Then she thought, to hell with that, let *her* look for *me*, and seated herself defiantly with her back to the door.

Her peevish mood, born of exhaustion, lasted only until Fedra appeared five minutes later. She looked tired, too—tired and scared—and Antonia's resentment soon softened.

It was not the shock of her brother's arrest that had upset the girl, Antonia quickly discovered.

"Oh, he'll be all right," she said. "The worst they can do is put him in some kind of home or something. And maybe that wouldn't be such a bad idea either. For him *or* us. I'm afraid it was Yanni that jumped Professor Randolph last Saturday, though I don't know why. Probably something just panicked him and he attacked the first thing he saw moving. I'm glad Professor Randolph wasn't hurt, but the next person he picks on might not be so lucky. Several nights last week, including Saturday, Yanni was gone for several hours. We don't know where he went, but I bet he was hanging around the museum hoping to see Ari. Usually she comes home to see him pretty regular, once a week or so, but these last few months she couldn't because of working so hard on that thesis or whatever you call it. So she taught Yanni how to take the bus from our neighborhood to the museum and back, so he could visit her whenever he wanted and not feel like he was abandoned. Made him feel real proud too, moving around the city by himself like that. At first he went back and forth a lot, like he was just showing off that he knew how."

"But I don't understand why you . . ."

"Look, I went down there this morning and saw him. Mamá wasn't about to go, and there wasn't anyone else to do it. He wouldn't talk to me, I didn't really expect he would, but I know that look he had. I never saw it but once before, but I never forgot it either." She paused, frowned, took a pull at the mug of ale Antonia had ordered for her.

"Maybe it was because I was just a kid myself at the time. It must have been about ten years ago, while Ari was still in high school. Well, one day she got appendicitis and they rushed her to the hospital to get operated on. Seeing it was her, naturally they made a big fuss about it. If it'd been me, I probably would've had to walk myself to the hospital.

"So anyway I was left at home to take care of Yanni. I didn't pay much attention to him, but after a while I began to notice something was wrong. He never talked much anyway, but that day I couldn't get him to say anything. He just sat and stared and brooded till I thought

I'd go crazy. I finally got so mad I threw something at him. Not to hurt him, you know, just some little thing to bring him out of that trance he was in. Well, I hit him all right, right on the cheek, and he never even blinked. After that I left him alone. I think it sort of scared me, him sitting there like a statue, not moving or making a sound no matter what I did to him. Like I said, I was only a kid—I must've been about ten at the time—and I couldn't understand what was wrong with him. But I know now, and that's what's worrying me."

"I'm afraid I don't quite follow that."

"It was Ari. Nobody bothered to explain to him why they were taking her away so suddenly, or when she'd be back. Probably Ari wasn't in any condition to talk to him herself, and it never would've occurred to the rest of us. So he just sat there like that for six days, until they brought her back. When she finally did come home, he acted funny too. At first it was like he was scared of her—wouldn't look at her or talk to her or stay alone in the same room with her. Afterwards, when he got used to her being back again, it was just the opposite—he wouldn't let her out of his sight."

"That's very touching, Miss Pappas, but I still don't see what it has to do . . ."

"The point is, Professor, I finally found out what it was that was bugging him. Somehow he'd gotten it into his head that Ari was never coming back. As a matter of fact—he thought she was dead." Fedra bit the end of the sentence off savagely, as if it had a bad taste that she wanted to get out of her mouth as quickly as possible. For good measure she also took another gulp of the ale. They were both silent for a long minute.

"But surely you're not suggesting that your brother is thinking that *now*."

"Yes, Ma'am, that's exactly what I *am* suggesting. Of course, he's probably got it all wrong, just like he did that other time, but I think he *thinks* she's gone away forever or died or something. I think he *thinks* he'll never see her again."

"Look, Miss Pappas, before we start speculating about what may or may not have become of Ariadne, and what your brother may or may not think has become of her, I'd like to know more about their relationship. I've gotten some rather conflicting impressions about that." She was remembering Caracci's words: *My guess is, he forced her to cooperate. . . .*

Again the calculating look passed over Fedra's face as it had Sunday afternoon. But this time her mental arithmetic seemed to go more quickly.

"All right," she said, "I don't see what good it'll do, but then I don't see anything else that's going to help either. You're the brainy one at this table. Maybe if you had more to go on you could figure something." She fortified herself with another swig of ale, tossed her black hair, and plunged ahead.

"Yanni, see, he's our half-brother really. It's not a pretty story and I don't know all the details, but apparently Mamá went on the warpath one time when I was about two. She and my father weren't exactly an ideal model couple, and she was always getting mad about something or other. Anyway, this one night she walked out, and when she came back a few days later she was pregnant. Naturally she didn't want the kid, and personally I got an idea she tried to get rid of him, maybe even messed him up some seeing how he turned out. Anyway, Yanni got born in spite of her, and when Babás saw him . . ." The long black eyebrows lifted eloquently.

"You mean your father knew from the beginning that the child wasn't his?"

Fedra snorted. "He'd have had to be a lot dumber than he was not to see *that*, Miss Nielsen. Whatever problems my father might have had, black blood wasn't one of 'em. And this kid was black.

"Now what you have to remember is, Babás didn't really live in twentieth-century America like you and me. At heart he was just an old-fashioned Greek farmer, a small olive grower from one of the most out-of-it parts of Greece. Practically a medieval peasant. So you can imagine what he musta been thinking every time he looked at his wife's black baby. I mean, it was bad enough she was cheating, and it was worse she got knocked up—but a *black baby!* I think that was what he died of, even if it took him nine years to do it. Not that he ever said much. Maybe if he had it wouldn't have eaten at him like it did. Only once or twice that I can remember did he drink a little too much *ouzo* and start in on Mamá. Just words, of course, he'd never have laid a finger on her, but he sure knew a lot of words. He'd start with the one for whore and never stop till he hit omega. Didn't hardly ever repeat himself either. Greek's a hell of a language for cussing, you got to give it that." She grinned appreciatively at the memory of her father's eloquence, finished her ale, and signaled to the waiter for another.

"There was one name he used to call her," Fedra went on, "that I never could figure out. Maybe you'd know what it meant. Passy-something."

Antonia saw that there was no hope of ignoring the implied question. The girl was looking straight at her, waiting for an answer.

"Pasiphaë, probably. She was a queen. A queen of Crete who was unfaithful to her husband."

"Yeah, that was it." Mercifully, she seemed satisfied with this bowdlerized version of the legend of Pasiphaë. But Antonia might have saved herself the trouble of trying to spare the girl's feelings. Ignorant though she was of Greek mythology, Fedra had long since recognized instinctively the depth of her father's bitterness against her mother, as her next words showed.

"Anyway, like I said, it was Yanni's blackness that messed up my father's mind more than anything else. I used to wonder if he wouldn't have been less hurt and less angry if it'd been an animal Mamá was with."

"And yet he raised the child."

"Not really. Oh, he let him live in the house all right, but it was Ari who raised him. Just about the earliest thing I can remember is her taking care of both of us. She must've been about nine, and already Yanni was nearly as big as she was, but she fed him and played with him and kept him quiet so he wouldn't call attention to himself. Attention generally meant trouble where Yanni was concerned. Things were pretty peaceful as long as our parents weren't reminded he was there. As long as they didn't have to actually *look* at him. When they did—you remember the sign? You saw it the other day when you came to the *taverna.*"

Through the gathering mists of exhaustion and strong ale, Antonia conjured up an image of the crude bull's head on the childish body. The vague distaste she had felt for the painting turned slowly to horror as she realized what Fedra was driving at.

"You mean that—thing—was supposed to be your *brother*? And it was your father who painted it?"

"Yes, Ma'am, that's what I mean. When he *had* to look at him, that's what Babás saw, I guess. Like he was half animal. I told you it was sort of a joke. Like calling me Fedra. That's not my real name, you know. But Babás had this crazy idea we were like a family in some old legend. The mother was that Passy-what's-her-name, and Ariadne was her daughter, and there was this bull-monster mixed up in it someway. My father said there was a younger daughter too, but she didn't have anything to do with the story. And I pestered him to tell me her name too, because I hated being left out all the time. Finally he told me it was Fedra, and that's what he always called me after that."

"I can't say I care for your father's sense of humor."

"Yeah, me neither. But it didn't used to bother me much when I was a kid. Like I said, that sign made a good target. You know how kids are to each other. Insensitive, like. Ari was the only one that ever saw things from Yanni's point of view. All the rest of us—me, our parents, the kids in the neighborhood, even the teachers—all we saw was this huge, ugly kid that looked dangerous and acted stupid. Ari somehow knew he was just a little kid, and hurt and lonely and scared because everybody hated him and he couldn't figure out why. That all seems pretty obvious now, I guess. But it didn't look so obvious when I was only eleven or twelve. What was obvious *then* was, if I didn't join the other kids in teasing Yanni, they were gonna think I was as creepy as he was. And I didn't have that kind of guts, and Ari did.

"Anyway, now he's in trouble and she's not around to help him, and there's no one else he trusts. Certainly not me or Mamá. I know what Ari'd do if she was here. She'd march right into his cell with one of their old books and . . ."

"*Books?* Now wait a minute—surely your brother isn't the intellectual type? I had the impression . . ."

"Yes, Ma'am, it's true Yanni isn't what you'd call real bright. But this is different. I was talking about *their* books, the ones Ari used to show him when he was little to keep him quiet. I don't know how much he understood of the words, but they had lots of pictures and I always thought it was mostly the attention he liked anyway. It was almost like he was hypnotized or something. He'd just sit there looking sort of dreamy, staring at those old pillars and things, and listening to her voice."

"Pillars. You mean these books were about Greek art or archaeology—temples and so forth?"

"Yes, Ma'am. And legends too, I think. He liked the parts about Crete, because Ari told him that's where our ancestors came from. I remember some of the pictures—gold cups, and those funny-looking axes they had, and all sorts of things with pictures of bulls on 'em. He loved that stuff—it'd always calm him down faster than anything else when he was upset. That's what Ari would do now, I figure—talk to him till he was calm and dreamy and ready to tell the cops what really happened to that museum stuff."

"Unfortunately, they already know what happened to some of it."

Once more Fedra gave a derisive snort. "Yeah, sure. But for my money that stuff they found on him just proves the opposite of what they want it to."

"What do you mean?"

"Come on, Professor, did you ever hear of a thief so stupid he lets the fuzz find him, eating supper in his own house four days after a burglary, with the stuff in his *pockets?* All *that* proves is, he isn't bright enough to rob a museum. Which he isn't."

The fog in Antonia's brain was closing in fast now, and the logic of Fedra's argument seemed irrefutable. The corollary occurred to her with preternatural swiftness.

"Then," she observed brilliantly, "all we have to do is find out how those things *did* get into your brother's pocket!"

There was an embarrassed silence while they both tried to decide how to deal with the fatuity of this remark. Antonia finally concluded that honesty would be, if not the best, at any rate the most dignified policy.

"Miss Pappas," she said, "I'm sorry, but obviously I'm no earthly use to anyone right now. I've had no sleep since night before last, I've drunk two and a half mugs of ale I didn't need, and I have classes to teach tomorrow morning. So let me go home now and sleep on all this, and I'll call you tomorrow noon." She rose to go, but before she started for the door—slowly, with immense dignity and no staggering—Antonia said, "I think you may be right about your brother. That he's hiding something, I mean. And not the museum burglary, either."

12. A Rope of Paper

ARIADNE WAS DANCING. HER LONG BLACK HAIR, NO longer pulled severely back into a ponytail, swung heavy and shining about her bare shoulders and down her back. Something that looked like a golden tiara gleamed dimly on her forehead, just above the long straight eyebrows. The smile playing about her lips combined triumph with a hint of mockery, but her great dark eyes were unreadable.

Behind her, appearing, disappearing, reappearing from what looked like heavy banks of yellow fog or mist, was a motley little band of men and women. Motley, Antonia decided, was the only word for a group that included Caracci in the dark blue uniform and peaked cap of an ordinary patrolman. Win Randolph in his inevitable tweed jacket and slacks and with Gillian at his side, Bennie in faded jeans and a sweatshirt with "Property of the University Museum" printed on the back. Oddest of all was the old man with disheveled gray hair and beard carrying a large roll of papyrus under his arm, his ankle-length chiton draped over one shoulder leaving half his chest exposed. Behind him, at the very end of this ill-assorted procession, came a tall caftan-clad figure with caramel-colored hair piled high on her head and a fistful of glossy travel brochures in one hand. (That, thought Antonia with objectivity, is supposed to be me.)

It was hard at first to make out what these people were doing, but gradually she realized that they were performing a kind of primitive dance, a chain dance or serpentine with Ariadne at its head. It wound its way monotonously in and out of the yellow mist that turned out to be a maze of forsythia hedges in full bloom.

It seemed altogether natural and unremarkable to Antonia that the dancers were linked together, not by joined hands but by a long tannish ribbon of what she somehow knew were strips of papyrus glued together. (That, observed Antonia severely, is *not* what Theophrastus means when he says that papyrus was used for making rope, as well as paper and a lot of other useful things.)

Ariadne held the end of this unlikely strand loosely, even heedlessly, in her left hand, seeming not to take very seriously her role as leader or guide, if that *was* her role. She seemed more intent on something she was hearing or trying to hear. Perhaps the *aulos*, which was the dance's only accompaniment. Or a bell tree?

A telephone. Definitely a telephone. Someone ought to answer it. Antonia ought to answer it. Antonia answered it, fighting one arm free of the twisted bedsheets in order to reach it.

"Hu'o?" she grunted into the receiver.

"Professor Nielsen?" The voice was brisk, alert, cleanly articulated. It had obviously been awake for hours. "Steve Caracci again. Look, I don't intend to make a habit of phoning you every morning, but I'm afraid I have a favor to ask." If he was expecting her to make encouraging noises before he continued, he was disappointed. The sound that came over the wire was more in the nature of a muffled groan.

"Yes, well, as I told you yesterday, our psychiatrist has examined the Pappas boy. He got practically nothing out of him, which is unusual. But he thinks the kid is probably slightly retarded, and he did find out one other thing that's kind of interesting. The boy is extremely sensitive to any mention of his sister—the older one, that is, Ariadne. It seems he . . ."

"Yes, I think I know something about that, Lieutenant. But what do I have to do with all this?"

"Just this, Miss Nielsen. The shrink thinks there may be a chance, just a chance, that the boy would open up to someone—a woman, preferably—that he could identify with his sister, someone who knows her and cares about her. The mother or the other sister would be the obvious choice, of course. But Mrs. Pappas flatly refuses to co-operate, and when the girl tried . . ."

"Yes, I know." *He wouldn't talk to me, I didn't really expect he would.* "And you think it would be public spirited if I were to come down and stick *my* head in the lion's mouth, right?"

"Yes, Ma'am, that's about it. It's a long shot, like I said, but . . ."

"All right, Lieutenant. But it'll have to be after lunch. I have classes to teach this morning."

"Of course, of course. At your convenience, Miss Nielsen. We'll be expecting you sometime this afternoon, then. And thanks."

After this unpromising debut, the morning turned out surprisingly well. Antonia always liked Wednesdays anyway. By Wednesday one has settled back into harness, the stress of reentry into the working week has passed, and Friday still seems too remote to be tantalizing. Moreover, on this particular Wednesday the weather continued springlike, she had had a good night's sleep and a hearty breakfast, and one of her students asked an intelligent question in class.

It was therefore in a more buoyant mood than she had enjoyed for several days that Antonia collected her coffee and returned to her office after her second class. She tried to concentrate on a long-neglected batch of quiz papers, but her thoughts kept returning to the tangle of incidents and personalities that surrounded Ariadne.

At the moment, she was inclined to view the situation in a relatively optimistic light. Ariadne herself, Antonia was increasingly certain, had simply gone on a trip related to her great discovery. Her study of the papyrus contained, for example, no reference to radiocarbon confirmation of the date she had assigned to it on paleographical grounds. Sooner or later this confirmation would have to be obtained, and it was easy to imagine the excited girl rushing off to the nearest carbon-14 lab, five-millimeter scraps of papyrus in a plastic envelope in her purse, prepared to

bully and badger and wheedle the technicians into doing
a rush job on her precious manuscript. Ordinarily it would
take months to get a dating out of the overworked labs,
and this surely was one time Ariadne would have no patience with orthodox procedures. It would be interesting
to know what account she had given the lab people of
herself and her papyrus. The least devious of women under normal circumstances, Ariadne was undoubtedly capable of prodigies of invention in such a case as this.
Antonia grinned to herself, wishing she had been there to
witness the scene. Wherever "there" might be.

She also wished Ariadne would come back from "there"
and straighten out her brother. His disorientation, not to
mention the golden artifacts found in his pockets, was
disturbing, though even the police had to admit that poor
Yanni wasn't likely to have planned and carried out the
museum burglary unaided. But who had used him, then,
or coerced him into collaborating? Certainly not Ariadne,
but what about her sister, Fedra, whose sense of exclusion
and deprivation was so strong, and whose determination
to "get out" was so ruthless?

But if not Yanni and some unknown confederate, then
who *had* stolen the Aegean Gold? The question seemed
as far from being answered as ever. Unless, of course,
one entertained the possibility that Bennie Thompson . . .
She thrust the thought aside. Still, it was true he had
seemed jumpy and irritable Monday night when she went
prowling in the museum. Could there be something there
he was afraid she might find out? Hadn't he said something about not having any secrets left after she and the
police got through snooping around? But on the other hand,
he hadn't made any move to prevent her leaving the museum, hadn't in any way threatened her the next morning
when he came to the apartment. If there was anything that
Bennie was anxious to conceal, she evidently hadn't found
it.

Twenty minutes into the quizzes, Antonia was interrupted by the arrival of Doris, the Classics secretary. She
was looking puzzled and a little anxious.

"Mr. Sandler asked me to ask you if you could stop at
the Randolphs' on your way home to lunch and . . .
ah . . ." She stopped in confusion.

"And what?"

"Well, the fact is, Professor Randolph never came to work this morning. He had two classes, at nine and ten, and he didn't show up for either of them. His students have been . . ."

"But couldn't you phone him?"

"Oh, yes, I tried that, of course, Several times, in fact. But there was no answer."

"All right, Doris, I'll look in on my way home." Antonia's voice was casual, almost cool. She did not think Doris was deceived, though. They both knew that, while it is not unheard of for a teacher to turn up for a class half prepared, half asleep, or half sloshed, it is extremely unlikely that he will fail to turn up at all without offering at least some shadow of an explanation.

"Probably something about the phone," said Antonia, looking Doris straight in the eye. "Probably isn't ringing at their end, something like that."

"Yes, there's been a lot of that lately," said Doris, looking Antonia straight in the eye. "Lots of people have been having trouble with their phones."

The neighborhood was quiet at this time of day, with only the preschool children and their mothers at home, and they all seemed to be indoors eating lunch. The Randolphs' house was no more deserted looking than the others, but its curtains were still closed as if the occupants had forgotten to get up that morning. Gillian might have gone out to shop, of course, but Win—what on earth could have induced him just to dump those two classes without a word of explanation?

When she rang the doorbell there was no response. She waited a minute and tried again, with the same result. Concluding that they had indeed gone out, she was about to turn away when she noticed that the inner door was not closed but standing ajar about two inches. Funny, she thought, they're both so compulsive about things like that. She opened the screen door and was about to pull the inner one shut when on an impulse she pushed it open instead and peered into the living room. With the curtains drawn, the interior was so dark that at first she could see nothing except the dim outlines of the larger pieces of furniture.

"Gillian! Win!" Her voice was startlingly loud in the

silent house. But at the sound of it there was a faint stirring in a large armchair that faced the door. Uncertainly,
she said "Win?" again and stepped into the room, groping
for a light switch.

A lamp went on beside the armchair, and the man huddled in it winced away from the light and covered his eyes
with both hands.

"Antonia? Is that you?" Win's voice was almost a croak
and his face, when he finally lowered his hands, looked
ten years older than that of the man she had talked to less
than twenty-four hours earlier. His eyes, which were
avoiding hers, had a dull staring quality that frightened
her.

"Win, what on earth's the matter with you?" She tried
not to sound as disturbed as she felt.

"I'm . . ." He cleared his throat and his voice became
almost normal. "I'm all right. It's . . . oh, my God."
Once more he buried his face in his hands. Involuntarily
Antonia glanced at the staircase that ran up one side of
the living room.

"Gillian?" she said in a very low voice. There was a
barely perceptible movement of Win's head.

Antonia's life had not been crammed with physical dan-
gers or violence. Like most of her peers she had had a
comparatively sheltered and secure existence. Yet there
had been a few, a very few occasions when death had
brushed past her, and each time her reaction had been the
same. An overturned boat at the lake one summer. A car
that flipped over on a snowy highway and left her hanging
upside down by her seat belt in the wreckage. The mountain on which she got lost as a child, wandering for six
hours among snowfields two thousand feet above timber-
line. And every time she had responded, as she did now,
with an odd sort of emotional coldness. No hysterics, no
heroics. Just a cool, numb efficiency that was almost ro-
botlike. She swam to the shore, she crawled out of the
wreck, she walked down off the mountain. She was neither
especially courageous nor especially quick-witted in an
emergency. In fact, her mind worked, if anything, more
slowly than usual. But it worked. It was as if a switch
marked Emotions had been thrown to the Off position and
left there until the crisis was past. It was the only way

she knew of surviving the few moments of real terror that had come her way.

And so it was now. The switch clicked off, a kind of deadly calm settled over her, and she turned toward the stairs. Win protested feebly from his armchair but she ignored him. She was setting one foot methodically before the other, climbing the stairs. They seemed very steep, and her feet very heavy.

When the stairs finally came to an end she found herself facing Gillian's bedroom door, which stood a few inches open. Still at the same deliberate pace, neither fast nor slow, Antonia walked to the door, pushed it open, and switched on the light. Without pausing on the threshold she walked to the bed and looked down at her friend.

The most disturbing feature of the scene was its utter normalcy and peacefulness. Everything in the room seemed to be in its usual place. Gillian's clothing was not even disarranged, and her features were composed. The masses of dark mahogany hair were coiled as gracefully as ever around her head. The small cylinder of transparent plastic that lay on the bedspread beside her looked innocuous and ordinary.

Antonia had intended to feel for a pulse or a heartbeat, but she found that even through the protective numbness that enveloped her she could not bring herself to touch Gillian's body. It seemed a superfluous gesture anyway.

On a small table next to the bed, on the side away from Gillian, there was a white princess telephone. Antonia picked it up, dialed, and waited for what seemed a long time before someone answered. When she finally spoke, her voice was clear and steady but the words came very slowly.

"I want to report a suicide. . . ."

13. Mystery of
the Lost Consonant

"WHEN I WENT BACK DOWNSTAIRS WIN WAS PACING aimlessly back and forth the length of the living room. I took him out on the front porch to wait for the police. I don't think either of us could have stood the atmosphere in that house much longer."

Antonia took a rather intemperate gulp of Barry's Scotch.

"We just sat there on the front steps until the police came. I don't think we said much, either of us. When the cops got there, I told them what I could, which wasn't much, but Win"—Antonia shook her head grimly—"Win was in no condition to talk to anyone. And then when they—they carried Gillian's bod . . . body down the—oh, Barry, it was horrible!"

Greenfield, fearing she might be about to cry, hastily thrust her drink back into her hand, but this time she didn't taste it.

"I keep thinking there must have been something I could have done that I didn't. Some way I could have showed that I cared about *her* even though I couldn't take her suspicions and accusations seriously. I *knew* she was upset, Barry, that's the worst of it, I *knew* she was overwrought about the Ariadne business, and I just didn't take it seriously enough. I thought Win was just being melodramatic, refusing to leave her alone in the house like that. And I thought Gillian was only trying to inject a little excitement into her rather empty existence." Antonia shivered and glanced down at the drink in her hand as if she had only just noticed it.

"It's terrifying," she said slowly, "how little we really know about people we think we're close to."

Greenfield was spared the effort of responding to this gloomy truism by the arrival of Marsha. They had been expecting her home from her student-teaching job for the better part of an hour. She burst in now, breathless and excited.

"Oh, Barry, have you heard? They're saying that the wife of that Classics professor . . ." She caught sight of Antonia and stopped short.

"I didn't know you were here, Miss Nielsen," she said quietly. "I'm so sorry. They must be friends of yours."

Antonia nodded. "I gather," she said with some bitterness, "it's all over campus already."

"Yes, I'm afraid it is. I stopped at the English department to leave a paper with one of my professors on the way home from school, and everyone was talking about Mrs. Randolph. But the craziest thing is the *reason* they say she killed her . . ."

"Marsha," Barry interrupted hastily, "wouldn't you like to get yourself a drink? Antonia and I are having Scotch." And gently but firmly he began to shepherd her, still wearing her coat, toward the kitchen.

But Antonia was not to be put off so easily. "Wait a minute," she said. "What did you start to say, Marsha?"

Barry shrugged his shoulders resignedly and started for the kitchen alone, muttering, "All right, *I'll* get your drink and you can extract your foot from your mouth by yourself."

Marsha continued reluctantly, "They're saying—it's idiotic of course—but they're saying Mrs. Randolph was insanely jealous of one of her husband's graduate students. I was startled because I used to room with the girl, and I know how ridiculous the idea is. But that's what they're saying anyhow."

Antonia was glaring angrily at no one in particular—the

impersonal "they" of Marsha's remarks, presumably—
when Barry returned with three fresh drinks on a tray. He
set them down, handed one to each of the women, and
put an arm around Marsha's shoulders while sipping his
own highball with his free hand.

"Ariadne is a friend of Antonia's, Marsha," he said.
"No one has seen her for several days, and Antonia's been
concerned about her."

"Oh, I *am* sorry, Miss Nielsen, I didn't realize. But
surely that part of it doesn't really bother you, does it? I
mean, it's such a stupid rumor. I don't know Professor
Randolph but I do know Ariadne, and it's just impossible."

"Yes, of course it is. But that doesn't prevent it from
being the reason Gillian killed herself. She was obsessed
with the idea that there was something between Ariadne
and her husband. But what bothers me is the thought of
Ariadne having to face all this when she comes back."

"Not to mention," Barry put in, "that it must be pretty
awful for Randolph himself—or will be when he hears the
rumors."

"Yes, I suppose so. Except that in a sense he's been
asking for it for years, cultivating that ridiculous Lothario
image of his so assiduously. The horrible irony of it is,
now that we've been forced to take it seriously at last, the
scandal has attached itself to an innocent woman."

Barry said, "Isn't it a bit morbid, dwelling on it like
this? Unless there's something we can do for Win."

"I don't think there is, no. When I finally left the house,
the Sandlers had come to spend the evening with him. I
was afraid I was going to lose my grip before long if I
didn't get out of there. And we've covered his classes,
one way and another, for the next couple of days. So I
can't see that there's much more we can do, not tonight
anyway." Antonia leaned back wearily into the masses of
soft cushions that Barry, with unprecedented solicitude,
had placed behind her back when she first arrived and
collapsed onto his sofa.

"At any rate, you've done more than *your* share, old
girl. Tower of strength and all that." Unaccustomed as
Barry and Antonia were to the exchange of compliments,
they both looked slightly embarrassed at his last words.

"Thanks, but could we talk about something else?

Something utterly dull and ordinary? I cannot . . . *cannot* think about the Randolphs anymore for a while." On the last words Antonia's voice rose several tones and quavered slightly.

Marsha broke in with a soothingly practical suggestion.

"Look, Barry," she said, "I'll get dinner tonight and meanwhile you fix us all another drink. You'll stay, won't you, Miss Nielsen?" It sounded more like an order than an invitation, and Antonia made a grateful noise from the depths of her cushions.

From the door of the kitchen, where he was mixing her a very weak Scotch, Barry kept a watchful eye on Antonia. She seemed, he decided, allowing for grief and fatigue, to be holding up pretty well.

When he once more returned to the living room bearing drinks, there was a dark blue book wedged under his left arm. With choreographic precision he set the right-hand drink in front of Antonia, extracted the book with the hand thus freed, set the second drink beside the first, and opened the book.

"Since you specifically suggested changing the subject, there *is* something I've been meaning to ask you about. It's my Greek." And he began to thumb earnestly through the dark blue book.

For the first time in many hours Antonia smiled, albeit a bit wanly.

"Barry's Greek" was something of an ongoing joke among his colleagues in English and Classics. Like many another literary scholar, Barry Greenfield had belatedly decided that for the true understanding of English literature it was essential to return *ad fontes*—to learn, that is, a good deal more about the Greek and Latin classics than he had picked up in two years of high school Latin and one undergraduate mythology course. He therefore badgered Antonia for several weeks until in self-defense she gave him the name of a Greek grammar "suitable," as Barry put it, "for autodidacts."

His own specialty was Henry Fielding and his theory of the comic epic. Knowing this, Antonia had put him on to a Greek text that approached the language through Homer, Fielding's great exemplar, rather than the more traditional Plato and Xenophon. Delighted with this method, Barry had plunged in and mastered in rapid succession the alphabet, the present indicative active, and two noun declensions. Thus far his progress was sufficiently typical of the autodidact's enthusiasm.

But at the first whiff of the optative mood, the dual number, and the middle voice—perils undreamed of in the philosophy of your average English professor—Greenfield's true mettle was revealed. To the astonishment of all, Antonia not excepted, Barry kept going. The middle and the dual he took in stride, the optative left him temporarily stunned—but he kept going. Doggedly he plodded through the mined fields of second aorists and passive subjunctives and contract verbs. Through a deadly rain of enclitics and particles, *nu*'s movable and *alpha*'s privative, Barry kept going. Eventually even Antonia, though noted for her skepticism on the subject of self-taught linguists, was moved to a grudging admiration. It had begun to look as if Barry Greenfield might actually read the *Iliad* in Greek one day.

He was standing before her now, dark blue book in hand, and he was saying, "It's these crazy hexameters. I can't get 'em to scan right. Look here—already in line 7 . . ." He shoved the open book under Antonia's nose and began to read.

"*Atreïdēs-te anax andrōn . . . Bum* ba-ba, *Bum* ba-ba, *Bum* ba, *Bum!*"

"So?" said Antonia. "Three and a half dactyls. So what?"

"So there's a perfectly *shocking* hiatus between the fifth and sixth syllables, that's so what. And hiatus," he intoned terribly, "is Not Permitted. Except, of course, sometimes. Only this doesn't seem to be one of the times. Explain, please." And he settled back on the sofa beside her with his drink, looking expectant.

Thus appealed to, Antonia was of two minds. On the one hand, she felt a vague, guilty sense of disloyalty at turning away from the painful thought of Gillian's death. But on the other, what a relief it would be to talk shop for a while—and besides, what useful purpose would be served by further dwelling on the Randolphs' misfortunes? She had done what little she could—surely the healthier impulse now was the one that urged her to turn back to her own life for a while.

With an attempt at their usual bantering tone, Antonia

began. "I gather you've never heard of the Phantom Consonant Digamma?"

"That," said Barry brightly, "sounds like an Electric Company reject. Is it anything like the Silent E From Outer Space?"

Ignoring this impertinence, Antonia continued. "In primitive Greek alphabets there was a letter that looked like a capital F but was pronounced like *w*. It was called digamma or double-g, but it got lost somewhere along the line and doesn't appear in the classical Greek alphabet, which is what you've learned. Now apparently this *w* sound was still part of the spoken language when the Homeric poems were being composed, and the rhythm of the verse sometimes reflects this. In other words . . ."

"Look, Perfesser," Barry drawled, "just show me how to make that verse scan, wouldja?"

"Oh, very well," said Antonia with the testiness of the pedagogue whose lecture has been interrupted in midflight. "That phrase *anax andrōn*—Agamemnon's famous epithet, Lord of Men—was originally *wanax andrōn*, with a digamma. Therefore and QED, there is no real hiatus between *te* and *anax* because it's really *te wanax*."

"Unless," Barry observed, "you philological types just made up this Magical Mystery Consonant to pull old Homer's eggs out of the fire. Or is it chestnuts? Anyway, had you thought of *that* my girl?"

"Sorry, but they've found digammas in primitive inscriptions from the islands: Thera, Crete . . ."

"Found what?" cried Barry enthusiastically. "A digamma? An actual charred-but-still-recognizable digamma, its bronze fittings all intact and . . ."

But Antonia refused to be diverted. "And in the Linear B tablets they've found the very word you're so exercised about, *wanax*. Unfortunately, in the tablets *wanax* doesn't seem to refer to anyone quite so grandiose as the Supreme Commander of the Allied Forces Against Troy. In archaic Crete a *wanax* appears to have been more on the order of a country squire or . . ."

To Barry's relief, with the philological waters rising icy about his chest, Antonia's lecture was interrupted once again, this time by Marsha's voice from the kitchen.

"Hey, could one of you erudite types possibly set the

table and open a bottle of wine? This chili is just about ready, and I'm trying to put a salad together."

As he manipulated the cork out of a bottle of burgundy, Barry reflected with satisfaction that he might well go to his grave without ever finding out precisely what a *wanax* had been in second-millennium Crete. But at least he could now move on, with a perfectly clear conscience, to line eight of Book One of the *Iliad*.

It was three hours later, back in her own apartment, that Antonia remembered her promise to call Fedra Pappas. Even through the shock and disorientation of finding Gillian's body and helping Win through the first few hours of his ordeal, she had had the presence of mind to phone Caracci and postpone her interview with the half brother. But the boy's sister—Ariadne's sister—had completely slipped her mind.

In her present state of drowsiness, induced by a heavy dinner, three highballs, and a glass of wine, Antonia felt a guilty yearning to fall into bed and go right on forgetting about Fedra. But she remembered the girl's anxiety— though that, come to think of it, had been more for Ariadne than for the boy—and the implication of last night's conversation, that Fedra was on the point of accepting some responsibility for her brother. It would be a shame to discourage this impulse, which seemed to be long overdue. Better to reassure her that one had not forgotten one's promise to try to do something for the boy.

Antonia sighed, tried to feel virtuous, succeeded only in feeling exhausted, and picked up the phone.

Her apology and explanation for her failure to call earlier were quickly delivered. Fedra was grateful for Antonia's promise to talk to her brother, conventionally sympathetic over the death of Gillian.

Perhaps there had been nothing between Fedra and Win before. But Antonia suspected it wouldn't be long before he received a call of sympathy in his bereavement, of apology for losing her temper with him, of invitation to share a dinner or a drink. Because Professor Randolph was now one of those whom Fedra saw as her legitimate prey: an eligible man, a man with a future.

14. The Minotaur

THURSDAY MORNING DAWNED—OR RATHER, FAILED TO dawn—cold, rainy, and hovering on the edge of snow. Last week's daffodils and forsythia blossoms were now no more than yellow stains on the muddy tracks that students had worn in the grass with their boots and bicycle tires. On tree trunks and kiosks all over campus, Aegean Gold posters flapped soggily in the wind.

The exhibition was still scheduled to open in just over two days, on Saturday afternoon. Miss Lilly and the museum staff were frantic, the police baffled and a bit defensive, and Yanni Pappas, after two days in jail, still uncommunicative. It was assumed that he had stashed the missing pieces somewhere—unless, of course (unthinkable thought), it was after all Ariadne herself who had spirited them away. But whoever had them and wherever they were, Caracci and his men were no closer to laying their hands on them than they had been six days earlier.

Antonia, trudging drearily toward her nine-thirty class, remembered wryly how she had felt while making the same trek the previous Friday. Then she had found the neatness, the orderliness, the pleasant respectability of the campus oppressive, and had felt both stimulated and unsatisfied by the vernal prettiness of blossoms and new grass and budding trees. She remembered how she had longed to go to Crete with Ariadne, to savor the island's violent contrasts of color and light and contour, its uncivilized harshness. Now—was it only six days later?—she only wished the familiar campus would go back to being tame and pretty and superficially predictable. As it was now, it only looked the way she felt, trampled and soggy. It did nothing at all to console or distract her from thoughts of a student missing, priceless works of ancient art stolen and perhaps destroyed—much less a friend dead by her own hand.

She got through the class. She got through her office hours—during which, miraculously, not a single student showed up in search of attention, sympathy, or justice. She managed a quick lunch in the Faculty Club, then returned to her office, packed up her briefcase, and started out the door. But before the automatic lock could click behind her she turned back, a thoughtful expression on her face, and stood for a minute before the floor-to-ceiling bookshelves that lined one wall of the room. Running a fingernail across the spines of the books on one of the lower shelves, she found the one she wanted, stuck it under her arm, and left the office.

She was remembering something Fedra had said. *I know what Ari'd do if she was here. . . .*

"Appreciate you coming down here like this, Miss Nielsen, especially under the circumstances. I'm sorry about your friend." As an expression of sympathy it was certainly brief, Antonia thought, but it sounded genuine enough.

Caracci went on, "I hope we haven't brought you down here for nothing but, I'll be frank with you, we aren't too optimistic about your chances of getting this boy to talk. The shrink's got a lot of fancy words for it but what it amounts to is, the kid's scared, he's dumb, and whatever he knows—if anything—he's bottled up inside himself and jammed the cork down good and tight."

"I may as well try anyway, Lieutenant, as long as I'm here. Besides, I promised his sister—the younger one, I mean, Fedra. She seems to be genuinely concerned about the boy, though from what I can gather it's a pretty recent development with her."

Caracci said dryly, "Yeah, well, I can understand her feelings. He's not exactly the cuddly type. As you'll see."

"He hasn't exactly had a cuddly life, Lieutenant."

"Yeah," said Caracci ambiguously, "that I can believe too. And what," he added, "might *that* be?"

Antonia glanced down at the book in her hand. "Oh, just something Fedra thought might get the conversational ball rolling."

A bushy eyebrow rose skeptically toward Caracci's receding hairline. "He doesn't strike me as the bookish type, Miss Nielsen. Still, anything's worth a try at this point, I guess, considering what we've got out of him so far—which is nothing. Well, here we are." He opened a small view hole in a metal door painted battleship gray and peered into it before turning back to Antonia. "Don't be alarmed by the size of him. He doesn't seem to have any tendency to violence, despite appearances. Problem is to get any reaction out of him. Like I said." He stepped aside to let Antonia take a look for herself.

She looked.

All this time, she suddenly realized, she had been thinking of Yanni, with sympathy, as "the boy," ignoring Bennie's and Caracci's references to his size and—yes, there was no other word for it—ugliness. She had assumed that the detective, at least, was prejudiced.

It was therefore with something of a shock that she saw that Caracci had been minimizing Yanni's weirdness, not exaggerating it.

The "boy"—actually he was about eighteen, Antonia recalled—was sitting on the cot in his cell, knees apart, hunched over, forearms on thighs, hands dangling listlessly between them. The posture made his huge shoulders look even more massive than they must have ordinarily.

In his eyes, which were motionless, was nothing but a blank hopeless stare. As Bennie had said, he seemed to be looking through everything that surrounded him, into some other, more bearable world.

He bore a disturbing though distant resemblance to the grotesque figure on the sign at the family *taverna*. Like the painted Minotaur, Yanni's head looked overlarge for his body, perhaps because of the huge mop of curly black

hair that seemed to engulf his face. Though he was not
noticeably darker in complexion than his sisters, Yanni's
features were heavier than theirs, less sculptured. That and
the hair were all that suggested his black father.

But the most disturbing thing about Yanni was something less tangible. It had something to do with his eyes,
as Bennie Thompson had suggested. There was a certain
lack of understanding in them, an unawareness of his surroundings—or was that only a reaction to his present surroundings? He looked—old man Pappas had been right in
a way—not inhuman exactly, but imperfectly human. Of
course, Antonia reflected grimly, he had been treated from
infancy with very imperfect humanity. By everyone except
Ariadne, at any rate.

She shook herself out of this unprofitable reverie and
withdrew her eye from the little window. Pity and sympathy were easy enough from the near side of a steel door.
Shut up inside the cell with him, alone, how would one's
liberal sentiments hold up?

Only one way to find out.

"I guess you'd better open the door, Lieutenant." Antonia had the impression that her voice sounded a shade
less calm and resolute than she could have wished.

As she swung the door open Caracci said, "I'll be right
out here with Joe if you need anything." No doubt he
intended the words to be reassuring.

Yanni raised his eyes to hers for a second, and Antonia
thought she saw a flicker of hope in them. But it died
instantly when he saw who she was—or wasn't—and he
went back to staring through the floor as before.

Not knowing what else to do, Antonia sat down on the
edge of the bed beside him, leaving about two feet between them.

"Hello, Yanni," she began. No reaction. "My name's
Antonia." Nothing. "I'm a friend of Ariadne's." A small
muscle at the corner of his mouth twitched at the sound
of the name, but that was all.

"She's my student at the university," Antonia persevered. "And a very good one, you know, one of the best
we've had in Greek." She opened the book in her lap.
"The others all envy her the way she can read poetry
aloud, the tragic choruses and so forth." She didn't add

that the other graduate students also avoided Ariadne for the most part, sensing that outside the classroom and library they would have little in common with her.

Absently, as she babbled on about Ariadne, Antonia was turning the pages of the book that lay open in her lap. She saw the pictures herself only peripherally, since most of her attention was concentrated on finding fresh topics for what was obviously going to remain a monologue rather than a conversation.

But she knew, almost without looking, what the pictures were. The "Parisienne" fresco. The ivory bull-leaper. The Throne Room with its griffin murals. The relief of the young Priest-King in his feather crown. The gold and ivory Snake Goddess.

She was saying, "She'll have her doctorate finished soon, and then she can get a proper job and a nice apartment where you would . . ." Suddenly a massive shoulder touched hers, and she flinched involuntarily with surprise. She hadn't realized that Yanni had gradually been closing the gap between them. She glanced up at him now and saw the black unreadable eyes fixed intently on the book. He still seemed oblivious to Antonia herself, but at least he was looking at the pictures. Whether he had heard anything she had said was anyone's guess.

Softly she began to comment on the pictures.

"Those are the ladies of the court. They would have worn necklaces and earrings of gold, like these. (You'll have to tell the police where the rest of that jewelry is, you know—Ari would want you to.)

"And these are the little gold axes they gave the Goddess of War, like the one you found in the museum. They aren't for people, Yanni, they were meant for the goddess.

"This one looks like a queen, doesn't she? Or maybe a princess. Did you know your sister was named after a princess? Thousands of years ago the king of Crete had a daughter named Ariadne. She fell in love with a foreigner and helped him to find his way out of a sort of maze. The next part's sad, because he abandoned her and left her to die. But in the end . . ."

"He knows that story."

When the deep, harsh voice finally broke its long silence, Antonia realized she had not really expected Yanni to speak, perhaps had even doubted that he *could* speak. He went on in a sort of lumbering singsong.

"She was a princess and she lived on an island and the sun was always shining and there was this beautiful palace and it had a dark basement and no one could get out and she was a princess and she helped him and when she died."

The flow stopped as abruptly as it had begun. It was not a pause for breath or thought, it was an end.

Was it perhaps a dim recollection of the adult's trick of pausing in mid-sentence when reading a familiar story to a child, so that the child can finish it for himself?

To humor him, Antonia prompted gently, "And when she died . . . ?"

Which version had Ariadne told him, she wondered. Catullus' romantic maiden on the beach, hair blown in the wind and pale feet in the ripples of incoming water, watching her lover's ship disappear over the horizon?

No, more likely the more ancient version, in which the princess was no lovesick girl but a goddess triumphant, bride of a god, her wedding chaplet translated into a starry constellation.

Yanni had fallen silent once more.

Antonia had been keeping her eyes on the book that lay open in her lap, but she turned now and looked up into his face.

His eyes were bottomless and black with pain. There were tears on the ugly cheeks, but his face was unmoving as stone. The sight was as shocking as if one had come upon a gargoyle weeping.

And looking at the stony gargoyle-face, she knew.

It was not after all vague anxiety or idle curiosity that had been driving her these last six days. It had been mortal fear, unwanted, denied, finally undeniable.

The cloak of cold, deadly efficiency settled upon her once again, shutting out horror, grief, anger, everything but the determination to find out what had happened.

She said again, less gently, "And when she died?"

At first there was no response from the mountainous body beside her. Then the hoarse singsong began again.

"He buried her like a princess like the Old Ones and she needed some things and they were right there and he took them and . . ."

"But where, Yanni, where?" She forced herself to keep her voice low-pitched and calm.

". . . gave them to her and she looked beautiful and he felt better."

"Yanni, where is Ariadne?" Again the small muscle twitched near his mouth.

"Like the Old Ones. Like the lab . . ." A note of doubt crept into his voice for the first time. ". . . laboratory?"

Antonia knew what he was trying to say, but for practical purposes her question was still unanswered.

"Yanni, we have to find your sister! Where . . ."

A look of immense cunning came into his face. *"Sometimes,"* he said slowly, as if he had not heard her, "they *rob* them and take *away* their things and then they have *nothing* and . . ." He paused as if to let the scattered pieces of his idea fall slowly into place. The thought, when finally completed, seemed to horrify him.

"No!" he roared. *"No! Don't* find Ari! *He hates that!"*

And without further warning the huge hands were around her throat. Just before she passed out, the last shreds of the cool detachment took note of the incongruous softness and smoothness of his hands. It was as if they had never worked, never been exposed to wind or sun.

Pale, hairless, soft hands, the hands of one who had lived in lightless places—they choked the light from Antonia's eyes and brain, and she lost consciousness.

15. The Princess Ariadne

WHEN SHE CAME AROUND, WITH A NECK THAT FELT broken and a throat that felt as if it had been worked over with a coarse rasp, Antonia had what was to be her first and last glimpse of Caracci looking chastened. The sight was, under the circumstances, no consolation.

"What . . . ," she croaked, then stopped because it hurt to talk. Caracci held up a monitory hand.

"What happened was, Sleeping Beauty finally came out of his trance and went for you. It took us a few seconds to get the door open and pull him off of you. And by that time you were—ah—unconscious. I'm afraid we underestimated that boy." Which was as close to an apology as Antonia ever got from him.

"I know you don't want to talk much," Caracci went on, "but can you tell me roughly what he said? We couldn't make much sense out of it. What was that about a laboratory, for instance?"

Antonia shook her head to spare her throat, which made her neck ache. So once again she croaked, miserably, using the fewest words possible.

"Not lab—labyrinth—remembered only first syllable— very confused—can't distinguish sister from princess in myth—lived in palace called Labyrinth—also thinking of

131

ancient burial chambers—underground—dark—oh God."
She buried her face for a moment in the pillow on the
couch where they had laid her in someone's office. The
pain, the despair, the objectless anger were physically nau-
seating.

Almost gently, Caracci said, "That's the next thing I
was going to ask—he said something about burying her,
didn't he?"

Antonia nodded, very carefully.

"And he said the place was 'like a labyrinth'?"

Another cautious nod.

"And nothing more?"

"I think—somewhere in museum—basement probably—ask Bennie—knows—building."

"All right, it's worth a try." He stood up heavily. "You
try and get some rest and . . ."

Antonia sat bolt upright and swung her legs off the
couch. She felt dizzy and faint but stayed vertical.

"No!" she said, so forcefully that her throat felt as if
liquid fire had been poured down it. "I'm going too."

"Now, Miss Nielsen, don't be ridic . . ."

"I tell you I'm going, Lieutenant." She spoke more
quietly this time in deference to the throat, but there was
a murderous look in her eye. Caracci wondered if it was
meant for him but decided it wasn't.

Antonia slid her feet into her shoes, which had been
removed and set beside the couch. She stood up and sat
down again immediately, feeling light-headed. Doggedly
she tried again, and this time she stayed up.

"I'm ready," she said, and her look dared him to con-
tradict her. Caracci shrugged with a mixture of annoyance
and grudging admiration and opened the door.

She was vaguely aware of being driven to the museum
in a squad car, sitting in the back seat beside Caracci.
The swaying hurt her neck, but the pain was drowned in
grief and anger. She had not even realized another police
car was following them, until it turned off and Caracci
said, "They're gonna pick up Thompson at his place—*if*
he's there." Antonia was too exhausted to resent the in-
sinuation.

They reached the museum just before closing time,
though it seemed later because of the masses of charcoal-
gray clouds that darkened the sky and the drizzling rain

that somehow managed to make everything look greasy rather than cleansed. Caracci had his driver park across the street for a few minutes until the museum guard had ushered the last visitor out and was beginning to lock the main doors. Then Caracci crossed the street, spoke briefly to the guard, and came back to the car to collect Antonia.

"The museum's all clear now," he said. "No point getting a lot of people in a flap if they're going to be gone in five minutes anyway. The director's not around, but Miss Lilly is still here. She seemed like a sensible lady when I talked to her the other day, and I figure she knows the building as well as anyone, so . . ."

"But I thought Bennie—your men—"

"Yeah, we'll let him take the tour too if he gets here in time. Come on."

As they climbed the long flight of shallow steps that led up to the entrance, Caracci put his hand under her left elbow to steady her, but it wasn't really necessary. Terra firma instead of a swaying car, the cool evening air, and the rain were rapidly clearing her head.

Miss Lilly, looking weary, greeted them at the door of her office.

"I'm sorry the director's not here at the moment. As a matter of fact he's gone to a meeting at City Hall. It's about the burglary, I'm afraid. I don't suppose you have anything new for us?" She didn't sound very hopeful.

Antonia said grimly, "There isn't any burglary, Miss Lilly. There never was." Miss Lilly looked mystified.

"I suppose," Caracci cut in, "you know this building pretty well, Miss Lilly. All the nooks and crannies, I mean, not just the main rooms."

With a trace of her old pride in the intimacy of her relations with "her" museum, Miss Lilly said, "From top to bottom, Lieutenant, from Tower to Dungeon. There aren't many nooks in this old place I haven't explored at one time or another."

"*Dungeon*, Miss Lilly?"

She smiled. "That's what the students call it sometimes. It's really just a subbasement—large but unusable, alas. Some years ago when the humanities departments were so desperate for office space, I prowled all over the building hoping to find a few square feet of overlooked space where we could stash an instructor or two. When I found the

Dungeon—only one ancient janitor even remembered it was there—I thought my prayers had been answered. I could have put the entire Romance Languages department in there. But it didn't work out."

"Why not?"

"Too cold. It's way underground and unheated. The average temperature down there is about forty-five degrees—it would've cost a fortune to . . ."

"Miss Lilly," Antonia interrupted gently, "would you take us there, please?" She sounded faint.

"Of course," said Miss Lilly, looking slightly bewildered, "but are you all right, dear?"

"She's had a rough afternoon, Miss Lilly," said Caracci, "and she needs to rest. Do you have a couch or . . ."

In a firmer voice, Antonia said, "No, Lieutenant, I'm going with you. As I said before."

Caracci's protests were interrupted by the arrival of his men with Bennie Thompson. The boy looked sullen and a little scared, and he glared at Antonia and Miss Lilly without speaking.

"Sorry we took so long, Lieutenant," said one of the men. "We hadda haul him outa bed. He was sleeping." His tone implied that he was bringing a highly suspicious circumstance to his superior's attention.

"Yeah, I do that once in a while," Bennie muttered resentfully. "I was gonna get up at six and—look, what the hell's going down, anyway?" But no one bothered to answer him. Antonia was too miserable to make the effort, Miss Lilly was as much in the dark as he was, and the policemen were preoccupied with the business at hand.

Miss Lilly disappeared into her office for a moment and emerged with a key, and the odd cavalcade set out. Miss Lilly took the lead, Caracci and Antonia followed her, Bennie followed behind them, and Caracci's two men brought up the rear.

They trooped first through the Main Hall, where a dozen posters were still bravely announcing the imminent opening of the Aegean Gold exhibition. The eyeless sockets of the Agamemnon Mask glared down at them as they passed.

At the rear of the hall was a small employees' staircase leading down to the main basement. On this lower level the corridors looked familiar to Antonia, but she couldn't be certain whether they were the same ones Bennie had led her through on Monday night. Halfway down one of them Miss Lilly stopped at a narrow door and turned to Bennie.

"Bennie, aren't there some flashlights in here?" Her tone was businesslike but not unfriendly. It was obvious that she, at any rate, still trusted him.

"Yes, Ma'am," said Bennie. "They're all working, too. I checked 'em just the other day. You want me to . . . ?"

"Yes, please. Four ought to be enough, I think."

Bennie rummaged on the top shelf of the storage closet and handed the large flashlights out to her one by one. Miss Lilly issued two to the rear guard, took one herself, and gestured to Bennie to keep the last.

The march resumed as Miss Lilly explained, "The so-called Dungeon, as I recall, is lighted by two bare bulbs of about forty watts each, and I've no idea whether either of them is working. But even when they are it's extremely dim. The place was originally a furnace room, I'm told, though the furnaces are gone, and I suppose one didn't need much light to shovel coal by."

No one replied, and her voice sounded small, diminished rather than magnified by the faint echoes from the dingy corridors.

At last she turned into a side passage, darker and shorter than the others, with a door at its end marked "No Exit." She stopped in front of it, then turned to Caracci, who was just behind her. "It isn't locked, Lieutenant."

"No, Ma'am," he said grimly, "I didn't think it would be. Now if you'll excuse me . . ." Taking her flashlight he brushed unceremoniously past her and through the door. Antonia could hear his hand patting impatiently at the wall inside the door, searching for the light switch. The next moment she heard a click and saw a dim glow from beyond and below him, and he started down a narrow flight of stairs. She followed close behind.

One of the predicted bulbs was still working, the one at the far end of the long empty room. The floor seemed damp and uneven to Antonia. For a minute she wondered if it could possibly be made of beaten earth, but she decided it was probably her vestigial light-headedness and the semidarkness at the near end of the room that made it seem so. Shivering, she stumbled after Caracci and the jerking slices of light from his flashlight, only vaguely aware of the other three men and flashlights behind her.

The old furnace room was dusty but not cluttered. No doubt it had been cleared out at some remote period to avoid fire hazards.

There was only one thing, clearly not a fire hazard, they hadn't bothered to remove. It stood at the far end of the room, under the feeble bulb. As Caracci stepped a little to one side Antonia saw it.

It had been the footing for the huge furnaces that had heated the building during the first fifty years of its existence, a low concrete platform nearly eight feet long and about five feet wide.

It was a catafalque now.

Antonia stopped ten feet away from it and stood there, swaying slightly, eyes closed, willing herself not to scream or faint. She became aware now of an odor she had never smelled before and hoped she never would again. For a few head-clearing moments, with her eyes still shut, she concentrated ferociously on the details of the inlaid blade, remembered from a hundred art-book illustrations.

Only one of the lions had turned to face its pursuers, tail thrashing in fury over its golden back. The other two were fleeing toward the blade's point, silver bellies gleaming and paws outstretched in the graceful "flying gallop" position. Behind them, silhouetted against a background of blue-black niello, four tiny golden huntsmen with figure-eight shields stood poised to fling their silver javelins. They had stood so for thirty-five centuries, ever since some nameless Cretan artist had fashioned them to adorn the grave-goods of a Mycenaean warlord.

Antonia opened her eyes, forced herself to look. It wasn't the original, of course, hiltless and ragged-edged, but the reproduction. And the girl who held it was no Mycenaean princess, no Electra or Iphigenia sacrificed to the ambition of kings. She was wearing sneakers and faded jeans like any other college student, and her long black hair lay undressed and disorderly about her shoulders.

Yet perhaps she was after all, as she had seemed sometimes to imagine, descended from a line of kings even older and darker than those of Mycenae. Her face had shed the look of fatigue and timidity it had usually worn in life. Her expression now was serene, almost arrogant, and the long straight lips curved in the faintest suggestion of a smile, as if she had taken with her some triumphant secret.

And all around her, arranged in the thick dust that furred the concrete slab, stood her grave-goods—the golden cups and the silver jug, the engraved goblets, and the royal diadem. At her feet stood the huge pottery jar from Knossos, at her side a little tangled pile of gold jewelry. Her hands, clasped on her breast, clung to the embossed pommel of the Shaft Grave dagger. And on its brown-stained blade the golden lions and the silver hunters gleamed dimly just beyond her fingertips.

Ariadne had been found.

16. Nocturne

AFTERWARD, THE ONLY EMOTION ANTONIA COULD remember feeling during the next few minutes was a desperate longing to sit down. It seemed somehow unendurable to stand there, hands at one's sides, and do nothing. Why it should be any easier to sit and do nothing she could not have said.

But there was in fact no place to sit except the dank floor, so Antonia stood. And the mixture of anguished thoughts and feelings that had washed over her were mercifully erased from conscious memory, leaving only the rueful recollection that she had yearned, most unheroically, for a chair.

With the exception of these first few shocked moments, she remembered the rest of the scene clearly enough. In front of her, Caracci and his men bent over the corpse, talking in low voices. Miss Lilly caught up with her, peered over Antonia's shoulder, and caught her breath sharply at what she saw. Bennie in turn came up behind the two women, silent and unnoticed until Antonia became vaguely aware of a muttered curse from him.

Antonia strained her ears to hear what the detectives were saying, but all she caught were disjointed phrases.

"Damnedest thing I ever . . ."

"Pulled the blade out and wiped it—the *blade* but not the *handle!*"

"Won't be any prints on that . . ."

"Piece of paper, sir."

Antonia only became aware that Bennie was gone when she heard the click of the latch on the old door at the top of the stairs, and the whisper of his sneakers and the bang of a door far away down one of the corridors in the basement above. The policemen noticed it at the same time.

"Thompson's got away, sir!" said one of them unnecessarily.

Caracci was staring at a piece of paper that he was holding gingerly by one corner. "Won't get far," he said absently. Then, turning to Miss Lilly and Antonia, "Ladies, how many words in the English language begin with the letters *FIV*, do you suppose?"

They looked at him uncomprehendingly.

"This paper was in the girl's hand, and that's what it says—*F, I, V*—and I can't make much sense of it. I thought maybe it might mean something to one of you."

"Five," said Antonia, her voice still a little hoarse. "That's the only word I can think of. Plus derivatives, of course. Fivefold, that sort of thing. But what . . . ?"

"But maybe it isn't *five* at all," said Miss Lilly. "I have an unabridged dictionary in my office upstairs—we could check."

"Yeah, we'll do that, Miss Lilly. Could be a name too, I suppose. Well," he went on heavily, "we'd better get on with it. You stay till I can get the lab people over here, Kominski. It'd be really funny if Miss Lilly's gold got stolen *now*, wouldn't it." It wasn't a question and Caracci didn't sound amused.

He took each of the women by an elbow and steered them back upstairs. Antonia didn't bother to protest this professional solicitude.

Up in Miss Lilly's office, Caracci used the telephone, the other detective disappeared on some mysterious errand, and Miss Lilly herself pored earnestly over the *fiv-* section of an unabridged dictionary, announcing from time to time that she knew it wasn't much help but she couldn't bear to sit and do nothing. In a low monotonous voice she recited *fiv-* entries like an incantation, punctuating Caracci's terse phone conversations.

Only Antonia was left without a function. So for a while she sat quietly in a chair, holding herself rigidly upright, trying not to think about anything. But try as she might she could not drive from her mind the sight of the young body on the concrete slab surrounded by all that incongruous magnificence of gold.

Ariadne had sometimes taken solace in the fanciful notion of herself as scion of the most ancient royal house in all Hellas. At the same time she had been thoroughly American in her conviction that hard work was the clew that would lead her out of the maze. If she had thought of herself as a princess, it was a princess in the tradition of Homer's Nausicaa who went down to the seashore with her serving maids to do the royal laundry.

Yes, Ariadne had worked long and hard. And then—again with good Greek precedent in legend and literature—she had had a fabulous stroke of luck, had stumbled upon a treasure as dazzling in its way as the bits of gold and silver strewn about her body now. This Ariadne, like her namesake, knew a good clew when she saw one. She had seized it without remorse or hesitation as hers, by right of blood as well as discovery, hers not to keep but to give back to the world.

The Euripides papyrus would have wiped out forever the family curse of fruitless anger, retaliation, and despair. It would have carried her once and for all out of the sad destructive Labyrinth her parents had built. And she would have taken poor Yanni with her, into a better life.

What a nice fairy tale, Antonia thought bitterly. So what went wrong with it? Some unscheduled dragon or wicked sorcerer came along and spoiled the ending.

Legends and fairy tales were supposed to have an enduring meaning, that was the trouble, and the ending of Ariadne's story didn't have any meaning at all. Not only was it sad and cruel and wasteful, it was incomprehensible as well.

Caracci's voice broke into her gloomy thoughts.

"Yeah, the Thompson kid. Bennie, yeah. I want him . . ." The voice dropped lower and Antonia made no effort to hear the rest of his words. Caracci's vendetta against Bennie Thompson, Bennie's reasons for bolting at such a moment—none of it mattered, none of it would bring Ariadne back.

Antonia rested her head on the back of the old armchair and stared up at the shadows on the ceiling.

Then there were other men in the room, a man with a camera and a bald man with a doctor's satchel. They were talking in loud voices, asking which way to go, and Caracci was asking Miss Lilly if she would mind. But Miss Lilly was bending over Antonia, shaking her shoulder gently, saying, "Come along, dear, there's a couch in the director's office. This place is getting so noisy. Come rest in there." Antonia went with her like a child and sank with immense gratitude into the cushions and the darkness and the silence.

She was dimly conscious of muffled voices and shadowy figures moving beyond the pebbled glass of the director's old-fashioned office door. She remembered Ariadne's face, waxy and pale and oddly shrunken, on her gold-strewn concrete bier. She was aware of her own bruised throat. Then she wasn't conscious of anything at all.

When she opened her eyes, the pebbled glass was dark and there were no sounds at all. She sat up, feeling chilled and stiff, and saw that the reading lamp on the director's desk was on, though it was turned toward the wall to dim its light. She rose and felt her way through the darkness to the desk. There was a note on it, in Miss Lilly's firm, elegant handwriting:

Why don't you sleep here the rest of the night, dear? I'll be in early tomorrow to make coffee and then you can go on home for a real sleep.

They've taken Ariadne away. [Antonia felt a pang, oddly muted now, at the thought of Ariadne as a thing to be "taken away."]

I'll see you in the morning. Maybe both our heads will be clearer by then.

Emma Lilly

Miss Lilly's note was good advice. She should stay where she was until morning, she told herself, turning back toward the couch.

Only it was so cold. The day had been wet and blustery, more like fall than spring. And since Buildings and Grounds had finally gotten around to turning off the heat

the day before, the office was chilly enough to make anyone long for a warm blanket. But there was no blanket in
the office. Antonia fumbled her way to the door and
stepped into Miss Lilly's office next door.

She looked around her, her eyes gradually adjusting to
the thin starlight from behind the window. There was the
scratch paper next to the open Webster's Third: *five-and-
ten, five-day week, fiveling, fivepence. . . .* No other words
in English that began with *fiv.* She felt her head clearing
slowly as she squinted at the old alarm clock on the filing
cabinet. One-thirty in the morning. And no blanket, not
so much as a shawl, anywhere in the office.

Antonia hugged herself to control a shiver and decided
there was nothing for it but a brisk stroll back across the
campus to her own bed.

She closed the door of Miss Lilly's office quietly behind
her and set out in almost total darkness to find her way
to the Main Exhibition Hall and the front doors. It wasn't
far, and she was soon feeling her way toward the pale
glass rectangles of the entrance. Within a dozen steps of
the door, she almost walked head-on into the golden Mask
of Agamemnon, peering at her out of an Aegean Gold
poster hung from a pillar.

"Oops—good evening, Lord of Men," she murmured
as she circled round the pillar. *"Kalispera, anax andrōn."*
I must be a little giddy still, she thought.

She reached the nearest door, laid her hands upon the
bar, and stopped. The bar didn't move. The museum was
locked up, and she was locked in.

"Damn," she said aloud.

There was a car parked under a street light across the
street that might be a police car. She could try banging
and shouting. And make an even bigger fool of herself,
she thought irritably, than she already had, passing out in
Miss Lilly's office like that.

Then she thought of the little door Bennie had let her
in and out of, the night of her last midnight visit to the
museum. It would be locked, too. But it had looked much
more old-fashioned than these steel-and-glass main portals.
Perhaps it would open from the inside.

She turned back into the darkness of the museum.

Eventually she found a stuffy little corridor that somehow felt like the right one. A small, square, head-high

window straight ahead of her looked very familiar. She could almost smell the damp grass outside.

Suddenly she noticed something else. On the left-hand side of the corridor, between her and the outside door, a vertical line of light revealed another door standing a couple of inches ajar, with a small dimly lit room beyond. Without thinking, she pushed the door open—and froze on the threshold.

It was a cubicle no more than ten feet square, lit by an old gooseneck lamp set on a battered desk. The only other piece of furniture in the room was a disreputable old swivel chair.

On it a long loose-jointed figure sprawled rather than sat, his feet propped up on the desk, his head lolling back, chuckling to himself in a low rich voice. It was Bennie Thompson. On the desk between his outsized feet stood something that looked rather like an ornamental doorknob with a long round shank. Except that it appeared to be made of solid gold.

Bennie looked up at Antonia with eyes that seemed to have trouble focusing, and his chuckle turned into a harsh, unsteady laugh.

" 'Lo, Professor," he said, waving a big hand vaguely in her direction. "C'min and joina party."

17. The Hottentot King

"WHAT ARE YOU DOING HERE?" ANTONIA TRIED TO make the question sound matter-of-fact. "We thought . . ."

"Yeah," Bennie grunted, "I gotta damn good idea what you thought." Suddenly he swung his feet down off the desk and his sullen air vanished and was replaced by a kind of tipsy graciousness. It was hard to tell whether he was actually as far gone as he appeared to be.

"Mattera fac' I'm jus' relaxing in my"—pause for dramatic effect and comprehensive sweep of arm—"office. 'Course it ain't quite what *you're* used to, but us black trash jus' gotta make do with whatever's left over after they get through putting in the broom closets and the bathrooms. If I was a white bitch, now, with a fancy *dee*gree like you or Miss Lilly—" He bit back the words "or Ariadne," but they hung unspoken in the air while the sullen look again replaced the mockingly cavalier one on his homely face.

Ignoring his bitter outburst, Antonia said, "Bennie, are you—are you sure you're all right?" Probably the boy was simply drunk, but she couldn't forget what Caracci had said about Bennie's former addiction—and the horrendous odds against his cure being a permanent one.

"Whaddya mean?" he said without interest, his consonants thickening once more. Then a glimmer of understanding seemed to come to him and he gave a short bitter laugh.

"No, Ma'am," he said, "you guessed wrong again. No way I can afford *that* stuff no more, not on what they pay me around here. Sometime I get to feeling so goddam straight I can't hardly stand being in the same *room* with myself."

He reached down and hauled at the lowest drawer of the battered old desk. It came out with protesting squeaks, jerks, and a loud clanking of empty bottles. One that was only half empty he held out to Antonia, whether in demonstration or invitation was unclear. In case it was intended as an invitation, Antonia shook her head. With a grunt Bennie withdrew the bottle, pulled the cork with his teeth, and took a long pull. Then, wiping his mouth with the back of his hand, he said, "Just like Ari, ain'tcha? She wouldn't drink with me neither." He raised the bottle to his lips again, then lowered it as he noticed the direction of Antonia's gaze.

Having reassured herself that Bennie was after all merely drunk and not stoned, Antonia had turned her attention to the gold object on the desk in front of him. She recognized it now, with sudden dismay.

It was a scepter, or the business end of one, of gold and colored enamels. It had been found in Cyprus but was attributed to Mycenaean craftsmen, and was famous as the earliest known example of true cloisonné enamelwork. Since it was only about eight inches long, it had probably been attached to a wooden staff, to which it would have formed a kind of elaborate finial. It consisted of a golden rod surmounted by an intricately enameled orb on which two hawks were perched. They were also of gold, but their feathers were indicated by dozens of tiny cloisonné cells filled with green and white enamel.

As Antonia stared at the exquisite little object, it was suddenly engulfed by a huge hand. Startled, she glanced at Bennie's face. He was holding the scepter up, squinting bleary-eyed at it as though trying to figure out what it was. For a moment he had a crazily regal air, like some nineteenth-century cartoonist's version of a Hottentot king.

"Pretty li'l thing, ain' it?" he said dreamily. "Mus' be

worth a pretty li'l pile o' bills too. Thing like that, a cat wouldn' hafta work for a whole year maybe. Git hisself some fine-looking chick with *real* class, not one o' these stuck-up bitches like—" He switched his tack abruptly. "Thing like that, lotta dudes woulda done more'n jus' take it, laying out there like that. Lotta dudes'd go outa their way, go to a whole lotta trouble t'get hold of a pretty li'l thing like this. A whole lotta trouble. *Maybe even kill somebody,* huh Professor? That's what you're thinkin', ain' it?" He glared with frightening intensity at Antonia for a moment, then shrugged off his melodramatic air and began again.

"Wasn' like that, though. Jus' laying out there for any-one to take. Jus' laying there. I could tell some o' the other stuff was missing, seem like one piece more wasn' gonna make no difference. They ever caught the cat that done it, they'd jus' figure he awready fenced this. An' if they didn' catch him—well, no sweat for ol' Bennie that way neither." He belched luxuriously, tried to take anoth-er swig from the bottle, found it empty, and dropped it back into the drawer with a crash. Then he fished up another, opened it, and took a long pull at it.

"Gave me a turn, seeing her like that again. Looked like a goddam queen 'er something, didn' she? Suited her too."

He took another long pull at the bottle.

"Yeah, she was a lot like that. Some people mighta thought she was stuck up. Kep' to herself mostly, didn' have hardly any friends. 'Less you count me, o' course." He emitted a short bitter laugh, which he promptly drowned in still another gulp of wine.

"Thing about a girl like that, she's making it, making it right straight outa wherever she come from, and she don' have a whole lotta time for people that ain't. Even people that are maybe trying but ain't getting nowhere. People like me, f'r instance.

"Specially the las' few weeks. Musta been a month since she said more'n three words in a row to me. Really ignored me, y'know? She'd jus' grunt 'uh-huh,' or nod her head in this sorta dreamy way. I hadn't of known better, I'd thought she was on something. Got so I was beginning to wonder if I was turning invisible or some-thing. Gave me the creeps. Like talking to yourself, y'know? Well, I was getting sicka that shit, see, and then one night last week I stopped by her office and she damn near poured boilin' coffee on my hand stead of in my cup. Made me so goddam mad I—"

"Bennie," Antonia broke in grimly, "how did you really get this?"

"Told you how I got it, damn you," he snarled. "Like this, nothin' to it." And the big hand once again swallowed up the tiny hawks and their enameled orb.

"But Ariadne must have been in the workroom that night, and she would never have let you . . ."

"Wasn't *like* that, I tol' you," he muttered. Then his voice rose again in anger. "But you got it all figured . . . got it all figured out, ain't you? Everything about me, all figured out nice and neat. You're two of a kind, you and that mother Caracci. I had you and her figured different, though—just goes to show you shouldn't never trust no white bitch, don't it?" He half rose from the chair behind the old desk, and to Antonia the movement, after his bitter words, seemed like a threat. Nervously she backed away, and such were the dimensions of Bennie's minuscule "office" that she quickly found herself outside in the corridor.

Then she ran, stumbling and panicky, in what she prayed was the direction of the main entrance.

Behind her, echoing weirdly through the tangle of halls and stairwells, came Bennie's laughter, angry and mocking and hopeless.

18. *Anax Andrōn*

HER STEPS SLOWED AS SHE HURRIED ONCE MORE ACROSS the Main Exhibition Hall toward the rectangles of light that marked the front entrance to the museum. There were no footsteps behind hers. There had been none, from the moment she had bolted from Bennie's tiny cubicle, only the fading echoes of his laughter, far away in the bowels of the building.

She moved still more slowly as she crossed the Main Hall. She knew she should hurry on, pound on the glass doors, attract the attention of the policemen in the car across the street. Tell them what she knew, or thought she knew, about what had happened to Ariadne just one week ago in this building.

It had been two or three in the morning (as it was now), they had both been tired and irritable, the tensions between them had been accumulating for weeks. What had begun as a strictly business arrangement between two night owls had developed into a one-sided—what? She didn't think Bennie had been in love with Ariadne exactly. It was something more complicated, and potentially more explosive. It was a desire for acceptance as an equal, a desire to be admired by Ariadne as he admired her; it also in-

148

volved envy and self-doubt and a lingering sense of unworthiness.

He had thought, quite simply, that Ariadne was his friend. Perhaps it was even her friendship that had kept him from—what was Caracci's word?—from falling, kept him for six difficult months out of that horrifying 80 percent who never escape the clutch of heroin.

Then gradually over the last few weeks she had withdrawn further and further into that other world of hers where she was alone with her papyrus and her dreams. And when Bennie, seven nights ago, had come along for his usual cup of coffee, Ariadne had ignored him one last fatal time, looked right through him or failed to answer some trivial question, perhaps even refused a drink he'd brought with him.

And all that gold was "just lying there."

Perhaps Ariadne had somehow gotten hold of the smaller items and laid them out around her for inspiration as she worked. It had never been clear how the gold had come to be lying around unprotected in the workroom, and it was the sort of thing one could easily imagine her doing.

Everything must have hit him at one terrible instant: temptation, a sense of friendship rejected, the inevitable suspicion that it was all somehow mixed up with race, and perhaps underneath and more painful than all the rest, the feeling that nothing he did—his gallant struggle against his addiction, his steady work at a decent job—nothing was good enough, not for Ariadne.

He had been wrong, of course, utterly wrong. But that was how it must have seemed to him, at least for the few crucial moments when Ariadne's life hung in the balance.

All this Antonia should tell the police. Or at least the simple fact that Bennie had a piece of the Aegean Gold in his possession, however and with whatever motives he had acquired it. So why was she hesitating?

She paused once more at the pillar with the Aegean Gold poster, the death mask of Agamemnon staring spectrally at her out of the darkness.

"Good evening again, my lord," she saluted the golden face sadly. And once more in words older than Homer's, *"Chairè, wanax andrōn:* Hail, Lord of . . ."

She stopped as suddenly as if the ancient king had struck

her in the face, stopped appalled at what she had said, at what it meant, at the word that could not be unspoken now.

Not *anax* as in Barry's *Iliad*, but *wanax* as in the Linear B tablets. If you went back far enough—not just to classical Athens, but to Mycenae and Pylos and Cretan Knossos a thousand years before—the Greek language had had a *w* sound. And, over the centuries, various ways of writing it. Slowly she turned away from the entrance, back into the museum.

She wondered dully what had caused her to make the connection at last. It had not come to her when Miss Lilly was chanting her meaningless litany of *fiv-* words. ("There are no other words *in English* that begin with *fiv* . . . .") She had not seen it when she had blundered into the Aegean Gold poster the first time that night and hailed the ancient lord by his Homeric title *anax* instead of *wanax*. Nor yet at the moment when Bennie had raised his stolen scepter and looked for one instant like a drunken lord from some undiscovered kingdom still underground, awaiting the spades of archaeologists as yet unborn.

Antonia never knew precisely why or at what moment the truth drifted up to the surface of her consciousness. She only knew that she had to be sure, that she could never voice her suspicion to Caracci—let alone to the nameless patrolmen in the car across the street—unless she was sure.

She threaded her way through more familiar halls now, found the stairs, and began to climb.

The staircase was not actually as steep and tightly coiled as those in medieval castles, but it was a fair imitation. With her neck still sore, her throat still rasping, and assorted dull aches throughout her body, Antonia found it a real torment to climb to the top. But climb she did, slowly and systematically, with frequent pauses for rest and breath.

As she climbed she tried again to think about nothing at all, and again she failed. She was afraid that she knew now what the tiny smile on Ariadne's dead lips had meant. She had taken it, perhaps fancifully, as an expression of triumph, of pride in achievement, of serene confidence that her life, however brief, had counted for something.

No doubt Ariadne's smile had meant all those things, she still believed that, but it meant something more too.

Forgiveness was not the Greeks' most conspicuous virtue. "To harm those who harm you" seemed to many Greeks the only natural and rational behavior, for woman or man. Achilles, Clytemnestra, Electra, Orestes, Medea, Oedipus—the list of noble vengeance takers in Greek tradition is endless.

Ariadne was smiling because she had joined that ferocious band of the unforgiving. She had lived long enough to destroy her destroyer, and few Greeks find that a bad bargain.

Was this also too fanciful an interpretation of a dead girl's smile? She didn't think so, but of course it had to have something more substantial behind it than a flash of intuition concerning three letters scrawled on a scrap of paper.

Antonia reached the top of the stairs at last. The door was unlocked.

The tower room was square and low ceilinged as she remembered it from her few previous visits. Yet something had changed too, something intangible that had nothing to do with the dimensions of the room or the arrangement of the few pieces of furniture. The narrow bed still stood against one wall, though now it looked as if it had been recently slept in and carelessly made. Two elderly armchairs still occupied one corner, sharing a floor lamp between them. It was, Antonia realized after a moment, the desk that was different.

It looked, quite simply, like a working desk, and it never had before.

Win was sitting behind it, looking haggard, unshaven, and startled. He stared at Antonia for a long moment without speaking. Then he pulled himself wearily to his feet, came around in front of the desk, and sat on the edge of it with his arms crossed over his chest in a parody of his old loose-limbed casualness. It was the posture in which he had charmed a hundred downy coeds, but now it looked more defensive than social, as if he were somehow protecting the desk. When he spoke at last it was with the same combination of fatigue and wariness.

"Well. Antonia. Unexpected pleasure and all that.

Though I must say you look as fagged as I feel—are you sure you're all right? I've been up here since midnight last night, after the Sandlers left me. Couldn't seem to sleep in the house. Didn't get much sleep here either for that matter, but at least—damn it, Antonia, what *is* the matter anyway?"

"We've found her, Win." She watched his face carefully.

"Found? Found who? This is hardly the time for riddles, Antonia."

"Ariadne Pappas."

"Oh, Ariadne, yes. Good. I told you she'd turn up."

"She's dead, Win. Murdered."

"She's—good Lord! But—but where? When? I mean, it's hard to imagine why anyone . . ."

"The police will assume it was her brother, I expect. We found her lying in state in a subbasement beneath this building—surrounded by bits of Aegean Gold. The boy has admitted doing that. Giving her a proper burial, he called it. But I don't believe he killed her. I think it was precisely the shock of finding her dead that has made him lose touch with reality to the extent he has. He's coming out of it now, but for a while I think he actually was confusing himself with the Minoan aristocrats he and Ariadne used to read about in picture books when they were kids. Some form of regression, I suppose they'll call it— a hated and rejected child, taking refuge in the only time of . . .'"

"Antonia, stop it, you're babbling." Win sounded calmer and less disoriented now, and his voice was like a therapeutic slap across the face. "I don't know what you're talking about, and I don't know why you've come here. I'm sorry the girl is dead, of course, but if you're looking for a shoulder to cry on I really think you might have found someone else right now."

As he spoke he uncrossed his arms from his chest and brought his hands down to rest on the edge of the desk on either side of him. The new position looked if anything even less relaxed than the old. But as his right hand swung down it flicked across some of the many papers that littered the surface of the desk, those papers that gave it the uncharacteristically busy air that had struck Antonia so forcibly when she first entered the room.

One of the papers swooped to the floor between them, landing with a strange click.

Startled at the sound, Antonia glanced down. Win had stooped swiftly to retrieve the fallen paper, but not quickly enough to prevent her recognizing it. Once again their eyes met, this time in a long painful gaze of mutual comprehension and horror. Finally Win straightened up, leaving the paper where it had fallen and resuming his posture of mock casualness before the desk.

Strictly speaking it was not paper he had knocked off the desk. It was a Plexiglas sleeve containing something that looked like a large dead leaf, except for its roughly rectangular shape and the faded spidery writing that covered it. Though Antonia had never seen it except in photostat, she was quite certain it was a folio of Ariadne's Euripides papyrus.

19. Theseus

ANTONIA STARED HYPNOTIZED AT IT FOR A LONG moment, while the throbbing in her head grew more insistent. She wondered vaguely whether Yanni had perhaps banged her head against the wall while trying to strangle her. She moved carefully toward one of the elderly armchairs and dropped into it with a moan of relief. Win followed her, but instead of sitting in the other armchair he remained standing, still between her and the desk.

"So it was you who had it," said Antonia. "Only the photostats were in Ariadne's desk. I assumed she'd put the originals away somewhere for safekeeping. You stole it from her literally as well as metaphorically. What did you intend to leave her, Win? Credit for compiling the index and checking the footnotes?"

"Don't make it out worse than it is, Antonia. I shall present Ariadne as my equal, my partner, my colleague, whatever you like. I fully intend to share the credit with her."

"You will share with *her."* Antonia's voice was bitter.

"It would have been to her advantage, Antonia. That's what I wanted to explain to her that night when I went to the museum. At *her* request, you will remember. But when I got there—God, what a scene! She was sitting there, with all that gold scattered around her. She said she'd

154

learned the combination of the safe long ago, more or less by accident—she had absolutely no sense of professional ethics, Antonia—and she'd been taking the stuff out every night since it arrived, for what she called 'inspiration.' She said it helped her work, and I must admit she looked as if she'd been working hard. She was thinner, exhausted looking, almost hectic.

"She said, 'My people actually *touched* these very things, Win. Some Minoan lady wore these earrings, these rings, this diadem. They drank wine from these beautiful cups and took these knives to their graves with them. When I have them around me I feel strong, I never seem to get tired, I can work all night.' She raved on like that for quite a while. I told her she was talking nonsense, tried to get her back onto the subject of the edition.

"For weeks I'd been trying to make her see what a lot of flak she was going to get from the profession if she tried to publish the papyrus under her own name. I mean, she had no *right* to this manuscript, Antonia. Everyone would have resented her appropriating it like that, a mere graduate student. But all she would say was, 'I've done a good job with it, everyone will see that.' I told her she was underestimating the pettiness and greed of our revered profession. But she just smiled in that superior way she had.

"I began to realize it was all slipping away from me, Antonia, my last chance at real eminence in my field. If only she hadn't been so greedy, so selfish: there was plenty of glory for both of us, in a thing this big. I tried, really *tried*, to make her see reason, but she was so stubborn. Finally in frustration I grabbed that reproduction of the Lion Hunt Dagger. I never intended to harm her. I don't know what I meant to do.

"But she only drew herself up—I swear she looked about six feet tall—and she said very calmly, 'My work is finished, Professor Randolph, nothing you can do will change that.' Then she muttered something in Greek. It sounded like Euripides' line about Jason being every kind of coward and no real man.

"I could see there was no reasoning with her, she was too stubborn and too arrogant. That bit from Euripides hit home too, I suppose. Anyway I must have lost control completely for a few seconds and stabbed her. I've had nightmares all week about the feel of that blade sliding into her flesh. . . . That snapped me out of that moment of temporary insanity and I just ran—left the damn knife in her body and ran. I think she was dead but I admit I didn't stop to make sure."

"But you weren't too disoriented to pick up eight folios of papyrus and take them with you."

"She was *dead*, Antonia, those eight scraps of papyrus couldn't do anything for her anymore. But yes, I did take them. Even so, I was in a sort of animal terror of being in the same room with a corpse. By next morning when I came to work I was much calmer, more or less resigned to the idea that I would be arrested. But then in the lounge they were talking about a burglary. I couldn't make sense of it at first, but eventually I gathered that some of the Aegean Gold had been stolen from the room where Ariadne's body should have been, only no one was saying anything about a body. I was baffled, of course, but I decided to keep quiet and see if she really had disappeared for good. I couldn't believe my luck, but if there was a chance of getting off scot-free—well, I intended to take that chance. Because this manuscript meant everything to me and Gillian."

"It meant everything to Ariadne too, Win. Her involvement with this papyrus was more than just a scholar's dream-of-a-lifetime come true, more even than a neurotic girl's obsession with the culture of her ancestors. It was this specific play that had such a profound appeal for her. She and her family had played out in their lives a tragedy very like the one in that papyrus, Win. Any sensitive reader finds that the story of Oedipus or Electra is his or her own story writ large. For Ariadne the parallels between her life and *The Cretans* were a little closer, that's all. And the catharsis that tragedy is supposed to give us— the sense of pain and grief and waste transmuted and transcended—that must have been correspondingly more powerful too."

"I don't know what you're talking about, Antonia." Win sounded bored.

"I've learned a good deal about Ariadne's background in the last few days, and it's a pretty grim story. Her father hated and despised her mother for what he saw as an act of unspeakable depravity. Her half brother, the offspring of that act, was hated, rejected, regarded as something less than human. The father himself underlined the similarities by calling his *taverna* The Labyrinth and nicknaming his other daughter Fedra. Ariadne somehow managed to survive all this and 'get out,' but even so, in spite of all she could do, the others might have dragged her back into that Labyrinth. But she found a clew, not a string as in the legend, but eight tattered scraps of papyrus. I dreamed about it one night, Win: Ariadne leading you and Gillian and Euripides out of—I don't know what exactly, obscurity, oblivion, despair—by means of a long ribbon of papyrus. That dream was trying to tell me something, only I didn't understand it at the time.

"Because the parallels between Ariadne and her namesake break down at this point. I wonder if she herself saw the irony of it. The maiden in the legend only used her clew to help the hero in *his* career, to get *him* safely out of the Labyrinth. But our Ariadne rewrote this part of the story. She refused to hand over her clew, insisted on keeping it for herself alone, to lead her out of her own personal Labyrinth. To be blunt, Win, she didn't fancy you in the role of Theseus."

"Ingenious, Antonia, if not very flattering. You always did have a nimble imagination where literature was concerned. Accounts for those critical papers you're so good at, I suppose. But it all seems a bit finespun to me. My need for that manuscript was every bit as great as hers—mine and Gillian's. To us it was the difference between—between—" His voice had been gradually rising, and for a moment he seemed on the verge of hysteria. Then he paused and again seemed to pull himself together.

"You haven't hit it yet, Antonia, you don't know what it's like. What are they calling it nowadays, the midlife crisis? Most men survive it one way or another, probably I would have too. Even though I had the additional burden of a wife whose self-esteem was all bound up with my success or failure. Gillian had set her sights high, and I hadn't measured up. She blamed everything she could think of—me, the university, the sex-starved students who were supposedly draining my energies. Sometimes she'd even blame herself. But most of the time she was just quietly miserable because we weren't living in Princeton or New Haven or Cambridge.

"As I say, we probably would've muddled through all this, like most couples. But unlike most men, I was suddenly presented with a way out, a second chance to end all second chances. I didn't see it that way at first, didn't realize what was happening to me. I never dreamed of killing Ariadne, of course, and at the time it didn't even seem to me that I was injuring her professionally. She would still have had a piece of the glory, better job prospects, the articles and lecture invitations that naturally grow out of a thing like this. Only Gillian and I would've shared it all with her, that's the way I saw it."

"And the way Gillian saw it?"

"No. Gillian knew nothing about it. Oh, she sensed my excitement—what wife wouldn't after twenty years of marriage? In fact, that was probably what gave rise to her suspicion that Ariadne and I were lovers. She could tell that something important was going on between us, and not unnaturally she assumed it was sex. It wasn't, incidentally.

"She hammered at me about it all weekend, and Monday, and Tuesday when I stayed home. Finally Tuesday afternoon—shortly before you arrived, in fact—I couldn't take any more and I yelled the truth at her, I said, 'You can stop worrying about Ariadne, she isn't going to bother us anymore,' something like that. Then she started in again and eventually got the whole story out of me.

"She didn't say much after that. I tried to tell her I could publish the manuscript as my own discovery now and probably eventually it would mean the kind of job and the kind of life she'd always wanted. But she didn't seem to pay much attention. She just sat and stared and stared—not at me, not at anything. We went to bed early that night, and woke early yesterday morning—so early that I had time to go to the store for a newspaper before breakfast.

"When I got back she was—looking pretty much as you saw her, I suppose."

"But surely she can't have died of an overdose of Seconal in the few minutes you were out of the house buying a newspaper?"

"I didn't say she was dead. She was lying peacefully on the bed, not quite asleep. I think she saw or heard me come into the bedroom, but she didn't speak. After a minute or two I went downstairs and sat in the living room, thinking. Gillian was the only one who knew what I'd done. Everyone knew, or at least suspected, she'd tried to kill herself once before, and half a dozen people had seen how unstable she acted at the party Friday. They would all assume without question that she'd finally gone over the edge. Which of course she had, only not because of jealousy. No one would know how soon after she'd taken the stuff I had found her. I was perfectly safe. And the sense of *relief*, Antonia—my God! For years I'd been playing the role of devoted-husband-martyred-by-neurotic-wife. I was used to it, almost comfortable in it. But then suddenly, when she offered me the prospect of freedom—I took it. I just took what she offered me, Antonia, that's all."

Antonia heard her own voice without interest. It was dead and unfamiliar. "You sat there and waited for her to die."

"Remember what I'd been through in the last five days, Antonia. After that godawful dinner party on Friday I spent most of the weekend huddled in my house, waiting for the knock on the door. When I stepped out for a breath of air Saturday night I nearly got myself mugged. Sunday I went downtown to try to get Fedra off my back once and for all; I was beginning to think more clearly by then, and I wanted as little visible connection as possible between me and anyone named Pappas. On Monday I had classes to face, wondering all the while if my students or colleagues could tell that they were looking into the eyes of a killer. And all this time Gillian hammering at me about a nonexistent affair with a girl I knew was dead. If I had to defend myself in court—which I won't—I could plead temporary insanity, Antonia, in all good faith I could."

As the torrent of self-justification flowed over her, mostly unheard, Antonia slowly absorbed the horror of what he had done. All too easily she could imagine the details of Gillian's last hours and Win's gruesome vigil in the room below.

"You left her to die. Just as you left Ariadne to die in that workroom. Because she wasn't dead when you ran away, Win. She wasn't dead, she . . ." Antonia felt a wave of hysterical revulsion rising to overwhelm her, took a deep breath, and fought it down. Carefully and soberly she went on.

"She lived long enough to write something on a scrap of paper. It looked as if it might have come out of a wastebasket. Probably it was all she could reach. She wrote in Greek, perhaps to disguise the message in case you came back, perhaps because she was delirious and like her brother she fled back into the only world that had ever offered her much comfort. They were both so alone, those two, except for each other.

"What she wrote looked to an American detective like the letters *Fiv*. But the last words she spoke were Greek, and she was thinking in Greek when she died. The classical Greek alphabet has no *w*. But there was the old letter digamma that had dropped out of use by classical times. It represented the sound *w*, though it looked like a capital *F*. And of course Caracci mistook the Greek *n* for a *v* because it looks exactly like one. But to Ariadne those three letters were digamma, iota, nu. *W, i, n.*"

He stooped again to retrieve the fallen sheet of papyrus and when he stood up to face her, papyrus in hand, it was as if he had heard nothing she said. For a moment he frowned at the mottled brown page as if trying to remember what it was. Then he looked straight at her and said, "You know, Antonia, what this edition still lacks is a good preliminary assessment of the *literary* qualities of the play. Just the kind of thing you do so well. You could think of it as your contribution to a sort of mem . . ."

"Oh, Win, for God's sake *don't,*" she choked. The next minute she was back in the precipitous stairwell, groping her way painfully down the dark steps.

Seconds before she reached the bottom and entered the Main Hall, she heard the faint crash high above her. It was several more seconds before she realized what the breaking of a window on the top story of the Tower probably meant.

Caracci and one of his men found Antonia a few minutes later, sitting on the bottom step of the great staircase that led from the Main Hall up to the second exhibition floor. Antonia and the golden Mask of Agamemnon were staring blindly at each other across the dim hall, and tears were sliding unnoticed down her cheeks.

20. Aegean Gold

THE PHOTOGRAPHER HAD GRUMBLED MIGHTILY AT Miss Lilly's request for a three-by-four-foot blowup, to be made from a mediocre eight-by-ten portrait on something less than twenty-four hours' notice. She had had to tell him enough of the story behind this outrageous demand to fire his imagination and his cooperation.

The result was surprisingly effective. One had to stand back from it, of course, as from a pointillist painting, so that the thousands of meaningless gray dots could blur into recognizable cheeks, nose, and lips. It was only then that one saw the huge dark eyes and wide unsmiling mouth of Ariadne, brooding above the scraps of papyrus she had died for.

Her face now, at two removes from the life that swirled confusedly beneath her portrait, had taken on something of the androgynous serenity of a Phidian Athene, otherworldly yet faintly menacing. It would have to be an unimaginative thief, Antonia thought, who would try to steal those eight sheets of Plexiglas-sheathed papyrus with Ariadne's eyes upon him.

The manuscript was displayed in a simple glass case just below her picture. One page had been transcribed by the staff calligrapher in accordance with Ariadne's edition, and the whole play translated in feverish haste by the Classics chairman, Roy Sandler, who had been up most of Friday night finishing it.

They had commandeered a fourth-century marble bust of Euripides from its home in the Greco-Roman Statuary Hall, and it stood now beside the manuscript. The old man's deep-shadowed eyes gazed gloomily at the tattered sheets of papyrus, the flowing beard and moustache half-concealing what might have been a smile of mockery at the frenetic activity lavished upon a play that had been off the boards for twenty-four centuries.

Antonia shook herself out of her reverie. Odd that a girl dead for nine days and an old man dead two millennia should have so much more solidity, so much more presence, than the throngs that milled around their images. She forced herself to shift her attention from the dead to the living.

It was Saturday afternoon and the Aegean Gold exhibition had opened, on schedule and with a sensational unannounced addition. The mounting of Ariadne's discovery, in conjunction with the originally scheduled exhibits, was the triumphant result of an exhausting thirty-hour campaign organized and led by Miss Lilly. Under her redoubtable eye, from dawn Friday till shortly before the opening, nonstop, the museum staff had argued and telephoned, sketched and lettered, hammered and sawed and hoisted and shoved. The media people, caught off guard, were in conference downstairs with the museum's public relations department at this very moment, negotiating a filming and interview session to be held that night after the glittering special-preview crowd had departed. But the crowd was showing no inclination to depart just yet. It still filled the Main Hall, with the densest concentrations near the manuscript and the portrait of Ariadne. Champagne was still flowing freely, though Antonia's own glass, barely tasted, was growing warm in her hand.

Her eye fell on Bennie Thompson, resplendent in a gold-braided green uniform. His assignment was to guard the papyrus, but it was clear that his allegiance was at least as much to Ariadne's picture as to her discovery. Antonia watched as a well-dressed child of eight or nine—apparently a scion of one of the high society families that had turned out for the opening—daringly stood on tiptoe and

tried to touch the lower corner of the portrait with one
fingertip. Bennie was on the boy like a swooping hawk,
and Antonia smiled sympathetically at the useless gesture
of devotion. It would be good to feel that one could still
protect Ariadne from something.

Caracci had found Bennie in his "office" just before
dawn Friday, snoring drunkenly. He was still clutching
the little scepter, so tightly in fact that Caracci could not
wrench it out of his hand without risk of damaging it.
Since it also proved impossible to wake him, the detective
finally abandoned him to his alcoholic stupor, left a man
to guard him, and went about the grim business of reporting Win Randolph's suicide. Four hours later, Bennie
awoke, looked long and fixedly at the tiny treasure in his
hand, and insisted on being taken straight to Miss Lilly's
office.

He handed her the scepter without hesitation, saying,
"This is yours, Miss Lilly, got separated from the rest.
I'm sorry."

They had gazed at each other, according to the cop who
told Antonia the story, "like they were doing some kinda
telepathy or something." Finally Miss Lilly said, "Bennie,
we're going to need all the help we can get around here
for the next couple of days. I'm counting on you to help
us."

So Bennie still had a job, and Antonia envied him for
having an official function, an assigned task that concentrated his attention on something outside himself. Her own
presence there in the Main Hall seemed to her utterly
pointless, even a little indecent. She looked around, trying
without much success to focus on something besides her
own morbid thoughts.

Then she saw Ariadne's sister.

Fedra was standing beside one of the huge columns that
ran the length of the hall. She looked as if she were forcing
herself by an effort of will not to hide behind it. Though
it had clearly been her intention to look inconspicuous, it
was equally clear that the effort was a dismal failure. Her
simple black dress, the French twist in which she had
confined the mane of dark hair, had only succeeded in
making her look more stunning than ever. She wore no
jewelry, but as Antonia drew closer she saw that Fedra
had applied makeup rather freely, not for adornment but

to conceal the traces of weeping that were still apparent in the puffiness around her eyes and lips.

She was causing, Antonia could see, a kind of subdued sensation. The men eyed her with interest, the women with suspicion, until one by one they found out who she was—"the sister of the girl who died"—and then both sexes moved quietly away in embarrassment.

Fedra had apparently misinterpreted this neglect by the assembled academics, socialites, and museum officials. When Antonia approached her, it was Fedra who spoke first, a mixture of apology and defiance in her voice.

"Hello, Miss Nielsen. I hope it's all right, me crashing the party like this. I mean I did have an invitation from Miss Lilly, so it wasn't really crashing. But all these people . . ." She gestured around her with a sad little smile. "Anyway I hope *you* don't mind. I know this isn't exactly my scene, but coming here's about the only thing I could do that would've meant anything to her." She glanced up at her sister's picture, and her chin rose a barely perceptible fraction of an inch. "It isn't much, but it's the last thing I'll ever be able to do for her, now."

Antonia put an arm around the girl's shoulders, as much for her own consolation as for Fedra's. "Look," she said, "there's someone over here I think you ought to meet. He was a friend of Ariadne's." And they threaded their way slowly through the crowd to the other side of the hall where Bennie was standing, uncomfortably splendid in his green uniform, beside the papyrus display case.

Five minutes later, unnoticed, Antonia excused herself and left them talking together, sadly but with obvious relief, about Ariadne.

Antonia circulated morosely, speaking now and again to one of her colleagues but not feeling equal to any real conversation.

Barry Greenfield approached, and Antonia realized with a little shock that he was the only person in the hall she really wanted to see. She held out one hand to him, the other still clinging mechanically to the glass of long-dead champagne.

"If that," he said with unaccustomed gentleness, "is the same bubbly I saw you clutching forty-five minutes ago, I really think you could abandon it now with a perfectly clear conscience. You've done your duty by it, old girl."

He took the glass from her, set it aside, and put his arms around her.

For a few seconds she let herself be comforted, but the effect was too insidious. She pushed him gently away and gave him an awkward and foolish little pat on the cheek.

"Another minute or two of that, my friend, and I would simply collapse at your feet. And for once that is not a joke but the literal truth. I'm afraid comfort is more than I can take right now. I have to hang tough just a little longer, till this is over. But thanks."

"Any time, old girl," he said, and for once there was no irony in his voice either. "Any time at all."

Antonia felt a hesitant hand on her arm and turned abruptly away from Barry.

"Miss Nielsen," said Fedra, "I'm just leaving now, but I wanted you to know . . ." She paused as if in embarrassment, then made a fresh start. "I wanted to apologize for what my brother did to you. I know you understand that he wasn't responsible for what he was doing just then, but still—I'm sorry. Especially when you tried so hard to help us and all."

"How is he now? Have you talked to the doctors?"

"He's still kind of confused, but they say he'll pull out of it eventually. Especially if he's got someone he can count on like he did Ari." She paused again, and when she continued there was a new note in her voice. It sounded as if Fedra had done a lot of growing up in the last forty-eight hours, and it had left her with fewer certainties about life but more determination, even perhaps a dawning sense of pride.

"And I guess that's got to be me, Miss Nielsen. There isn't anyone else now."

"I suppose your mother . . ."

"She's retired into her bottles. I figure we can't expect much help from her." Fedra spoke sadly but without rancor. "So I think I'll just try making my own life for a while, Miss Nielsen—for me and Yanni, I mean. That's what Ari always meant to do, and now it's what I'm going to do. Even if it takes a little longer than some of the ways I had in mind before."

Touched, Antonia put an arm around the slender young shoulders and squeezed affectionately.

"Ariadne would be proud of you, Fedra. And so am I."

"Thanks, Miss Nielsen. I have to go now—I'm supposed to talk to one of the psychiatrists at four-thirty, and it's nearly quarter past already. I won't forget you, Miss Nielsen."

When she reached the big double doors that formed the main entrance to the museum, Antonia saw her pause and turn back. For a long moment the girl stood there, gazing down the hall at her sister's portrait. It seemed to Antonia as heartfelt a farewell as any that was likely to occur at funeral or graveside.

At the thought of Ariadne's grave, Antonia's mind turned with a kind of grim relief to the next practical problem confronting her.

It had seemed at first more quixotic than practical. Antonia had put the suggestion to Miss Lilly with much misgiving, almost as a joke. But Miss Lilly had taken it seriously, had stared unseeing through Antonia's right shoulder for a full minute while she thought it through.

Then she said slowly, "I like it. I think—yes, I think we might just pull it off." And then, with the ladylike little smile that figured so prominently in the nightmares of the museum staff: "I'll have a word with Mr. Koutris if you like. And put me down for ten dollars, dear."

Thus abruptly had Antonia become treasurer of the unofficial Shaft Grave Dagger Committee. Its sole purpose was to purchase, from the National Museum in Athens, the reproduction inlaid dagger that had killed Ariadne.

And to lay it with her, like ancient grave-goods, in her coffin when she was buried.

Diffidently at first but gradually warming to the idea, Antonia began to canvass her colleagues and the graduate students who had known Ariadne. Without exception they responded generously. From Bennie came a pledge of thirty dollars, payable in three installments. Antonia hadn't the heart to discourage so princely an offer, though she suspected it represented several lunchless weeks.

The little fund had grown, in the brief span of twenty-four hours, to quite respectable proportions. And with it had grown not only the certainty that they would be able to meet the National Museum's price, but Antonia's own belief in the rightness of the gesture.

The lovely reproduction, like its prototype, would spend the centuries in darkness, outlasting Ariadne's flesh and probably her bones. Eventually, no doubt, it would fall prey like the original to grave robbers or archaeologists. (And what on earth, wondered the professional in Antonia, would an archaeologist in the sixth millennium A.D. make of it?) But time could not touch it and—suddenly Antonia saw just where the rightness lay—as Ariadne had snatched the Euripides papyrus from oblivion, so would the golden lions and the silver hunters carry her with them into a kind of immortality. Her flesh, her bones, perhaps even her name would perish. But those unknown diggers of the fifth or sixth millennium, though undoubtedly they would puzzle and argue and speculate over the presence of such a thing in a twentieth-century grave, could hardly doubt that they had here discovered the tomb of some very special person.

ABOUT THE AUTHOR

CAROL CLEMEAU has been a classics professor for fifteen years. She lives in Virginia with her husband, novelist and historian Anthony Esler, and her two sons. THE ARIADNE CLUE is her first novel.